THE THREE FACES OF ZEMBETH

BOOK I

By
ROWAN CANTERBURY

This book is dedicated to:

JOHN GEORGE CANTERBURY

Cover Art by Rowan Canterbury

ISBN 978-1-257-81329-2

Index

From the Author

A story is a wonderful thing. At times it comes from the imagination. And then again it may be birthed by the sheer onrush of events in such a manner that if the one lived does not divulge, then the observers feel compelled record such tales.

I now take this opportunity to share my story with those who will take the opportunity to read it. I am but one of trillions, or so I have recently been made aware of. I am unique in the fact that my people are out of the written documentation or "data" of the known universe. I am an elf. I am an immortal by birth and my body and blood retain an everlasting knowledge and relationship with all that is physically and kinetically currently in existence. Sounds important, but in truth I had NO idea. Nor did I have the vision to foretell the events that would unfold and eventually motivate me to put these words to parchment.

I have always kept a journal. We in the royal family are required to do so for historic purposes. I doubt, however that any of my kith and kin will skim through these pages. For, although I am the Princess and rightful heir to the crown of Zembeth, I am now an outcast, and happy to be so. The habit of documenting my days was however, a valuable one as you will soon see.

I had a great deal of assistance in the final product you hold before you now. In the writing and publishing of this, my adventure, I have also been vastly educated by creatures beyond my wildest imagination in the cold black of space, far beyond the gilded mirror in my sleeping chambers. I am now an alien in a cosmos of exaggerations.

Here and now, I am simply striving to suck it all up as water in drowning lungs.

I digest it as to nourish some unforeseen hunger in a search to validate my existence. This total completion of the destruction and reconstruction of my psyche (and must I mention, very physical being) would not be silent until I submitted and scratched it down, primitive and naked, bared on the open road amidst the tall grasses of my home as my feet once were. In the mud, covered and smelling like skin sweat and dead insects, the writing persisted when nothing else was stable or sure, thus the birth of this saga through the fluids of my undertaking cold and clean and copied for the masses.

The decision remains then for the reader as to whether it is worth the read or not. All life is a story. Every movement an adventure in the slanted viewed ideals of the one involved. Many cultures have quested for the spirits of the stars, only to stare deeply into the sky, impotent of purpose and unable to achieve the goal of contact. As such, many souls have flocked to the written word in its billions of forms in search of a truth or a fantasy lost to childhood fables. For whom and what are we, if not scattered? Where is the story without the villain, the hero? What is life itself without the same players? You see, even as an immortal and like those whom are mortal, I am but a slave to fable and a child of energies fair and foul. I will always be, to the end of my long days, if such an end should come.

Take this gift if you will. Pick it out from the chaotic multitude on a risk and a dare and read on. For reading is like making love. In opening the cover you unveil the source of intimacy with your author. You may expose your inner villain.

If luck favors, and you have walked the path clear and sure, you may just discover your hero in the mirror.

Meriden of Fairfax

Zembeth, Princess of Elves

PROLOGUE

You can't make galactic goop without the larger, if not largest, species of Thernixian desert cockroach. The trick is trapping them. Dom had seen some of the less fortunate street brats riding them like air scooters with multiple legs. If you could get a stout cable around the thick helmet by way of looping it under their road-buggy-tire-sized heads as they charged one of your friends, all you had to do was jump on and steer. He knew some of the older kids trapped them. They had been selling them to him by the dozens at hideous prices. They had to be trapping them! If you took aim at one of them with a laser cannon, you would either miss or just dent the armor (in which case, it is suggested that you drop the laser cannon and run). If said desert cockroach were to turn on you, call the wife and kids and say your farewells. Istill had told him he had seen it done.

A box is constructed, just large enough to fit one tip to tail, with a latch catch and some rotten meat. When the beast was restrained, one had to take a syringe full of acid and aim up under the frontal plate, going forward toward the brain. When it stopped kicking, the action had to be quick in order to chop the head off before the acid got into the prime cuts. Istill, upon explanation of said butchery produced a sharply curved fifteen-inch blade and demonstrated how it was designed to shift under the nearly unbreakable armor and slice the head off.

Dom was up early this morning to check his first traps. He wasn't planning on opening the tavern early, but somehow knew it was going to take some guts (no pun intended) and a bit of fighting room to get used to harvesting his own vermin for the lunch rush. He would have to close the Burning Hand Saloon if he kept throwing money away on something he could easily do himself, he complained in a low grumble. (This, of course, is a ballooned overstatement. He had no money problems to speak of, but had been raised very poor and was always jumping the economic gun.) Out of habit he waved on the intergalactic news. He wasn't planning on actually watching it, but was accustomed to listening in once in a while. The rest served as background noise to keep him focused.

Miguel would not be in today, it was doubtful he would be able to make it to the other tavern (the Blood Jack) they co-owned either. It seemed Dom would have the full responsibility of cooking the special until Istill crawled in for short order duty, and managing the customers. Dom would have to jump a speeder and check on The Blood Jack at some point that afternoon. It was just as well. He despised attending Thernixian merchant guild meetings. As full partners and lifelong friends, they were well aware of each other's strengths and weaknesses. Miguel's strengths were negotiation and long winded debates. Dom preferred the silent but deadly roles of management and the persuasion of clientele.

They were important meetings. Dom loathed them but he had to admit that, because of the business guilds, Thernix had become the most productive merchant planet in the system. The more they communicated and negotiated, the longer they would avoid entanglement with galactic politicians and law enforcement specialists. It was, after all, business on a galactic level. They were obscenely wealthy, and none of the outer rim systems volunteered this wealth with the core systems. The rim systems were not taxed the same as the core systems. They operated independently and required no services from the core systems and upheld none of the same laws and restrictions. Although it had at one time been debated in the galactic senate, it was quickly overturned. Instead an agreement was reached and in return for their sovereignty, the rim systems had one job and one job only, to protect the core systems against invasion and possible takeover from the two sister galaxies that sandwiched the Andromeda's far rim. This was accomplished through procedures that would not exist in a "civilized" interstellar environment.

It was the same in all galaxies in the end. Life forms evolved and adapted to the situational living conditions they were given. This social gestation was common in aspects unnumbered from the smallest planets to the largest galaxy clusters. The rim planets were separated by a substantial distance from the core planets able to sustain life. They stretched in a spackled ban of independent systems along the curve of the great Andromeda. The closest institution to government known to these at times hostile floating orbs was the Zenerian Empire. Neither the core government nor any other risked an outright entanglement with any planet under Zenerian protection, and this encompassed 68% of the rim system planets.

Thernix was, although not part of the Zenerian empire, very much part of the trade and livelihood of the empire and thus enjoyed an unspoken "brother" contract of protection. Amazing as it seemed, Zenerians did not convert or overrun systems by brute force. Even with the largest and most vicious fighting armada ever recorded in galactic history, Zenerians were considered a mysterious people of recluse pirates. They could be found everywhere and nowhere. They operated under a strict code of perfection, oddly mirrored by a questionable moral agenda.

Dom knew his share of Zenerians. He had been working hand in hand with them for several of decades. He ran a tavern, but above and below were safe houses for abandoned children who would be either candidates for the lifelong education of a Zenerian, or found suitable homes elsewhere in the galaxy. Scoundrels often wear many faces.

Although he loved the life of one who provides adult entertainment, he was also an orphan of Thernix. He was well aware of the survival rate of a child alone on any system. He had seen it firsthand. After so many years in the business of "child relocation" he now served drinks to the very children he had once taken in off the streets. Many of them wore Zenerian black. The last thing any of them wanted was the involvement of a bureaucratic system stepping in and mucking things up. Apparently some life forms were aware of the historic and epic failure of such systems. On the rim, they took care of their own. Hard formed statistics did not float on the rim. Zeneria was peopled by orphans and emancipated slaves. In spite of what they were fed from the core, on the rim, the underdog had the advantage. These were the quick flashes of information that splashed around in his questionable mind as he prepared to work on the bugs.

The newswoman was rambling on about long range financial goals for colonizing some rock a billion miles away in the center systems. He opened the back door and grabbed the first trap after putting on his thick leather gloves. It wasn't good for his back to haul the heavy insect and box across the floor. He was going to tell Ystill if Istill wanted to keep his job, he would have to start hauling something else in early and stop drinking late.

His mind shifted back to his business partner and the guild meetings as he filled the syringe, ignoring the chewing sound of the roach tearing at the steel plated planks of the trap.

It had not always been this easy for them. Like any small businesses that started here, they had lived through the starving times. Miguel would have no problems at the meeting, he was, after all, known as "Uncle Miguel" to all the right people. Yet this meeting would be very different from the rest his partner had attended. Therefore, Dom had reason to be concerned, he volleyed back to the nagging emotional state he was working to overcome.

The syringe drove violently under the head plate, puncturing through the tough skin like a blade through thick tendon. Thank goodness there was so much meat under the armor; otherwise this would be too much of a hassle.

He craned his neck and wiped his clean bald head with a cloth, watching the roach kick and quiver. Somewhere in the back of his mind he heard something that had caught his attention. Cautiously observing the giant roach, he snapped his fingers and cocked an ear toward the speakers.

He liked his kitchens kept very clean. He often reminded everyone that he was a clean man with a dirty mind. Those who knew him believed it. Every utensil was in its place, as if the kitchen were run by a daunting net-haired spinster. He would rather be drinking, was all he could think, as the 15" knife slid silver and sharp from the box specially designed for it. His face creased with a frown. The noise the helmet made as it shifted to allow the edge of the blade to splice open the tough under flesh was not the cause of his frustration. Once more his thoughts shifted and swearing, he shoved the box over the sink, allowing the black blood to drip down the drain instead of all over the counter. The stress of outside events was playing havoc on his ability to concentrate. Thankfully he had remembered to put a pot of water on to boil the meat once he succeeded in ripping the shell off. He frowned, and snapped his fingers to turn up the volume on the speakers, realizing this was the true source of his irritation.

The woman on the screen, reading from a teleprompter, robot voiced the overtones of the true source of his agitation. Another system, just outside the rim had been taken possession of by a group that had one time been considered a flash in the pan nuisance from the Eliptica galaxy. A small team of thugs had been pushing the few planets that floated between galaxies, just on the borders. It seemed that the "mergers" they had professed to be facilitating, were becoming increasingly physical. Their leader was named Nahasam Inondet, in the common tongue he was known as Jeff Kolbert, a name he chose to support his delusion of being a humanoid. The only name Dom could think of for him was "stupid bastard". Jeff had yet to approach Thernix, but from this morning's news reports, he was gaining courage.

The amount of courage needed to mount an assault on the rim systems would appear to be much larger than Kolbert had strutted in the past. Dom reflected on Miguel's premonition that this dim tit had been handpicked, run through his mind.

"You just don't find obnoxious greed like that walking around." Dom remembered Miguel commenting after the second recorded attack on a small system.

"Think we should bring the kids in on it?" He asked Dom.

"I think they've been in it and come out the back side already." He assured his business partner that their Zenerian associates were well aware of the threat.

"Do you think they will step in?" Miguel had asked him.

"Hard to say. We never signed a contract with them. We go on faith. Now the question is, can faith win us a possible galactic conflict? If not, I sure hope they like us a whole hell of a lot." Dom replied.

Miguel was correct, Dom mused now as he sliced the wings off the dead roach. Jeff was a special kind of idiot. He didn't take no for an answer. He was born believing that he was just a laser slice above everyone else in the universe and if he worked at it, all the simple creatures he attempted to overtake would eventually succumb.

It had come to the point of some of the systems petitioning the core government, that they were technically part of, for assistance. Jeff had been wise enough to go around the back door. Past the protected rim systems, if one had the funding to fly that far, one could approach the Andromeda from another angle, one that was "protected" by the core government. They were offered minimal assistance, and with the small showing of military presence Jeff had backed out of the picture to lick his wounds. As of yet his bravado had not reached the point of actually attacking a rim operated system.

Dom dumped chunks of pink and gray meat into the boiling water and got ready for the next roach. Kolbert's disappearance had been some time ago. Dom was in tune with physical energy and could foresee changes through the energy of others. He knew they had not seen the last of Jeff Kolbert. Something in the shifting eyes of this particular idiot told Dom that once again, the Andromeda would be in need of the rim systems' intervention, to keep themselves safe.

A short time later (as Dom had predicted), Kolbert returned. This time he chose a planet much closer to the rim systems. Hearts were held petrified at the sight of his much larger flight command. He returned with enough firepower to overtake the planet with ease. Cries for help went out en masse to the core with sluggish response. It became clear that by the time the core mobilized, Imtua would be taken.

Imtua was a green and lush planet of quiet farmers. She was natural and peaceful, primitive in her innocence. She was the perfect pawn, for sadly she was not valuable enough to warrant the beginning of a galactic conflict. She did not generate enough revenue. She sat five clicks galactic south from the last planet protected by rim law. Imtua was unaware that she was hiding ten space-black Zenerian pirate fighters waiting like wasps for a chance to settle the dispute once and for all.

The incident was publicized galactic wide and broadcast on many of the Elipcitcan and Stinette networks. It took a total of twenty-five standard galactic minutes for the event to begin and end. Kolbert had finally been introduced to Zeneria. His reinforced numbers escaped with a total of two ships after starting the campaign with over fifty. It was speculated that two were purposefully left to take back the message. The Zenerian ships circled Imtua a few times then disappeared without a word, leaving a pair of ships to escort Jeff over the galactic divide. That day, countless families on Imtua gave thanks for their lives to individuals they had no kinship to. This is how Gods are made.

On a more important note, no attempts were made by the Zenerian people for compensation or payment. No attempts of negotiation for possible Zenerian occupation were initiated. They simply vanished.

After the incident an Imtuan fighter pilot had visited The Burning Hand. He was free flowing with information about the historic incident, unaware that the pub was frequented by Zenerian pirates of every level.

The Zenerian ships placed themselves between Imtua and the invaders, reported the pilot. The Imtuan pilots were told by a single transmission from one of the Zenerian ships to hold back. They had heard Jeff attempting to communicate with the almost invisible black ships he had only heard stories about. No reply came. At one point an Imtuan Admiral stated that Kolbert's ships were a direct threat and he requested they stand down. A stunned lull ensued due to the black line of single and silent fighters that floated between Imtua and Kolbert's mass of readied warships.

Then a voice came over all open channels, the fighter pilot from Imuta informed.

"It was a female. We could all hear her. She was calm and creepy. Hell, I knew she was protecting my ass and *I* was terrified of her."

She said, "I don't think they want you here. I'm giving you one last chance to save the lives of your crew and turn around. If I ever see you anywhere near the Andromeda again, I will personally rip your heart from your body."

This provoked more silence until Kolbert's ship fired an unsuccessful shot at one of the black ships before them. The next broadcast to be heard by all was simply: "We'll save you for last." The Imtuan pilot narrated.

The pub erupted in laughter, many of the patrons fully aware of who the message had come from.

Dom giggled at the memory. It was a miracle that Kolbert had gotten out alive. Captain Devarelle wanted to skin him and hang one half of his hide on a flagpole above the Stinette and the other half on the Eliptician Galactic Federation Building.

The squads had come to his saloon after the incident to celebrate in their own fashion. The Zenerian 23rd had been assigned this mission.

Their captain, a beloved friend to Dom, stepped away from her squad mates for the customary private meeting with the tavern owner. She took advantage of the rare opportunities to partake in Dom's kindness and wisdom. She was the most feared being in several galaxies. She made it a rule to seek out such wisdom, 'for the survival of her people depended not on the strength of their squadrons, but on the humility of their leaders', she had been quoted saying.

"I don't know, Dom. I think there's a backing force here. I know Miguel thinks so too."

She was easing into the discussion. They were playing rip tow, a favorite card game on Thernix. He loved to see her with a cigar in her mouth, concentrating on her hand. It was like watching someone put hard whisky in a cup of fine sand spun crystal.

"Whatcha thinking, kiddo? Ya think he has more military force than we originally thought?" He puffed and set down his stogie.

"I think it's worse. He's got some pretty big balls. I mean, like Galactic Prime Minister sized balls."

She looked at Dom over her hand, allowing her impressive forest green eyes to scrutinize his expression. She knew it wouldn't take him long to follow her train of conversation.

"Ya think? That's kind of risky. Big bad. Lots of messy entanglements." Dom speculated.

"Ya know I'm dating him, right?" She attempted to blow a smoke circle and failed.

"Dating who?" Dom was surprised to hear she was dating anyone. He realized she had never really dated to his knowledge. Unlike many living beings in the galaxy, he had always had a hard time reading her. Her energy was somehow overflowing and encompassing. It confused him. It was unique even among her Earth brothers and sisters. Earthlings were very rare and could only be found in the ranks of Zeneria society as far as Dom was aware. It was not as if he had many of them to compare her to. Earth had been completely destroyed some time ago, so it was unlikely he would meet more. Even next to her species, she was vastly different. Her feel, her smell, her energy was like nothing he had encountered.

At The Burning Hand, Dom had the distinct advantage to run into just about every form of life in all three galaxies that could pilot a space ship. He had often marveled at the fact that even the countless life forms he had run across had a thread to each other. But Britt was set aside. He had never mentioned this to her. He had no idea how to broach the subject.

"Jeff." She grinned.

"Nah! Are you pulling my leg?" He set down his cards and took a swig from his flask.

"How do you think we know so much about his operation?" She called his bluff and took the hand.

"And get this: I even got to go to a fancy dinner with Szelezenda. Things were really tight if you know what I mean?" She winked.

"I was allowed to come into the parlor after dinner, being the fragile and simple bit of arm candy that I am." She leaned back in her chair and propped her long legs on a stack of boxes.

Dom was speechless. Szelezenda was the Prime Minister of the Eliptician Galaxy. From what she was telling him, she had just paraded her Zenerian Pirate fanny around in front of the upper echelon of the Eliptician Galaxy without so much as a slight fear of imprisonment!

She had to know that she was wanted for numerous crimes in about 700 systems in Eliptica alone. Furthermore, this meant that it was official, Eliptica WAS involved and the core systems were none the wiser.

"Now Dom, just because *you* are smarter than the average duc lizard doesn't mean they are. The people that make the rules in that galaxy think I'm related to Zenerio." Britt shuffled the deck for another hand and puffed on her cigar. Zenerio was a giant monster with a large white head full of teeth. Dom occasionally had nightmares about him and they had been close friends for years.

"As a matter of fact, I am engaged to Jeff Kolbert, or so he thinks." She choked a bit with glee, leaning her head back farther and swigging a shot down.

"That my dear is just wicked. I love it!" Dom was truly impressed. He had obviously been a good influence (or bad). Either way it was working.

"Anyway, there's something else going on here. Szelezenda has been wanting a chunk of our pie for some time, but just hasn't had the brass to admit it, so he finds Kolbert all hot and raring to go and whamo! He's got himself the perfect little scapegoat." She started dealing out the next hand.

"I bet Szelezenda would just shit his drawers if he knew who you really are." Dom was still musing over the visual. His face wrinkled in concern. "Do you think they will keep pushing?" He asked knowing full well that he was talking to the future leader of the Zenerian Empire and captain of the most notorious Zenerian Pirate Squadron ever to hit light speed.

"Yea. I know he will. He has been trying for some time. He knows he has to get through us to get to the core. Your systems are the loophole. It only makes sense." She waited for his reply, knowing that she was talking to one of the most influential businessmen in this system.

"Hmm." Dom grunted and reached for his walking stick. "You gonna tell me if we're gonna be hanging our asses out there alone? I'm speaking strictly unofficially, of course."

"Remember a few years ago when I got in that jam? You know the one; the time I got accused of treason?" She asked him.

"Sure, how could I forget? What a load of shit that was." He knew where this was going and it made him feel something he rarely felt in the energies around him: true loyalty.

"I gotta admit it was a nice try. My true brothers knew better. But then again you are not Zenerian." She hesitated to take her turn. "You didn't have to stick your neck out for me." She grinned, parting her plush lips in a brilliant smile and winked at the older humanoid male. "I got your back. Unofficially speaking, of course."

"Well whatever they decide to do next, it should be interesting." Dom commented, now completely disinterested in the card game. "After that last event, I can't imagine what else they would try to get through the cracks."

He stretched his legs and looked across the table at her. He had known her since she was very small. He had watched her grow into a female humanoid second to none that he had tried to seduce. She could charm a sand lizard out of its sex organs, yet she held herself with an unconscious relaxation unexpected in a woman of her physical attributes. He knew this was due to a lifetime of training to be a Zenerian Mercenary Pirate. They didn't come tougher than that. Britt Devarelle might be able to charm the sex organs off a sand lizard, but Dom knew after seeing her in action that she was the last creature in this galaxy he wanted on the other team.

Dom was on his third bug now. What a mess. He knew the stew would sell like mad so he kept pulling tendons and shell fragments from the mixture. He decided to use the left over Dardasian vegetables from last night's salad bar, why cut new ones? He made his way to the walk-in cooler to pull the tub of vegetables from the shelf while trying to shove a large canister of blood juice out of the way.

The next news report that came punctured his heart before it captivated his ears, causing him to drop the entire canister of blood juice. With as much grace as he could muster while sliding in the spilled blood and condensation, he latched onto the steel door handle and swung around into the kitchen fighting to turn up the volume.

"This just in: An explosion on Thernix has allegedly killed Captain Devarelle of the Zenerian systems. A bomb was allegedly believed to have been planted within a regularly used Zenerian port hangar sometime last night under security surveillance, making this assassination appear to be an inside job. Tib, more on that story as it unfolds." The normally blank faced female seemed to tremble when delivering this last bit of information.

Dom remembered hearing a loud noise just as he had awakened. He'd thought nothing of it. Large freighters often flew over the merchant areas and shifted to full engines in the process, causing the houses and shops to shake.

Dom slammed the monitor off and raced for the corridor leading to the basement bunkers. He knew it was no use to go upstairs. By now every pirate that would have checked in last night was in flight. He nearly ran into Celeste on the way to the hidden stairs.

"I take it you have heard the news?" The wispy pirate asked.

"Why didn't anyone tell me?" He was frantic.

"We've been busy, friend. And as you have heard, the incident has just happened. We think the perpetrator tipped off the news crews. We are evacuating all the children to Lambelin. I'm on my way to the shuttle now." She had the way of a wind racer, always moving. He had wondered why she had not chosen combat pirate over social worker. She would be a real stinker to catch, with her body made of 85% oxygen.

Dom was visibly paling. Was his concern for the children overtaking his emotions? He leaned against the wall, wiping his forehead. His empathic abilities were painful at a time such as this. The fear of every living being within a five mile range was floating in the very atmosphere. He coughed, trying to dispel the smell of smoke from his lungs. He could not escape the feeling of movement and shifted involuntarily.

"You really should stay here, Dom." Celeste floated around him. "We will come for you very soon. Finish with your business, close your accounts and keep the tavern locked up. With the way things are going I wouldn't answer the door for anyone who doesn't already have a key."

Dom's heart was shifting in a way that made his chest hurt with pressure. He had no doubts that he would be taken care of and that all the children would be safe. His spirit was falling ever farther into a pit of desperation. His head felt as if it were on fire. He could still smell smoke. His stomach churned with the vile plunk and swig of bile and booze. He braced himself against the wall.

"What's wrong, Dom? What do you see?" Celeste asked.

"Britt. I can *feel* her." He bent down and she became solid to support her long time friend. Under the hangover, he knew this must be Britt. Her memories flashed before him. Her soul shot through his skull. He felt as though he would erupt with the power of her flame and the force of her departure.

"Dom, tell me what you see!?" She clicked her gauntlets hoping to contact Byron Dawson or another member of the 23rd.

"I can't explain it. She just vanished." He choked as he spoke. "The pain ended as soon as it began. It was not death. It was not explosion or slow burning."

Dom clung to the doorframe. He still wore his apron covered with cockroach entrails. Celeste worked to rid him of the sickening aromatic cloth. She contemplated as she worked to get the apron off the slowly sinking man. It was nearly impossible to kill a Zenerian with a flight suit, and they all wore flight suits, pilot or no. Britt's gauntlets would have activated her protective full body armor. This special outfit was fireproof to super nova temperatures. Now Dom was telling her that Britt had just vanished. He had actually said, "It was not death. It was not explosion or slow burning." She struggled to seat him.

"Just like that?" Celeste voiced her confusion. She waited for a few moments to allow him to settle the constant swirling of nausea that now crippled him. Once Dom could stand, Celeste helped him to his quarters and pulled his feet up to lie back. She would call Zingara, Dom's love, to keep watch over him until she could arrange further travel plans for both Dom's and Miguel's families. She knew that this planet was no longer safe for them. This was a history-changing action. This was the straw that broke the camel's back.

Celeste stepped away from the bed and used Dom's communication monitor to contact Zingara. After she ended the call she touched her gauntlets and requested assistance for the tavern. It was clear that Dom was in no position to handle the details of closing down and bugging out. It would be imperative to get him to Zeneria as soon as possible to assist in unraveling the mystery of their missing captain. Many of the pirates knew the finite intricacies of this business.

"You have to rest, Dom." She floated over him. "I am needed with the children. This place is crawling with Zenerian pirates. You are safe." She kissed his forehead with tenderness. "When you wake, we will make arrangements to have you taken to Zeneria. I will see to it. I know you trust me." She smiled down at him.

Dom nodded. He knew Celeste was about to put him to sleep for his own good. Of all the pirates, she understood the tremendous amount of energy it took to connect with another living force. When he awoke, Zingara would be there. When he awoke, life would change.

Celeste waved her half invisible palm over his tired eyes, sending him into a deep restful sleep. She floated down the hall, through the kitchen and up to the roof top, looking beyond the tavern to the large cloud of smoke just a few clicks away. She would only slow long enough to make sure the team assigned to this tavern knew what must be done. She shook her silver blond waves and cast her brilliant blue eyes to the burning sky. She struggled with the belief that Captain Devarelle was dead. It was a cold day in the desert indeed. She would have to make sure they got Dom and Miguel to Zeneria, and fast. If Dom was right and Britt was still alive, someone was going to be in dire need of protection when they found her and brought her home.

Chapter 1
Meadow Witch

"One pinch of salt. That should be enough." SWAT. "Damn swamp suckers!" Ma Fafella labored toward the ancient circle of stones. Walking had become increasingly difficult with age and weight gain. She opened her tusked mouth and belched, killing every insect in a three-yard radius.

"Serves the vipers right." She giggled. It was a good five hours to sunrise. She needed to move her monster-sized legs a bit faster if she were to complete the transformation spell and make her way to the meadow before SHE woke. The goblin sorceress approached the giant stones embedded on the murky swamp shores of the Deneb Sea some two thousand years before when the "first" of her kind immigrated to this home.

"Salt, and a fresh lunar moth. Or should I use a butterfly?" She wiped under her breasts with a rag she had wisely remembered to pack in her basket. One must keep such places dry and clean. "I wonder which I packed. I suppose that is the one I will be using in any case." She mumbled to herself as she positioned the night-sized hourglass atop the largest of the western inner radial stones. Sifting through the basket she came across a lock of raven hair. Holding up the thick curl, she contemplated if it would be needed. If her visions were accurate, layering the spell was a waste of precious time. Matters of the heart were so unreliable and unreadable. She frowned, pursing her thick wart covered lips. It was a long shot. In the end it did not matter, someone was going to be heartbroken one way or another. It was unfair for her to protect either or.

The giant goblin sow scratched her thinning, greasy hair and snorted. Her mind would have to be more focused for this spell. The energies of late had been like an irritating relative that refused to leave. Even when you had booted them out of your dwelling, somehow their influence was still hovering, annoying and noxious. She positioned her green gargantuan backside on a stone for just a bit of a rest. It was a testament to the slack jawed stupidity that the elfish civilization had degraded to, that they had not picked up on this blatant shift in the energies of Zembeth entire. She had been contacted by ogres, goblins, centaurs and black mountain elves, but the elite of the elfish race had stayed clear. She could not blame them. If she remembered correctly, she'd given the last elf that had dared show his face at her door, oozing genital sores. She once again giggled, the sound rumbled through the trunks of the trees not far behind her.

Pointing her knotted green finger, she stoked the fire to full force under the cauldron that had been simmering for three days. Time to get back to work and stop fretting unnecessarily for those that chose to be blind. She was far more concerned for all the secondary races and Zembeth herself. Whatever these energies were telling her, it was just as foreign to her mind as it was to those of less magical ability. This fear was something she could not conjure up or materialize until she understood it better. Fear was only fear until understanding took its hold. This fear was beyond what she knew her old head could wrap around. The only thing she had managed to see coming was HER. Any dream that came more than once was worth investigation.

Ma Fafella had been dreaming about the same female for months now. She could pick this woman out of a crowd in an instant, the visions had been so clear. They had awakened her from a dead sleep more than once. Tall, pale she was, nothing like the creatures that walked Fafella's world. She was neither elf or human, goblin or troll, and she was wicked. In the dreams Ma Fafella got a flash and a glimpse, as if looking through piss water. The woman in her dreams was deadly in all the right ways and in no way even a seasoned witch like Fafella had ever encountered. And she was coming here.

Thinking back now, it was also hard to understand how dropping this human in the middle of a society that practices human slavery was going to help.

"Tits on a bore hog, useless." She often mumbled upon waking. Who in the great names of the Gods could handle a package like this vixen? It was not her obvious strength Fafella worried about, it was her diverse mind that would flip Zembeth on its' backside. What could she do here other than stir up the forced natural order of things? If Ma Fafella did not believe SHE could help, she would not be out here eating the heads off moths. Being a great magick worker meant that you had to know when you were out of your league, and sit back and learn. It was the only way to grow. If the energies said SHE was the one, who was Ma Fafella to argue?

Only a few more things to be added then a drink, a shrink and a long walk. As she worked to position a change of clothing and continue tossing milkweed into the brew, Fafella rehearsed her plan of persuasion. It would be no easy task to convince this one to take the road to Garath with an Ogre. SHE was no ordinary human. Fafella grinned with anticipation of the coming introduction. This was becoming the most interesting situation she had encountered in at least fifty years. Life had been boring since the boys had moved out. The boys. She looked at the brew and then the cascading waves of the sea.

"The boy." She mumbled.

There were times a mother had to do things she would rather not, knowing all the while that the future would divulge more pleasant times.

"That boy." She started to hum and walked toward the fire to start the transformation spell. He had stopped by not too long ago, her elf son, one of two. The younger was most often a silly git, but it was who he was and they loved him for it.

Her eldest was the worry. He had known she was hiding something. She had not known she was hiding something until he had walked in the door right off the road. She had known he was coming, but somehow seeing his face made everything click. She had already planned to come out here and do the spell and then waddle to the meadow to meet HER. When Roderick showed up for a random visit, she had even planned to tell him of her future escapade. It was not until he was actually in her kitchen looking at her that it hit and she slapped her trap shut. Perhaps if she were lucky, she was developing the aging sickness and losing her skills. In this case she hoped so, but for now silence was the best plan. Every action has a reaction. Ever living creature is affected by another. This was the way of things far beyond her and older than time.

So it was to be a lunar moth. She bit the head off the bug and continued chewing on the squirming torso, sending her thoughts to change.

Not far from where she worked, the sun was coming up on Zembeth prime, licking the darkest points of their homeland first. The golden goddess's light skimmed over the black peaks of the Kloter Mountain Range, only to wake the dankest of Zembethian civilizations, the goblin city of Kloter Mass Arosa. From a city that would rather hide from the light of the sun, the great warm goddess would spread her loving touch over the Arosa plains. These plains are so vast; a good horse could not span their girth in three moon phases of solid running. The grasses are twice the height of an elf, sending the tallest tips to heights of 12 feet above firm soil. Under the canopy of dense foliage, the sun sheers through in bright strips of exotic prison bar stripes to the infant shoots struggling for warmth. With the morning comes moisture that illuminates the wide blades, bringing out the translucent veins that feed the green giants. The ooredna birds take flight from their nests in the early morning to greet the golden mother, their cobalt wings causing a riot of color as though a deep cut in the imagination. As they spin to warm their bellies, their silver feathers reflect the sunlight sharply, flashing light back into the pastel sky.

Throngs of large herd animals live inside the Arosa grasslands. Among the many, are herds of unicorn, bison, and small grounded griffins. The larger griffins fed on the herds themselves instead of the small prey of the under canopy. They could be found nesting in the black cliff walls of the Kloter mountain range, and rarely submerged beneath the grass carpet. They watched from the pitch hematite cliff face that shadowed the expanse of the western border of the known realm of Zembeth prime like giant living statues, large and fierce enough to carry off a full sized bull. Other less desirable creatures skulked in the grasslands. Among these were harpies. It was not uncommon for a male of any race to be lulled into the next of one of these winged and infested beasts. They were usually found in small bitch clutches of two or three, fiercely fighting over male souls and devouring anything even remotely female that happened by. In the consumption of a female, the magick of a harpy could use the fluids if the female were young enough, to firm her own flesh or tip up her sagging feather covered breasts.

They would seem to be the worst of the worst to most, but they dulled in comparison to more than one species of creature under the Arosa grasses.

Once the solar illumination cleared the mountains and melted into the grass lands, it was not far to Fafella's meadow, nestled at the foot of the mountain's south talon. It is completely bordered by wise trees that are as old as any elf can remember. Under the solace of these giant Hallafawn trees one can find a host of fairy villages and gnome havens that began to stir in the early morning to sing the song of dawn. The lilting tune hovered above the soft carpet of mosses and ferns.

With this song, Father Night flees to his shining stars, and Mistress Moon. He dances among the trees and over the small lake, evoking diamond reflections of cool goodbyes. His denied lover comes to wrap her molten arms around his great thighs, to swim with him to the surface of the heavens in her golden gown to kiss him farewell. The meadow comes alive, so to speak, at dawn.

********** * * * * * * * *************

From a morning glory rose a tiny green dragonfly fairy. Her name was Bella and this was the day of her birth. She was so excited she wished to be the first out on the lake to skate and chat, in appreciation of gifts and gossip. Her delicate wings beat swiftly to lift her from her bed of blue and white. She was deep green and her wings resembled those of her brother dragonflies, in sound and appearance. Aloft, she could see the lake amidst the morning fog and hurried to be around the buttercups and cattails. Low and behold, as all of her fairy brethren in the meadow that morning, she was cut short just of the white sand by a sight that stopped the beating of her wings.

All about the lake, toads, gnomes, brownies, pixies, butterfly fairy, and the like, circled to stare at the visitor that had come in the night.

Before them lay a figure that seemed to be dead, face down in the sand. It appeared to be a human female, yet some argued that it was far too large. Although shaped like a female, this creature had what appeared to be reflective black skin and was as long of limb as an elf male. It had a mane of red gold curls that spilled out over the sand in long waves. No human any of them had ever seen had hair like that. Yet it was not so much the color of the hair that confused them. Many expensive companion slaves had different shades of golden hair, although Grimstone argued that he had never seen one with red hair. The chances of a priceless companion slave flopping face down in the sand of their meadow were slim to none. Leave this alone and there was still the issue of sheer size to grapple.

Grimstone was a very prominent and well thought of pixie dwarf. For some reason today, he was suddenly the resident expert on humans. He took to a moss-covered rise near enough to the creature to intimidate all others.

"Of course it is not human! I have seen dark humans all, and none have skin as dark as yonder wench. It must be a goblin of some sort." He folded his fat little arms over his belly and huffed.

"Silly Grim, 'tis not a goblin, 'tis too thin to be a goblin sow, unless she is beyond death. If that be her pains, how did she come from Kloter in such a state to drop here? She would have no magick or be thicker. Have you ever seen such a banner of sun-like fire about the crown of a goblin sow?" Recia, the blue lizard maid, challenged.

"Well then, what in the three moons is it, if you be now our wise woman!?"

Recia stepped to a closer lily pad for a better look. "I doubt that is her skin. See there, her hands are of the color of cream." She reached dangerously close.

"Step back, you daft git!" Bella barked warning to her sleek blue friend.

Just then the creature started to move, sending all fleeing into the taller grasses. From the cattails and luck stones they watched in awe, as the dead seemed to groan to life and sit up.

"Well," whispered Grimstone, "That is definitely a female of some sort."

Captain Britteny Eden Devarelle sat back to wipe the sand from her eyes and shove her hair out of her face. Her stomach heaved in rejection of the ridiculous amount of alcohol she had consumed earlier that night.

Being conscious of little else, she turned her head and vomited on the grass. Still holding her hair with one hand, she supported her weight with the other against a boulder next to the lake's edge. Her convulsions soon become dry and painful. In her mind she kept repeating her (often broken) vow to never, never drink again. Her stomach did not seem to be satisfied; nor was she sure she cared.

She willed herself to stop heaving and started breathing slowly. When she could move, she held her right arm before her and touched the black gauntlet on her forearm. From the glass like shield rose a pill. She popped it into her mouth and looked around. Spying the crystal clear lake, without testing the water for toxins, she dropped down on all fours and started to drink. Once she had her fill she splashed her face with the cool water and pulled her hair back into a tie. The dawning realizations of her surroundings were now beginning to permeate the hang-over haze. She slowly lowered her arms and looked with wonder and confusion at the meadow paradise.

She seemed to freeze where she sat and her eyes turned to the patch of cattails directly in front of her. Beneath the cover of the weeds, Grimstone gasped. This creature had enormous eyes as green as the color of a dark forest. He glanced at Mipinx, a brownie that had moved next to him. The little fellow shrugged his shoulders and grimaced in ignorance. Grimstone whispered sharply assuming most humans had very bad hearing.

"Would someone please like to tell me what in the name of Ren' Fordel that thing is?!" He hissed.

Panic paralyzed the lot of them when the creature, only a few feet away, heard them. Its line of sight now directed at the cattail that hid Grimstone. It started to survey the lake and surrounding area without moving a muscle of its athletic frame. Slowly it sat back, as if in anticipation of an attack. Her leg muscles bulged and twitched, preparing to flee if need be. By now it was apparent to the enchanted audience that this sleek black film was some sort of clothing. The rest of her skin that showed was a pale peach color; her cheeks were flush from vomiting. As if in suspended animation, the human started to rise. Grimstone gasped again in spite of himself. She was a giant. Her stature was that of a warrior, her poise was beyond that of any human slave. She removed her jacket and placed it on the boulder next to her, avoiding her previous mess in the grass. She wore only a black tunic of some sort that had no sleeves and clung to her frame. Around her neck was she wore a very fine silver necklace with a tiny tear shaped deep blue sapphire supported by delicate ivy leaves. Her only other adornment were the strange black gauntlets on both her wrists.

"Oh, this is just amazing. Byron, you have outdone yourself this time. I mean it is so real. O.K." She took a deep breath, "so real." Captain Devarelle whispered to herself.

For a moment she drifted off in thought. She had not seen a planet like this since Earth. If what she remembered from Earth, so many years ago, was still correct in her memory, this place was perhaps a flush on the astounding side. She was aware that she was being watched but, as yet, was not sure by what.

"I can't believe how well you programmed this. I can smell the grass and even feel the mud." She hesitated. "But you were from New York City and I thought you said you had never been to the country. I know Central Park couldn't have been this beautiful." Britt turned about slowly, her head rotating from mountain to stream and back to meadow. "Ok you have convinced me, we need a vacation and I promise if you get me out now, we will all take a long one." She rubbed her chin thoughtfully. "Although I don't know where we'll find a place like this in the Andromeda." She started walking toward the cattails. "Hell after seeing this, we can just stay in the virtual program." She continued talking to herself.

To the horror of all the little people hiding in the thick cover, she was heading straight for them. Grimstone reacted the only way he knew and stepped out from behind the giant plant.

"Hey now, who are you little fella? Are you part of this program?" Britt asked.

"I am Grimstone, Lord and high protector of this swamp." He lied. "I do not know what a program is but I would like to be the first to welcome you to our home, in peace." The little man bowed so low his gray beard fluffed the soft moss at his feet.

"Ha! This is great! Yea! This is too damn cool!" Britt smiled broadly. With that she reached out and lightly touched his shiny bald head. "My God, you are so real!"

"I beg your pardon my lady, but I am totally real and have been so since the day of my birth!" Grimstone huffed. "I would like to introduce you to the rest of my meadow family." He waved his hand behind him to coax the rest of the populace out of the tall weeds. From every cool dark shadow emerged a multitude of creatures. Heads spy hopped the lake's placid azure as mermaids bashfully surfaced to be introduced to this strange guest. Britt stood up and stepped back.

"Whoa". She kept backing slowly and commenced in a series of confused glances in all directions. Lifting her right arm, she started to tap her gauntlet. "Why do I feel like I am not in Kansas anymore?" She repeatedly tapped the gauntlet. Her broad smile turned into a scowl and she stopped walking.

"Is there a problem lady? Have we offended you?" Bella asked, lofting herself to nearly Britt's eye level.

"I'm just a little confused. I don't know how I got here, and from the looks of it, I may have some difficulty getting home." It had become clear that she was not in a virtual chamber, and that this was not a joke by her squad mates. Her weapons gauntlet computer was not responding to a simple location inquiry, only offering "Destination and location unknown." She tapped it again and it produced a handful of crackers. She rubbed the two gauntlets together and then extended her arms wrists down to allow a red laser to strike the ground and produce a small fire.

"Huh, they seem to be working just fine, and still I'm not picking up any location." She commented as she ate the crackers and put out the fire.

"It seems your powerful magick has also damaged your lovely hair my lady. You should not meddle in the affairs of the elves." Bella observed. The dragonfly fairy hovered near Britt and touched a fiery curl to show her. Indeed Britt's hair was singed in some places. She sat down on the boulder and tried to think. Her audience watched in anticipation.

If her memory was correct, she had been at a party with her squad members. Their ships were a few clicks down the way on Dead Sands Lane in their assigned hangar. Kolbert had been sent packing back to the Eliptica. Everyone was happy. Yay. Drink, drink more and stumble back to your ship. She itemized in her mind. Pass out and wake up in fairyland? It didn't calculate. Something was terribly wrong. The party consisted of the 23rd squad and a number of the other long-range fighter squads. They had decided to meet on Thernix, celebrate, and then rendezvous back on Zeneria for their next assignment.

Thinking so hard that it made her frontal lobe hurt, Britt could remember walking into the hangar and seeing her fighter in the dark building. After that everything was a blank, until she woke up in Oz that is. She looked closely at the mythical creatures around her. They were closing in to get a better look at her. Perhaps they had deemed her harmless enough to risk it. If her weapons gauntlet was not reading a location, but was still functioning fine, it could mean one of two of things. She was either in a totally different dimension or she was out of range on a galactic level. Even if she were out of range of the Andromeda, she should still be able to pick up Eliptica or Stinette. No signal would basically put her in the next universe.

None of these options comforted her. Looking at her new friends, it was obvious that they would have no information regarding local space transportation. She tipped her head to look at the morning sun. It was obvious that she had to wait a few hours to get a look at the night sky to get some type of bearing on her location. This was not the first time she had encountered such a situation, although usually her equipment worked well enough to get her home right away. She tried to summon her ship to no avail. If Opus was not picking up her signal it was worse than she thought. Her options were now limited to doing as the natives did until she could surmise a plan. She was too well trained to panic just yet.

"Would you mind telling me what you are?" Grimstone asked, cautiously attempting to touch her leg.

"Well, I'm a woman." Britt offered snorting.

"I know that. What I mean is, are you an elf or a nymph or some sort of celestial spirit?" He asked this as though it was a perfectly natural question. Britt looked around once more.

"My lady! Are you ill, I asked you a question?" Grimstone demanded.

"Oh, ha, well you see, I'm a human." She replied. She knew his question was valid. She was used to being an endangered species. She then asked, "Did you say elf?"

"Yes, I said elf and I cannot believe you are a human. Are you sure? You must have been transformed by some powerful spell." Grim stated. All the other fairy creatures murmured in agreement.

"Of course I 'm sure. How many other humans have you seen? Elves, now that's one I haven't heard in a long time. I thought they were only in bed time stories." Britt laughed.

"I'll be supposing you don't believe in fairies either?!" Grimstone blurted out. "Besides, only elves can do magick like yours, so you must be an elf." He seemed confident with this statement.

"I don't know how to do magick, little man. That wasn't magick. That's technology. Science, get it? You speak English." She stated in delayed surprise.

The odds of an English speaking creature being discovered off Zeneria or strictly rare systems were unheard of. The language had been derived from her home of Earth by aliens about a thousand years ago and used widely throughout the Milky Way due to voice translation devices. In the Andromeda it was not so popular and thus the human pirates were all installed with translation chips. This being's lips were moving with his words. Devarelle was starting to truly worry.

She bent down and was almost nose-to-nose with him. Grimstone's face turned bright red. She wasn't threatening him; she just needed to get a better look. It was a nearly daily event for her to encounter new life forms. She had often encountered life forms that her human mind could not comprehend and, from time to time, had to spend a day or so in a mental conditioning seminar to help her brain adjust to the stimulation of the experience. Here, in this meadow it was not her brain that ailed her. It was a creeping pain deep in her heart. Wherever she was, she knew she would definitely be coming back to once things got sorted out. In all her travels she had never seen creatures so close to anything from Earth, and these creatures were not necessarily indigent to Earth at the time she had left it. These creatures were fabled to have lived on her home planet hundreds of thousands of years before she was born and largely regarded as either extinct or make believe.

Before she had time to consider expounding on the subject, she noticed the din of conversation dying down. Many of the meadow party chose to retreat and those that stayed seemed reverent. Her instincts told her that there was a being approaching her from behind. She rose and turned to see the vines and larger plants close to the tree line swaying in the wind-free meadow. Through them emerged a crippled creature trudging along with a twisted walking stick. Britt waited, wondering if she should advance and offer assistance to what she now recognized as a bent old woman. The hag seemed intent on approaching the lake looking up every so often to get her bearings. It took some time, but eventually she reached the gathering by the water. She neglected to introduce herself at first. Instead she chose to rest against the boulder, taking off her hat and fanning her wrinkled, slightly green face.

"Grim, there's a good lad, fetch me a drought." She requested. The pixie dwarf moved to action instantly. Britt thought she heard him mumble the words, "thank goodness." The crone slowed her fanning to take a gander at her company doing her best to seem unaffected.

"Well now, so you have finally arrived and a good thing it 'tis as well." She took the shell full of water from Grim and drank deeply.

"I'm sorry. I don't believe I know you." Britt respectfully replied.

"Well of course not, how could you? You have never been to Zembeth, have you?" She chuckled.

"Well then how do you know me?" Britt asked.

"I cannot say that I *actually* know you, child. I only know that all the signs were pointing to something." She looked about. "And seeing as you are obviously the only "something" around, I can only surmise that YOU are the something."

She patted the slightly smaller rock next to her. "Have a seat, dear. You look a bit flushed."

Britt sat beside the woman never letting her guard down. Old women could be just as dodgy as young women or the most evil of men, and usually smarter.

"Now, knowing you are new to Zembeth, and you *are* new to Zembeth, are you not?" She asked.

"Yea." Britt answered, her frustration starting to seep through her usually controlled voice. Her impatience got the best of her and she blatantly went on, not allowing the hag to finish her statement.

"Hey how about you tell me your name for starters." Britt's voice was firm. While it was not wise to offend natives, it was also not prudent to allow them the instant upper hand.

"How rude of me!" She bellowed out a laugh that was far too dark for such a crouching old bag of bones. "You can call me Ma Toad, 'tis what all my friends call me." She reached out a gnarled hand.

Britt took the hand, marking the unusually solid grip. "I am Britt." She relinquished.

"Back to business then?" She asked. Britt simply nodded. "Right then, knowing you are new to Zembeth." She rolled one slimy eye Britt's way while keeping the other on the tree line. "You are new to Zembeth are you not?"

"Yea. I already said that." Britt fought her impatience, although it was hard not to giggle at the eyeball trick.

"I would guess you are not educated in our culture or ways. Therefore, I took it upon myself to hike out here and give you a bit of advice. In a few moments, through those trees an ogre will lumber. Now this ogre is a slave trader. He is a good man, but a slave trader nonetheless. He will not harm you if you harm not him. He is going towards Garath this very day." She stopped to huff.

"And this concerns me how?" Britt asked.

"Well, my love, on Zembeth all humans are slaves." She stated.

"Well I guess as of today only most humans are slaves. I'm not the slave type." Britt was guarded.

"No, but you are the lost type." Ma Toad tipped her head. "We have only large cities and a sprinkled few villages here. In each, humans are slaves. I find it sickening myself, but that is that. So it is my piece of advice that if you wish to get to a city and find what it is you need, you will need an avenue that will suffice. I will be the first to tell you, and I am sure not the last, that you are a very rare find. It just so happens that Osizio has been banished from Garath and separated from his family. I would be willing to bet my bottom he would take you to the city if you would agree to be traded to Prince Sholendor for his freedom." She took a moment to catch her breath. Britt instinctively backed a bit.

Around this frail woman Britt could feel a very encompassing weight that seemed to tax the hag beyond obvious physical limitation. She watched Britt as if she could see into her thoughts.

"Now child, we both know that few creatures in any world can best a pip like yourself. What is there to lose? What better place to be a slave than in the royal palace?" She pulled a loaf of bread from her bag and handed Britt a chunk. Captain Devarelle took a brief second to pass the bread over a gauntlet to check for poisons and found it safe, if not horribly high in fat content. She ripped off a smaller piece and popped it into her mouth.

"You seem to know more about me than you let on." Britt tested.

"Just look at ye." With surprising speed she propelled a thick goblet from her bag at her human companion. Britt caught the item without hesitation. "Tell me yer not a bum kicker. Convince me you would have a tough time ripping off my noggin before I could spit." Ma Toad prodded. "Besides, just because I am old and my eyes are bad, does not mean I can not see in other ways." Fafella's bushy eyebrows rose and she looked up at her guest. The disguise was becoming increasingly uncomfortable. There was only so much fat you could shrink down before it started cramping up. The sun was not helping matters. She was now concerned if she did not get on with her business the white moon spell would fade. Her skin was already a sick shade of green through the spell.

"I guess you could say that. Why do you care where I go or what happens to me?" Britt challenged. She did not dispute the see comment. She knew well that there were forces in the universe that she barely understood.

"Hum. Well. You dropped, plop, into my meadow. You look like death. You are human. I may be green with age but I am no beast. What kind of Ma would I be not to at least give you a bit o' a head start? I keep no slaves. If ye stick around here, my meadow is sure to be crawling with elves before I can wipe the flies from my ass crack." She stood and shaded her strange eyes. "If ye choose not to go, so be it. Osizio will be coming for a drink soon. I suggest you get out of sight before he arrives. After that, I have no other options. You will find no peace here in a world where you are a thing of great value. And trust me, lass, they *will* be chasing the likes of you in no time. Better to be guarded by an Ogre than ogled by a goblin, 'tis what I always say." She contemplated some goblins that she wouldn't mind being ogled by, but decided that was also for another time.

Britt looked down at Grim. He refused to meet her eyes. "What do you think, Grim?" She asked.

"Ma Toad is very wise and she speaks the truth. I dunna wish to see the likes of you a slave, but there's nothing for it. Better a slave in the palace than a slave under the mountains. I can only imagine that the dwarves would be wealthy enough to purchase the likes of you. I do not wish to think of who else under that mountain that could afford you. I suffer from nightmares as it is." There was no lie in his voice.

Britt took a moment to run things through her still foggy head. From the looks of the current company, technology in any form was a distant wish. In such a case, her next plan of advancement would be to locate some type of learning facility where the stars were mapped out and studied, or perhaps be introduced to a scholar of the sciences. "Is there someone in the palace that studies the night sky?" She asked.

"Why of course. Our Lord Gherkin of Sid O'Sala is an expert on the movement of the night sky. He is the royal astronomer and a right fine elf as well if I do say so." Ma Toad offered. Britt seemed to mull it over for a brief moment longer.

"I guess I don't really have much of a choice." She submitted.

"Ye should not worry lass. I get the feeling, and I get a great many feelings, ye will be fine. A nice lass like you they will treat like a queen." Ma Toad patted Britt's knee just in time to feel the ground quake ever so slightly. With the coming of the Ogre, Ma Toad waddled toward the tree line. "I'll be talking to the beast to prepare him for this. He be not all that bright and ye be a bit much. No sense giving the old lad a heart attack on such a fine day." Britt watched Ma Toad lumber off, all the while wondering if this were a good idea.

While she was somewhat alone, she tested her weapons gauntlets again to no avail, trying every moment to fight the sick feeling growing in her heart. She had been lost before, but never so lost that her high tech toys could not find her way home. She had never been out of communication range of one of her family members. She worked to calm her center and control her emotions. The thought that she might be dead had occurred to her. Now that her mind was clearing, Britt seemed to remember her flight suit being triggered by something. She shifted on the stone, again looking at her singed hair. Somehow she doubted that in death her hair would be singed and she would resort to riding with an ogre to a fairy tale city to become the slave of an elf prince. Even her imagination was not that fringe.

She woke from her stupor when, from the tree line emerged a giant mass of flesh. He was nearly completely covered with nappy black fur, moles and epidural disfigurations. His lips were wide and moist as if saliva constantly dripped off his expansive black tongue that hung out one side of his maw behind a half rotten tusk. The head of this ogre seemed nothing more than another unnatural lump of hairy flesh atop his mobile mass. Osizio's giant ears twitched this way and that to slap the buzzing insects that swarmed around his stench and filth. Britt could see his eyes from where she stood and decided the ogre was, although large, no threat to her. They harbored a dim light of limited intelligence and a simple soul. She surmised creatures of his ilk got by on sheer bodily mass.

The nagging fact that she was standing in a fairy tale continued to plague her. She had not seen any of the elves they had spoken of but she was looking right at a fairy. There was an ogre walking right for her. The old woman was definitely a witch. Her mind burned to figure out this mystery, yet her heart cramped with the first and most natural conclusion. These creatures, as far as her very ample galactic education had proven to her, could only be found in Earth folklore. This would nearly eliminate the possibility of these events NOT being a dream. Again, was she dead? If she were dreaming, it meant she absolutely *had* to stop drinking. The day she started vomiting in her drunken dreams was the day she became scared sober.

Osizio lumbered up to Ma Toad. It was clear he was almost blind, but his nose flared and he tipped his head in her direction.

"I made it, Ma Fafella. If it t'were not ye telling me, I woulda set off and been on me way by the now." He replied gurgling in his deep bass voice.

"Osizio you cut me to the quick. I told you I had a human that could get you back into the city and I do. You must promise to treat her with respect and kindness. I have told her your dilemma and she is willing to go peacefully. Do you understand?" Fafella spoke slowly as to not confuse her aromatic friend.

"Do ye think I would to harm the poor lass? What kind of ogre do ye take me fer? I wasna born in Kloter like the rest o' them brutes." He huffed and tromped in the direction his boil-laden nose directed him. He smelled so horrid that for a moment Fafella considered grabbing him by the filthy tunic and dumping him in the lake. Then she considered the probability of this killing off all the mermaids with some organic form of toxic shock. He must have come close enough to get a good look at Britt because he stopped, mouth agape. His brown, cracked, boar-like tusks jutting up from his pork fat lips framing the cave sized hole that served for his mouth.

"Sweet mother o' me hide!" He spun to look at Fafella then with a bit of effort, turned that masterpiece of horror of a head of his back round to make sure he was not seeing things. "Oh! Me own eyes an ol' heart." He clutched at his tunic. "She is of fairy magic no doubt! Ya know I canno' take a magical lass to that bastard Sholendor. He will skin me fer sure!" He looked as distressed as an ogre can look.

"Osizio, she is real enough and lost. She does not know where she is or how she got here. As a matter of fact, I do not even think she remembers where she came from." Ma Toad shot a knowing look at Britt. Her education and understanding of Britt's history disturbed the captain and set into motion another nagging feeling that her arrival here was indeed a conspiracy of some sort. With the amount of information the hag had of her though, it reassured Britt that she could not be all that far from the reach of the Zenerian Galactic Empire. Millions of civilizations knew of the Zenerian pirates. Granted, few knew which pirate she actually was, but all one need be is Zenerian to evoke either fear or respect.

"Tis she a runaway?" Osizio fretted, bellowing loud enough to shake the leaves from the trees.

"No, you idiot!" Ma Toad slapped him sharply upside the head. "Now you're getting on my last nerve. Pay attention when I am talking to you, you simpleton." Ma Toad started walking toward Britt again. "I told you, she is lost. She got dropped here by accident from some far away land. I have no idea how the magick works. I only know that we have to help her. Imagine the bad luck! Do you want our crops to grow, you selfish bastard?" She skirt whipped the brute with such proficiency and courage that now Britt was sure this bent old witch was more than meets the eye.

Harassed into being convinced, Osizio approached with cautious disbelief. He started to reach out and touch Britt's breast.

"Not so fast, fat boy!" She backed away quickly. "No one said anything about fondling on our first date." Britt warned.

Osizio gasped, "O kracky it talks!"

"Of course I talk." Britt laughed in spite of herself, slyly turning her torso sideways.

"And look at those teeth! Blimey I nev'ra seen a wench with all o' her teeth, and as white and all." He was talking so fast his jaws looked as though they were attached with surgical rubber bands. All the while he dripped saliva and chunks of something he had eaten in times past. Guessing it was breakfast was a forgone conclusion by the color of it.

His statement, when registered, distressed Britt a bit. If she was all that, then what were the other humans like? This situation was beginning to look more like a mission than a mishap. She was always on mission and more times than not it was because of mishap.

"Oh Ma I canna thank ye enough!" The ogre was actually crying! "I'm goin' to see my Censci this very day! And my sons! I getta see my boys again! First time in no' 50 years!" He was almost dancing as he cried out.

This statement cemented the deal. Even if she did not want to be a slave, she would do what she could to help the ugly fool see his family again. "I'm such a sap!" She mentally chastised herself. It seemed a small price to pay. She would play with the prince for a time, and give a man back his family. At the very least she needed nightfall.

"Oh all right already, can we get going please, you're making me sick." She smiled and at Grimstone. The small man looked sick to his stomach. "What's wrong Grim?" She asked.

He looked terrified. "You are such a nice lady. I really hate to see you off to the high elf prince. I wish you could stay." He was trying to sound brave.

"Trust me Grim, I can take care of myself far better than you could ever imagine. Besides, I'm not afraid of a little elf." She bent and kissed him on the cheek. "Bye everyone, thanks for everything." She waved and started to walk again for the road. She hesitated at Ma Toad.

"I suppose I should thank you." Britt said.

"I have no doubt ye will find yer way. Be sure not to mention to that big lug that ye plan to skit outta there the minute ye get the chance. He may not take kindly to the knowledge." She winked once again. Britt looked back and Osizio looking forward at her backside giving it quite the once over.

"I'm not too worried about it. I'm sure when things start to fall in place I will make some sense out of it and get home. Believe it or not, I have been lost more than once. Maybe I will swing back by and visit one of these days. Are you up for company?" She asked.

"Sure! That would be brilliant. Did I mention that I have a son?" Ma Toad took her hand and started to escort Britt to the road.

"None of that, you slick old witch." Britt giggled. "Trust me, you don't want your son stuck with a wild spitfire like me." Her mind went over the possibilities of a male that was part of Ma Toad's gene pool and decided that the chances were more than likely very slim that she would want a kiss.

At the tree line Ma Toad said her goodbyes and watched as SHE finished the journey to the rutted road. She remained still as the two unlikely traveling partners mounted the wagon and were well out of sight. Absently stroking the lock of ebony hair she still held in her pocket. The sick feeling in her gullet was not from the shrinking spell.

She started to walk back to the tree line so she could explode back into her fantastic goblin-sow self. This feeling, foreign and terrifying, a first for her, was the feeling of a malicious magick that she had no power to fight. As each day passed, her nightmares became more vivid. She had seen the fields of the Arosa black and burned. As she walked, she wiped a silent tear from her now bulging eye. Everything would die.

"May the great Mother Goddess guide her feet for the sake of us all." Ma Fafella prayed, looking over her now broad green shoulder down the road.

Chapter 2
Bipolar Fey

If the world ended while she slouched on the pot, would it make a difference? Better to evaporate here on the chamber dump than have to face her mother, the Queen.

She despised the woman; it was just that simple. This morning, as the sun spilled its light over the pale limestone battlements atop the palace walls and found its way into her bedchamber, she cringed.

Princess Meriden of Fairfax was at a zenith. This was the morning. It had been coming. Something had been coming. Now that it was here, she decided it would be better to die on the pot. She bit her blue lip and shifted her bottom.

This particular chamber pot was so cold to the touch of her alabaster buttocks it made her wince in displeasure. She loved to inflict these petty discomforts upon herself. No elf needs to bear such humiliating circumstances.

Yet she, crowned princess of elves, felt it her just reward forever having been born and often used displeasure as a way of validation. Again today, Meriden fretted, as everyday, that her mother, the Queen of the realm, would summon her to the main chambers, only to express her royal displeasure for the weak daughter she had borne. She leaned forward and put her finely sculpted face in her hands and blew a stray strand of stark white hair from her cheek. As this lecture continued, it would evolve into a grand appraisal of her royal niece, the Duchess De'Loria of Havaland. From that point it would wonder to Meriden's deserting father, the once great King Ren' Fordel of Garath. Her mother made it a point to criticize the desertion of the king. This point was duly followed by remarks of Meriden's resemblance in personality to her weak father. Alisi ranted on and on of Ren' Fordel's shiftless behavior and the fact that Meriden was turning out just like her father. All this was done, as so often before, in front of as many members of the royal court as the Queen could summon or force into earshot.

It happened constantly in private as well, Meriden reminded herself. Meriden then wondered if her self-absorbed mother realized that she had developed a pattern of abuse that literally everyone was familiar with by now. The entire court, servants included, knew from there her comments would trail along with adjectives like "weak minded" and "fickle" as well as "untamable". If Meriden's feelings were correct, the Queen was about to get a bit more than she could handle.

Meriden sat, the picture of misery and self-pity, still secretly wishing she could sit on the crapper all day. She started naming the small lumps that dropped from her bum to the water in the pot, after her mother. It made her giggle. She glanced up from her cold hands and insane laughter. Across the great bed chamber, mounted on the stone wall, loomed a giant gilded mirror. Why it had been positioned directly across the room from the chamber pot was, as yet, a frustrating mystery that Meriden had not had the time or motivation to solve or rectify. This mirror served no other purpose than to remind the young princess that she was indeed her mother. Her skeletal knees jutted out, suspended above the ample ceramic pot like skinned potatoes stuck on birch sticks. Her skin was stark white luminescence and in every way free of blemish. Reflected from a distance, the slightly warped blown glass of the mirror made her face seem even more narrow and sallow than it actually was. The torches had yet to be lit. In this dull light she resembled one of the prisoners of the dungeon. Her face was that of a depressed famine survivor. Whatever the fabricated situation of her own self loathing, the mirror mercilessly created the image that helped her naturally large ruby colored eyes look almost grotesquely disproportioned in comparison with the rest of her face. In truth, she looked like a big white bug.

Despite the matter or means, here she sat, the naked vision of rebellion. "Watch out Fairfax, here I shit!" She mused to herself. Her white hair was matted to one side of her head. She slept very soundly and for long hours at a time. This enraged her mother. It was completely unhealthy to sleep so. Just as with food, elves required very little sleep. Meriden, however, made it a ritual to lock herself away in the tower and sleep for days. This alone had earned her a great deal of scorn and scandal at court. Due to this and other social weaknesses, like the inability to watch slaves being whipped, she was known as a threat to the kingdom. A weak child could never be Queen of the elfish people. She would be expected to rule with an iron fist. Meriden lazily pulled her hand away from her face to examine it. It looked more like a cage of bones held together by paper and thin purple thread, so much for the old iron fist. She continued the appraisal, tracing her finger over her protruding ribs as they slid in a slow rhythm back and forth under the clinging skin. Her hand rose to her scant breasts resting high atop the washboard that passed for her rib cage. She tried to warm her petite blue nipples. They were supposed to be pale pink. They would be if she had been healthy.

She never looked up when the slave door in the south curve of the room creaked open. Her maid, Sara, quietly walked 'round the bed to look at her mistress sitting alone and naked on the pot.

"'Tis yer mother callin ye, lass. We canna have ye for to sit here all the morning and bring about her anger. Come now, off of this silly perch ye have fasted yerself to and up to dress."

Sara had been Meriden's personal slave since birth. Her voice was dry and quiet. She was very stout and even on the tall side for a gnome. She had thin yellow hair and completely yellow skin. Her teeth were sharp little points that she used like scissors. She was a fortunate gnome to have these gifts as well as the gift of hearing and speech. Many palace slaves were relieved of their tongues when they were birthed or purchased, especially those that attended the royal family. It was much easier to cut out their tongues than to damage their ears. As it were, the ears of a gnome were scarcely more than small holes in the sides of their bulbous heads. The creatures were considered horribly ugly to begin with. Visually scarring them further would make them too repulsive to bear. On another turn, this was a sturdy breed, able to survive through nearly anything, including the wrath of their elfish masters. They were known for their incredible strength despite their small frames. The only other creatures so small with such strength were dwarves, and of course a dwarf could not be a slave. They were related to elves and revered as nearly equal.

Sara reached over and hoisted the young princess off the pot. "I'm not supposing ye think 'twill be me that will be wiping yer backside. 'Tis best ye snap out o' it quick afore ye are off to yer mother. Ye know how she is on these days. If I canna be telling ye for warnin, she did summon Rowland this morning. Ye know what this means, my love." The gnome talked on as she watched Meriden wipe herself with a cloth and silently walk over to the dressing stool by the wicked mirror.

Rowland of Sid O'Sala was the royal scout. In truth Alisi used him to spy on other elves. It was fact that an elf could see much, but when inquiring after other elves, the game got a bit complicated. Most elves could block energy and inquiry to their whereabouts and doings. Yet it was usually only the whereabouts of one, Roderick of Darmuth Anor, which concerned Queen Alisi of Fairfax.

For the past one hundred years, Roderick had done everything in his power to avoid Alisi. The thought of him actually coming to the palace was unheard of. Even he knew this. Meriden had to respect the fact that he knew he was not welcome, even when her mother did not. Meriden would always welcome him because she knew it was his insistence on living on his own terms and his refusal to kowtow to the gentry that bubbled with social contempt for him. "Hurrah for Roderick" she would often whisper. When he was very young, he would come to speak to King Ren' Fordel, who seemed to favor him. He was a fish out of water among the elite of the elfish people. His freakish appearance could stunt the court from its constant chatter. Meriden remembered him standing in the main court hall. His hair was complete black. Long curls hung down, spilling over his broad shoulders. His strong, square face completely contrasted the normal fine features of a truly exquisite elf. His mouth was wide with full lips and his teeth were larger and square. His eyes however were elfish. They slanted upward in a completely elfish fashion. Their hue, enhanced and brilliant bright green and ever keen like jade illuminated and animated.

He had the ears of an elf, yet his body was heavy and thick with muscle, seeming odd in tandem with his magick born grace. Upon entrance of any room, he towered over his wispy kin. He moved with the precision of a hunted beast along the stealth road of elfish ancestry. This energy parted crowds and inspired songs. He never looked down. Meriden pondered this. He never looked in any direction he felt uncompelled to. He plowed through social barriers to deal with those that would scorn him head raised, intention calm and purpose prepared. He had been the uninvited, yet sought after, company of each tribe of elfish worth. For each he was unique and for each he was welcomed at a trembling arm's length, despite contradiction of terms when he left. If he were to show up in any Duke's court it was considered, under whispered hands, good fortune for the house yet uncomfortable circumstances for those of less internal metal. So it was, that Roderick of Darmuth Anor lived in chosen limbo, never in the world of his people and never completely outside of their curiosity. Meriden envied this power, noting that few elves that she knew of realized their potent un-eclipsed freedom.

In reflection, Meriden remembered how much she loved when the young rogue was at the dinner table. He would laugh. This mesmerized her. The only other elf male that she knew that could burst into laughter was her father. When Roderick laughed his face glowed and his deep voice boomed and vibrated. He was always very kind to Meriden and would truss up her white hair and ask her of her day and her school, then proceed to listen to her replies rather than look over her frail head and ignore her. The only member of the family that he rarely talked to was Alisi. There were many times Meriden would wander down the halls of the palace with him to end at a game of gammet only to surmise that the rumors of this man being an evil killer were wholly fabricated. She had heard from many that Roderick was callous and evil, capable of feats of malice unheard of for even an elf. He seemed to use this cloud of fear to his advantage. Never admitting to it, yet never denying either. Once her father disappeared, Roderick did everything he could to avoid the palace. He refused to hold company with the Queen alone. He usually did her bidding to save trouble, then was done with it and lost again from her grasp.

Sara hobbled on her short, bowed legs to Meriden's wardrobe. As soon as she finished digging through the undergarments, she turned to see Meriden had dressed herself by way of magick.

"Now there is no need to be difficult, lass! Ye could of told ol' Sara that ye were of a mind to help yerself." She patiently folded the cloth shift and placed it back in the wardrobe drawer.

"You sly old girl. You know perfectly well why my mother is up in arms. She knows." Meriden sounded almost gleeful.

"Knows what?" Sara tried to sound indifferent.

"Really, Sara. Act not simple for my concern. You know Mother knows what is on the wind. Granted, she is not skilled enough to read it correctly. That is why she has sages." Meriden slumped over and puffed. "She knows that today is the day."

"And what day would that be?" Sara did know. Even the slaves were talking about it. Every half penny witch in the market was spouting off about the end of the world.

"Strange, even I can not quite grasp it. I know that it is something I have no understanding of. I only know that things are going to be very different around here very soon." Meriden hoped her conversation would keep Sara occupied and interested. She knew the longer her slave stood, arms akimbo, the longer she avoided her mother.

"Tis it the end o' the world?" Sara ventured.

"No. I do not think so. Pity, really. I have no idea what it is. That is why mother wants Roderick. I will bet my little blue bulb of virtue Ma Fafella knows what it is all about."

Sara slapped her for mentioning her maidenhood in such a way.

"How dare ye speak so? Who was it who taught ye to curse like that?" Sara badgered.

"You." Meriden answered honestly.

"Well ye hadda better be backing offa that kind o talk. Now let's get ye down to the main hall afore the guards are up here again. Remember last time?" Sara barked as she started making the bed.

"It does not matter Sara. One day is the same as the next. One day of this life to the other to another, there is no end to this cycle. Would that I could, I should think to leap from the window like a mad slave. I am learning what their notions are and why they do such things."

Meriden's morbid tone, and ridiculous assumption that she had any real idea of what it was to be a slave, gave Sara the nearly uncontrollable urge to strike her off the dressing chair with a blunt object.

"Oh! Enough o' that. 'Sides, who would it be that t'would cause me to have such a pain in my arse everyday?" Sara moaned as she threw up her knotted yellow arms.

Once the slave combed and braided her hair, Meriden walked to the door and started down the tower stairs. Every window brought a gentle breeze that wisped her fine white hair about her face. She walked as slow as she could without arousing a jolt from Sara. The gnome followed her down the stairs just below the level of the wind.

Meriden had magically added a gray cloak and a woolen gray corset to her plain white muslin chemise. Now she appeared the vision of elfish royalty. Perhaps it was true what her mother had said, "The older you become, the less your mind shifts to those things better left to humans and gnomes." Walking down the dank tower stairs, she could not expel the feeling of numbness that was overcoming her more and more, year after year. Perhaps she was becoming truly elfish.

Below in the main hall, the sounds of the harp and flute could be heard. It floated up the winding stairs and filled the passage. Meriden paused at the next window. This special opening looked over the walls and out to the great white Tree of Truth. One more spiral round and the only thing one could see was the great vine covered palace wall. This land was beautiful, and in that natural beauty Meriden found a spark in her blue heart.

The tree was the largest of its kind in the entire realm and hosted the Temple of Life. Elves were a fellowship of the circle of life and therefore their calendars, holidays, and all other functions, were aligned to this great cycle. This Hallafawn tree was the hub of their spiritual rituals. The tree still had the telltale skin textured white bark. The leaves were copper colored, red and gold and glinted with a metallic reflective effect. The window framed a picture of this tree atop a deep green rolling hill of grass so rich it would appear to have been painted in the window by a master. This special hill sat atop the northern peninsula, surrounded by the aqua sea waves, thrashing amidst limestone break walls under a clear blue sky laced with breath taking manicured gardens that hosted flowers of every color of the imagination. This vision never failed to give her hope.

"Ay, every morning ye stop to wonder at her. Tis as I tell ye my child, ye are more than yer mother thinks." Sara, in saying so, reached forward and touched Meriden's frail hand.

The princess turned and looked down into the yellow eyes without speaking. She used her powers to embrace Sara, giving her nanny slave a feeling of warmth. If she were ever seen holding the gnome in an actual embrace, Sara would be killed instantly. Many times as a child, Meriden had hurried from her spacious bed through the slave tunnels to Sara's chamber. The cold nights in the tower had been too much for her to bear. She would often wake screaming of dreams she could not explain, or did not wish to contemplate. It was unheard of to seek solace with her mother or another of her kind. Even if she had the courage to creep into an elf's chambers, no matter whose it was, they would have her removed and whipped. It was rare that an elf got whipped. She did not wish to be the first to break that record after so many years. She had succeeded in ranking at the top of the "history's worst members of the royal family" list thus far. At least she was wise enough not to secure the "number one of all time" place for herself.

So it was that she had become familiar with the slave tunnels beneath the palace. They seemed to accept her. At first they were terrified, but amazingly enough they were more afraid of Sara than they were of Meriden, so she was allowed to stay. As time wore on, the slave populace began to welcome her. She changed when she passed through the stonewall doors and went to the bowels of the palace. Deep down she knew that their acceptance of her was largely due to the fact that she would one day be Queen and this could only help their circumstances. She was treated as an equal; this was the agreement that kept her visits regular. She was made to sew and cook and help with harvest. She loved every minute of it. She was allowed to hear and tell stories during their secret social gatherings. She was never permitted to use magick in any form in the tunnels or to speak of this crime. There were plenty of gnomes on Zembeth. It would be an easy action to slaughter the entire staff and replace them with new stock from Sid O'Sala. They would all be sold for dried meats in the market and the money used to enhance Queen Alisi's wardrobe.

She was aware that the entrance she wished to steal into was not far down the stairs. Knowing Sara would have none of this, she mentally willed her slave to become preoccupied with duty and become overwhelmed with the urge to trot off and bark orders elsewhere. Sara was in no way a weak-minded individual so this had do be done with precision and grace. A stark mental intrusion would be instantly identified and then it would be war. Instead she flashed images of pots falling and fires burning unattended by incompetent kitchen slaves as if slipping notes into the cache of her mind.

"Well lass, I musta be off now. No telling what will happen to me hide iffin those lazy layabouts foul up her morning meal." She started down the stairs. "It's best ye just get yerself straight to that throne room, ye hear!" She pointed a little finger at the princess.

"Yes, Queen Sara." Meriden bowed.

"That'll be enough o' that, spoiled wench." She patted Meriden's behind and waddled down the steps.

The tunnels were designed with pixie-sized races in mind, run and set before Meriden was born. Dwarves were known for their skill with such affairs having carved the blood of their culture in stone. Meriden slipped like a pale vapor into the familiar tunnel, closing the heavy door behind her. She had no fear here in the earth and now stopped to pull in a deep breath of the stone and torch oil air. As always she was reminded that her childhood imprinted memories marked the slave caves as a place of comfort and acceptance, a place where the fires were truly warm, where she was greeted with smiles. Being the royal disappointment she was, she was given the courtesy of respect married to rank, yet she had only managed a few true friends in her 199 years and they were, all of them, slaves. Because of this hidden relationship with the common folk, in their rough tongues she had been named "air lily" or Lelienach – meaning "the pale air flower."

It was necessary now to slink near to a crawl along the passages. None of the gnomes jumped at the sight of glowing red eyes. She began to prepare her body and mind for the spy mission. It was important that she lower her overall body temperature prior to approaching the peek hole she planned to use. The palace was full of such intrusive crevices. There were chutes for food, dead bodies, nearly everything one could think of. Dwarves were brilliant and efficient.

She must, also, dwindle her emotions to silent memories. She had to quell the angst that welled so easily in the presence of her royal mother. Alisi, like all elves, could pick up on all of the above and more, even in a crowded room, if her focus was precise.

She approached, sliding on her belly without fear of filth. The tunnels were kept in better shape than the palace. Meriden almost had to stifle a snicker pushed forth from this irony. What little revenges they could afford, the slaves rejoiced in. At the spy hole she immediately shoved one of her eyes into the light causing its' reflective power to dim the red glow and closed the other. Her mother was seated on her elaborate throne, her royal advisor Misinki taking the auspicious position of sitting in Meriden's assigned perch. The two were chatting softly as the rest of the court buzzed with intrigue. Alisi raised her bone-shadowed hand and signaled the pipers to play. Meriden could never understand her mother's attraction to these ghastly windbags, better suited for war and ogre orgies.

Around the main hall, silver slips and sheets of fine fabric had been strung with lavender ribbon over the small hallafawn trees that had been grown between the great marble statues of kings past. Chairs of pale marble adorned with silver work and white suede cushions surrounded elaborate tables covered with goblets of carved crystal and plates of white gold.

All three palaces were designed differently, yet each of them housed a great hall that echoed the nature of the city's magick in sculpture and style. This palace was home to white elves or the lighter races and its great hall mimicked the theme of light magic. Shots of pale yellow gold flowered molding carved as fine as natural vein wrapped around the support pillars next to hand selected plants chosen for their color and fragrance. The spacious floor of this hall was a moving recreation of the northern sky, ever changing, in the center of such a room, mysterious as its inspiration. Clouds could be seen from time to time shifting in the magical skin of the walls of pale blue and silver. Here in the north, elves were lithe and slight as air and snow. Their customs were prim and serene if not suppressed, lacking in the primal urges that seemed to pepper the other elfish tastes. Thus, Meriden's pipe issues.

The palace at Garath was designed by jeweled elves that predominantly inhabited the southlands. Although they were of the same race, the elves of the south tended to be larger and more physically structured. The definition given to jewel toned referred to the rainbow of colors these elves seemed genetically prone to. Rowland was a southern elf, Meriden pondered, recalling his white streaked blood red hair and amber eyes. She had seen many southern elves, some with purple hair, some with green, even some with pink. Skin tone for these elves tended to veer away from the ghost white of the northern and western elves. These elves were tan and peach, their skin living with color and able to change with exposure to sun and shade. Garath was a hall of earth tones and primitive simplicity. The tall oak grew within this hall, covered with fragile golden figurine offerings. The twin thrones were cast of wood and stone. Their seats were woven from Arosa grass worked until soft and forgiving. The great floor sunk to a rock bed lake, alive with fish and plants and easy for any elf to glide over.

The dark palace at Kloter Mass Arosa boasted black onyx walls polished to a mirror finish, carved with magick to show fighting dragons throughout. The mountain elves, although un-rare, were seldom seen outside this city and were believed to be close relatives to the ever-elusive Gothica elfin clans that lived deep in the Shalnas forest. They were the largest and strongest of the breed. Although their skin was as pale as their cousins in the north, their demeanors were dark and brooding. Meriden could very well remember looking into the eyes of solid ink black. Their magic contrasted and completed the circle. And so it was that their hall was dripped with scarlet and deep purple, embellished with detailed iron works, their floor a macabre spiral of magical symbols constructed to maintain balance within the darker surges that dwell in all.

Meriden had never been to Kloter Mass Arosa. From what she had been taught, she was quite certain she would never willingly visit. Her cousin De'Loria had already graduated into the grim duty of Prime Elfish Sorceress and Duchess of the city, as was her birthright and responsibility. Unlike Meriden, her education had been heavily seasoned with knowledge of the dark arts. As well her personality had been colored by life within a city lacking of order and virtually pregnant with compromise. Meriden had been required to learn the same, yet practiced it only when absolutely necessary. Her bloodline and training must be universal in nature if she were to rule Zembeth in its' entirety. Her mind was used in ways that De'Loria could not comprehend. Meriden must understand all and focus her powers on a much more diverse level. It was imperative that De'Loria maintain and focus the sum of her strength on the relentless struggle of dark energies cyclone spinning constantly in the goblin city.

Now Meriden looked from a slit in the stone wall at the statue of her father. He seemed to have more adornments than the other kings, she mused. This must secretly enrage her mother. Pulling her eyes back to the throne, she rested her chin on her hands, exploring a feeling she had been exploring now for months. It was the same that she had spoken to Sara about not long ago. At first she speculated it to be little more than marriage terror. However, omens revealed a different story and she had chosen to dissipate each as well, not daring to reply when her headmaster questioned her.

"My lady Princess, have you the feeling of chaos looming ever so, as if it were to be plucked from the very air before you?" Eldewyn asked as if in passing. Meriden knew her powers far exceeded her most advanced masters. This was not a question of concern for her education, but an attempt to validate the visions of one less gifted.

"Why master, I have felt so constantly from my day of birth." She replied, knowing he would accept her usually blue doom and gloom answer. He would then shake his head in disgust and get back to the task of keeping the princess busy.

Searching now, she struggled with the term "chaos". It could be described so, yet it exhilarated her. Magick affected every living creature differently. Reading omens and auras was a matter of personal priority and opinion. One sees what one chooses to see unless one is trained to let go of selfish motivation to view the naked truth. Eldewyn must still be terrified if he indeed felt the same disruption that Meriden was now exploring. It was the feeling she may experience if she had enough courage to run through the hall, right that moment, ripping cloths off tables and dancing like mad before her mother. It made her contemplate strutting up to the throne and prostrating herself before Alisi and the entire court then sailing away. Away? Where? Where did she wish to sail? She coursed her mind, urging it to answer her question, knowing it had other plans. Nothing came, as if the magical voice she was so used to speaking with had no words for such a location. What fun! The best part was that she knew all the elders were feeling this way, as well, and it did not sit with the gentry. In the scholars' halls, she could fair near cut the air of tension. It cheered her to see her superiors in such a state, especially her mother. Alisi hated being out of control, and this magick left no room for order or form. It was the magick of wild change and unending possibilities. It was something new to all of them. Meriden knew that even the average of the gnomes felt it. Now that was powerful, she thought as she lie on her stomach in the tunnel looking at her mother's harried expressions.

Alisi was a mess. Her usually cool and calculated nerves were shot. She screamed at EVERYONE now. She screamed before, but never at her counsel or members of her immediate staff. Meriden was deep in gleeful thought of her mother's distress when she was jarred by the incoming presence into the great hall.

Just then Rowland was announced. Meriden hissed with displeasure at forgetting her journal back in the tower. She liked to jot down notes and draw pictures. She had been waiting for another chance to see Rowland of Sid O'Sala and study him. She waited like a fool for each of his visits, hoping he would request her company. Often they would sit and take tea. He had been assigned as a guard on many a journey. She was hoping with all her heart that her mother was planning on assigning him to the princess for the upcoming trip to Garath. Now he stood before Alisi. He was windswept and wild like burnished gold and hard leather.

"My lord Rowland! What a pleasure to see you in good health after your long journey." Queen Alisi greeted. Rowland bowed ever so slightly. He had learned to keep his eyes on the queen many years ago.

"My Queen. I bring you news of Garath. The city is secure and prepared for the games as well as the wedding. Prince Sholendor has seen to the last minute details of city security and awaits your arrival." By this time, many young elfish had gathered. Rowland, like Roderick and Amaranth, were special treats of masculinity for their starving spirits. Most courtly gentlemen primped and prodded. It would never be admitted that they gossiped like old maids, yet all men of court were involved in intrigue. Rowland spoke with conviction and presence. From time to time he would dodge a glance around the room, erupting a spray of giggles.

"Is there news of the whereabouts of Roderick?" The queen tried to sound aloof.

"None, my lady. Even I must guess to his location." Rowland lied. He knew perfectly well where Roderick was and what he was about. His own magick was strong enough to conceal it.

"You would think being summoned by the Queen would be enough to bring our recluse from his hiding." She was simmering.

"He enjoys a quiet life, my lady. I am sure if he were really needed he would appear." Rowland tried to sound firm yet assuring.

"What do the seeing tell of these events in Garath?" She inquired.

Rowland shifted at this question. Apparently even he had caught wind of the unsettling vibrations. "I have not spoken to the seeing, my lady. I was not permitted into the private chambers of the palace. Sholendor chose to keep me in the front hall." He would not have paid mind to what they had to say either way. He would wait and take a visit to Ma Fafella if he needed to understand the comings and the goings of Zembethian energy. This was a privilege Alisi was not privy to.

“Is there something amiss, my lady?” He asked in curiosity. He had felt much the same waves within the presence of their untamed forests. The land spoke louder than the cold stones of the castle and Rowland was a man of the fields and forests.

Alisi huffed and started to fidget with the ornate throne armrest. As he watched the Queen stew, Rowland resisted the urge to ask why Meriden had not reported such an event. He did not see her in the crowd, yet he felt her not far off. She had been the reason he agreed to this position. She was the reason he ran into this cold room. He looked up to the platform and noted the reason she was hiding. It occurred to him to reach out to her mentally, yet he would not risk Alisi picking it up. Meriden was safe for the moment and if her mother knew she was crawling about eavesdropping, Rowland might end up in the royal dungeons. He chose not to think of what Alisi would do to Meriden.

“Well then, be off to Garath.” Alisi ordered.

“My lady?” Rowland had hoped to stay for the night.

“You heard me, messenger. If Roderick is going to show up anywhere, it will be Garath for the games. Even if he chooses not to, Donavan and Amaranth will surely make an appearance. You can question them and bring me back the information however you see fit.” She noticed the hum rising from the courtiers. “Roderick has his hand on and in every political corner of this nation, dark and light. I know he sits with the military generals of Kloter Mass Arosa. He has their ear and their loyalties even and ever more so than my own niece, the RULER of Kloter Mass Arosa.” She loudly stressed the word RULER. “Your own father holds him in high regard and confides in him, does he not?” She asked, hoping to intimidate him into admission.

“Roderick has been like a brother to me and surely a son to my father, yes lady.” Ferrin practically helped Ma Fafella raise the boys when none would assist. They had grown to manhood together and Ma Fafella depended on Ferrin of Sid O’Sala to teach the boys the way of their people, knowing at one point they would be elf men. There had never been a situation in Zembethian history where two male elf infants were left at a tavern in Kloter Mass Arosa, then picked up by a goblin sow and taken to be raised in the seclusion of an elf-free – magickal meadow. When the boys were very young, Ferrin of Sid O’Sala had asked at all the royal elfish courts if anyone would take the boys in. None offered, to his embarrassment. Fafella gladly kept the children and raised them.

“Who better to divulge information if a revolt were submerged in the peasant whispers? As well he, as you I think, have the well of wisdom that is Ma Fafella. She is the most powerful sorceress save my own daughter known to the thinking people of these lands. I feel we must be wary of times to come. My own dreams foretell an unveiling. I see Meriden in these dreams. She is floating away into the clouds.” She noted the skin-thin twitch in Rowland’s animal amber eyes. “Surely this concerns the kingdom entire.”

“I assure you, my queen, if I hear the slightest of such whispers, you will be the first I speak of it to.” He answered, being wily enough to know that Alisi was using his affection for Meriden to draw out information that he had no business giving her. Even if Ma Fafella, or any other commoner for that matter, would have told him something worthwhile, he was wise enough to feel the shift as well. If Alisi was so incapable of suppressing her greed and anger that she could not deal with these energy shifts, it was her own inadequacy.

"You have one foot in my court and the other in the wild, Rowland of Sid O'Sala. I enjoy your treachery. It keeps me sharp." She waved her hand as if dismissing a child. "Be off now for Garath and announce my arrival. I must now send a guard to find my worthless whelp of a daughter."

Meriden needed to hear no more. Using her mastery of the element air, she lifted her body off the stone floor and hovered herself back to the passage and out to the stairwell. Chin set firmly for the moment, she trudged down the long descent to the high hall. Soon she would be off to Garath with Sara to be married to Sholendor of Garath. The hell she lived in now, of constant negative appraisal and never ending ridicule was nothing compared to what was to come. In her hand she fondled a stone. Later she would set it upon a black mirror in her private chambers. She would light a blue fire and tap the glass three times. She would call to the spirits of the future to bring about this elusive shift all seemed barely aware of. She would spit on the stone and drop a pin prick of her own blood to ensure her personal entanglement in any event that would free her of the privilege of being queen. As she trudged down the tower stairs now, she made a note to use her same blood in the ink of her journal. If a spell were to be cause to change her stars it would have to start with her. The written word had its own power. A tale once set down for all time was a more powerful truth than one spun from the voices at campfires. If there was going to be an upheaval, she was going to be part of it. She sauntered through the crowd that had assembled at the bottom of the tower stairs. For the first time in almost two hundred years, the Princess of Fairfax had a gleam in her eyes.

Chapter 3
Dead Questions

Many trillions of miles away, through the anomalies of outer space, on a desert planet, stood Canga of Zeneria. Time is a tricky thing in different dimensions. This story must struggle with that distance. She stood struggling with her ever-volatile emotions. Her thoughts wandered. Space. The universe. A Galaxy. Millions of years of research and searching for many civilizations had been totally devoted to the discovery of the giant void. It is strange how things are lost to some and kin to others. Canga could not help but wonder at this from time to time. As a child she would lie atop her fighter and look at the stars. For her this was simply looking at a living map. She knew the patterns of this galaxy as well as she knew her own heart. Her people lived among the stars and enjoyed a life of boundless exploration. At times this would frighten her. It was most often the times or the moments she really took to contemplate such things, that the reality of how insignificant she believed herself to be would stifle her. How easily her life could end. The horror of being stranded to one planet and not being able to escape its destruction was a theme that had haunted many of her dreams, second only to the fear of having her spirit controlled and molested into servitude. These were among the very small list of things that Canga of Zeneria could truly be said to fear.

Earlier, much earlier that morning, actually just past the mid of night, she had been walking behind her best friend. They had been out drinking the entire long Thernixian night. Canga knew Britt had consumed far too much Dardasian Brew to be left alone. Canga had stopped a few paces behind her captain to haul a pail from a well for a drink, trying to rid her mouth of the coming morning's film. It had only taken a few seconds. She knew Siggurd was close. They always traveled in groups or at the very least pairs. One second she watched Britt walk into the hangar. The next second her flight suit had activated and she had been blown a few hundred yards back down Dead Sands Lane.

She had charged into the inferno, not fearing for her safety with her flight suit in full survival mode. She had searched through the fire-engulfed piles of roof that had fallen and then the molten ashes and amber glowing floor. She had cried for help and was answered. More searching, more tears, followed by unbelievable numbness and disbelief. There had been bodies moving around her but she looked through them, pain pushing past clarity and comprehension. She did not remember walking into the open desert.

She wiped at her bright yellow eyes. She called on every meditation lesson she had ever attended to keep her calm. She was a cosmic cut-out of slim black amidst the orange waves of heat on the Thernexian desert landscape that swirled around the city. She was of an animal nature, her legs long and strong, her mind connected with the living force of the universe. Her every movement reflected stealth in the darkness that was her shadow, she was Canga. She must stay in control. The fires were still burning. There was no reason Canga could conceive of, after slapping her weapons gauntlets so many times that her hand ached, that Britt would not answer her. Eventually her twin brother Billy had had to drag her out of the rubble before she zombie-strolled off alone. He had shoved her forward onto the street. That was when she had started walking in a haze of shock. He followed slowly. He was the only one present that dared.

She could hear Byron Dawson before she could smell him in the smoke. It was strange how she felt in a dream, unable to move. Her mind would not accept him running toward her, or the fire, or the hangar in flames.

"Canga! Come on, we gotta get out of here!" He shot a cautious glance toward Billy whom had chosen to simply hang back. He pulled at her arm. She turned her dark face to see him. Her smooth black skin was streaked with soot and tears. Dawson looked into the sharp cat eyes, the pupils wide, and their rims bloodshot. This wasn't going to be easy. He had never seen Canga cry. He had been her partner for years, after he had been taken from New York and brought to Zeneria. He, like Britt, had made the trip through the wormhole to the far galaxy of Andromeda. This one was old and had been studied by many other systems. Zeneria was only one of these systems and one of the few to make use of it on a regular basis. Many other systems refused to risk the trip, arguing that the Milky Way was a rotting graveyard of dysfunctional systems and Earth was the worst of them. It was a game of {don't talk to the neighbors, as a matter of fact don't even look at them and least of all don't give them our address or phone number!

When wormhole travel started, most of the Andromeda systems got involved. It didn't take long in the Earth study program for them to figure out that opening the door was a very bad idea. Some species were adaptable to Earth and made advanced studies and observations of the society and its history. The findings were plastered galactic wide and it was voted by an overwhelming majority that the Milky Way and her primitive systems were an infectious cancer that, if allowed to seep into the Andromeda, would spread like wildfire and destroy what little peace they were able to maintain.

The ecology teams followed suite and when the findings of blatant lack of respect for healthy systems was displayed in such a short time as a "developed" system, the lid on the coffin was sealed. The contact had been made. Earth people were now aware there was life on other planets, or at least some of them. Their television and movies began to reflect this vision of the future with countless expressions of life on other planets constantly being displayed as either inferior or terribly feared. So, in the end, Zeneria was the only large Andromeda system that saw the need to risk the wormhole and attempt to save something of this eclectic primitive planet. As usual they went against galactic policy, but only long enough to do what they had set out to do.

Canga had seen Dawson cry a number of times. She had helped him to bed the day Earth was destroyed and listened to him go on about Earth music, cuisine, and how much he never realized he missed it until now. He had told her of all his Italian cousins and the wonderful food his grandma would cook. How you could smell it in the street. He barely remembered going to kindergarten and was almost 6 years old when they had taken his mother to prison for child endangerment and drug possession. He was supposed to go live with his

Grandma Rizzo in the lower east side. That is what the social worker had told him before the strange man had taken his hand and walked him out of the condemned building he had called home. At first he thought the man was from his father's side of the family. He had Native American relatives that lived in Arizona that he had never met. Little did he know that the man was from much farther away than Arizona.

Now she was crying. He knew it would take more than his slim body, even with his extensive combat training, to get his partner away from the burning hangar and back to Zeneria. Billy had retreated for some emergency, leaving his sister in her emotional coma, knowing full well none would disturb the legendary Zenerian warriors. Dawson slapped his weapons gauntlet against his one leg reaching for Canga with his other hand.

"Orin, I think you better get over here and bring Billy back with you. I don't think she's gonna move without help." He positioned his arm around her shoulders. His hopes were that the gentle Orin Wolf would be able to get through to her in this time when they needed to be pirates. If not, her brother was the only member of the squad strong enough to physically move her if need be. Maybe he should get Meadows and her bag of tricks first? He looked around them. The people of Thernix were pulling still-hot sheet metal from the wreckage to sell for scrap with gloves and prongs. They all gave the pirates a wide berth, and then scurried past into the dust clouds. Canga stared ahead and once the smoke cleared enough for Dawson's human eyes to see better, he could make out the black form of Britt's ship floating just behind them. He knew the ship would still be intact.

"Canga, I am putting Opus on auto pilot now. I am sending him home. We have to go too. Come on, kitty girl, don't go psycho on me now, not here!" He begged his squad partner as quietly as he could, hoping the bystanders were intelligent enough to keep walking. When Canga was in this state, everything and everyone was a strip steak side dish. His voice jarred her. She tensed and started to squat down. She was going to kill some civilians if he did not get her out of there soon. To his horror, she bared her feline incisors and started to scream in anger.

"Oh Damn! ORIN!" He yelled into his communicator.

Meadows, the squad medic, came running from behind them, moving her hands in a snake charmer's fashion as she spoke to distract her shock stricken pirate sister.

"Dawson, get Billy! We gotta get her outta here NOW!" Meadows turned Canga to face her.

"O.K. Kid, look at me! Snap out of it!" From her jacket Meadows drew a vial of liquid. Before Canga could react in her state, Meadows injected a high powered muscle relaxant into Canga's neck. Above them came the hum of Orin's conversion engine. The hatch opened. Orin leapt out and took hold of Canga's shoulders.

"Give her here, she can't fly and her ship's already been sent home! Let's go!" He hauled the six-foot female up the wing of the space vessel and almost tossed her into the back compartment, while Dawson shoved her legs over the sideboard. Canga seemed to start assisting, sensing the need to vacate the premises. Meadows turned to see Opus, Britt's ship, engage its red flight lights and start its conversion engines.

"Meadows! That is our cue to get the HELL out of here!" Dawson yelled as he jumped to the ground and started running for his own ship.

From the south, she could see a squadron of enforcement ships clearing the horizon. Soon the area would be crawling with Galactic police and news crews. Most of the civilians scurrying about had little if no knowledge of what this explosion represented. Although they all watched the news, the conflicts were hard to separate from the regularly scheduled programs. Thus, ignorance was bliss, until it blew a hangar apart in your little section of the galaxy, ripping out your front windows and charbroiling your skunk lizard and a few of your kids.

Canga still watched as the sand beneath Orin's ship began to swirl with the force of the engines. She looked forward. Now it would happen to them. Blank faces shielded by shrapnel hid from her glare. They avoided stepping too close to the fighter, even though the cockpit was well above their heads. Many of them had seen Canga eat up such a space in a matter of seconds with deadly grace and speed. The look of her features read sorrow and pain, yet the sting of her glare sang revenge. This explosion could very well mean the destruction of their planet. The death of Captain Devarelle would puncture a hole in the iron condom of support that enabled them to busk about unmolested. Thernix was the primary trade hub for larger business between Eliptica and Andromeda. A small explosion to ignite an unfathomable war seemed to be all it really took.

As her squad partners prepared to leave, she could make out information through the haze of medication that coursed through her brain. Her mind, sifting out unnecessary information, seemed to locate on statements concerning her closest friend. She pulled her slumping cranium from the rim of the cockpit and dropped it into her hands. Nothing had been found. No suit, no gauntlets, no Britt. A chemical test of the area would need to be performed to be sure, but to Canga no evidence meant that she somehow escaped. For most individuals this would be filed as a miracle. Many psychological tendencies would state that it was the pain of loss that led the pirates to believe that their captain could survive such an explosion. Canga looked up, wiping the tears from her face and smiling ever so slightly. Those were the educated idiots that had no clue to the ever-evasive, always-miraculous Devarelle. Orin jumped to the ship and closed the front hatch. She sat back and allowed the stinging air to rush over her face, breathing deeply.

The pirates stayed low until they cleared the stratosphere then charted a course for home. All Zenerian ships were illegally black, reflecting light and making cloaking devices almost unnecessary, save the deception of plasma or magnetic detection devices. Because of their hull armor, these too were invisible to the point of likening them with little more than floating meteors. Depending on the level and location of galactic law enforcement officials, their departing would be tracked only by those with specific interest.

"How's she doing?" asked Siggurd over the communication system.

"Well, she lost her best friend, and got drugged. I would guess like shit." snapped Orin.

"O.K. Enough of that. Where's the rest of the gang?" Meadows replied.

"I sent them to tail a ship that left orbit just before the explosion." Answered Siggurd. He was now in command, in a situation he would have rather not been shoved into. It would be up to him to formally tell Zenerio that Britt was gone. He would then be expected to assume his role as the replacement of the captain of the most successful pirate squadron in the galaxy. Contrary to what most believed, he had hoped this day would never come. In all his dreams for the future, he had only hoped to replace her when she was named Empress of Zeneria. He shifted in his cockpit punching the air control to nearly freezing.

Overwhelming pain shot through his face threatening to crack his skull. It was the reality fairy come to call, rapping just behind his eyes. He imagined her dressed in holocaust robes with a giant cycle. The numbness of responsibility would have been a welcomed diversion to the pain. He wished he had been a member of the civilian fire crew at that moment. Anything would be preferable to the fact that he would be the one that must tell Zenerio that Britt had been killed. Unfamiliar fear swirled in his stomach, leaving it rotten. Killed. Killed. Died. Dead. She was dead. He needed to keep repeating the gruesome fact to accept it as a possibility. Women like Britt never die. That was the delusion. Pirates never die. That was the lie. Somehow someone had figured a way around the flight suits. Alcohol seemed to be the Achilles heel of their defense. If she had been sober, the suit would have reacted in time to save her. He shivered, suppressing a scream of pain. The suits were designed to automatically react to a direct threat. He did some calculations, noting the unreal amount of Dardasian ale Britt had consumed. She had been drinking as if they had lost the skirmish with Kolbert. She had been drinking on and off for some time without reason. Without reason, he nearly slapped himself for the insensitivity. Zenerio was dying. Her responsibilities were limitless. She seemed apart from all but her squad and even then a bit different from the other Earth humans she lived with. Could it be called lonely? Leaders often were.

He had zoned into thought and was pulled out when his navigation computer signaled their arrival at the farthest Zenerian prime outpost.

None of them had expected she would do what she had done. There had been plans to infiltrate Kolbert's operations. Zeneria had extensive resources and special teams for just such a job. Devarelle grew tired of waiting and antsy at the thought of being discovered. She had taken leave one evening dressed to the nines. No one had noticed, not even Canga. It was not uncommon for each of them to don civilian clothing and spend a night out with the "normal" people.

Devarelle did her best spy work in this way. Legends spread fast. Distance distorts legends, sprinkling salt and peppered variations with every mile and each specific culture. For as many systems one could visit in the outer rim there were three times more descriptions of the great Captain Devarelle. In Cilicopi she was said to be a giant beast with acid for blood. On Belladonna she was akin to the reptile creatures of that area. Never in their history had Siggurd visited a planet and picked up a legend of their captain that was accurate. In a skintight dress with her hair down, she was the very LAST individual any life form would take for the infamous Captain Devarelle. And so she used this and her natural sexual attraction to slip right through the security cracks of the Kolbert operations. It was a big galaxy.

The next thing they knew, she was engaged to Jeff Kolbert and accompanying him on nearly all business ventures. Photo opportunities and media ran rampant at the stunning new female the most eligible bachelor in the Eliptica systems had picked up. Her name, or so they were lead to believe, was Kitty. Siggurd had spit his coffee everywhere when he had heard it.

"Kitty?! You're kidding right?" He could not believe his eyes or ears. He had picked up a galactic rag magazine and had to step into an alley to hide his shock. Kitty, a secretary from some obscure planet in the Stinette galaxy, the pages read. She was noted as soft spoken, demure and totally obedient to Kolbert. He leafed through the pages, gawking at pictures of her on the steps of the Eliptician Senate House, smiling at the prime minister. He had gone straight home and questioned her.

"Come on, Siggurd. I told you I was working on something. Well it worked."

It had worked to a degree that surprised them all. She held a meeting with the entire investigative team. Apparently she knew everything anyone ever needed to know about Kolbert operations.

"Did ya do it?" Siggurd asked later.

"Of course! How do you think I got him to propose?" She rattled it off as though it were a card game maneuver. Dawson was proclaiming her as brilliant. Canga just smiled. "Come on Siggurd, tell me you've never just gotten busy with a babe for the hell of it." She poked at him. "You're acting like an Earth male." She dismissed the subject.

They were nearly home now. The flight had been silent except for the occasional inquiry to Canga's health. Multi colored lights flashed as they passed the first outpost on the system's borders. Zeneria could be seen only as a faint blue dot in the distance. Canga shifted in her seat as her head continued to clear. The fighters' cruising speed in open space was 5 times the speed of light. Upon approach they slowed to light 3 then sub light speeds for final orbit. The clear skies of Zeneria prime welcomed them, each one swallowing a lump of pain as they raced over the perfect ocean to the tall white docking port suspended above the thick forest.

From the observation deck Zenerio watched the 10 precision black ships break the blue and white of the heavens, coming ever closer. He had already received the information. There was not much that the 23rd squad did that did not become galactic news in hours. He was ill and old. No longer a hungry slave searching for a home; nor a hell-bent scientist insistent on the survival of the universe. Now he was a father, something he had never dreamed of being. He was dripping in his tank. He had recently begun decomposing, as all his kind did. At least he would die of natural causes.

Heartbreak is so contagious when a loved one is lost. He had run from his camp at a young age and never looked back. He had never known a female and therefore never procreated young. His children were those that he brought to this paradise. He touched the glass with his pale gray tentacle. His assistant hovered behind in the shadows, not knowing what to say. Was she really dead, or just misplaced? Devarelle had been the most tenacious and challenging student they had ever had. She had defied science and behavior statistics for human children and completely baffled his best teachers. She had worked her way to the top of their military. She had presented herself to Zenerio at the age of 8 and approached him without fear. He was 9' tall and she about 3 ½. She looked up at his fan-shaped cranium and sharp teeth and asked to stay and not be taken back home. It was then that she had taken his heart as well. He knew that now.

"My lord, the 23rd has docked. Shall I have them sent to your quarters?" asked Milo.

"Yes, of course." Zenerio replied flatly.

Once he was off the com link, Milo started to wheel the sustaining tank that carried the Emperor of Zeneria to his personal quarters, for a very unwanted meeting.

Chapter 4
Osizio Unhinged

Some humans had to be tied. Some knocked over the head. Osizio was not sure what to do with this one. He was still not sure what he was doing in the meadow and how he got talked into taking her, or even how he came up with the plan. The only thing he knew was that once Prince Sholendor got a look at the lass, he would grant the ogre's freedom without question. So here they stood, knee deep in soft grass, staring at each other.

"Well?" Britt shrugged her shoulders, "Shall we get going? Or do you propose we stand here like fools?" She continued up the soft bank and walked past the ogre. He was still in a bit of shock and let her pass, trying not to let his gaping mouth drip spit.

Beyond the small hedge of trees he had parked a wooden oxen- drawn cart, positioned on two dirt ruts that must pass for the road to Garath. He watched as Britt walked around the oxen, staring as if she had never seen a bovine creature in her life. In truth, the nagging in her memory was itching at the back of her mind. Across the road grew the giant stalks of grass that carpeted the Arosa Plains. Without approaching the cart, she made for a stalk. Gripping it with both hands, she forcibly broke it off at the base, causing the five-inch blade to sway and timber, falling to the ground with a wispy thud.

"Wow, that is one hell of a piece of grass! I wonder if it's a form of cane?" She touched the thick white sap bleeding from the base. Osizio watched dumbfounded. He looked back at Ma Fafella, who shrugged and smiled from a distance. Britt moved her fingers to her nose first to smell the liquid then stuck her pink tongue out to taste it.

"Mmmm, good." She proceeded to break of a portion of the plant and stick it in her mouth. With the cane sticking out of her lips she turned to look in the cart and climbed into the passenger's side.

She was silent as the cart lurched forward, aware of the ogre staring at her. Her head was still in pain from the night before. She cringed, remembering her behavior in the tavern. She could hear her drunken voice now, causing her brow to knit and pride to shrink.

"What's so wrong with wanting to be freaking normal for a change?" She slammed her glass on the table.

"Britt, you're freaking everyone out." Loco warned her. Loco, of all people - the queen of freaking people out - was warning her.

"Okay I've apparently had too much to drink! I'm going home and sleeping it off." She stood up and nearly fell back down. Billy followed her to the street and she told him she wanted to be alone. He hesitated until she screamed at him. She knew she was writing a one-way ticket to the counselor's office in the morning. She had been working on it for a while. Maybe they decided to dump her off here because she had been such a jackass? Folding her hands on her lap, she knew she wouldn't have blamed them. She had been quite the pip lately. Pip or no, she reassured herself, when it came to professionalism she had not faltered. Her only real embarrassing moment of vulnerability being last night in the tavern. All other times, she had been the ever-in-control Captain. She swallowed forcibly on her own delusional perception of personal denial.

The ogre continued to fuss and grunt every time she breathed loud or moved. She would need to know more about her role here to blend in with the natives, if that were possible. Until she could find a mode of communication suitable for space she would follow the hag's advice and go to the palace. So far there had been no signs of such technology. Deductive reasoning told her that to divulge the fact that she was not from this planet, would only serve to alarm these creatures. She had to think of a lie quick. Memory loss was always a good ploy.

It was hard to concentrate. This planet seemed familiar. It was not like Zeneria. Her home planet was lush and moist. It was young and prehistoric. This planet had been around a while. If there was one thing she had gotten used to, it was judging planetary evolution. This planet was clear. The air, the soil, the temperature; were all very well developed. Of course she could not be sure without a complete geological and global survey. Still, this was a rare place. Good planets were so hard to find, especially those that could support life like this. At the moment there was nothing to see except grass. She decided it was time to pump the Ogre for info.

"So, what exactly is the plan, Osizio? " He started rocking the entire cart. "Calm down big guy, I should think it would be me that needs to be on edge." She giggled.

"Tis I'm not used to wenches that can talk like you." His crusty, bulbous eyes rolled from side to side, trying to look at her and keep an eye on the road. As if the overweight oxen were going to suddenly take off in a fit of undiscovered energy. He was trying so hard to appear in control.

"Well, I would really like to know about this place before I am shoved into the palace, if you don't mind." She insisted hoping he was smarter than he looked.

"Whaddya mean about this place?" he asked.

"You know, the planet, the people, the whole place." She moved her arms in a large circle, hoping the visualization would help.

He stopped the cart and shifted to look at her. His mouth hung open in a stupid, dripping, gape and soon she was to discover that this was a usual look for Osizio. Britt decided she liked this ogre, if only for his comical expressions.

"Surely yer not asking all that, 'ave ya never been around, or did ye grow up in that meadow?" He bellowed so loudly it made the oxen jump.

"Listen up, fat boy. I can climb out of this cart right now and the deal can be off. You want that, or can we establish some sort of understanding? I told you I have no clue where I am, remember?" Her voice was unwavering as she confronted Osizio. Her spunk and courage surprised him and shoved him into submission against his better judgment.

"Aw now lass, donna get a going crazy on ol' Osizio! I'll tell ye all ye are wanting to know." He offered in earnest.

So he began. They rode on in the fresh spring air. Britt leaned back and looked at the clear sky, took a deep breath, preparing to store all necessary information she was given. She noted to always keep in mind that all opinions were different. The ogre may very well have his own slant on history and events. As he rambled on, she was able to sift out that this planet was called Zembeth. It had three major cities and a few small settlements. The first of these cities that he spoke of was Garath, their destination. It was, by far, the largest of all the cities, as well as a trade hub. It was the only city that allowed all walks of life to live without borders or "problems".

The second largest was Kloter Mass Arosa. This was primarily a city for goblins, ogres and those that practiced dark magick. The only reason it was still functional was the constant presence of a strong elf monitoring over the magical energies of the area. This never-ending task was performed by the niece of the Queen Alisi, named De'Loria. She had been trained from birth for the job.

"I know how she feels." Britt slipped. Fortunately Osizio was so busy talking, he had not heard her.

The smallest and most powerful of the cities was Fairfax, the city of Elves. It was nestled between the great ocean and the Shalnas Forest. This forest was off limits to just about everyone, due to a deep enchantment. The magick it held was said to be the source of all magick on the planet. Fairfax was the religious and spiritual capital and totally off limits to most of the inhabitants of Zembeth.

"Yer either a slave or an elf in that city, or you're there on very important affairs." He bobbed his head in a matter-of-fact motion. "Iffin' ye find yerself there for reasons of criminal activities, yer wishin' ye were ne'ar a birthed." He snorted.

The social structure thus far seemed: Elves were the top of the food chain and everyone else was there for amusement. Britt just grinned at this. She posed the question of human involvement.

"Well lass, most humans are either slaves, or food." He blinked a fly away from his lashes. It had been walking around his eyelid for some time now. "There are certain humans that are used as companion slaves ye know. They are specially bred for this. Noin I aint nev'ra seen one other than Cameron. He looks a bit like you, and costs more than a poor Ogre like I will ever see." He huffed for emphasis.

"And who owns him, the Queen?" Britt asked.

"Na, she hates humans. He is owned by a good ol' elf named Ferrin of Sid O'Sala. He is used for breeding others like him." He stated.

"Well, I'm just sure he hates that job." She chuckled.

Osizio snorted. "Yer allot o' fun lass." He was starting to feel a bit guilty about the whole deal, but his longing to see his wife again kept washing it away.

This line of discussion gestated the more political and social intricacies of the planet. Osizio expounded upon the upcoming wedding of the Princess Meriden of Fairfax to Sholendor of Garath, that very month. Osizio seemed distant when talking of Sholendor. He then went into detail on the entire story of his banishment.

Apparently it was just an accident involving Sholendor's brother Gabriele and another elf named Roderick of Darmuth Anor. It seems Gabriele had fallen for one of Osizio's human slaves and it had started driving him mad. Her name was Marsiz and she still lived with Osizio's wife in Garath. One night Gabriele had come to the tavern alone. Being a member of the royal family should have been enough to keep him from such an establishment, but he had claimed that Marsiz had cast a spell on him. Osizio appeared completely disgusted with this accusation.

"Marsiz canna barely do the dishes, let alone cast a spell on an elf, fer the love of Ren'Fordel!" He bellowed.

It was a summer night and the tavern was full. Gabriele was seated at a table close to the bar. It just so happened that Roderick and his band of ruffians were in town that night and, as always, staying at Osizio's inn. The entire situation made Osizio's wife, Censci, very nervous. She begged Osizio to summon the royal guard to escort Gabriele home before things boiled out of control. As usual, Marsiz was paying an embarrassing amount of attention to Roderick, as all women did. Cup after cup of Censci's homemade brew helped Gabriele's courage and one thing led to another. Before he knew what was happening, Gabriele was standing behind Roderick, sword raised to kill. Osizio did not think. He only knew that Roderick had been like a son to him and he raised his giant ogre fist and smashed Gabriele's unsuspecting, drunk skull.

Things were very severe after that. Of course Sholendor wanted Osizio skinned alive. Due to the fact that his little brother was in a tavern, fighting over a human, and had attempted to kill an elf, (even if it were Roderick), the elfish counsel elected to banish the ogre to the outside world for eternity, never to see his family again. It had been 50 years now and he had given up all hope of winning his freedom into the city again.

"Wow, sounds like a soap opera to me." Britt offered.

"A what?" The ogre spat.

"Never mind. So I imagine it must have been a sight, seeing you slug a little elf, must have been really messy." She said.

"Whaddya mean, little? Gabriele was as tall as ye are." Osizio informed her.

"Oh, I though elves were small things with pointy ears." She said flatly.

"Ohhhooo." he roared, "Roderick is taller than me! The only elves that are that small are wood elves that live in the north, and other kinds o' spirit elves, like water spirits and the like. I should warn ye to stay away from brownies though, nasty little lot that." He advised.

Britt tried to picture an elf taller than the ogre. That would be one intriguing creature, judging from the pictures she had seen of elves. Although the illustrations she had seen in Earth Studies class were probably not close. She doubted these elves looked like Earth elves. She was sure she was not in the Milky Way. Her communicator would have picked up something. She had only heard minor static, as though any near systems were scrambled, denoting a sparse interstellar population. Whatever the case, elf or not, this place seemed full of petty dramas. She again vowed to find her way off this planet as soon as possible. The last thing she needed was to get caught up in some love triangle on a planet full of mythical creatures. She laughed to herself at the very sound of it.

Osizio had started to explain how a human should behave, when he stopped the cart. His sweaty head tipped back and the round nostrils flared, catching the wind.

"Balls! I smell an elf!" He panicked. "I canna have you seen afore you get to the palace, I gotta find something to do with ye!" He started falling out of the cart. Once he was on the ground he reached to the back of the wagon and shoved a couple of old bones that still had rotting meat clinging to them aside to retrieve a dirty gray cloak.

"Here, put this on!" He demanded.

Britt obeyed. The cloak completely encompassed her lean body.

"Damn you look silly! He's gonna wanna see who you are!" Osizio looked like it was killing him to think of an idea quickly. He shifted again and took another gale force sniff. "Just my luck! It's Amaranth! I gotta hide ye in the woods! Can I trust ye, lass?" Osizio pleaded.

"Well sure, I think." She was in awe of his ability to smell the elf, and actually determine which elf it was. He seemed terrified, and she did not think it was a good time to argue.

"Promise me ye will not leave!" He begged.

"Where would I go?" She offered with a snide glance. She stepped off the cart and over the small ditch. She proceeded to walk into the forest just far enough to be out of sight, but close enough to get a good look. This was, in fact, a fantastic turn of fate. She had to relieve herself in the worst way. She shimmied out of her pants and squatted behind the largest tree she could find, looking for large leaves. She watched Osizio climb back on to the wagon and take hold of the reins trying hard to look nonchalant, if it were in the power of any ogre to do so. She giggled when he leaned back and rested his thick arm on the rear plank of the seat and started to whistle.

It only took a few moments of the silence and off tune ogre air to hear the beating of the approaching hooves. She stood and pulled her pants back up, moving in for a better look. Now she stood behind a slender white tree and focused her vision. The elf was mounted on a brown horse, nothing to get excited about. At first she could not get a good look at him. He rode up and his horse stepped down into the rut beside the cart, hiding him behind the oxen. When he cleared the back end of the beasts though, and she could see just his upper torso and head on the other side of the ogre, she stopped breathing.

"Holy shit." She hissed.

In all her time as a space pirate, even as a child on Earth, she had never dreamed of such a creature. His hair reminded her of milk slowly poured into water, cut short and flying in blizzard waves on his head. It floated ghostlike around him in a halo of pearl. His eyes were so silver she could see them from such a distance.

It was not just his physical appearance that struck her, it was the aura of such a magical creature that eluded her grasp while consuming her. As with most humans, it is a type of shock to the senses to see an elf for the first time. No matter how often human eyes look upon an elfish face, they lose memory of the beauty for a time. It is like a dream within a dream that leaves the human a bit dizzy and confused. She turned around and put her back against the tree trunk. Taking a deep breath, she closed her eyes.

She could hear the two talking, but the elf's voice was like a drug. She commanded her senses to regroup. Mental control was essential to survival. She had encountered many life forms that had strange effects on her. Although this one was pleasant, it was not good to be so "off base". She peered around the tree again to see Amaranth and Osizio standing on the road, arguing. Amaranth was dressed in snug fitting light gray breeches with a soft black tunic. He was looking Osizio in the eye and poking the ogre's chest.

"You have to be kidding me! I cannot believe you are such a fool!" He paced back and ran his nimble fingers through his white curls. "It must be some type of spell or curse. That's it. Who have you talked to lately? You were in that fairy meadow, weren't you?" His silver eyes sparkled with mischief. "That's it! I know it! You ogres are very susceptible to that type of thing. Don't worry, we will take this thing back where you got it and everything will be okay. Now where is it?" The elf demanded.

Osizio was going to cave. His face was sullen and Britt could smell the brain cells burning with the effort of thinking. Perhaps the elf was right. Maybe he had been buffaloed into taking her to the palace. The old witch was very sure of herself. She wondered if there was some type of trick or agenda the old crone had chosen to keep secret.

Osizio continued to look at the ground for a moment and then kicked the dirt. Britt noted that he never mentioned the old woman. Even when Amaranth had asked him whom he had spoken to, Osizio defiantly refused to offer the information. Instead he seemed to try and shift the focus of the conversation in a very un-ogre like fashion.

"Ahhh, well ye would know, now wouldn't ye? After all, you are a wily little bastard. If I show her to ye, ye have got to promise me to keep an open mind!" He begged.

Amaranth tipped his head, "Osizio, I know how much you want to go back to Garath but you have to understand, Sholendor is just waiting for something to kill, all the time. He would skin you in the public square for making a joke of him." Amaranth stressed.

"Amer, I know this. Can ye just have a look? Fer me? If not fer me, then for the sake of Ren'Fordel, for Censci? She canna go on alone forever." He begged.

Britt had never heard of an ogre begging before. She had always been lead to believe that they were brutish and cruel, and ate small children. She suspected if it were to a creature like this, Osizio had little chance but submission. Amaranth touched his horse's nose, his white brow troubled.

"Well, I suppose a look will not hurt, after all, fairy magic cannot work on me so at least you will know the truth, and know to avoid that damn meadow from now on."

"O.K. So it is then. Britt, ye can come out now." Osizio called into the trees.

She was not sure she wanted to. For a moment she stood frozen, holding the hallafawn sapling. This was getting a bit out of hand. Then when she thought about it, when was her life *not* a bit out of hand?

She numbly pulled off the cowl and started walking toward the two men. Amaranth was staring before she reached the tree line. He did a crazy little dance of stepping back, then forth, then back again.

"Roderick has to be told about this." He said in a soprano spastic tone. "This is big. I think things are about to skit to chaos." He said as he approached Britteny.

The two of them stood in the middle of the road, ogre in tow. For a long time they simply observed one another, like apes in a cage at the zoo looking at simple people. Normally Amaranth was known as an immature joker. His life was a never-ending string of pranks and smart cracks that always landed him in the hot seat. In the 100 years Osizio had known the boy, he had never seen him this serious.

"Well! Did I not tell ye?" He blurted, shocking the pair back to reality.

Amaranth slowly reached out to touch Britt's hair. She inhaled sharply and backed away.

"Well, she is a shy one. Are you sure she is human? I mean she looks; well I do not know what she looks like. Maybe she is a spirit incarnated into flesh. A tempting demon perhaps, sent here to steal our souls." This was no jest; Osizio knew that Amaranth meant every word he had said.

"No, I've been in this skin since birth and as far as I know, there haven't been that many visitors that I'm not aware of." She offered.

Amaranth squeaked. "She talks!"

"I seem to be getting that reaction from quite a few natives lately. Yes I talk. I walk, I sing, I dance." She twirled around. "And I really want to get to the palace and get this over with, if you don't mind." She bowed low.

"Will you excuse us for a moment, my lady?" Amaranth grinned and grabbed Osizio's thick arm.

He pulled the ogre a few feet away, as if he doubted Britt could hear that far. He folded his arms and put one hand on his chin. Removing the hand he again, racked his white hair nervously. He uncrossed his arms and put his hands on his hips looking from Britt to Osizio, and back again.

"I honestly have not a clue as to what to do." He admitted.

"Shut up and let me take her to Garath." Osizio offered flatly.

"Yes, well OSIZIO! Since when did you start giving orders? I am only trying to save your life, again." He spat.

"Iffin I remember correctly, t'was not you that saved my life the first time, it was your brother. And iffin I recall as well, you, my boy, have neither children nor wife. Aside from killing yer old friend, I right well doubt there is anything ye can do."

Osizio turned at that and started for the cart. He looked back; "An' I don't care if ye tell him either. If ye all cared about me as much as ye say, ye would let me either try this or die. So off with ye, besides, elves aren't supposed to know how to care about nothing anyways!" He labored into the driver's seat. "Come on Britt, we have a prince to see."

She looked at Amaranth and shrugged her shoulders. "He is much bigger." She said and jumped into the cart.

"I am off then," said Amaranth, "and we will see what Roderick has to say about it, you stubborn old fool." Britt did not see him move and the next instant he was mounted and riding like a mad man towards the city.

"That didn't go well." She said.

Osizio snuffed. He was clearly disturbed. He slapped the reins on the sleeping oxen. Britt could tell now was not the time to ask more questions. She looked around and tried to act nonplussed.

It was doubtful that even with her extensive training she would have confronted a creature like Amaranth with such defiance. However, she did not have a family either, so what did she know. Then she thought of the countless times she had gone mad defending her squad members. At times all it takes is the memory of those you care for to understand the actions of a person insane. They drove on in silence to the wall of Garath.

Chapter 5
Ruddy Mudders

Wood seemed to keep the smells of life, forever. Sometimes old wood was like a storybook with its stains and scars, a road map to the past. Ruddy Mudders Tavern had a museum of wooden artifacts that told the tale of Garath's finest. From the wooden tables, to the trodden floor, the entire tavern smelled like life on the other side of prestige.

The front window of the tavern just next to the front door housed a round slab of driftwood fitted to legs making one of these tables. Some say this table was used to see the sludge of the city crawl by. Others stated to like it for its early warning, escape vantage point. Roderick liked it because of the sunshine. He had no enemies, save possibly the Royal Guard and the Prince, and maybe his future father in law, none of which would come to this tavern. Thus he felt relaxed drinking his ale and kicking back for a day of darts and doddering.

He did not really want to be in Garath. Donavan and Amaranth insisted they come for the games. He could not deny that he enjoyed the festival and the life of this city in the spring. The dancers, the food, it was a good change of pace from traveling the plains. It was the royal wedding that upset him. He had told his friends that as soon as the games were over, they were off to Sid O'Sala. The others had agreed, wanting to miss the wedding as well. Now he watched as a little human girl carried bracken to the hut of her owner. Her hair was filthy and her skinny little legs buckled under the load. For a moment she looked up at him, but looked back at the mud quickly. All elves had that effect on humans, even Roderick.

Donavan had told him to meet here before mid-day. Roderick looked at the sun; as usual the lobolack was late. He watched other wolf-like creatures milling in the street to see if he could pick Donavan out. His friend was almost silver gray with blue eyes. He should stand out among the black and brown wolf-man creatures. Marsiz approached the table.

"Ere ya are Roder, hot bread and porridge. Iffin' ye need anything else just yell."

He looked up, "No Marsiz, thank you, that will be all for now." He said in an unusually deep voice for an elf, and went back to staring out the window. The human sauntered back to the kitchen dejected. Since the killing 50 years prior, Roderick rarely talked to her other than to give simple orders or say thank you. It did not occur to her that he did not talk much to anyone, but Marsiz focused a delusional self-centered opinion that Roderick was denying his feelings for her, or at least that is what she told the other slaves.

His sharp, lime colored eyes squinted to see a pair of gray ears above the crowd. Finally Donavan was about with money and news. He waited for his friend and adopted brother to enter the tavern. Donavan stepped onto the wooden planks, taking care not to get his claws caught. This only occurred when he was drunk, and was usually the subject of much laughter for days after. Censci had learned to move all the tables at least 7' from the door, in fear of him wiping them out again. She had insisted that he make her 3 new tables and 6 new chairs. Of course Donavan cheated and just paid the local carpenter to do it, but still, Roderick and Amaranth cherished the memory and brought the subject up every time a female lobolack was about. Roderick automatically moved the table closer to him to allow his large friend space in the small alcove.

"Good morning Roderick, thanks for pulling the table over." He said.

"No trouble, I figured with all those gnomes you have been eating you would need the space." Roderick snickered.

"I will have you know, oh witty one, I have yet to shed my winter coat, thus my extra girth." He waved his hand-paw to summon Marsiz. "Just let me have a drink without your torture." He winked.

Marsiz nearly ran to the table. Donavan was careful to make his order quick, as not to have her lingering about and putting Roderick in a foul mood. This served to send her stomping back to the kitchen.

"You know that girl is incorrigible. I doubt the decision to have taught her to talk." Donavan remarked.

"She is only confused, she cannot help it. Think about it, because of Gabriele she will never fit in with her own kind, nor ours. We can only humor her now." He swallowed a bit of his drink. "So, have you seen my wayward brother?" He asked.

"Yes, as a matter of fact I have. He is heading out to see Ma Fafella. He said he needs to get a spell for memory spheres. He claims they are the latest things and he wants to record a few women he has encountered." They both laughed at this.

Creatures were milling about at the bar and more patrons were coming in every moment. Garath was always packed to the top of its great walls at the time of Beltane. If the games did not draw folks from all around, then the wedding would. As they sat and talked, citizens of all walks of life passed by the window. A centaur bartered feed prices with a faun across the road. Despite the wedding, Roderick loved being in Garath. There were peasant festivals, great food, and merry making of the like one could not find elsewhere. He gazed out of the window as Donavan talked to him. For some odd reason his mind would not focus on one thing or another. Instead it seemed to find a place in reality that was not common to him. It was as though his eyes were working independently of his mind, and somewhat detached from the strange empty feeling in the back of his soul. He shifted in his chair, searching his memory for anything he may have missed. His stomach felt warm from the base of his lower abdomen, with a heat that lingered and stretched to his chest. Was he becoming ill? This was likely not the case. Elves never fell ill unless the sickness was the result of a spell of sorts. For all the people that could be strong enough to cast such a curse, he could not imagine one that would attempt it for fear of retaliation. Besides, he was very close to most of those individuals, and those that he considered adversaries, he had taken the precaution to guard against.

So what could this feeling be. He scanned the storefronts, noticing every detail that had for years evaded him. Most of the buildings in every city of Zembeth were made of cut and cured Arosa grass. The largest stalks could be 2' in diameter, and when cured, were not only waterproof, but very strong. After some time in the sun, their outer husk turned a simple gray, marble color. The house roofs were made of the same material, but cured with a black tar. His sharp eyes could pick up an insect on a roof top 100 yards away. Today the moist heat brought in not only travelers, but also large swamp mosquitoes and other little vermin. He watched a green dragonfly hover over a dwarf that was shining armor a few shops down. It all seemed so dead before, somehow mundane. Today it woke up, today it had color again; there was definitely something afoot.

"So are you going to ignore me all day, or for just a few hours, my boy?" Donavan already had his drink and even some food. He was looking across the table, a chicken leg wedged in his canine fangs. "You seem rather off your game today, what is it?" He asked

"If I knew, I would be happy to tell you." He said. "Donavan, do you ever wonder what end there is?" Roderick asked.

"What do you mean?" Asked Donavan.

"We always seem part of an unfinished puzzle, all of us. I think I have always felt this way, deep down, but lately, well today most of all, this feeling of apprehension fills me. "He stared into the eyes of the wolf-man.

"You are starting to frighten me, Roderick. Every time you say something like that, there is some catastrophe a few days later and we are running for our lives." The lobolack was so shaken by this he had stopped eating.

"No, it is nothing like that. It is nothing like that other time." He sighed, "Thank goodness. No, this is kind of a good feeling. At first I thought I was ill, but it does not feel like I am losing anything or becoming weak. As a matter of fact, I feel like a fresh blade of grass after the rain, sitting in the sun." He offered a quirky smile as he shrugged his shoulders.

"Now you really do disturb me! Since when are you interested in soppy cliché's?" Donavan barked.

"What do you mean, soppy cliché's?" Roderick cocked his head to one side and raised an ebony brow.

"Grass growing? Sunshine? What does that sound like? I am the poet of this little family." Donavan reminded him.

It was true. Of the five of them, Donavan was the poet, the writer and the dreamer. Amaranth was the clown, and Roderick, the silent dark figure in the corner. Rowland was the one testament to sanity the group possessed, or at least the closest thing. When Roderick was younger he was more open, but as the years had progressed and his appearance and upbringing set him apart from those of his kind, he started to find solace a much needed companion. Only his adopted family knew he was a very multi-dimensional person that was capable of compassion and mirth, but they never told him that, lest he deny it.

Just then Amaranth burst through the door. The youngest of their traveling family skidded to a stop on the polished wood, causing all the tavern patrons to turn and look. This action did not create any serious curiosity among the crowd. Those that frequented Ruddy Mudders were quite used to Amaranth's antics. The white elf spun on his heels and spied his older brothers in their usual corner.

"Roderick! We have to get to the palace lane as fast as we can!" He raced to the table. Not bothering to sit down, he reached for his brother's bow and bag, as if to just escort him from his table. "Well, come! We have little time!" He hissed.

"Sit down!" Roderick demanded. "What is wrong with you? Did you eat some of the herb from that shifty goblin peddler again?" Donavan laughed at this comment.

"NO! I mean it! This is no joke!" Roderick grew concerned with the strong tone of his usually shiftless brother. "Osizio is entering the city as we speak, with a human he found in the meadow. He is going to take her to Sholendor and see if he can trade her for his passage back into the city." He slapped his slender hands on the table and loudly whispered, "Is that serious enough for you?"

Roderick jumped up and looked into Amaranth's metallic silver eyes. "This had better not be another of your pranks, or so help me I will beat you like a spoiled whelp." The larger of the two elves growled. Roderick stood almost a full head taller than his pale brother.

"Nay brother, I have come as fast as I may." Amaranth held Roderick's arm and tried to keep his voice down to protect Censci from hearing the news. "I have seen this human, and he may just succeed." The three companions traded glances.

Roderick pulled Amaranth into a chair roughly. "You have lost your senses! You agreed with him!? You allowed him to come?!"

"Listen, he told me I could try to stop him, but I would have to kill him first. What was I to do? His feeble mind is set. Besides, this human, I have never seen the like of her. I mean *never*. If Sholendor does not go for the deal, he can sell her for such a price as to buy his freedom either way." He jerked his arm from his dark brother. "Do you think I am thick in the head? I did tell him I was going to tell you and Donavan and he did not care. He is on his way to the palace as we speak."

Donavan had noticed that the only two elves in the tavern were starting to draw attention. "I think it wise that you both keep your tone down until we can reach some sort of an agreement." He growled the warning.

Marsiz was hovering near the table and Censci had stopped wiping the bar down to inspect the arguing brothers. She was the last person that needed to hear this discussion.

"We leave then, slowly. I will go up and pay our debt." Roderick rose from the table and adjusted his long sword. The hungry onlookers moved to let him pass with respect as he made his way to the main bar to pay.

Donavan sighed, "Yet another meal half eaten, when will we ever dine in style?" He had always wished for a candle lit dinner with soft music and good company. Life on the road never afforded such finery. The two companions at the window seat turned to hear Censci's questions to their leader.

"Leaving so soon are ye Roderick? Did ye need a room for tonight?" she asked, looking over his shoulder to try to make eye contact with Amaranth. She had always been able to read the boy; his older brother was another matter. Roderick stepped in her line of vision and smiled politely.

"Yes dear, I think we will need a room. If we are not back before you close the doors, give the room to another traveler." He handed her five silver pieces, then turned to be off with his ravel. The ogress craned her massive neck and flared her nostrils. Marsiz approached the bar and set up a tray full of wooden tankards.

"Something is up in the air today," Said Censci, "Roderick is acting far too gentlemanly for my liking. I wonder what it is those heathens are up to this time?" She waddled to the door and watched the three of them make haste down the crowded lane towards the palace.

Chapter 6
The Gate Breakers

If the raven that flies from his perch atop the walls of Garath could speak, what would he say? In the soul of the wind, a place few ever truly go, wings alight a view of a timeless land. Hundreds of feet down, from his origin, skimming along the endless stone and mortar wall, his heart anticipates the clearing of the white sheath of clouds. Farmlands stretching beyond even his sharp powers of observation only hold his interest for a moment, their patchwork precision and color contrast, a slight diversion.

None of the hundreds of life forms milling about below are aware of him, for he is one of many blue-black ravens that nest in the highest torrents of the great wall of Garath, amidst only the elfish dwellings. If he so chose, he could slow half way down the straight drop to perhaps snitch a crumb from an open window. Many flats were built into the 2,500 ft thick wall, making it a living honeycomb of families, lives, deaths, and scraps for the ravens. Today he had no such time for these games of farmer's wives with brooms and clay pots to toss at him. Today he was venturing to find a mate in the breeding grounds of the Arosa Plains, where all life is born, lived and devoured. If he had a care to learn, he would be enlightened to the fact that the grass alone of these plains supported a substantial part of the Garathian economy. Everything from the ground huts to the furniture that adorned hovels and mansions alike was made from old growth grass. At different stages of growth, the Arosa grasses were used from an array of medications to the simplest stews and flour. Blankets and rugs were woven from finely stripped veins of the soft summer first year shoots then dyed for color.

He had no time to ponder the peasant uses of Arosa Grass. Now he was reaching foliage. The thick morning glory vines clung as far up as 100ft, in their attempt to take over, only to be thwarted with the constant disappointment of being thrashed with scythes from the lower level windows of the wall. If he chose to fly farther north he would need to avoid entanglement with the hearty dwarfs that were constructing the new addition from the north gate. Apparently Garath was outgrowing its' own colossal walls. Little did this raven know that the walls were also buried deep in the soil and housed the darker life forms that held the cold and damp sacred over the bright sun light. That is no business for ravens. For now he would be content to whisk through the smoke from the drying house, and savor the smell of the pungent cured flesh.

Three goblin whelps barked at one another from behind their wide sow, fighting over what appeared to be a human forearm. He tipped his wings and aligned his body with the strong draft that banked off the Deneb Sea. This gust against the wall would provide him with a more than sufficient boost to the outer grass fields. With the new power behind him, he chose to steal the raw arm from the goblin pups. It would make a fine gift for his mate to be.

He would now follow the well-trodden road that lead west toward the Deneb Swamp and Ma Fafella's meadow. He passed over two centaurs conversing over the impending birth of their spring foal, a dwarf farmer, hauling his seed supply out to his assigned lot, and an old witch gathering herbs from alongside the forest. He flew on to the crest of the last hill of turned soil that marked the line of vision, and thus the line of safe workable land, before one entered the Arosa Plains. Travelers were few and far between from one city to another. The few that traveled with ease were strong elf males and usually only those from Garath or Kloter. The white elves of Fairfax preferred to stay well within their pale city walls. Although their magick was more than sufficient for protection, they simply chose not to mingle with the common fold unless absolutely necessary. Aside from elves, the rare ogre could be found and even they usually traveled the plains in pairs. If a dwarf were found it was within a very large group of dwarves, usually escorted by elfish guards. Centaurs traveled in herds and again would often hire an elf warrior for protection. All others traveled in caravans or only on short day trips, or simply never left their home city.

It was not unheard of for a large ogre to brave the plains alone. There had been reports of the larger species of Zembeth setting out on such journeys and found torn to shreds and spread out over miles. The trick was to stay close to the tree lines, even that of the Shalnas if you were traveling in the north. Those that traveled the plains knew that this was not necessarily a safer route, but the predators that lived in the grass and the predators that lived in the trees made it a point to avoid one another. If a journeyman were fortunate they would kill each other, allowing a brief time to run, as if on fire, to either the next disaster or some type of delusional safety.

Today, the raven was to pass over just such an unusual sight. He had encountered Osizio on many an occasion on all roads, but none so close to his home city of Garath. The oxen drawn cart was dull brown against the brilliant shades of green, and our raven passed too late to see the passenger before she was cloaked for protection.

********** * * * * * * * * * ************

Britt watched the giant black bird glide by, shaken by the shape of the prize it held in its talons. She chose to ignore her suspicions and looked back to the ogre. Osizio had responded to a few more inquires from the human, but for the most part stayed preoccupied with the coming danger of entering the city. From their location he could now see the entire western view of the wall of Garath. It had been almost 50 years to the day that he retreated over this very same hill, to save his life. In truth, ogres are horrifically covered with stench, grotesque, and very strong, but history and fiction, like so many other races, had painted them stupid and heartless as well. Britt glanced over at the creature next to her. His bulging eyes surveyed the walls as if playing over memories long suppressed. She could remember reading a great deal about ogres in her Earth studies class. Her favorite subject was Earth folklore and fairy tales. The ancient and pre-holocaust literature, written from pure imagination by the people of Earth, always amused her. OmJoIb had assigned a number of fantasy novels as required reading. Of these, her favorite was a story written by a man named Piers

Anthony entitled "Ogre, Ogre." Smash had been a childhood hero. Osizio looked very much the same as she had imagined Smash.

Amaranth, however, had stirred her in a way she could not explain. It was not a sexual feeling, not completely, but a deep knowing. The thought escaped her as she took in the sight of the wall of Garath. Her amazement at the pure masterpiece of architecture that was the wall of Garath would be kept to herself. Silence was her only equalizer at this point. It does not serve one's purpose to have an emotionally unhinged ogre to deal with. From her standing, her only hope was to locate some type of communication with the outside world. This ogre was her ticket to the royal family. This trip through the city was business for her, for the ogre it went much deeper.

"Osizio, no matter what happens, I want you to know that this whole situation is fine with me. I only hope you get your family back."

She reached out and touched his thick hand. The ogre sucked in a deep breath. He had never been touched with compassion by another creature outside his wife and sons. Beautiful creatures simply did not touch ogres. He looked into her sharp eyes. An overwhelming feeling of guilt settled in his stomach. "Don't worry about it Osizio, I can take care of myself. If it makes you feel any better, I would have it no other way. You only have one family." She stared directly into the muddy brown and yellow eyes. "Now let's go meet this prince." She patted his shoulder and looked forward, leaving him confused.

Human slave trading had been a lucrative business for him for many years. Breeding farms in Sid O'Sala had provided him with a number of quality slaves to transport and profit from. He was never privileged enough to trade in companion slaves, and usually stuck to general labor and feeding slaves. Perhaps this was the way of companion slaves. If so, he thanked all the spirits of the mother world that he did not make his living from such a venue. He did not have the heart for it, ogre or no. The cart jutted down the dirt path to the busy thoroughfare of farmers and hunters riding for the nearby woods while daylight was new. A band of dwarves set for their mountain capital of Borgendoch marched in military precision, only turning in haste to cast fearful glances. Osizio sniffed and slapped the oxen on. Every manner of creature cleared their way. It was very evident that Osizio was well known in the city. Whispers buzzed all about and some creatures even fled from his sight.

"Why are they all so afraid of you?" Britt whispered.

"Tis not me they fear lass, 'tis the army of elves that will be a waitin' fer us soon." He chuckled, "Hee. I almost am hoping that Roderick shows up. He may be our only chance of getting to the palace in one piece."

Britt absently tugged the cloak hood farther over her face and tilted her head down, observing her surroundings from the shadow. No need to start a riot. Soon they were in front of the gates of Garath. Britt made a promise to herself that once she was home on Zeneria she would have to come back to this place if only to observe from afar. OmJolb would be just silly with excitement. The streets of Garath were crammed with shops of every kind. Chickens hung upside down from butcher shop awnings alongside things she could not quite place. Children of all types raced up and down the carts. This was always a good sign. Britt had learned to look for children in any society that she first encountered. Civilizations that cherished children were usually more compassionate. Some of them tugged at her cloak only to get a glimpse under the hood and stare in wonder, then run off to tell their unbelieving mothers of the woman and the ogre. Many females upon sighting Osizio nabbed their children into safekeeping and locked their hut doors.

"Magick! Black and White! Get your potions!" yelled a fat goblin wench from a run-down shack ahead. She forcibly snapped her head around to see the cart that everyone had been gossiping about.

"Osizio! A doomed Ogre! You bring us a child of the stars! You bring us the child of fate and destiny! EEEEEEEAAAA!! You bring us the child of freedom!" She was hysterical. Britt jumped in alert defense. From the ragged building came a larger goblin male who grabbed the slobbering witch by the neck and dragged her, screaming into the shop.

"Crazy old bitch! Stars! Imagine! Tis a shame they don't stop those phony crones from lunacy afore they rot in the brain. They ruin the trade for the skilled witches." Osizio barked.

"Yea, just imagine! Silly old girl, Ha, ha…" Britt sounded off weakly.

They had been traveling for a number of hours and now could see the wooden gate that would take them to the private lane to the palace. Osizio was sure by now that Roderick was on his way. In truth, he was amazed that he had made it this far into the city without meeting the royal guard. Britt was growing very warm in the thick cloak and was actually looking forward to meeting the prince and getting the whole thing done with.

Ahead of them on the road stood three beings of which only one was familiar to Britt. She recognized Amaranth, the breathtaking elf that she had met on the road. She noticed the wolf first. She had seen many creatures like him in space. Osizio slowed the cart. Britt could only guess that this fine trio was none other than Roderick and his gang. She had not taken the time to look at the quick moving cloaked figure that approached the cart on the Ogre's side. The beasts grew nervous at the approach of the werewolf. Britt toyed with the theory that such a creature was this way all month and turned human on the full moon. She watched as he padded next to her and peered under the folds of her cloak. All of the beings that had been following them cleared out. Her stomach quaked in a strange foreboding way. She reached for the ogre and looked past him to the man that stood on the other side.

We all have alarms. Later, if the two of them thought back, each would be inclined to admit that the alarms worked and went off. Britt's told her to run. Get out of the cart and run in any direction but toward the pale, dark haired elf that gazed at her over Osizio's lap. A strange discomfort settled over her, making her shift in her seat. He had much the same effect on her as his brother Amaranth had to her internal organs the first time she laid eyes on him. For a brief moment she filed it away as the human reaction to elves. As Roderick continued to talk to Osizio, she remained under the protective awning of gray fabric; working on the classification of the turmoil she was experiencing. It occurred to her that she may have multiple reactions when being introduced to these creatures and she was either going to have to gain some type of mastery against their effect on her equilibrium, or just topple over every time a new elf came into view. Roderick looked away from Osizio's face and looked directly at her now.

Suddenly the light headed feeling of nausea from her recent hangover dulled in comparison. Something new and abnormal was happening to her. Something the entire Andromeda galaxy had never been able to accomplish with its vast, unnamable life forms.

"Lass?" Osizio nudged her. "Come on, take off the hood for him, I promise he will behave." He requested kindly. She then realized she had not heard a word they had been saying. Her instincts were clearly becoming dulled. Britt doubted that it mattered how he behaved, he only needed to be standing there to be toxic. She straightened her back and took a deep breath, angry at her lack of focus. Her hand moved to the coarse gray material and she eased the hood back. Donavan was the first to let out a sharp gasp, or yip, she was not sure which. She was looking right at the werewolf, to avoid the gaze of the elf.

"Hello, I'm Britteny; it's a pleasure to meet you." She extended her hand to the lobolack.

"Oh, truly, the pleasure is all mine, dear lady. I am Donavan of Darmuth Anor." The werewolf bowed and kissed her hand. She willed her stomach to sit still and turned to face the elf. She darted a glance at Amaranth then back to Roderick. The feeling was definitely something attached to Roderick. Her gut instinct rarely failed her. Something was amiss. The feelings that came over her when she looked at Amaranth were that of a drug induced sleep. Her eyes lingered out of focus and then into focus. Her memory seemed to fail her for brief seconds and it was all quite pleasant in a strange, incoherent way.

Roderick, however, was another story. She would need to be constantly wary of Roderick until he proved not to be life threatening. He was actually causing the hair on the back of her neck to stand on end. It would not be like her however to not admit to herself that he was possibly the most beautiful male being she had ever dreamed of encountering. Playfully she imagined bringing him home and watching the reactions of her female squad partners, if only to give herself a slight mental retreat from the current insanity. They rarely had time to indulge in such frivolities. The life of training to be a Zenerian Pirate left little time for flirtation. Aside from this, humanoids were rare. Pirates rarely mated, and even more rarely bonded as mating pairs. It was however not unheard of, yet happened more readily for the more abundant races of the Andromeda. Britt was positive that nowhere in her extensive education of galactic life forms, had she ever encountered any to liken to the elfish race.

"And you must be Roderick of Darmuth Anor. I have heard a great deal about you. It's a pleasure to finally meet you." She held out a shaking hand. He reached out in kind and took her hand over the ogre's lap.

"My lady, I beg forgiveness for my rudeness and comments earlier.

I am only concerned for the life of my long time friend." He spoke in a monotone. Their hands clamped together and held for a long moment. She fought the urge to pull away when the shock spasm shot through her arm. He blinked in surprise.

"I completely understand." She lied; she had not heard a word of it. "I only hope the prince will agree to the bargain and we can both be on to our futures." She offered. Her head snapped to a comforting aversion. "Amaranth, how good to see you again!" She let go of Roderick and reached for his brother.

"Hello lady." The younger elf beamed and reached for her outstretched hand. He kissed it hungrily and held until Donavan growled.

"Well enough of this. We are off then, if you don't mind." Osizio huffed and slapped the reins.

"Not so fast." Roderick interrupted. "I think it best we escort you to the throne room. Sholendor may yet skin you without witnesses." He made a valid point but Britt wished he would shut up and leave. His presence was motivating her by the moment to find the nearest space station and leave this rock, curiosity and all. At least with him around, she knew now for sure this was not a joke played by her squad members. Neither Byron Dawson, nor any of the others could have imagined a being like Roderick. They were a creative lot, for sure, but the male humanoid standing to her left seemed custom made for her personal torture.

"If ye wish to come so be it, but ye better not try talking me out of it lad. I'm warning ye." Osizio pointed a fat finger at Roderick.

"No, I would never persuade you not to deliver this rare jewel into the hands of a mad lunatic." Roderick stepped away from the cart and retrieved a horse from the side of the road that had been standing in wait all along. Britteny smirked and her brow lifted.

Osizio bellowed so loud the oxen shrank in fear. "Oh there ye go. That is enough of that! You can just leave iffin yer goin' to be thata way, you black bastard!"

"Who, me? It was just a statement of truth." His incredible frame glided onto the beast of burden and he flashed a quick, devastating smile at the ogre. Britt felt her chest cramp. "Shall we be off?" He offered and glanced at the oxen.

They started walking without urge from the ogre, which told Britt that these creatures could communicate with animals telepathically. This action also quelled the anger of the ogre. Osizio cowered a bit.

"I am sure she will make a fantastic wedding gift for the princess." Roderick looked over his shoulder sending his raven curls and native, bone-beaded braids, flying behind him.

Osizio had not considered that action. He should have known that Roderick would read the prince in a way he could not. Who better to read Sholendor than his worst enemy? He had not considered the outcome of his decision beyond the prince's hopeful acceptance to grant his freedom. He had never worried about the lives of his slaves once they were sold.

Roderick rode just ahead of the oxen. He seemed stiff and focused. Osizio did not like his distant attitude. Amaranth gabbed to Britteny as though they were best friends while Donavan tried in vain to get a word in edgewise. Britt chatted politely with them, laughing at their jokes and smiling sweetly at their complements. Osizio looked from her to Roderick's back as he rode before them, again and felt a pang of regret. She was so innocent, frail and human, yet intelligent and beautiful. She would fetch a fine price on any market and if sold in Sid O'Sala would have made him a fortune far exceeding his wildest dreams. Perhaps she may have even been sold to a good home of dwarves or wealthy centaurs. Now she would be used for the prince's sick ambitions against the quiet princess. His perverse ideal of human degradation would take a whole new meaning with this prize. The royal guard would be here any moment; it was too late to turn back now.

Roderick glanced back at them. He looked like a painting. Britt stared ahead at the figure on the horse. The walls that guarded the palace lane were not the dark earth color of the main walls of the city. She had not noticed until that moment. The longer she was on this planet it seemed, the duller her memory of purpose became. It was as if she were forgetting to look for home. Looking at Roderick before her again gave her that feeling one gets just before passing out.

She slowed her breathing and attempted to focus on her surroundings. The palace lane walls were marble engraved with strange figures and symbols, hidden by the thick grapevines. Only hallafawn trees grew along the side of the white graveled road, wafting soft red–gold leaves in a ballet of currents above his black crown of long curls. Roderick set in her memory in that moment amidst the marble and tones of emerald. Everything was so vivid. One never knows color or awakening unless one lives the life of adventure, or so she had been told. She had not known color and smell, nor sight until this moment. She forced her mind back to Canga, Dawson, Meadows, Siggurd, and the rest of her squad in a desperate attempt to remember where she was needed and belonged. Roderick meet her gaze for a fleeting moment, then turned his horse to continue on to the palace. Amaranth was still chattering in her ear when she noticed the end of the lane and the group of elves riding toward them.

Roderick galloped to meet them first. Britt could see one elf break formation to meet him midway. They spoke for a moment and Osizio slowed the oxen in anticipation. The blue haired elf waved the rest of the guard back to the palace and advanced with Roderick. Upon approach of the wagon, Britt got a better look at Demetri of Sid O'Sala. The palace guard stopped his horse, staring at her as everyone else had done.

"The prince knows you are arriving, Osizio and has agreed to accept your audience. " He spoke formally. "However, you will only be permitted to enter with Roderick and the slave. Amaranth and Donavan must wait in the lane." He nodded to Amaranth and Donavan.

The two companions nodded back in agreement and Amaranth dismounted his horse. Donavan had gone to all four legs to trot along beside them, but now erected to biped stance and waved his agreement to Demetri. Osizio started climbing from the wagon and turned to tip his giant head at Britt. She followed suit and got off the wagon. She unclasped the cloak and tossed the heavy gray cover back onto the wagon seat. When she turned to walk forward she stopped. Every member of the party was staring at her yet again.

"What?" She asked. "What did I do?" She held her arms out.

Amaranth swallowed and looked at Roderick.

"What? I swear to God you people are lame. Haven't any of you ever seen a female before?" She was having a hard time keeping her cool. Her attempt thus far had been polite. The actions of the males surrounding her were screaming for the battle-hardened leader she truly was.

"Not like you." Amaranth squeaked.

"Well, here's a news flash. I have never seen an elf or an ogre, but you don't see me standing around gawking like a perverted idiot. Didn't your mother tell you it's rude to stare?" She was clearly having none of it. She looked at Donavan who seemed to be the only one with a lick of sense. "Am I going to keep getting this reaction?" She asked.

"I am afraid so, dear. They are all rather unrefined." He walked to her and took her arm. "Personally I think you are too skinny. I like my females covered with fur." He patted her arm.

Britt visibly relaxed. Yet Amaranth was not finished.

"You....You are muscular." He said it with hesitation.

"I get plenty of exercise." Britt retorted.

"Britt. May I call you Britt?" Roderick was speaking to her now.

"Yea, sure. May I call you Roderick?" She asked in return.

"You may call me anything you wish." His smile cracked her consciousness. "I apologize if I seem to be rude. I, like my companions, am only attempting to adjust to a very abnormal situation. Please forgive us." He kissed her hand. He kissed her hand. He kissed her hand. He had only kissed it once. She felt like he had melted it off. She fought the urge to pull it away sharply.

"Sure. Can we get to the palace now?" Britt did her best to keep her voice steady. She turned to walk past the palace guard, Amaranth, Donavan, and

Osizio. She paced on for a few yards then turned around to glare at the lot of them. Her movements were calculated and stealth like.

"In case you haven't noticed, I'm not gettin' any younger and we all know I am only as good as my physical appearance." She growled and waved her hand in a circle around her face. With that she walked on, leaving the rest of them to catch up. Roderick trotted easily to her side and kept pace with her for a time. This made her very nervous, but she showed no sign of slowing. Osizio was having a hard time keeping up with the three of them and labored with ground shaking tremor like steps from behind.

"There's no need to storm off lass, hold up a bit for an old Ogre!" He bellowed. Britt was stalking down the lane. It was not until Roderick grabbed her arm that she shot him a venomous glance.

"Please don't grab me. I tend to get violent when people grab me." She looked down at his hand on her arm. He had sparked a very sensitive chord in her.

"Would you be so kind as to tell me exactly what I did to deserve this treatment?" He protested her sudden shift in attitude.

"For starters, none of you know a damned thing about me! For all you know Roderick, I could be some demon or virus carrying plague package. You assume a great deal for someone who has just met me. For a supposed intelligent life form, you sure draw quick conclusions. For the love of GOD…none of you even seem to be concerned that your friend just happened to pick someone like me up on the side of the road. You act like this shit happens every day. I bet if I were a big ugly male human you would have asked more questions." She turned and kept walking.

"Why would we fear a female human, no matter what she looked like?" Demetri asked.

"Oh, really?" Britt giggled. "Man, are you guys in for a big surprise." She commented as if addressing slow children.

Roderick moved in front of her. "I am not the one that got in the cart with the ogre knowing full well what his intentions were. Furthermore, I know Sholendor, perhaps *too* well, and I know life in the palace will be far crueler than anything I have said." He waited for a reply, crossing his arms.

"Clearly you have no idea what any of you are in for. I can only IMAGINE what the other human females in this place are like." She turned to walk on to the palace. Again Roderick grabbed for her arm.

"Listen, Spock, I'm only gonna tell you this one more time. Don't grab me like that, ever again. I know you heard me the first time. You can probably pick up subsonic vibrations with those ears." This was not said in humor, but in a threatening tone. "I *will* hurt you, and I won't feel bad about it. You have been told." She informed him.

"I am only attempting to help you and I only wish you to stop and listen to me. Just as us, you know now what you walk into when you step into that palace." Roderick kept his tone calm and removed his hand from her arm, in fear of having to restrain her in a fit of rage.

"Do I have a choice?" She offered. "Are you going to take me away? Promise me I will be set free and never become a slave to anyone?" He froze. "Well?" She waited a moment longer. "I didn't think so. I tend to be my own knight in shining armor. I have run across too many retards in tinfoil to wait for that crock of shit fairy tale. How about just trying to be my friend? How about treating me with a little respect, or like I have a brain attached to my tits and ass? You want a better attitude from me, start by giving it first."

She overtook his blockade with ease and walked on, turning back to reply, "And I am quite capable of taking care of myself, more so than you can ever imagine, and you can be very sure of that." She continued walking.

The group walked in silence toward the pearl gates. Demetri was shaken. He was a very young elf and this was his first real assignment. The prince knew Roderick was coming and acted ready for it. He doubted the prince had any idea what else was in store. Because he had been informed that Osizio was bringing him a human in hopes of an exchange, Sholendor snuffed of the severity of the situation as mere desperation, taking no time to see for himself what was now stalking up his lane. This human just strode to the gates of the royal village as if she owned them. Her magick was strong enough to quell Roderick of Darmuth Anor and Osizio. Even he, a palace guard, was finding it hard not to stare at her shapely backside and bouncing fire gold curls. Upon approach she tipped her head back to look up at the gates of Garath Royal.

"Wow." She muttered. She placed her hand on the finely adorned gate of silver and pearl. Each door was carved in the likeness of a female elf holding a spray of lilies that cascaded over her body and fell to the likeness of the ocean. "Now this is impressive!" She beamed at them. Osizio groaned at her smile. He was beside himself with guilt. She stepped aside and motioned to Demetri. "I suppose we should allow you to enter first."

Demetri walked past, his eyes never leaving the human. "Yes, My Lady." He placed his palm on the figure of a mermaid made of silver that must have been the gate latch. They opened with the sound of glass bells. She took a few steps into the royal gardens. Small silver bubbles floated over beds of violets and sweet peas. The path beneath her feet was a succession of sterling silver plates engraved with the same type of symbols she had seen on the exterior wall. She concluded that they must be part of the elfish alphabet. Her companions walked behind her, allowing her to take in her new home. She reached up to touch a silver bubble.

"No!" Roderick warned. He gently touched her hand. "You must never touch the bubbles. They are messages." He cautioned.

"Messages?" She asked.

"Yes. This is how some elves communicate from city to city and reality to reality. It is also how they store history and memories or send messages. This could very well be the history of our people, or even the princess sending orders to Garath for her wedding." He offered her a kind smile. "They are only meant to be opened by the one they are destined for. If you touch one, it may harm you." He educated.

"Oh. O.K. I 'm sorry." She looked at Demetri. "I am sorry, I had no idea." She apologized, not wishing to offend as she bowed slightly and walked on.

"It is quite all right." Demetri said unconsciously hoping to earn her trust. Roderick walked bravely at her side, explaining all she took an interest in. Osizio wanted to die.

"Those are poems written by elfish scholars." He pointed to the pathway. "And soon we will be in the village of elders." He pointed ahead at the low stone wall, adorned with all colors of flowers. She pointed to a large bird perched on a silver fountain.

"What kind of bird is that? I saw a number of them in the grasslands." She asked.

He approached her side and absently put his arm around her waist. If she noticed the action, she did her best not to show it. Apparently he felt the need to touch her. This did not escape Osizio's normally slow intellect. Roderick rarely touched anyone. He was after all, an elf.

"Those are ooredna birds. They are very common on the Arosa. Beautiful, are they not?" He inquired.

"Yes, I love the color of their feathers." She laughed as the bird flapped about in the water of the bath.

Demetri looked to Osizio for help to understand the behavior of the wild elf and the new human. The ogre frowned. He was completely baffled and only glad that Amaranth and Donavan were not here to see this. Amaranth would have passed out by now. Roderick and Britteny continued down the path talking of all they discovered. She the world around her and he the woman before him, running like a child to the smallest of insects for explanation. Roderick was alive with comments, jokes and stories. He picked an elfish buttercup and walked to her.

"Here, try it, they are exquisite. You can lick out the center and they taste like sweet butter." He held the flower to her. She produced a soft pink tongue from between her full lips and licked the flower as he stood still as death watching her.

"Oh wow, those are wonderful!" She clapped and took the flower for him to try. He pulled back his jet black curls and to Osizio's astonishment, licked the flower like a silly child.

"About this magick thing, how does it work?" she asked her new companion as she continued licking the buttercup. She had already forgotten the warning bells. Apparently fantastic eyes and full lipped smiles are the elixir for temporary mental instability.

"What do you mean, how does it work? I fail to understand." He focused his attention on this valid question. They both stopped walking and ignored the other two members of the party.

"I've been lead to believe that elves can do magick, but so far have seen no proof. I have some understanding of magick tricks but I think this may be something different. I was trained in the magick of nature and spell craft but that takes work and years of knowledge. I'm only guessing that your magick is something different." She bit her bottom lip in anticipation. He watched with wonder. She knew better than to expound on her substantial scientific education. It was clear this planet had absolutely no such technology so she chose to chalk it up to witchcraft.

"Well. No human has ever asked me that. I am not sure how to answer it." He confessed.

"How about, you stop thinking of me as human? Perhaps think of me as something different?" She presented.

"You are definitely something different." He winked at her flirtatiously. "Magick?" He rubbed his chin. "How to explain magick… Well first off, we are born with it. It is in our blood and all that we are. It is connected with all life and even the spirit world. For instance," He held out his hand to show her a bare, strong palm. She admired the long thick fingers and rough texture. "If I were to think of what you remind me of:" In an instant a gilded rose appeared from nowhere to rest in his wide hand. "At my will, it shall be so."

"Oh shit!" She gingerly reached out to touch the red and gold flower resting in his palm.

"Here, keep it. Consider it a gift." He gave it to her and for a moment they stood silent. He coughed nervously.

"That's incredible. That must be so powerful. Can you do that with anything?" She begged for further knowledge.

"Well, yes. Some elves have more ability than others, but we can all pretty much make things move, shape the weather, and make things grow. It is being in tune with all elements of life and being able to will them to do your bidding. Does that make more sense?" He asked patiently.

She started walking, staring at the rose. "That's so profound and overwhelming. What a gift! "

"I guess I have never really thought of it that way." He reflected.

"That's because you have it. If you had to live without it, you would." She walked on deep in thought. "Tell me more about elves, how, other than the obvious things, are they different from humans?"

"Well I am not sure what you mean by obvious but the basic things are easy. We are immortal. From what I know of most humans they only live for about sixty years." He jumped at her shock.

"60! Why so short?" She asked.

"Some of them are lucky to make it that long. Why, how long do you think you will live?" He asked.

"Well if all goes well I hope about at least 100 years. Wait, did you say immortal!"

"Yes, that is correct." He was amused at her bold reactions.

"When you say immortal do you mean really immortal?" Britt tried not to sound mentally challenged.

"I only know one meaning for the word immortal, Britt. If there are more I will need to be educated." He said flatly.

"Immortal to me means you will live forever." She explained.

"Yes. I will live as long as I choose to live. I will only die if killed, and that is no easy task, or when I choose to venture into the next reality. We have elves in the elder village that are over 10,000 years old." He informed her.

"Okay. Regroup." She held her hand up as if to stop him from talking. "You can do magick and you live forever. Is that right?" She was still having a difficult time processing the information.

"Yes. That is correct." For a brief terrifying moment, to his ultimate chagrin an image flashed in his mind of eternity without the human before him. To his discomfort it did not register as a desirable option. He understood her dilemma and did his best to smooth over the shock, hoping it would pull his mind from the path it now followed.

"You seem comfortable enough with it. Most humans are very disturbed by the fact." He held up his finger to silence her impending response. "But...But you are not most humans." He gawked as she playfully bit his finger.

"I have learned to accept all kinds of life forms. Ya never know what you will encounter from one day to the next in my life. But you guys, now that's something totally off the charts. I am a little stunned, but I want to learn more. Nothing comes from ignorance. Besides, I have a few neat tricks of my own." She returned his earlier wink.

"I bet you do." He smirked, and then from the corner of his eye he caught sight of Osizio and Demetri standing just behind them. He instantly straightened up. "My Lady, I think we are intimidating our companions." He gestured to the two figures behind them. It was comical to see a royal guard of the elfish palace standing next to a filthy ogre.

"Come now gentlemen, shall we be off to the palace?" He waved them ahead. Osizio slowed when he passed Roderick to examine him with an outrageous appraisal.

"Do you feel well, lad?" He asked. Roderick ignored him and pushed him playfully. Britt skipped ahead to the neat wooden gate leading to the elder's community. She halted at the gate and once again bowed to allow Demetri to pass ahead. He skirted around, avoiding contact with her and almost knocking Roderick over, and opened the gates.

Every silver head turned to see the incoming guests to the royal grounds. Demetri entered first, followed by Roderick, Osizio, then Britteny. She used the ogre as a kind of living shield to hide behind, absently latching on to his crusted vest. The action of familiarity and trust felt like a blade slicing into his ogre heart. She was truly in a state of wonder by this point, feeling the rush of a new and brilliant discovery, a planet of such rare qualities was beyond her expectations and the natural explorer in her came alive.

Each elf was graceful and ghost like. Each wore individually crafted silver circlets. It was difficult to separate the males from the females for they were all tall and slim, wearing long robes of intricate embroidered blue and silver, their enormous eyes shades of wisdom beneath wrinkled lids. Roderick had fallen back to walk behind her. She brightened further as she noticed some of these older folks were playing a game that looked like chess. They were all, however, distant. A slight breeze sent glittering dust floating up from the tables creating the only sound louder than Osizio's breathing.

Britt approached one of the game tables. She had been drawn to a particular old elf, sitting alone and watching the commotion. His expression had captured her. Instinct noted it was lacking the cryptic frigidity given by his peers. His wrinkles told the tale of laughter in his life. Something in his eyes was familiar to her as if she had known him in a past life. For the first time in her stay on Zembeth she felt very comfortable around a member of this species, even at home. She could not stop herself from approaching him, as if some unseen force called her to his side, fearless and wanting more knowledge of his existence.

"Sit my child, for I know you can only stay a while." His voice was so soft and soothing. Britt sat at the opposite side of the table and all the game pieces turned to look at her.

"I feel a bit like Alice." She hiccupped.

"But you are not Alice? Then what may I call you?" He asked politely. Before she spoke she was aware of the slightest feeling of potency within the interaction. This elf knew her as well. Everything about his mannerisms told her that he was of the same mind as she.

"I'm Britteny Eden Devarelle." She whispered, cautious of his magick. She had been told there was magick in a name and that at times it was better not to give one's name to a worker of such. Something told her this elf already knew more about her than she knew about herself.

"You need not fear me girl, for I am an old fool and nothing more. I am surely a fool for such beauty and spirit." He waved at her. "I am Gherkin, king of fools and master of the stars." He extended his skeletal hand.

"Master of the stars?" She took the hand without hesitation and grasped it warmly.

"Yes, I am the court astrologer. I chart the night sky and keep track of its movements." He said. "It has become quite an obsession of mine." He added. "Perhaps I am just an old fool searching for something I will never find but have always yearned to know, as if in search of an old friend or loved one." Again his smile warmed her.

"Well in reality, you are moving as much as they are. You are spinning in an orbit and will see a different view from night to night." She slipped.

He beamed. "That has been my theory all along! So you know the nature of the stars?" He was a little too calm for her liking. Most scientists that were passionate enough about their work to devote a lifetime, especially a very long lifetime, to their craft seemed to make giant productions out of even the smallest findings. But his smile was of pure love.

"Oh, well I just figured since there is day and night the world must move away from the sun somehow to face the night sky. Like a dancer spins for an audience." She attempted to sound dull witted.

"I am sure that is what you meant." He replied dryly. "Perhaps once you have the prince in the palm of your hand, you can visit and we can compare notes, if only for the amusement of an old fool?" He asked.

"I'd like that very much. " Roderick had approached and put his hand on her shoulder.

"I see you are in the best of company, most excellent!" He chuckled. "Most excellent indeed. Why Roderick my boy, how is my favorite scoundrel?" Gherkin laughed lightly as if greeting an old friend.

Britt was relived to see Roderick adored the old man. "I am well, Gherkin. It is a pleasure to see you still vibrant." The old elf stood and hugged Roderick.

"You always were a fine judge of character." Gherkin tilted his head toward Britt.

"Oh, no, you see, we are taking this human to Sholendor for the freedom of Osizio. You remember Osizio?" He motioned to Osizio.

"I am sure you are." Gherkin elbowed the young elf in the ribs. "Hello Osizio! It has been some time since our last Gammit game." He greeted the ogre.

"Well Gherkin, you old codger! Fancy meeting you in Garath. Decided to come live with the bone bags after all?" He blurted out forgetting his whereabouts.

"Yes, I gave in. Besides, the prince is very interested in my latest notions of the new moon. He wants me close by. Speaking of which, you all must be off before the guard comes out and ruins all our fun." He shooed them away from the table. Before they parted, Britt looked down at the table and moved a game piece.

"Goodbye then old man, be well." Roderick turned to walk off.

"By the stars! I have been trying to win this came for 25 years. You come along and in one move. . . Won't Belphin be furious?" He slapped his thick robes. Again his appraisal of Britt was openly warm, even proud. "I will insist on our time." He promised with sincerity. "Worry not, my child."

Britt hovered, temporarily being pulled by a strange desperation to stay in his company. Eventually she allowed Roderick to take her hand. "I hope to see you again soon Gherkin." In a strange and unusual gesture for someone of her skills she kissed his cheek in farewell. The old man touched her face lovingly.

Once they had all walked on a bit further Britt offered an observation. "All this slave stuff makes no sense to me. Every elf I have encountered has been very nice to me."

"Yea! I was wonderin the very same thing!" Osizio settled his ham fists on his hips glaring at Roderick. "But then Ol' Gherkin is as sweet as these devils come." He contemplated.

None of them had time to comment. They had reached the royal courtyard and were being greeted by a full fleet of guards. These elves were obviously Demetri's superiors. The platoon formed a circle around the little group and the leader spoke to Roderick.

"It seems you took your time arriving, Lord Roderick." He bowed.

"Yet I am here. I thought it wise not to damage the rare gift the ogre has found for the prince." He stepped aside and motioned to Britt, who smiled as sweetly as she could. The captain of the guard stepped back and looked at Roderick.

"We must be off at once!" He reached for Britteny.

Roderick blocked his action. "That is not a wise move friend." He moved in front of Britt. "There is no need, she will come willingly. She has, after all, come this far without so much as a struggle." He nodded and gently took Britt's elbow. He then nodded to Osizio and together they walked with the escort into the front atrium of the palace. All above, green and gold flags billowed from the vaulted ceilings. Roderick knew the palace well and continued walking through the main room, past a court of elfish onlookers, to the solid oak doors that lead to the throne room. As they entered and ascended the stone steps, Britt moved to walk behind the ogre and the elf. She could see the colossal triangle shaped openings in the ceilings that showed the daytime sky, allowing a multitude of vines and plants to spill into the chamber. From one opening, a silver stream of water cascaded into a pool that dominated the great floor. Small creatures scampered here and there, holding fabrics, jewels and foods. Each stopped quickly to glance at her. They were the same creatures she had seen carrying packs and pulling carts in the city.

The company walked around the magnificent pond and mounted the marble stairs to the throne platform. From over the shoulders of her companions she could see the seat of power. It was worked of solid wood and gilded with light gold, seated amidst giant rocks, adorned with green plants and sparkling fountains.

Upon this throne sat an elf male. He was much thinner than Roderick. He sat neither like a king nor a prince. Instead he slouched back in the, should be position of respect, with his knees crossed and a sly smile on his shrunken face. His nose was sharp as was his chin. His eyes radiated a cruel glint that Britteny had seen too often. He wore a simple circlet of silver entangled in his white curls.

When Roderick got closer to the throne, Sholendor sat up a bit. "Well now, this is quite a surprise." He scowled at the ogre. "You are more daft than I first presumed, Osizio. I am disgusted that you are in on this little parade of fools, Roderick." He hissed. "All this way, to think I, of all elves, would accept ANY human, as payment for my brother's death. Are you out of your mind?" He almost laughed.

Roderick reached over and gently shoved Osizio aside to let Britt come face to face with the prince of Garath. Without fear, she walked forward to face Sholendor. Sholendor stood up in slow motion. His eyes sparked as he magically stripped Britt of all her clothing. She stood, head raised and a sure smile on her lips, confident that she was now completely being underestimated. Roderick could not help but look and Osizio blanched.

On Zembeth, the fashion of the brassiere and bikini panties had yet to be conceived. Most human females wore peasant dresses and chemises. Her buttocks rounded under the light fabric dimpled with muscle. Her stomach was softly rippled with strength and her voluminous hair hid her scantily covered breasts.

"Where did you find this?" Sholendor whispered. "What form of magick did you use to create her?"

"He didn't create me." Britt answered him. "He offered me a ride to your palace. I was lost and alone. I have injured myself and cannot fully remember my past." She stated.

Sholendor started for a moment, blinking at the sound of her deep female voice, as every other creature had done upon hearing her annunciate. He walked down the few steps to the floor to stand before her. He then walked around her to inspect her.

Sholendor's voice cracked. "Get out of my palace, ogre, you have your freedom! Do not let me see you here again." The order only had to be stated once. Osizio turned and hurried off. Sholendor was standing nose to nose with Britt. "Why are you still here Roderick, you have acquired what you came for, the ogre is free." He barked.

"I will be leaving as well my Lord Sholendor. I am glad to see you are pleased with the ogre." Britt turned to look at him one last time.

"Thank you for your help Roderick." She walked to him, standing as close as she would allow herself. "I hope to see you again very soon." She whispered, despite conscious unease with this man. It seemed the proper thing to do was bow, so she did so. He lifted her chin gently.

"You must never bow to me, Britteny. I am but your servant if you should request my services." He smiled at her then turned to go. She watched him stride out the door, ever aware of the odd occurrence he had enacted in her ever vigilant emotional blockade. She turned to see the prince staring at her. Now she was dressed in some type of short dress. It was forest green and made of very light fabric that clung comfortably to her body. Sholendor never let Roderick out of his sight.

"I want everyone OUT of this room NOW!" Sholendor commanded. "Shall we?" He held out his arm to her. She took it carefully. It was well known to her that any male that accepted her with such sudden interest was clearly interested in one thing. It had also not escaped her keen female sense that he was not above raping a human female and/or using one for physical pleasure. Why else would he treat a slave so? He led her to the throne mount and advised her to sit in the place of the future queen. She shot him a questioning glance. "Don't worry my love, it is not time for court and after all I am the prince, unless you would rather sit somewhere else?"

"Demetri!" He yelled for the young elf. Demetri came running to the throne. He looked at his feet in shame at the sight of a human female sitting in the princess's chair. He had guessed this situation would turn to ill fates. Sholendor spoke in the elf tongue to not upset his new pet. "I want you to have the ogre skinned alive as soon as Roderick leaves this city. Better yet, wait until after the Beltane games. I shall present his hide to my new queen." Sholendor ordered.

"Yes, sire." He obeyed without question.

"And make sure to tell the guards I want to be ALONE for the night on your way out the door." He stated in human tongue.

Everyone left the hall. She was now alone, with the future King of Zembeth.

CHAPTER 7

MISFIT SHUNNING

Amaranth paced in front of the sleeping oxen. His brother, friend Osizio and Britteny had been gone for a very long time. Much longer than it should have taken to get Britt to the palace and come back. He was starting to think Sholendor had not gone for the deal and perhaps he and Donavan should set off to rescue them. He was starting to feel claustrophobic. He did not like being surrounded by walls, no matter how much room was between them. Donavan was sitting in the grass next to a hallafawn tree reading a book he had found in Osizio's sack of things to sell in the wagon.

"How can you read at a time like this?" Amaranth insisted. "They have been gone forever! Do you not worry for their safety?" He stomped over.

"I know your brother and I have some good idea of the natural attraction that human possess. If there is anyone I am concerned for, it is Sholendor." His ice blue eyes looked up from the book of elf prophesies to the eager young example before him. "Just calm down. If they are not here by night fall we will go looking for them." He rose to his hind paws and started back to the cart. Just before he reached his destination he put his sensitive nose to the wind.

"I smell an ogre." He grinned, baring his fangs. A few seconds passed until the pair could feel the ground trembling. "I smell a running ogre." The lobolack said with a little more concern in his tone.

"Do you smell an elf?!" Amaranth begged. "Or perhaps an army of them?!" He insisted.

"No. One ogre and, just faintly, one elf. No army. I wonder what this can mean?"

Just then, the silver doors burst open farther down the lane to belch out Osizio, running as fast as an ogre can run. His thick arms were pumping in earnest to propel his girth forward. Each leg labored forward, shaking the ground upon impact.

"IT WORKED!" He screamed, waving his arms. "BY BUGGERS IT WORKED! I AM FREE!" Upon his approach, the oxen woke from their usual state of restive slumber. He slowed a bit and took hold of the side of the cart with one hand, while he placed the other on his hairy knee and tried to catch his breath. "He just accepted! Cannya believe it! Woohooo!" He started to climb into the cart then reconsidered. "Damn ox are too slow, must go faster!"

Donavan noticed that he was talking like an ogre in his glee and haste.

"Amaranth, let us borrow yer horse, lad?" Osizio asked.

"You will kill it Osizio! You will break its back. No, you can not borrow my horse! Now slow down and tell us what happened." He yelled

"Not on yer life, boy! I am goin' home to me wife!" He jumped ahead and started running again. His bulk teetered this way and that in a ridiculous rocking and running motion, making Amaranth conclude that it is better to leave running to elves and humans.

"At least tell me where Roderick is!" Amaranth demanded.

"He is right behind me! He will be here soon." Osizio yelled back.

"What about your goods?" Donavan yelled.

"Keep 'em, sell 'em, I donna care! Bring 'em to the tavern fer me!" They could barely hear him now, but they could still feel the tremors from his weight. To their surprise, he turned around and came back.

"I must warn ye, yer brother has lost his bleedin' mind. I owe ye at least that, friend." He waited till he got close enough to not have to holler it. His breath smelled horrible. "Ye shoulda seen him! Holding hands! Eating buttercups! T'was enough to make me sick!" He waved his hand. "Just keep an' eye on him, I'm a goin' now." He huffed one more time and turned to trot off.

"What do you mean by that?" Amaranth was livid.

"Ask him yerself! I'm a goin' home!" He kept going this time. Donavan put a paw on Amaranth's shoulder. Amaranth looked past him to see his brother walking through the gates. The black elf of Darmuth Anor was trudging along like a dead man. He did not seem to notice them and kept walking. When he approached his horse he handed the reins to Amaranth.

"I am walking the rest of the way. I will meet you at the tavern." He mumbled.

"What the demon is wrong with you?" His brother insisted.

Roderick did not answer; instead he started walking past the cart and toward the city.

"RODERICK!" Amaranth yelled. Donavan barricaded his pounce.

"Let him go, Amaranth. I think this is something he does not want to talk about." Amaranth pulled his arm from Donavan's grip. The young elf closed his eyes and suspended the oxen and the cart in the air and turned them around to face east.

"It would have taken us all night to get that cart turned around your way." He huffed and climbed onto his horse. He grabbed Roderick's horse's reins and started for his brother. Donavan mounted the cart and slapped the lazy oxen into motion.

"Fine." He looked down at his brother from atop his steed. "Have it your way. We will meet you at Ruddy Mudders." He kicked his steed and sped down the lane with both horses. Donavan approached Roderick in the wagon.

"Is all well my brother? Roderick?" He seemed to be able to read Roderick's mind.

"Yes old friend. I just need time to think." He patted Donavan's paw.

"She really made an impression on you?" He asked.

"I have not the faintest idea what just happened." Roderick looked up at the sky. "I just feel strange. I feel as if there is an undiscovered place in my energies that has been in slumber these two hundred years."

"I think it is called love." Donavan offered.

"Donovan. You are aware that such mention is folly to my people." He reminded his friend. "Let us not begin to think of such a word attached to a human female. Is it death you wish for me?" His words reflected his current features.

"Well, you have yet to be classified as normal." assured Donavan, attempting to lighten the mood.

"I understand that well. I just feel less than noble for handing over such a wonderful woman to such a snake. I may be an elf, but I do have a conscience. I am going to take a long walk and think it over. I will see you at the tavern. I am sure there will be a party." Roderick guessed.

"Yes, there very well may be." Donavan slapped his companion's back and headed for the city gate.

Roderick watched his friend drive away in the cart meant to haul slaves. He could walk faster than the oxen, but he stood still instead and watched Donavan and the beasts lumber out of the gate. He strode to the gate and instead of turning south, towards Ruddy Mudders, he ventured north, toward the slave traders' end of town. He had no intention of pricing humans, or sizing up breeding stock.

As he moved through the streets his mind raced with all manner of quandary previously forgotten. He questioned life. Absently he ran his fingers through a laundry basin. Five human slave women stepped back as expected in complete submission. For a moment he looked at them. For truthfully the first time in as long as he could recollect he actually registered their existence. He had never been for slavery, yet what had he ever done to prevent it? Was it that he had accepted this as a social monument, unmovable and ancient? What made one race superior from another? What was superiority? Was it superior to have power over another living thing, or just a sadistic game played by the powerful? He had never been considered an elf as a child because he had been raised by a goblin. He had the ears, the eyes, maybe not the body, but he was still an elf. So was it race or upbringing? Who gave those in charge the right to rule, or better yet, what? Was it the ability to kill and destroy more efficiently and without remorse? He turned from the well and walked slowly through the slave quarter of town. His whole life had been riddled with these social theatrical productions. Was he really safe from slavery? What kept the other elves from making his life a succession of pain and labor? It was his strength and magical ability, nothing more. Children in rags scampered out of his line of sight. They had no need to fear him. He knew no matter how he tried to tell them this, they would still shrink in terror, like a small animal held in the hands of a hunter. Years of suppression can wear away all hope of trust and burn every bridge that separated two races.

No one, not even an elf, knew for sure what would happen the next moment of every day. It would be too tiring and entirely too boring to have control over it. If the elf race was so magical, why is it none of them saw Britteny coming, or had they? He pondered this for some time. He had known that there had been rumors of something coming, yet he doubted the frail female he had just deposited at the palace would equate to the discord amongst the seeing of late. If any being had foreseen this event it would have been Ma Fafella.

He had just visited her not but five days past. She had fussed and huffed more than usual. He had never seen the cottage so clean. Absently he willed a blade of thick straw into his hand and placed it in his mouth. She had said nothing of the sort, yet he had felt an air of expectation permeating the entire cove. He had passed a number of butcher shops that sold human meat as well as human hair used for coats and lining boots. He had passed a brothel that used human females for the sexual release of just about every race he could think of, only to be sold when their use had run its course to the butcher. He had not been approached by any of the street front vendors. They were all very wary of his presence. The slaves in this part of town were not sold to elves. They were purely labor and trade slaves and not of the quality to be sold to an elf. He had had quite enough of the slave quarter.

What would happen to him tomorrow, or tonight? He had gone quite far west and turned to his left down Brewers Road towards the middle of town. He was entering the industrial section of the city. Garath seemed to be divided into trades rather than races. This was yet another reason he loved Garath. The city continued to grow if the people that lived there were productive. Ogres lived next to goblins. They worked together, raised their pups together. He wandered past a silversmith shop and peeked in at the fine jewelry. He felt inclined to enter the shop, for the first time.

Behind the stout wood counter sat a dwarf woman. She was busied with accounting the sales and shushing a babe at her feet behind the wooden showcase. He took a deep breath of the sweet smoke coming from the brass incense burner hanging in the corner near the door. It was wise to purify the air at one's entrance, lest evil find its way into one's place of business. The shop was very well kept. Roderick took advantage of the fact that the dwarf dam had not noticed her unusual patron and for a few moments wandered around the shop. There were trinkets of all sorts, made by every type of race he could think of. He admired a blade cast from the hands of an old troll. The hilt was griffin bone and carved in the likeness of a troll sow. As he walked, he admired the fine craftsmanship of a pendant in the showcase before him. He set the blade back on its hook and walked over to the case. The dwarf wife popped from her stool and became flustered.

"My lord, you elves are so quiet! I am so sorry sire. I did not hear you enter! Is there something I can assist you with?" She was having some trouble holding the toddler dwarf from climbing up onto the glass to see the elf.

"Yes, my lady. I was wondering at that pendant. There in the front." He pointed to the deep blue tear-shaped stone.

"Funny you should ask." She reached in to pull out the tray that held the piece in question. "I have had that thing in here for so long I had almost forgotten it was here. My husband bought it off of someone on a trip to Sid O'Sala." She placed the ample jewel in his hand. "It is strange; no one has seemed very interested in it. I think it is one of the most perfect pieces I have ever seen." She commented.

Roderick held the stone to the candle. "How much do you want for it?" He asked.

"Well it depends, who am I selling it to?" She smiled up at him.

"Why do you ask?" He set the stone back on the glass and in a friendly manner, squinted his eyes as if he had need of caution.

"Well, if you are who I think you are, I would be willing to give it to you." She said.

"That is rather generous! And who do I need to be for that?" He joked.

"Roderick of Darmuth Anor." She pulled out a soft leather pouch to place the piece in. The child was wild with excitement and ran to get her siblings. He could hear her announcing that Roderick of Darmuth Anor was in their shop, followed by a scamper of tiny dwarf boots.

"I only wish my husband was here to meet you, sir, he would consider it a great honor." She blushed.

"Really?" He was surprised.

"Of course! You are so humble. It is plain to see why you are so well loved." She cooed.

"I had no idea." He looked puzzled. "And how did a bastard like myself grow to deserve such generosity?" He leaned on the solid oak railing.

"The word has spread through the city already. You won Osizio his freedom at last. You are the only elf that would have bothered." By now there was an audience of chubby dwarf children hiding behind furs and hanging chain mail.

"I had little to do with it really. It was due to a human female named Britt. She was responsible for his freedom. I only escorted them to the palace." He assured her.

The dwarf wife seemed to ignore the last statement. She shoved the suede pouch in his hand. "Please consider it a gift of gratitude for the kindness you have always shown to the peasant folk." She giggled at touching his hand. "Your respect to all people is more valuable than any stone dug from the soil and polished up to shine. You are the only one of your kind to have such a soul. I am sure you know this." She tipped her head upwards to look at the face of a man she had always hoped to meet. He was more beautiful than the stories had let on, if it were possible. She frowned for a moment. His beauty was mixed with a solid feel, not like that of most of his race. Their beauty was stolen before it could fully penetrate any mortal soul. Roderick's seemed to linger.

"But my lady, I am one of the peasant folk." He reminded her.

She started walking back behind the counter. "In this house, Sir Roderick, you are more noble than the Prince himself." She insisted.

He placed the pouch in a pocket inside his worn leather vest. "I am very thankful for your generosity and I shall not soon forget it. I must be off now, there is merriment a' foot." He was becoming a bit uncomfortable at all the praise. If Sholendor ever heard a peasant, dwarf or no, refer to him as higher nobility than the prince, it would be the end of their shop, business, and perhaps their lives. Before he left he stopped to tickle a small dwarf female. She was just that sweet. Her thick yellow curls bounced about her plump pink cheeks. She giggled with glee and ran for the cover of her mother's skirts. He turned to see the family standing in the shop; most of them arm in arm. He could not help feel a sense of responsibility and belonging. He hadn't a family such as this. No elf did. There were never any real warm fires or laughter for them. He had never been in an elf keep that was not perfect and empty. He remembered the words of Ma Fafella.

"All that thinking leaves no room for loving." She had said behind a cloud of smoke.

He started to feel glad that he had been raised by a goblin. He knew the feeling of family and home. He had laughed as a child. He had held Ma Fafella and cried when he was very sad. He had chased his brothers through the fields in the sun and come home tired after a day's work. Those days vanished once he was enrolled in the military academy at Darmuth Anor and became an elf.

He waved and walked back into the street. Feeling better, he turned for the road to the tavern. He was not sure how he felt about the gift. He knew he was well known and liked by the common people but now they were giving him very expensive gems. That jewel could have feed the family for some time if sold at its fair price. What was he going to do with it anyway? He pulled it out of his vest pocket, dropped it from its pouch and looked at it again. He knew perfectly well what he was going to do with it. He was going to give it to the one person that was responsible for the freedom of a good friend, as soon as he had the chance to see her again. His only concern was that the prince would jade her before he could creep into the palace. He hoped she would be strong enough to survive. He popped the jewel back into his vest and smiled. Somehow he knew he would not have to rescue this human.

********** * * * * * * **************

For a few moments she just walked around the great hall. It was not until Sholendor had started talking to the other elf that Britt decided to just take a good look around. To her amazement, the entire chamber was a brilliant marble carved forest. How she had not noticed it before was a mystery. The walls themselves were carved in the likeness of mammoth trees. Along the hall, were placed long wooden tables, complete with ornately carved chairs. This must be where they held council. Sholendor had been watching her the entire time. He sat enthralled as she walked over and ran her fingers along the carved bark of a near tree.

She could not resist the waterfall or the deep blue pool. She sat on the rim of the indoor pond and dipped her finger in to tickle the fish, hoping all the time that they were only goldfish and not some rare breed of piranha. She must have noticed then that the giant room had grown too quiet, for she turned around to look at the prince seated in his royal chair looking at her. He crooked his finger, ordering her silently to his bidding. She rose and walked back up the deep blue carpet to stand before him.

"So, you speak." He asked.

"Why yes, Your Majesty, I speak very well. I can also read and write." She added.

"You did not keep your seat, as I offered earlier. You have chosen instead to stand." He patted the seat beside her usually reserved for the queen of the realm.

"I was not sure you wanted me to do so with an audience." She walked up the few stairs and sat in the throne.

"It suits you. Somehow you look like a queen." His smile was sly and calculated. She knew he would never be a person she trusted. Little did he know that queen was a gross demotion from her current rank.

"Thank you, My Lord." She tipped her head.

"So is there anything you require, my pet?" He was asking more out of curiosity of her greed than her needs.

"I haven't seen a slave dressed like this yet." She hoped to diffuse his visible interest.

"You have probably not seen a companion slave. They are rare and are only seen accompanying very wealthy persons. Roderick of Darmuth Anor is hardly wealthy." He gave a snide laugh.

"So." He began, leaning over to get a close look at her. "I should ask you where you are from. I should also ask you a number of other questions, but I think they would be a waste of time".

"Why do you say that?" She asked.

"You must be completely lost to have come willingly with Osizio. It is either that or you are in some type of trouble which you are running from. Say perhaps, slavery to another owner." He put his hand on her knee. "Fret not my priceless possession, none will come for you here. You are now property of the King of Zembeth, and in saying, above contestation from all subjects of the realm."

So he thought she was a runaway. That was wonderful. This was going to be much less work than Britteny had originally projected.

"I see you are wise, King Sholendor." She used the unofficial title that he seemed to equate to himself. "I am from far away and a stranger in this land. I am lost to its people and cultures. I fear I will not be an adequate companion slave for the princess."

"Nonsense! She is not very bright. Why, I would be willing to bet my kingdom that you already posses a sizable amount of intelligence that she will never obtain." He was rubbing her leg now. "For you my dear, seated in that chair of power, I will allow any education you may quest. I have a feeling we are going to be in close company for quite some time, if you choose to obey me as I wish." He bravely leaned over and kissed her cheek.

She turned her head and met his lips, lightly. The kiss was forced forward with false passion. She would leave no doubt to her abilities in order to reach her goals. "So I may have a teacher or teachers if need be?" She questioned.

"If that is all you require I am a lucky man indeed. I will summon our palace scholars to begin tomorrow." He kissed her again with growing lust. Her mind again amazed at the never failing stupidity of the humanoid male when presented with such a situation and their ability to throw caution to the wind, risking wealth, power, family, love, all for a few moment's passion with a strange woman, toxic as she may be.

"Sire, is there such a need for public embarrassments? I do not wish to soil your reputation." She did her best to sound at least a little concerned.

"What do you mean, pet?" He asked.

She wondered if he would ever use her name rather than these titles of useless affection. "I was thinking perhaps Gherkin, the elder I met in the village. After all, he is old and no one in court would even notice that you were educating your new human slave."

He pondered this a moment. "Yes, I suppose you have a point. You are shrewd as well. That is very attractive." He went into deep thought.

She had a feeling if she told him she ate live frogs; he would think that was attractive as well.

"As well you will need a guard. It would not be wise to post just any member of the staff with such a job. This guard will require a sense of isolation. A man that is able to protect himself as well." Britt was a bit eager to hear his decision. "This elf would also need to be able to resist your charms. I would not want the death of a royal guard marring my saga."

He contemplated a moment longer then the name came to him. "Rowland of Sid O'Sala. There is clearly no other choice. He knows the minds of thieves. He is an excellent warrior. He lives most of his days in solitude running the plains of the Arosa." He shifted closer to Britt. She had no concern for a guard only wishing to obtain enough knowledge of the man to best him later.

Aggressing contact Britt chose to slide her neck close to his lips while lightly kissing his pale neck. Sholendor was alive with fire and feeling. He looked down to see remarkably voluptuous firm breasts nearly bare and seductively rubbing against his arm. Breathing deeply, he inhaled a scent that must only be present in human females. The entirety of womanhood shivered his consciousness. Skin, smell, she slowly rubbed her cheek against his and placed her hand on his thigh. He was insane. His mind began to ramp up with savage need never felt and soon to become obsession. When she moved to kiss him full again he noticed her color had risen. She was vibrantly filling with warmth that encompassed his cold tones. Her eyes were hooded and intentional, her lips parted in instinctive hunger.

The doors to the room opened and a member of the guard apologized feverishly. The spell was broken as Britt sat back obediently. Sholendor found he was enraged and near to executing the guard.

"I have given orders not to be disturbed!" He burst out with no hint of shame.

"Excuse me, my lord. You have been summoned on an errand of urgency by the lady De'Loria of Havaland." He bowed so low he almost touched the ground.

"I will be there anon." He turned to Britt. His tone did not escape her. He answered the guard as if he were being reminded of a troublesome task he had forgotten to see to earlier.

"I must leave. This lady never summons me unless it is of great importance." He clapped his hands. A gnome came hustling out from nowhere. "Take the lady to the south tower room and see to her needs." He again seemed to be surmising a plot. The gnome stood ready, apparently used to his patterns of communications. "I want Sara sent for as soon as possible. She will be assigned to the care of this new slave. See to it the Lady Meriden is given a younger slave in replacement." He turned his head sharply and squinted his eyes. He must have communicated telepathically with another elf outside the door. Another white haired guard appeared. "Is Rowland of Sid O'Sala close?" Britt was mildly impressed with the speed of his delegations.

"Yes sire, he has left Fairfax and will be here soon to inquire for the queen." He answered.

"Have him report to the palace. He is to be personal escort to Meriden's new companion slave until the time the princess arrives. Make it known this is not a request. I will leave word to her needs upon his arrival."

"Yes my Lord." He was off as fast as he had come.

Britt could only conclude that De'Loria must be a very important person to spur this self-absorbed ruler into such sharp action. She looked down to see the terrified gnome bowing before her, hand out, bidding her to follow.

"There is no need to bow to me. I'm a slave as well." She informed.

"Britteny! Never tell another slave that!" His chastisement caused her muscles to tense battle ready. "You are above those creatures and shall treat them accordingly." He hissed.

There would come a day she would not need games. For his sake she hoped she was well into another solar system.

********** * * * * * * * * * ***********

He stopped for a brief moment just past Darmuth Anor. He only need have run a bit further and he would be at the northern most gates of his destination, Garath. Alone, at full run, a well-conditioned male elf, calling on the spirits of the wind, could make the run in nearly a day. This was without the help of systematic magick. Rowland of Sid O'Sala rarely used such magick. He had been born to Ferrin of Sid O'Sala and raised in its simple country court. His mother had died giving birth to him. He had never longed for the crowded city life or the company of other elves. Perhaps this was due to his association with Amaranth of Darmuth Anor and his decision to take to the road with Amaranth and his older brother that had changed Rowland. His father did not mind. Young Rowland had still made a name for himself as Royal Scout. So he would stay this way until the time came that the high council insisted that he get married and devote his life to a more secure vocation.

He wore the ritual bones of the mozeta braided into his thick blood colored hair. The bones were rare and only awarded to elves that chose to venture alone in the Arosa Plains at the onset of manhood long enough to hunt without magick for the mozeta. If an elf was strong enough in mind and body to achieve such a task, they wore three rib bones from the creature to keep this sacrifice alive in their souls. This would only add to their magick as a warrior and a male. The mozeta was the only creature on Zembeth that could best an elf in a match of physical strength. When hunting the beast without magick, it could creep into the minds of its prey and slowly drive the subject insane. Opening the mind of its prey, the mozeta was then able to capture the core essence of spirit. Historically a great number of elves had died young at this special ritual of manhood. Of all the men he knew, Rowland could only count 10 that wore such bones.

He leaned against a sapling and waited for the silver message bubble to float to him while he rested. He tried to remember if he had forgotten anything at the palace. What reason had any member of the royal family for taking the trouble to send him a message on the road? Judging from the direction of flight, this was a message from Garath. He was not aware the prince paid that much attention to his journeys. The fragile sphere approached and he held out a dusty hand to receive it. Placing it in his palm he brought it to his forehead, relishing the coolness of its touch. He closed his deep amber eyes and concentrated, only to open them again in surprise. He looked at the message globe and thinking he heard wrong, placed it back against his forehead only to do the same.

"Escort a human?" He trotted a few steps and stopped; shook his head and walked a bit further. What possible motivation would Sholendor have to assign HIM of all elves to guard a HUMAN? He was aware the wedding was close. He could think of nothing else. He had been hoping he would be given leave of the city. Long distant scouts would not be used when virtually every member of the royalty would be within the city. He wanted to be as far from Garath as possible the day Meriden was sacrificed to matrimony. Why a human, for the sake of the gods? There was little choice. He must do as ordered by the prince. He reset his plans to make Ruddy Mudders by nightfall. He set out with increased speed.

At this pace, other creatures would not see him pass. They may be vaguely aware that the wind shifted unnaturally. They would turn and look behind for a moment, only to shrug and move on. Rowland loved to run and rarely used horses or travel globes. He rejoiced in solitude. He was, even when forced to socialize, very selective with his company. The only elves he enjoyed being around were Amaranth, Roderick, Ferrin of Sid O'Sala, and Meriden. He hadn't the slightest idea how to handle a human slave. He was very in tune with the magick that was physical effort. His blood coursing through his veins, his heart racing red instead of blue he willingly chose this release and solitude, the focus known by those who run to live.

Before his thoughts could reach conclusion, he was at the northern gates of Garath. He slowed to a trot and sifted his way through the people eventually slowing to a walk. Ruddy Mudders was on the south side of town on the corner of Brewers Road and The Fenway. Rowland was sure, as they had done many times in the past, that his few close friends were staying at this inn. It was growing warmer each day. The roads that were not cobblestoned were draped with sheets of mud. Rowland danced to miss the larger puddles and keep from tripping over a dwarf. He stopped for only a moment to observe the crews, covered with mortar and grime, carrying large wooden buckets of water on yokes over their stout shoulders. They would sing a number of songs while they worked, many of which were as steady as the beat of the mountain's heart. This new addition would be a feat of masterful architecture. Scaffolding was being constructed in the outer field and transported to the work site. The chief builders had erected surveying points and stood as soldiers bent on a cause, waving arms and yelling orders. Some turned to bow to Rowland as he appraised the operation. Others could be seen moving the human slaves with whips toward the mud pits and rope slings designed for pulling the large building blocks. Enough dawdling, he must be off to Ruddy Mudders.

It did not take him long to reach the tavern. It never took Rowland of Sid O'Sala long to do anything. He hesitated to kick off the little bit of mud that had collected on his leather boots and lifted the iron doorknob, only to step aside and allow two male trolls to come crashing out onto the road in a fit of fists and daggers. Rowland stepped over one of their legs and proceeded into the tavern. He glanced around and noticed the dive was unusually crowded, even for Beltane and the games. Loud cries of laughter and swearing erupted from every corner. He squeezed his way past two ripe ogres and made for the bar.

To his shock, the first person to speak to him was none other than Osizio of Garath.

"Rowland! Tis a pleasant surprise to see you here, lad! I heard you were coming down for the wedding." Osizio gripped the hand of the palace scout with glee. Before he could speak, he was distracted by another hand on his shoulder.

"Don't worry you palace puppet, Sholendor gave him leave today. He will not be dragged out any minute." Amaranth moved around his long time friend and shook his hand. "How are you, old boy?" He greeted Rowland.

"What? How much have I missed in my absence?" Rowland began.

"Do not feel left out, my lad," Donavan injected. "It all happened just today. It is quite a surprise to all of us as well." He assured.

"But how, why? I can not imagine Sholendor being so forgiving." Before his question could be answered, Osizio gently pushed him onto a bar stool and Censci served him a drink.

"Here, I think you need this." He shoved the cold tankard of ale towards Rowland. "I found meself a human and made 'im an offer he could'na refuse." Osizio explained, waiting for Rowland's next, but anticipated question.

"A human? One human? Today? This is rather distressing!" He swallowed a large amount of ale.

"Why? Have you and the prince gotten closer since we last met?" Amaranth asked.

"No." Rowland wiped his mouth. "I was just sent a message about a human from the palace." He looked about. "Where is Roderick?" He asked.

"What kind of message?" Osizio seemed insistent.

"He let off to the north of the city for a bit of a walk. He should be here soon for the party. Is the lass in trouble?" Osizio asked with unhidden concern.

"It is a female?" Rowland asked in a very loud tone.

"Of course. What in the stars would Sholendor want with a male slave?" Donavan delivered from his corner, looking up from his book on ancient Zembethian art.

During the flurry of questions and conversation, Roderick strode through the door in a dream. Noticing Rowland at the front of the establishment, he sifted his way through the dancing sea hags that had come ashore for the festival. He was able to catch a statement by Rowland about being chosen as personal escort for Britt.

"What's this?" Roderick yelled. "What have I missed?"

"Well, hello to you as well, Roderick. I have just been informing everyone that I have been asked to guard this human female slave while Sholendor is off to Kloter Mass Arosa for a few days before the wedding."

Without greeting Rowland or responding to his statement, Roderick shoved his way past the tables and to the bar, and announced he was off to the palace as he headed for the stairs.

"Why is he going to the palace?" Amaranth asked.

A thundering heard of creatures assaulted the weak planks of the inn steps. The first one to mount was Donavan, being the closest and quickest thinking. He was tailed only a few steps by Osizio. If it were not for the girth of the ogre on the stairs, Amaranth would have passed them all. Next came Censci, then Marsiz and last, shaking his head, Rowland. Donavan bounded into their room in time to see Roderick stripping off his tunic and hopping about to pull off his boots.

"Just where do you think you are going?" He stumbled forward, being knocked over by the incredible force of the ogre.

"Put yer clothes back on, you silly bastard!" Osizio grabbed for Roderick's belt.

Soon the room was filled and Roderick continued to strip and head for the washroom to bath. Marsiz blushed to see his buttocks as he hurried past the dividing curtain. Censci had no such shame and followed the naked man into the small area. She walked up to the basin full of warm water and looked down at Roderick.

"Haul yer young ass out o' that tub!" She boomed.

Roderick ignored her and started soaping his armpits. Amaranth pushed past.

"Do you mind, Censci?" He asked with premature courage. Her glare changed his tone. "I guess it is your inn." He cowed at the glance only a wife and mother can give, leave free the fact that she outweighed him by three hundred stone.

Roderick had slipped under the water to wet his hair. When he emerged and wiped his eyes, pushing the soaked curls from his face, he was not surprised to see everyone crammed in the small space the inn afforded them for bathing. He was comforted only by the fact that at least Marsiz had the sense to stay in the bedroom.

"I know that each of you wishes to live. I strongly suggest that this conversation go on with all of you behind that curtain before I get out of this tub and acquire my blade." He reached to the small table next to him and touched the hilt of a dagger. Everyone stepped back simultaneously and disappeared behind the thin curtain. It did not quell their resolve for answers.

"Ye know lad, this is a trap of some sort." Osizio began. It was not long before they were all yelling and arguing. Donavan's canine nose poked through a hole and he voiced his opinion. Roderick ignored them and finished his bath. As if he had not heard a word of their plight, he wrapped a towel around his naked genitals and proceeded across the damp floor to the bedchamber. By this time they were all so engrossed in their own opinions of the situation that they moved to let him pass and kept arguing. Marsiz was the quiet one. She watched as he faced the wall and started putting on a clean pair of soft black breeches. She walked over to him and cleared her throat.

"Roderick." She spoke almost in a whisper. He turned to look down at her. She could feel her knees begin to give under the weight of his stare. "I…" Her eyes watered. "Please do not go. I could not bear to see you harmed."

The party of complainants ceased their chatter at the courage of the tavern servant.

"Marsiz, I must go. Osizio knows it. Amaranth knows it; even Donavan knows it. I am sure when I return with Britteny, you will understand as well." He was well aware that he could say just about anything. Upon producing Britteny to the people of Ruddy Mudders, Marsiz would allow little concession for compassion.

"But I do understand." She was crying. "Even if Sholendor does not kill you…" She was shaking. "He knows how to hurt you in many other ways. I know I have never said this, but I am so sorry for what happened. Please let it not happen to you." She begged. "You overtake us. Your kind gives us of human flesh little hope to resist. I care not who she is, Roderick, you have an unfair advantage and it will cost both of you your lives." She wiped a tear from her eyes. "If you care for her, you will not condemn her to an eternity of alienation." Her last words caused all of them to twinge.

Roderick hesitated to pull his vest on. For a moment he looked at the floor and only the floor. Censci reached for Marsiz's hand, holding it gently, preparing to pull her from harm's way if necessary.

"I never said anything would happen between the two of us." Roderick almost choked on the words.

Marsiz pulled free of Censci's ham fist. "You do not have to. It is written in your eyes and in your tone and in the rash decision to sneak into the bloody palace." Censci spoke first.

"I think you are all being outrageous!" Amaranth barked. "Marsiz! To assume MY brother would EVER do such a thing is worth hanging you for right here and now!" He moved toward her.

Roderick held his arm out sharply, stopping his younger brother from attacking the terrified human female.

"I think we all need to calm down a bit." Donavan offered.

Roderick continued dressing. "I must do this. I do not know why." He reached for a bone comb to run through his curls, avoiding his mozeta braids. Amaranth moved in front of him before he could don his best vest.

"You will not do this, Roderick. We will find a way to save her, I promise." He rarely challenged his older brother. Roderick turned and looked at the unlikely audience that had watched him bathe.

"I have rarely begged favors." He walked to the door and bent to tie his leather boots. "I have protected each and every one of you. I have sacrificed my own happiness at times, so that you may be safe. I know as well as all of you what Sholendor is about. This may be our only chance to help her. She is alone in that palace. She is out of her world and without friends. I refuse to lie here with a gut full of this guilt."

Osizio interrupted. "Roderick." He leaned forward and challenged his friend in light of disclosing his observations earlier that day in the lane. "Ye saved my life, sure, and fer that I will always be in yer debt. Now it is time for me to save yours. Yes, the lass is spectacular. I saw her as well. But you forget, lad, she is a human. You go straight into the bleedin' palace for a human. Do you hear me, son?"

"I have no fear of Sholendor, Osizio, you know this." The others all felt there was something unsaid. Osizio confirmed their hidden fears.

"I saw ye with her, lad." Osizio hesitated. "I saw the both of ye together. I may only be an ogre, but I know what I saw."

"Really, Osizio, and what was that?" Roderick inquired.

Osizio shook his head. "I saw what I ne'ar a would have never believed. I saw ye smile with a light I dinna know any elf possessed. I lied to yer brother to make it sound better as not to upset him, but now I canna lie more. She has her spell on ye, the same as Gabriel." He looked back at Marsiz and the girl nodded in numb agreement. "Don't be a fool, lad. That woman has it. Me pa told me once that females can blight ye till yer drooling like a fool. That wench has all o' it. I 'ave never seen such a woman. She is a lust witch, sure."

Roderick stood by the door, ready for his ride to the palace. He overlooked all of the faces before him. He looked at the silver eyes of his brother and then to the giant wolf in the corner. Censci had unfolded her arms. He considered the fact that because of such a situation, she had almost lost Osizio. He turned and looked out the window to see the tips of the palace flags atop the hill to the south of the city flying purple in the wind. A vision flashed in his mind's eye of Britteny standing in the palace, watching him walk away. Would there be a price to pay for this or was it only a lesson? His chest burned with the struggle. Osizio may speak the truth. He reflected on his emotion at the first sight of her. It was without a doubt like awakening from a two hundred year sleep. He knew that tonight would be the start of a new life, bad or good. He turned to leave the room.

"Please forgive me, this I do for reasons that are not yet clear, but I must." He walked down the stairs to the stable. None followed.

His horse trotted slowly through town. With each step he could see the face of Gabriel, yet in each step he could feel closer to something more like living.

Chapter 8
Bypassing Protocol

Britt followed the gnome through the palace amidst stares and whispers. She tried in vain to take in all that may be hidden around a corner or behind a tapestry. From every angle she could see slaves appear and disappear. The furniture seemed alive in its design and arrangement. In her heart she only hoped that soon the sun would set and she could find her way home. At the very least, she hoped to be alone for a time to gather her thoughts and perhaps rest. She absently rubbed her arms to ward off the chill of the stone. She had always imagined castles to be such warm and noble places. In truth they were drafty. Her own island hut on Zeneria was adorned in plants and works of art. The ocean breeze billowed white curtains across plank floors. A simple rough table was positioned in the middle of the small kitchenette. Dried fruit and herbs hung along the walls. She imagined she would have to venture to the slave quarters or kitchens to feel more at home. The yellow female walked ahead, every so often turning a terrified eye to the human behind her. The unlikely pair forged forward up the long hike to the tower. The way was narrow and steep. Stone encased the silo opening affording only narrow window slits allowing a rare glimpse of the outside world.

Finally they reached the door. The slave opened it with an old iron key. It appeared she was to be locked away in a tower. It was kind of romantic. It made her giggle a bit. She knew that the simple wooden door was no barrier for someone of her vocation. Once inside she surveyed the room. The space was no cell as she had contemplated. The round room was decorated with plush cushions and vivid tapestries. A fire burned within an ornate carved marble fireplace. She moved to the dinette set with silver flatware and fruit. Large doorways opened onto an encircling balcony. She was too busied with inspecting her accommodations to notice the gnome leaving.

To her relief, she could see the shadows finally falling over the gray stone and dancing across the room. Feeling the pangs of hunger and not completely trusting the food, she produced a sandwich from her weapons gauntlets, along with a cold Dardassian Beer (hair of the dog). She carried her small dinner to the balcony and set it atop the high wall. She hopped to sit on the ledge and marvel at the Deneb Sea. In an attempt to calm her nerves she let her hair down and inhaled the fresh air of twilight. Around the harbor, white houses were tinted pink. The sky was illuminated in spectral precisions of gold and reds. Moments like this assured her, that even death couldn't take away the power of the spirit. Meditation and absorption of energy became more pertinent that dinner.

Slowly the sun had set without breaking the hypnotic trance of the sea. Soon the night sky shone in a brilliant array of stars. The food and drink still rested on the stone. She looked up to the sky and paced the stone floor, searching for home. She blindly wandered around the entire tower. After three laps circling the monolith, she still had no idea of what the stars could tell her. Desperation began to grow in her stomach. To her knowledge there were very few systems in the Andromeda, Eliptica and Stinette galaxies that she could not navigate visually. Below, somewhere in the distance she could hear the faint sound of drums and pipes from the city. She steadied her nerves once more and attempted to get a location with her gauntlets to no avail. She sat in a finely carved chair and put her face in her hands trying to breathe deeply as she pulled her hands through her hair tightly, forcing her face back toward the sky. This left her but one choice.

She unclamped the black gauntlets from her arms. The gauntlets could be programmed to propel themselves beyond the atmosphere of this planet like a homing device or explode, sending a sonic wave. She would set one to jettison towards home and the other to send a sonic message. Its waves would carry billions of miles into space, in hopes that some advanced civilization would hear it, and allow her to hitch a ride. She had resorted to stellar hitch hiking. Sending the gauntlets would also be sending her last shred of technology. She would have to completely depend on her skills for survival. She looked down at the untouched sandwich on the balcony wall.

She programmed one computer for signal and the other for homing capabilities and stepped back. Taking one of the gauntlets in her hand, she thrust back her arm and, propelled it into the sky above the tower. A red light burst from the gauntlet and it shot off into the stratosphere towards open space. She followed suit with the second and watched in anticipation. She stood, hands on the walls, following the lights until she could no longer make out the glow. A short time went by before she saw the bright explosion pinprick, small in the ominous black canvas. The atmosphere of this planet would protect it from any damage due to the magnitude of the signal. She only hoped there were no space stations near by, least they blow out their sound systems, radar, and long-range communications.

Again she tipped her head towards town where the pipes were growing louder. Pipes? How did she know that sound? For some reason the strange drone uplifted her. It was a sound that made her blood pump and her hair stand on end, as though it unlocked some deep genetic well of energy within her. Grasping the now luke-warm ale, she dumped a healthy swig into her mouth and swished it around. It was unlikely she would have another for quite some time, best to savor it. Although it was prime ale somehow it always lacked that strong, pungent kick that came from primitive brewers. She should have zapped a few more before she tossed the gauntlets.

She rested her back on the tower wall and stared out at the southern tip of the city barely visible over the royal wall. It was becoming difficult not to panic. Regardless of what we have been told and read in legends, all heroes panic. Everyone panics. She reminded herself that it would serve nothing; it made no sense. She would do the best she could to keep her mission in sight and find a way home. The systems may have seemed unfamiliar yet this did not mean that they were not inhabited by a race that would pick up that signal. Her mind wandered to the events of the day and eventually rested on a pair of neon green eyes. She ran visions of his face over and over in her mind. She could see him urging her with his incredible smile to taste the flower. She took another drink and walked to the balcony wall. She may not get the chance to see him again. This was clearly a mixed blessing. Thinking of him again, she weighed the reaction to a second encounter with such a man. She entertained him standing next to her in the main courtyard on Zeneria Prime. What a vision that would make, he would be a showstopper. She was sure he was addictive.

Finishing her beer, she wolfed down the sandwich and belched. She looked around for a trash can to toss the bottle in. She resorted to tossing it in the fire and watching it melt. Turning around she noticed that the wind from the sea did not seem to come through the giant openings in the stone. The curtains that hung from iron rods above did not move and the room was warmer than the ocean gale. This must be some form of magick, yet another thing to fret over. This issue of magick would have to be studied very closely. Very little contemplation was needed to discover that it could be dangerous unless she learned to avoid it, or master it. Her schooling on Zeneria had taught her natural magick. She understood herbal healing and spells, the movement of planets and spirits. According to Roderick the magick these people possessed was something intangible. The ability to reproduce matter with the power of the mind was far beyond her education. What really wet her noodle was that it was done without apparent knowledge of quantum physics or scientific data and understanding.

She wanted to look at the city instead of the sea. She walked back out to the balcony. The torches lit up the wall and walkway with a soft glow. She did not hear Roderick enter the room. He stood in the shadows for a moment, watching her in the moonlight. When he decided to make himself known, he cleared his throat and approached slowly.

"Roderick! Jesus, you elves are too stealthy!" She winced more from the feeling of his nearness than the startle of his sudden presence. He walked past her to the southern portion of the balcony and looked out at the Deneb Sea.

"I have always loved the view of the sea from this side of the palace." He turned to smile at her sending a rush through her veins. "I am sorry for giving you a start, I should have knocked." He bowed before her. "Roderick of Darmuth Anor, at your service, my lady." Her imagination was going wild and she hoped elves could not read minds. He leaned back against the wall.

"How'd you get in here?" She asked.

"I have been known to collect on favors from time to time." She doubted he was embellishing.

"Really. So, why are you here?" Her hopes needed to be constantly suppressed by her logic.

"I thought it well and good to pay you a visit."

"You know Sholendor headed out tonight, don't you?" She skipped to the pivot point.

"I do." He walked to stand next to her, feeling his head empty of blood then fill again in break neck speed.

"So do you always make surprise appearances to the palace?" She quarried.

"No, not normally. I felt it necessary. You are alone and lost. I did not wish to not offer my services. I had no time to offer such when we last spoke, at least not seriously." Approaching her was devastating to his better judgment. "I am glad to see he has not harmed you yet." He added.

"He's not going to hurt me. He needs me to harm the princess." She stated bluntly. He was amazed at her perception of the situation. "And, he got called to Havaland to talk to the Duchess. He said he wouldn't be back until sometime tomorrow. I guess that means I am safe from his lust for one night, by pure luck." She snorted a bit in disgust, causing Roderick to laugh.

"I am sure his plans are very vile, I only hope he does not harm you or Meriden." Roderick gazed at the mirrored light on the waves to hide his frustration of the future.

"Well his plans, and what is actually going to happen, are two completely different things, I assure you, my charming companion."

"Are you always so forward with men?" He inquired.

"Only ones that sneak into my bedroom without permission." She vollied. He laughed out loud.

"Well said, my lady. Well said indeed. Oh, I almost forgot, I have a gift for you." He announced, doing all he could to avoid plotting to take over the palace.

"A gift? This better not be something disgusting." She warned. He gave her a look of impatience. "O.K. O.K. I trust you." She extended her left hand.

"You are left handed, my lady?" He asked.

"No, I am saving my right hand to smack you just in case." She opened her mouth in a comical "O" type smile.

"You evil little beast! Close your eyes." He laughed. Her lips parted slightly in anticipation. He was held spellbound.

"Can I open my eyes yet?" She begged.

"Yes you may." He consented.

The look on her face would have been worth his very soul for the joy it gave him. At first she just stuttered. Then she lifted the gem into the night sky.

"OH…MY…GOD!" She looked at him wide eyed. "Roderick! I mean…WOW! What did I do to deserve this? I just met you." She reminded him.

He leaned forward, almost touching her nose with his. "I saw Osizio before I came here. He was holding his youngest son. He has never seen the boy. Domboin was born a few days after he was banished." He looked back into her eyes. "The big idiot looked like a pup himself. I do not think I have seen anyone so happy."

Britt was silent for a moment. To Roderick's total surprise she embraced him. His heart went wild and he felt like laughing, crying and yelling for joy all at the same time. Her hair covered his cheek and he was lost in a fog of sweet softness. He had not been held for the sake of holding, since he was a child and never out of such emotion. When she released him, he felt cold as death. She sat back on the chair and examined the pendant.

"This is very kind of you Roderick. It is so considerate, but I think it's too much. This jewel must have cost a small fortune. It is almost....well...crown jewel material." She seemed mesmerized by the blue of the stone.

"I, in no way, mean to sound like a letch, or crook. I really wanted to pay for it, but a dwarf woman insisted it be a gift." He attempted to justify the purchase hoping she would not refuse the token.

"GAVE IT TO YOU?" She raised a red brow. "What did you do for her, you sly devil?" She chided.

"You heathen." He messed her curls. This familiar touch seemed natural.

"She said it was a gift for the kindness I showed in helping Osizio win his freedom." He faced her and spoke softly. "So I am giving it to the person that is truly responsible for that act." It took him a few moments to notice that he had forgotten to let go of her hand.

"Oh." He reluctantly let go. "I am sorry. Forgive me for my boldness." He apologized.

"No. Really, it was nice." Britt assured.

He turned and walked nervously into the parlor and seated himself in front of the fire, on an overstuffed chair. She followed, thankful for the slight distance.

"This woman was a bit strange." His voice woke her form her trance.

"How so?" she asked.

"She told me that I was far nobler than the Prince." He sniffed. "Can you imagine?"

"How is that strange? She sounds pretty damn smart to me." Britt commented offhandedly as she held the sapphire to the candle light.

Roderick blinked. "Well in any case, I am sure she would have done the same for Sholendor." He said.

"Yea, maybe. He is the prince and protocol would have called for it. She gave you this pendant because she wanted to. That act alone speaks volumes. What a gesture of respect."

Britt did not catch his look of revelation. "Anyone can demand what others hold dear. All you have to do is intimidate them enough. I like it when they give it because they really want to, don't you?"

"Yes. I guess so." He was set back.

"So.. Are you going to tell me why you really risked it to come here?" She pried.

"I felt something." Roderick ventured timidly.

"I felt it too." She admitted.

"So what do we do of it? Assuming you felt the same thing I felt, of course." He sounded like a sputtering idiot. In her eyes it got no better universally wide.

"We do what we want. There is a price though." She observed.

"I do not wish to cause you trouble. I would understand if you opened the door and insisted I leave this room. It may be the best thing for both of us." He could feel his heart attempting to burst through his rib cage.

"Nope." She stood and helped him up, wrapping herself in his strong arms. "Just remember to see it for what it is and nothing more."

She melted into his kiss. The longer he stayed the more she was aware that there was no hope of resistance. He could have had her on the road in the cart. She had no control.

"What is it?" He pulled away, the sexual energy overwhelming him.

"I am going to be leaving soon. You are an elf. We both know that this is way off limits, socially speaking. There's a good chance this is all we'll have. I want to take it for what it is. How about you?" She seemed very sure of herself.

Roderick started to speak again, confused as the woman before him seemed to be already striping him for the game.

"Blah, blah, blah…take your shirt off." She ordered. He laughed in response as he felt the last chains of his better conscience slip away. They moved to the large bed and were both well on their way to nudity in seconds.

Britt had been given an android when she had turned 18 for the sole purpose of sex. It was the Zenerian belief that providing organic life forms with clean, disease free sexual partners was a surefire way of keeping them safe and happy. She was even allowed to choose what the humanoid android would look like. She had grown quite fond of sex but had never had it with another carbon based life form. This was not sex as she had come to understand it. In the course of their lovemaking, Britt barely remembered getting to the bed. She remembered noticing that elves were anatomically correct, and this elf was anatomically gifted. She vaguely remembered ripping off his shirt and falling to the soft blankets in the light of the candles. Her mind did not exist separate from her body, as it had in the past. It seemed to fuse with the entire act of spirit, flesh and feeling. It was a Zen-like focus she had only known in extreme moments of adrenaline in life and death situations, never in acts of passion. Roderick became a part of her. She knew his heartbeat, and the taste of his soul. She urged to envelop him in a way that would end the madness of her actions, like air to fire, to light the fuse and marvel at the explosion. She had never known such blinding need. His body was corded lean power. The enchantment that he possessed coupled with raw male strength took her down and spread her out, devouring any sense of purpose. The amount of pent up ecstasy released itself in a series of soft moans and cries that filtered into Roderick's fire, deeper than she could know.

Roderick felt as though he was falling very fast toward a death he longed for. He had been aware that Sholendor might be watching. At this point he did not care if every creature in the realm was watching him take this woman. The death was closer with every movement into her. It was the death of darkness and solitude. Warmth would be his craving from this point on, his sickness and his sweet curse. He was frantically searching for her, at the end they would come to together, the climax of blinding light and release. This end would be the beginning of the way they both preferred physical contact. Some fruit is addictive and leaves all those in the past, wilted in comparison.

At the top they both cried out, only to stifle the unified voices in a clinging kiss. Lying in a heap of material, naked and dazed, they took a moment to reorient themselves to reality. It lasted for a short while before it had started again. He had hoped to maintain some type of composure. Every woman he had taken in the past had been enjoyable, the night memorable. One look at her bare breast and he found it would take a fleet of goblin warriors to suppress his urges. Again they entwined. Britt rolled on top of him and kissed his firm chest as though she had a millennium to seduce him. She worked her way up his neck, over his magnificent ears, and then to his nocturnal predator eyes. She sat up, naked on his stomach, looking down at him, her hair pulled to one side covering a single breast hanging low enough to tickling his nipple. His arms stretched back as she slowly started to rock with the control of intent. He gripped her thighs and arched to meet her. She released in a succession of shudders causing her head to spin from side to side, his passion left marks on her legs.

The third time was tender. They had decided to get in the tub and clean up. Roderick had never shared such intimacy with a female. He had already had a bath. He would take a thousand more if she were on his knees. She allowed him to wash her with antagonizing hesitation. He hovered over her breasts choosing to massage them with his tongue, causing her to slide farther down on his lap. Britt felt as though she had been drugged. Water had collected on her lashes causing the candle to blur color and light into psychedelic discs as her eyes rolled with uncontrolled pleasure. She washed his hair, tenderly cherishing each inch and line of his face, kissing him wherever the soap would allow. Quiet now, soaking in the glow and water, Britt felt more relaxed than she could remember feeling since childhood.

"One day you should tell me all you desire." He roused her from her trance.

"No. I think I have found a new desire." She pressed her body to his and kissed him deeply. He fondled her necklace.

"I saw it and thought it would look great with the one you have. Maybe we could get a ring of silver and attach it to the smaller sapphire on yours." He suggested. She crunched up her chin and looked down at her own necklace.

"Yea, I think that would look great. What a good idea." She said deep in her own thoughts.

"Did you get that from an elf?" He asked.

"No." She looked at him from across the tub. "It was a gift from my brother Aeyden. She touched the necklace she had not taken off in over 16 years.

"Did he get it from an elf? " Roderick reached out and touched the choker like ivy vines that encompassed her long neck.

"No. Where I come from, there are no such things as elves, only in stories and fables." She confessed.

"Is there such a place?" He was surprised.

"No. Not any longer. My brother and all of my people are dead. They were burned in a fire that consumed the entire race and destroyed the planet." She waited for his response.

"Oh." He naturally found it hard to know what to say to something of that magnitude. "I am sorry, I did not know."

For a few moments all conversation was lost as she stared into the bubbles around her knees.

"It was a long time ago. I've put it behind me, but thank you." She said sounding a bit bitter. "You have been so good to me Roderick. I want you to know that I will never forget your kindness."

"I could have sworn it to be elfish craftsmanship. It does not look like as if dwarves designed it. They are such earthy people and very good…." He did not finish.

"What did you just say?" She sat rigid.

"I said it looks like an elf…" before he could finish she interrupted him again.

"No! The part about the dwarves!" She was a bit frantic.

"Oh…They are earthy people and good at…" He was cut off again.

"Where did you learn that word?" She pleaded.

"What word?" He was very confused.

"EARTH! " She choked out a strong whisper.

"Well it is the dwarf word for soil, why?" He was attempting to avoid upsetting her.

She searched the water for an unseen answer. How strange that the dwarves would have that word, of all words, to describe soil. What were the odds?

"No reason, I just thought it sounded familiar. " She started climbing out of the tub, looking at her pruned hands. "It will be dawn soon. I think it best if you be off." She said while looking for a dressing gown.

"Yes, you are right. There will be much explaining to do back at Ruddy Mudders, for sure." He reminded himself aloud.

"Ruddy Mudders?" She had wrapped herself in a blanket and looked sensual enough to make him forget he was leaving.

"It is Osizio's Tavern. When I left there was quite a party going on. I will be willing to bet it is still going on, but now afflicted with passed out drunks." He laughed.

"I wish I could go with you." She really did.

"I would take you from this place, Britt. I would do anything for you." He offered.

"I think it best if I stay here, at least for a little while." Her voice held a hint of distance.

He walked to her, pulling up his breeches along the way. "One day you will. I plan to start working toward your freedom as soon as I return. I want that for you." He kissed her again, struggling to remember he was leaving.

"Roderick, I think I told you I won't be staying long. I mean not staying anywhere. I am leaving Zembeth. I have to." She warned.

"I know you were not meant to be locked up in a palace. I can see you romping about in the plains and swinging through the trees of the Kloter Forest." He slipped on his tunic.

"I know you're not deaf." She was doing her best to fight her heart with her head.

"What do you mean?" He stopped her from fixing the bed that she was only going to sleep in again.

"I can't stay here. I don't know how to make that more clear. I have people that need me at home. I am not supposed to be here, Roderick." She was growing frustrated.

"I thought you said they all died." He blurted out.

"They did, but I was saved by another type of people at a very young age, that is how I survived. I have an adopted family." She did not realize that she was giving too much away.

"So you do remember?" He inquired.

"Yes and no. I know who my people are, but have no clue how to get home from here. I think we should leave it at that." Her voice trailed off to a dead end.

He swallowed hard. He had not expected this type of goodbye. It was beyond him what had made him think that one night with a woman meant she was going to be with him forever. He was not that type of man. So she would be a miracle that appeared then disappeared again. His mind was racing against his better judgment.

"Well I understand. I must be going. May I visit you again before you take leave?" He donned his quiver and bow, then strapped on his broad sword and headed for the door.

The night was being jaded by the future and actions that had been better left undone. What had she been thinking to get this close to an alien life form? It needed to end. "I don't think it would be wise." She said flatly.

"Sure." He opened the door. "Farewell then my friend." The door shut on the last word, leaving her standing in her blanket in the middle of the room.

He raced down the lane towards the city, his horse giving more than was normally expected. His rage and confusion ran deep through an avenue of desperation. She was only doing what he should have and breaking the tie before it became unbreakable. He remembered Ren' Fordel telling him that the chains of habit are often not felt until they are too strong to break. They had used each other, plain and simple. What was the harm in a night like this? Looking back, he doubted he knew any male that would not have severed an arm for such a chance. He almost ripped the bit from the horse's mouth when he yanked its neck to turn the corner to the Fenway.

When he reached Ruddy Mudders he found the tavern quiet. He jumped from his mount and handed the reins of the lathered beast to the stable boy. He appraised the human lad for a moment. It made the male very nervous and the boy bowed his head low in submission.

In disgust for scaring the lad, Roderick gave him a silver piece and sent him to the barn, telling him to be sure to walk the animal down before giving him drink. The boy nodded and waved. Perhaps she knew that extracting sexual fluids from an elf would expand her life. He doubted it. She barely knew about the race of elves, let alone that now, after their love, she would be immortal as he. With all the fluid they had just shared, he wondered if she had put a spell on him as well. Is that why it was against the law for elves and humans to mate openly? Where humans evil and capable of bewitching magick? No. He knew better. If that were the case, they would not be slaves. Surely one of them would have figured it out in all this time.

He waited for his mind to clear before entering the tavern. Somehow he could not lose the image of Gabriel. He kept seeing the pale face and the enraged look. His companions had warned him and he had gone anyway. He would not go tomorrow, or the day after. He would not be cast out in shame and brought to the point of endangering the life of another elf. If she were an obsession, she was Sholendor's obsession. He would choose to dissolve the memories of this night. He would ask Ma Fafella for a spell to erase the vision of her flushed face against satin pillows or the feel of her flesh against his. It would need to be a very powerful spell.

He opened the door and stepped over a pickled body. It was his brother. Ignoring Amaranth, he walked toward the bar and told Censci he was going to bed.

"Wait just a bleeding minute there, lad!" She hollered. "I wanna know how she is? How is Britteny?"

He was hoping she would not ask. "She is very well Censci. Why do you ask?" He had never been told Censci admired humans that much, especially humans she had never owned.

"Osizio has been talking about her all night." The ogre squeezed from behind the bar. Marsiz had heard him enter and came out from the kitchen. "The lass sounds like a dear. After all these years he's feeling guilty fer trading her off for his freedom. She must be somethin' special fer ye to risk yer neck going to the palace." Censci glared at the man she had known since his youth. He hated the fact that she could read him almost as well as Ma Fafella. She lumbered up to him and sniffed him with her huge nostrils. Her face set like stone. He had forgotten that ogres could smell everything.

"Ye have had her. I can smell her all over ye." She whispered. He expected her to go running to Osizio and Donavan. Instead she stomped over to the linen cabinet and grabbed fresh sheets. She returned to dump them in his hands. She grunted. "Yer like a son to me, boy. Iffin it is possible fer our two peoples." She looked away. "I'm a thinking ye need to get that stench off of ye afore yer lil' brother notices it. I canna imagine what ye must have been tinking. A human? And what is worse, the poor lass just arrived today. She had not a chance. Iffin she did, ye have all but taken it from her now. Are ye any better than Sholendor?" She turned and retreated to the kitchen. Roderick whispered harshly to call her back.

"Censci." He began calmly. "I do not know what has come over me."

"Donna give me that sheit." She bit and hissed keeping her voice as quiet as possible.

"I'll be sick of hearing you rutting elfish bastards blaming the girls for dis. You all know the power ye have over humans. Besides, she wasna the one that snuck into the feckin' royal palace. Gabriel was bad enough. But you?" She grunted and turned to leave, fighting the urge to twist his head off. Roderick paled two shades lighter than his usual alabaster.

Marsiz stared after her. She looked back at Roderick, standing liked a marked man in the middle of the dark tavern. The expression on her face made him think she was looking at his ghost. One never remembers their friends and associates when one is in the thralls of passion. It was time for reality. He had mated with a human. Saying it now, it sounded like a hollow echo. In the eyes of the people of Zembeth, he was now truly an outcast.

He lit the candle in his room and flopped down on the soft straw mattress. He sat up and looked out the cracks in the shuttered window. Opening the wooden barriers, he could see the palace atop the hill at the edge of the city. He would need a very strong spell.

********** * * * * * * * * *************

"What the hell is going on down there!?" Jeff Kolbert had fallen from his chair to the floor of his conference room. It seemed the entire station shook from some type of blast. His nightmare would be a meteor or, worse yet, some space cowboy bent on invasion. He stabbed the control panel and demanded a response. "I asked what the HELL just happened!?"

Static, then a faint voice: "I don't know sir!" Static again. "Something…some type of signal." The voice broke off. Throughout every corridor, fire alarms were sounding. Jeff burst through the door. He had wished in vain that there were no flames. He pushed a short-range pilot into the wall.

"What in the HELL is going on down there?" He yelled.

"Sir, something just blew out our satellite." He cowered against the wall. "I don't know what it was, some type of sonic charge." Jeff shoved him to the side and stormed to the elevator. The door would not open. Damn safety codes! He cursed under his breath. He ripped open the door to the fire stairs and descended them at a break neck pace, sending workers toppling down in his wake. People from every prison and slum that had any technological knowledge of environmental mining came running up the stairs to avoid the flames. He watched as the fire doors slammed shut to allow the sprinkler systems and emergency robots to do their work. From the soot came his chief engineer.

"Baxter! What in the hell is going on!?" He approached without concern to the health of his highest paid, hardest working employee.

"It seems something exploded just outside the atmosphere, on the other side of this big rock." He was trying to clean his glasses.

"Was it a meteor or did one of our satellites just detonate? I want a specific answer!" He was frantic. This little accident would set him back indefinitely from his deadline. He was entering negotiations with Gigneot for raw materials that would earn him a fortune. This planet was loaded with every type of fossil fuel and many undocumented forms of flammable rare material.

"Well Jeff, I have no idea what it was, but I know it was not natural and it was not one of our satellites, if that helps." He put his glasses back on. "It appears to be some type of beacon or ultra-powered sonic message." He seemed quite calm. "I think someone was making a long distance call."

"That's completely impossible. We checked for intelligent life and found not a one." Jeff slapped the warming wall. He hoped those robots were worth the money he spent for them.

"We found life, Jeff. No one checked to see if it was intelligent or not."

Baxter started up the stairs. They had indeed found a few large civilizations. Each distanced from one another by thousands of miles or by large bodies of water. It had been guessed that none of these individual civilizations were aware of the existence of the other. No advanced communication systems had been established. Electricity had yet to be discovered. Lights coming from condensed civilizations had been studied and charted as fire or natural light.

Baxter had expressed his concern about one of the civilizations on this planet. He was ignored. This particular area had signs of a rather advanced culture. They had mapped roads, buildings and castles. Baxter had pleaded with Jeff to investigate further, but they were on a deadline for product. Baxter knew this was not the issue, but he wisely did not mention this at the meetings. He knew, in truth, they were on a deadline to escape the inevitable collapse of an unstable wormhole. Jeff was just lucky this gold mine was across the universal divide and well out of reach of the "Black Death" or so the seasoned multi universal crewmates called the Zenerian pirates. Jeff stayed on the platform and appeared to be thinking painfully.

"How long do you think the repairs will take?" He yelled up at Baxter.

"It was an impressive explosion. We will be lucky to salvage a portion of the sector. Whatever it was, it was beyond anything I have experienced. I think we are dealing with a very advanced technology here." He did not want to climb further and risk Jeff's anger, but felt the need to escape the heat coming from behind the blast doors.

"That is impossible!" Jeff started up after him. "Those bastards don't even have electricity!" He stormed past Baxter.

"Jeff, I know. You have to understand, I am not sure if this came from the planet surface or from outer space. The disruption has to be analyzed. I know for sure it was some type of signal and that is all I know now. We have to put out the fire first." Baxter tried to reason.

"Put it out fast. I want answers. Have the main helmsman set a course for the other side of this rock. I want a better look at all of these people!" With that he continued up the metal stairs and out of sight. Baxter started slowly after him. If it were not for the money, and the fact that Jeff had chosen to relocate his family until further notice, he would have been gone by now. He was a wanted man, but not a criminal. When he thought about it, every Zenerian he knew had the same record. He needed to find another vocation.

Chapter 9
Nobody's Baby

No one knocked. This could be the reason she almost sent the gnome flying across the room and over the balcony. The little beast had to learn that it was very hazardous to approach a sleeping Zenerian and start tapping their head to wake them up. Before Britteny realized what she was doing, she had the terrified female by the neck and was poised to propel her as far as she could. The gnome pissed on Britt's feet in fear. She dropped the woman and started hopping from one foot to the other in disgust.

"Son of a bitch!" She danced around frantically trying to get to the tub to rinse the urine off her feet. The gnome was on the floor in a ball by the puddle. "Oh man! Hey! I'm sorry, but you just can't sneak up on me like that." Britt felt horrible. She trotted across the room, urine soaked feet and all, to approach the frantic gnome on the floor. She cowered, but did not run. Britt reached out very carefully and touched the round, almost bald, yellow head. "Come on, it's O.K." She spoke gently. "See, we can clean it right up." She reached for a towel and started cleaning up the steaming, ammonia smelling puddle. The woman screeched, causing Britt to drop the towel and back away. She grabbed the towel and started scrubbing frantically, speaking in elfish or gnomish it was difficult to tell when one had only been on the planet for a bit over a day.

"All right, all right, you can do it, Jeez!" She walked around the crazed slave. She noticed a bowl of fruit sitting on the bedside stand. "Can I eat one of these?" She asked the servant. At first the gnome just looked at her as if she were stupid, then to Britt's surprise she spoke.

"Yes mistress, they are for you." She bowed down and backed to the door.

"Don't call me that please. Call me Britt, O.K." She popped one of the purple fruits in her mouth. The gnome hesitated.

"I may not use your given name mistress, I am a slave." She kept looking at the yellow towel and the floor.

"Well, I'm a slave too, so there you go. Call me Britt, or I'll try to toss you out the window again." She smiled. "What's your name?"

The gnome was flustered. "Uh, I am called Minakshi lady."

"That's a really cool name. O.K. Minakshi," Britt approached her holding two purple fruits in her hand. She gave one to her new friend. "I 'm Britt, its very nice to meet you, and that window thing, I was just kidding." She tossed the small grape like fruit into her open mouth. This time she must have tossed too hard. The fruit became lodged in her windpipe and caused her to choke. The gnome gasped. The very thought of killing the princess' new companion slave was beyond her comprehension.

"AAAAAAHHHH!" Minakshi screamed. Britt pounded her chest in an attempt to dislodge the fruit. She swallowed as hard as she could and walked to the table for a drink of water. She raised the pitcher to her mouth and guzzled the cold liquid. Regaining her oxygen, Britt addressed Minakshi.

"CALM DOWN!" She yelled. "My God you're spastic!" She took another drink of the water. She looked over at the slave. Minakshi was staring at her in a strange way and not eating the fruit. She looked back at the bowl. Had the fruit been poisoned?

"Did you just poison me?" She demanded.

The look on the gnome's face told her she was safe. "By the Gods, NO! My lady, I and my entire family would be put to death for harming the consort of the future King." She blurted out.

"Consort?" She laughed. "So that's what I am, huh?" She started dressing. She wished to say no more on the subject. Gossip was a given among slaves and servants no matter what galaxy you were in. She wanted to keep the stories to a minimum, lest she be burned for witchcraft next.

Minakshi understood her distance and bowed to leave. Before she vanished she informed Britt that a man named Rowland of Sid O'Sala was here to take her to meet with Gherkin this very morning. "He will be up shortly my lady. If you are in need of anything, all you must do is pull this cord and I shall come to your assistance." She pointed up to a white satin cord hanging from a hole in the stone.

"O.K. I should be fine. What's my name?" She smiled at the gnome.

Minakshi blushed. "Britt." She turned to leave.

"Have a nice day Minakshi." Britt offered.

Minakshi turned before she disappeared into the stone. "And you as well my… Britt." Then she was gone.

She finished dressing and went out on to the balcony. The sun was brilliant and from this altitude she had a spectacular view of southern Garath and the Deneb Sea. She giggled to think of Boomer's assumption during planetary survival class. The teacher had asked the 10 children how to tell the size a planet was without the help of their equipment. Boomer had bobbed up and down for the chance to answer, almost bursting with excitement.

"Yes Boomer." OmJoIb permitted.

"Well the way I see it, the longer the day, the bigger the planet." He said proudly.

He had been somewhat right if simple. Britt glanced at the section of the palace that she could see. This must be one big planet. She had no idea how long she had slept. There were no timepieces. She would have to watch the shadows of the sun and make her own assumption to the number of hours it took for this mammoth to rotate. She felt much rested in consideration of her extra activities the night before. She would watch the moon as well to get a better idea of location and orbit. Tipping back she tried to look in the direction of the sun. Well at least they only had one sun. Planets with more than one were usually very hostile. She had assumed it was a singular system. Plant life like this usually only grew in very select conditions.

Straddling the wall she tied her boots. It was an odd job to actually dress herself in fabric. Her bio armor was as easy to change as the push of a button. Her mind drifted to the prior night's pleasures. Her face was warming to the sun and it felt wonderful. Last night had felt wonderful. She absently rubbed her breasts, the erotic feeling still lingered. Was she wise for telling him not to come back tonight? She sighed. No matter how much she wanted to see him again, she knew it was better for both of them not to get close. She would not stop until she found her way home and from what she had been told it was a big, bad NO for the two of them to go on so. Still, she missed him this morning, and somehow it resonated beyond physical attraction.

This time she had her wits about her and could feel the presence of someone walking in the door.

"You people never knock, do you?" She turned to see another elf. This one was as striking as the rest. These people were so color coordinated. Rowland looked at her from across the room. She could see his bright amber eyes and in them, the depth of his intelligence. This elf had a strange stability about him. Unlike all the others she had met thus far, he did not flinch or gawk; he merely approached her and bowed. His hair was the color of blood; much richer than hers, and ever so slightly streaked with white.

"I apologize, my lady. I am Rowland of Sid O'Sala. I have been assigned to be your escort for the day." He held back a question. He felt somehow that he had seen this woman before.

"Oh. Well, alright." She nodded with a funny frown and walked past him to retrieve her jewel. She did not wish to leave such a wonderful gift out of her sight. She placed it between her breasts, snug in her bra. She wiggled a bit to set it in place, Rowland watching all the time. He had, without expressing it, noticed she was as spectacular as he had been warned. He tipped his head in the knowledge that he, however, did not find her spectacular enough to risk death for as did Roderick did.

This was perplexing to Rowland, for he had never known Roderick to act in such a manner, therefore his own lack of attraction marked a start for mental debate. Perhaps it was something he needed to analyze further, in light of Roderick's decision to breach the castle security last night. However, with his sharper talent of deductive reasoning, he also concluded she was very physically powerful. She did not move like most creatures, let alone humans. To an untrained eye it may appear graceful, but Rowland saw the warrior beneath the woman.

"I have been informed that we will be visiting Gherkin this morning." It was more of a statement than a question. "I was wondering if there is anything else you would like to partake in this day?" She turned to face him and thought for a moment.

"I take it you already know my name." She stated.

"My Lady Britteny, I think every living person in Garath knows your name by now." He assured her. "I am a close friend to Roderick of Darmuth Anor." He kept watch for her expression.

"That's nice." She looked around the room. He was almost disappointed that she did not inquire about the Black Elf of Zembeth. Judging from Roderick's mood that morning, something had transpired in this room that Roderick refused to talk about. "Ya know, I think there is something I would like to do before we go to see Gherkin." Britt offered.

"Your wish is my command Lady Britteny." He bowed.

"Just Britt." She said.

"Excuse me?" He asked.

"Please, call me Britt, the whole Lady thing creeps me out." She instructed. "I've been many things in my life, but a lady is not one of them." She joked.

He was pleasantly amused. "What shall your wish be then, Britt?"

"Is there anywhere I can stretch my legs and perhaps get a bit of exercise?" She asked.

Now Rowland looked like the others. Whatever she had said, it touched something in this rustic looking elf. "It would be my pleasure. After you." He opened the door and they started down the tower.

Britt was thrilled to see that there was an arena built a bit north of the palace. It was being decorated for the use of the coming Beltane games. Normally it was the training location of Garathian soldiers. Rowland escorted her to the dusty ground of the stadium.

"This is perfect!" She took off for a quick run around the enclosed area. Rowland set off behind her and was amazed at her pace. From what he could see she was merely jogging. He caught up to her with glee. He was only slightly taller than she and he noticed with no small amount of concern, that their strides were much the same.

"You are quite the runner, Britt. Where did you learn to pace like this?"

She kept her eyes in front of her and did not slow. "Running from bad boys." She sped up and he did likewise, enjoying the challenge. She slowed at the weapons that hung on the wall. Rowland looked about and noticed, luckily, that no one had arrived yet. He did not want the entire kingdom, especially Sholendor, knowing what this human was capable of. He was waiting for the right moment to bring up the princess. She reached for a long stick, blunted at both ends.

"Do you fight?" She asked.

"Yes, I am a trained warrior." He looked a bit surprised. "Why do you ask?"

"Would you mind sparring with me? I would love the practice." He did not know how to answer.

"Britt, I am a trained warrior. I would be mortified if I harmed you in any way. I am not like most of my kin." He backed up a bit.

"Oh. Well if you're afraid, all you had to do was say so." She set one end of the fighting pike on the ground and leaned her weight on it.

"Afraid?" Rowland laughed. "I am a member of the Royal Guard, trained in Darmuth Anor. There is little I fear, my sweet friend." He decided to play with her, if it amused her. He would take care to not damage the merchandise.

"Good. Shall we begin?" She spun the pike so fast it blurred then held it in a guarded position.

"My stars! You are full of tricks." Rowland readied himself. Even with his speed, he did not see her coming and was only conscious of being tripped and hitting the soft ground.

"Really, Rowland. If you're going to spar like a girl, I can find someone else." She offered him a hand. He did not accept it. Instead he leaned back and looked up at her.

"Forgive me, I was under the impression I *was* sparring with a girl." He jumped to his feet. He ignored his role as palace guardian and set his mind to the task at hand.

The match was more than exhilarating. She moved like a ghost, with the strength and balance of a predator. Every shot was blocked without effort, every assault a child's game. She was calculating, to the point of predetermination of every move he made. If he were not stunned enough by her agile battle contact, he was awestruck when she appeared to run straight for him then proceeded to vault over his head, only to spin around and nearly take it off with her pike.

"You'll have to be much quicker, my friend." She cautioned Rowland. "I could have killed you with that move." She was correct, to his embarrassment. He tossed down the pike and held out his arms for bare combat.

"Shall we begin, MY LADY?" His tone was not threatening, but eager for the thrill of a good match. Before he could breathe her body went into the air and she flipped backwards and over herself (he estimated three times) before she set her body in a squared-off battle stance.

"By all means, MY LORD." She waited for him to continue.

They fought so for a time unmarked, until the elf became winded as well as the human. They did not fight with the aggression one uses in a life and death struggle, but with the honor a true warrior uses with a respected partner. Still Rowland had only wished he had been watching instead of fighting. He was sure she had moved in ways he had never thought of, or had time to fully observe. He was only thankful this was not a real battle. Deep down, he was sure she would have finished him some time ago. He doubted Sholendor had the slightest idea of what he had accepted as a gift for Meriden. If she were protected from magick, she would be unbeatable in a battle.

She approached him and patted him on the back. "Thank you Rowland. You have no idea how much I needed that." She said it as though it was perfectly normal to fight with the skill of a master. She looked around for something to wipe her face with and absently started pulling her hair back to cool her neck.

"Whew! I think I need to clean up before we go to see Gherkin. Is that O.K. with you?" She started walking for the exit. He followed.

"Of course. Wait up a bit." He picked up the pikes and placed them back on their hooks.

"I'm sorry." She felt rude.

"No, that is quite all right, it is my pleasure." He approached her, still not commenting on his discovery, secretly thrilled. "May I ask you a question while we walk to the palace?" He ventured.

"Sure." She said, as she strode out of the stone archway back towards the palace.

"What do you think of Princess Meriden?" He blurted out.

"Well that's hard to say. I've never met her." She kept walking. "I don't think it is fair to make a statement until we have spent some time together."

Rowland stopped at the mouth of the royal labyrinths. "May I have a word with you in private?" He gestured to the stone bench just inside the tall bushes that made up the walls of the great puzzle. She peered into the opening then looked into his eyes. He was happy to see she was ever watchful as well as deadly.

"Yea, I suppose." She waited for him to enter first. He strode up and sat on the cool stone surface, then patted the place next to him. He knew she was wisely considering things she could not see as a danger. Once she was seated beside him, he took a moment before he began.

"I must be candid with you, even at the risk of my own life." He began. She nodded for him to go on, giving him her silent agreement that this conversation would be between the two of them. Each relationship that had developed in her waking consciousness had a format of sorts, even on this strange planet. Rowland eased into her as if he fit in the same skin and saw from the same eyes. She observed his facial expressions and gestures as he talked in familiarity. She was sure she could keep his secret as if keeping her own. He went on. "I have been with Meriden all of her life. I have grown quite fond of her. I am not sure if you are aware of this, but you were not just chosen to be her companion slave."

He paused to allow her to question. She seemed aware of this fact and did not speak. "I fear that Sholendor plans to use you as either a consort or a means to eliminate the princess, and if his plan is discovered, it would be all too easy to blame her companion slave for the murder." A strange cloud seemed to swallow her whole aura. He progressed. "I know I have no right to ask this of you, but the princess is merely a child and an innocent. She does not wish to be queen. I only ask for your assistance and your mercy in her dealings."

Britt appeared to be weighing the situation. "I did not know you were a warrior, or this intelligent, but now that I do, I feel I must be completely honest with you and beg you for your compassion. I know Sholendor is capable of none."

Britt looked at the grass. She was silent for a long time before addressing this new individual that had proven a worthy and honorable companion. "I'll tell you what…I can tell that you're an honorable man. We share the same sense of fair play and justice. I will give you my word, that I will do what is just and fair as I see fit. Will that do for now?" She asked.

"I cannot ask for more than that." He nodded. "Shall we be off to the palace then?" He rose and offered his hand.

"O.K. Off to the palace." She accepted and they walked out of the maze.

Britt's mood was growing consistently foul. It was apparent that things were escalating and the plot was thickening. She feared she would be tangled to the point of desperate measures before she found her way home. Now there were whispered conferences with a royal scout, hidden in the labyrinth. The safe conclusion to draw could be that her actions toward the princess may just decide the fate of this kingdom. She was not sure that was a bad thing. She could find no room in her heart for any government that allowed slavery, so perhaps stirring things up a bit may just be what the doctor ordered.

"What is she like?" Her question slowed Rowland's pace a bit.

"Meriden?" He asked.

"Well yea, silly, who else?" She smirked.

He reflected a moment. "As I have stated, I have known her all my life. She is quite a bit like me really. She likes to be alone, solitary. She is very small and thin. She is quiet and unassuming. I have had the rare chance to speak with her on occasion in private. She is sensitive and can even laugh when she is not around her mother." He gazed over Britt's head as if Meriden was floating in the sky above them.

"So I take it her mother is a bit overbearing?" Britt coaxed.

"The queen has had a troubled reign. Meriden's father was a great king, but abandoned them when she was quite young. Alisi has been forced to manage alone as sole ruler of the realm. She can sometimes be very stern with her daughter. It does not help that Meriden is so fragile."

"Just because she's small, doesn't mean she's fragile." Britt stated.

"In any case, you will know soon enough, they will both be here tomorrow morning to prepare for the royal wedding and attend the games." He informed her.

They walked through the palace and up the south tower stairs. Rowland hesitated at the foot of the long staircase to inform a kitchen slave that Britteny would need fresh garments, and then continued up the steps to wait outside the room for his new charge.

As they ascended the steps, Britt continued the subject. "Sholendor said something about someone named Sara becoming my slave. He acted as though it would upset Meriden. What did he mean?" She was a bit concerned when Rowland stopped.

"Did he order that to anyone or just say it in passing?" He asked.

"He sent word to Fair…Fare…Oh, I don't know the name of the place. I only know he sent another slave to get Sara for me." She elaborated.

He walked up the steps past her, obviously upset. "Did I say something wrong?" She pleaded.

"No, Britt. I am just set back. Sara has been Meriden's personal slave since her birth. I have never seen the princess without the gnome at her side. I think that Sara is the only person she trusts." Rowland continued up the steps. "It is just another attempt to weaken her spirit." He mumbled farther up.

She hopped up a few steps to meet him. "I didn't ask for that." She touched his elbow.

"I know, Britt. Please understand my concern." Rowland did not wish to meet her eyes. He needed to keep walking up the steps. "Sometimes the petty games are the cruelest." His words of wisdom helped Rowland of Sid O'Sala set firmly as someone Britt could grow to like.

They reached the wooden door and Rowland held it open for her. At first she stood on the landing. For a moment he assumed she might be apprehensive or fearful of him or the room. Then he felt his shoulder ache from the wrath of her strength and realized what an asinine assumption it was and dismissed it.

"Are you ill?" He asked.

"No." She said.

"Why do you stand so?" He laughed.

"I was waiting for you to walk in, you did open the door." She gestured.

"I was merely being chivalrous Britt, ladies enter first." He bowed and waved.

"Oh!" She laughed and scurried through the door, attempting an awkward bow on the way. "Oh, I didn't know. Ha, Ha. I'm sorry."

"Do you have no gentlemen where you are from?" He asked.

"Well, I'm not sure. Our men are kind but we treat each other equally. There's no door opening or bowing or that kind of thing." She stood in the doorway talking to him. Minakshi was waiting for her by the bed with a simple black dress and thankfully a plate of food. "I guess if there were, for my people, it would be like wasting time or something, if that makes sense." She found it embarrassing to detail in so many words that her people had no manners.

"Truly barbaric!" Rowland announced.

"So you do this for all human females?" She asked.

He started, eyes blinking. "Well no, of course not!" He half laughed.

"Well then that, my dear Rowland, is the very definition of barbarism." She abruptly closed the door in his face. He could hear her through the wood and iron barrier. "I will be out as soon as I clean up and change."

"Very well…" He did not know what else to say. The question was literally one that had never been asked to anyone that he had known. The concept never challenged. He leaned against the wall and looked at his fingernails. This would explain Roderick's behavior. Only a woman like this could color a personality such as Roderick's. When Rowland left his room this morning, Roderick was still brooding behind closed doors. Rowland did not feel the need to disturb him, so passed by and went downstairs. After breakfast Roderick made an appearance. He spoke little then retired again to his chambers. Rowland shifted. He knew not how long Roderick had visited. He was awake most of the night drinking and making merry. Still he could not remember Roderick coming back to the inn. He looked at the door and shook his head, dismissing the thoughts any male would entertain. He would be pleased to report her high spirits and good health to the lot of them. Rowland assumed that this would do at least something to ease the tension about the inn. Osizio was beside himself with worry. The least he could do was use his position to help the situation a bit. It also gave him the rare chance to get the inside story on what Meriden was truly in store for.

Rowland looked back at the door as if he were standing there contemplating his own masculinity. It was obvious that Roderick was attracted to this human to the point of risking much to sneak to the palace last night. It was, as well, obvious that the prince was willing to risk even greater public humiliation on the skirts of his dead brother for the same female. Rowland pondered a bit, digging into his male instinct, and again found no such blatant attraction to the creature in the next room. He agreed that she was a beauty, yet he felt they shared a familiarity that could not quite be defined as of yet.

A few moments later, Britteny emerged, dressed in a floor length, simple black court dress. Minakshi had piled her curls through a braded ring, atop her head. She was stunning. Now seeing her standing here, dressed as a true maiden of the court, he was not so much worried about Meriden, but Roderick was an ever-growing issue.

"Well I can say this is the first dress like this I have ever seen, except in history books. How do I look?" She spun around. The dress hugged every curve; the snug bodice uplifted her already healthy breasts. Her face was alive with life itself and glowed with warmth that enchanted the very stones around him.

"I could not speak the words, even if I could find them, dear Britteny." He offered his hand again to escort her down the steps.

"You are just too sweet!" She pinched his cheek and squealed. "Don't let Meriden hear you say that, she may get jealous." She called over her shoulder as she started down the steps.

"What?" He trotted down after her, noticing that she was having trouble walking, until she figured that a lady must lift her skirts to descend the stairs.

"Oh, you know. It must be hard enough for her to have to marry someone like Sholendor, when a handsome brute like you loves her." She stated it as though it was a known fact and kept plopping down the steps, wrestling with her skirts as if she had never worn the like in her life.

"Hold!" He stopped and thrust his hand forward. Britt spun around at his demand. "I just want to educate you dear. It seems you are very mistaken. You see, elves don't believe in love, and even if they did, I doubt it would be an issue in this case." He crossed his arms.

Britt's brows raised in amusement. "Oh, really?" She said.

"Well, yes. What a totally human notion! Of course human females are more noted for the infliction than the males, but that is beside the point." He patted her shoulder as if pacifying a small child.

"Are you loyal to the princess?" She asked.

"Of course!" He was now nervously amused.

"Well, loyalty is nothing more than a type of love." She waited for his reply.

He shifted uneasily. "You surely struggle to understand, dear, elves do magick; it is our belief and the support of our very spirituality. There is no room for base emotions, especially illogical ones like love."

She shrugged before turning. "Yea, you're right. It sounds like elves are more into denial than love." He shoved past her.

"What is that supposed to mean?" Once again, he was not angered, just challenged and from the look on his face, a bit uncomfortable.

"Wow! Hey, I didn't mean to get you all in a huff there, big guy." She smiled.

"No, what do you mean, denial?" He insisted.

"Come on, Rowland. Do you really think I can't figure it out? Are the humans here truly that thick?" She returned the childlike patronization and patted him on the shoulder. "Yea, O.K. You just agreed to come and escort me for what reason? You had nothing better to do? You are a royal messenger, or scout, or something and you have nothing better to do?" She put her hands on her hips. "You just happen to be a very bored royal scout, that just happens to be close friends with Roderick of Darmuth Anor and very fond of Princess Meriden. That is denial, if I have ever seen it. I think your whole race is completely delusional. It must be the magick thing." She walked past him.

He was becoming offended. He had to check his temper and remember that this woman was new here and ignorant of many things; aside from the painful fact that she had recently proven she could very well end him in a confrontation. He started down the stairs after her. Said ignorance taken into account, he still felt the need to argue the point.

"Britteny." He called to her.

"Yes, Rowland?" She asked almost sweetly.

"I think you will be in much need of your lesson with Gherkin. Perhaps he can explain it better." He offered.

"Rowland?" She asked.

"Yes Britteny?" He answered.

"Where do baby elves come from?" She asked. "As a matter of fact, do you even have babies? I haven't seen any baby elves around." She looked confused.

"You are unaware of how babies are made?" He insisted.

"Well, do you have sex or do you just wave your arms and blow some smoke, and "POOF" a full grown elf appears?" She was baiting him.

"Well, of course we have sex! It is the natural order of things and, no, we surely do not just wave our arms and big elves appear. We have children. They are kept in our homes until they are old enough to venture out into the world."

"So you are saying you feel nothing for each other and you just procreate, then you hide your children away from the world. I see. Well, that explains Sholendor."

She turned and walked on. She decided she was not going to discuss this topic further. It was clear that the elfish idea of love was either interpreted differently or the use of magick had really gotten to them and they were all swimming in different waters. Nonetheless, she knew better than to argue spirituality and emotions with a being that looked this much like Dr. Spock from "Star Trek". She was going to see Gherkin.

Rowland tried again. "Britt!" He barked.

She turned and held up her hand. "Nope. Conversation over. I have a wizard to see and questions to ask and you, young man, are at this point, beyond rational thought. I suppose you don't feel passion either." She knew she should not goad him further but it was too irresistible. She had mastered the skirt issue and was now making good time down the stairs. He had no choice but to follow. He did not give her the satisfaction of a response and somehow knew she would not bless him with an answer. She had stopped at the bottom of the stairs and was looking at something. When he came up behind her, he emerged into the main reception hall. Every elf in the room had stopped to look at her.

"What are you all looking at? It's only Rowland." She bobbed her head and proceeded out the front doors and down into the main courtyard. She could hear Rowland apologizing to the crowd behind her. She just shook her head and slowed at the bottom of the stairs. When he reached the bottom he seemed to be on his last nerve.

"You are really neurotic for someone that has no emotions." She pushed her luck.

"After you, my lady." He did not let her see his smile. His amusement was rooted in the thought that Roderick of Darmuth Anor was quite taken…he hesitated. He had wondered at the fact that Roderick was willing to risk his life in coming to the palace last night. What had motivated him? She saw his look of confusion.

"Now you're getting it." She proceeded to the first wall and beyond to the village of elders.

Gherkin's cottage was divine. It set just off a narrow path and was nestled against the smaller wall that separated the village of elders from the outside world. Perhaps elves figured when they were this close to death, they did not need as much protection.

The walk there had been almost hysterical. Rowland had tried in vain to continue the debate but Britteny stubbornly ignored him. This caused quite a bit of commotion to the elfish villagers that observed the two. It was disturbing enough to have a female like Britteny strutting about, let alone watching her torment a royal scout. Most of the higher-class people of Garath Royal had not seen her approach last night. The news was fresh in their cheeks and now leaking out in venomous gossip. Britt could not help but ponder fame. She was going to be an empress soon. One of her realities was the lack of a personal life. There were times she wished she was nobody and could just disappear. She imagined Meriden felt the same way. Rowland finally gave up when they reached Gherkin's little wooden fence, laden with sweet periwinkle ivy. Britt opened the gate and glided up the walk, as if she had been there a million times. She stopped to knock on the door, shifting from foot to foot with excitement. Having the chance to talk to someone that was over 2,000 years old did not happen every day. She could not imagine the things he could tell her. First she would extract as much information as she could, primitive as it may be, about the galaxy she was in; then it was on to the nagging question of magick. From inside she could hear two voices engaged in a heated discussion. Before she could raise her hand to knock on the door she barely heard the words "Quiet, she is here," before the door opened.

The elf that opened the door was much younger than Gherkin, but very handsome. He had hair just a shade lighter than Rowland's. His eyes were brilliant green, not unlike Roderick's. He had opened the door in mid-hammer and Britt had almost bopped him on the nose. She lowered her hand and waited for him to speak. He regarded her at length.

"Hello Britteny. I am Ferrin of Sid O'Sala." He introduced himself, holding his hand out. It did not go without notice. He was the first elf that did not bow. She reached for his hand and grasped it firmly.

"Hello sir, I am Britteny but I guess you already know that." There was something familiar about him that she could not name. Osizio had mentioned him, but he had not gone into great detail.

"Please, come in, Gherkin has told me about you. I can hardly wait to get better acquainted." He stepped aside to allow her into the cozy cottage. She remembered his line of work.

"I am not sure anything I could tell you would be of much use, I'm not for sale." She was standing in the middle of a wonderful room. Beneath her was a woven rug of colors that almost looked multi-dimensional. They were entwined in a strange three-part symbol. The fireplace was cobblestone and the mantle hosted a number of interesting statues. One caught Britteny's eye. It was a brilliant statue of a red dragon. She squinted to get a better look, not wanting to be rude and walk up and touch it. She had not noticed the pain she had caused Ferrin as a result of her last statement. She could hear it in his voice when he replied.

"I was more interested in becoming friends, if that will please you." He had shut the door after welcoming his son Rowland in.

"I don't make friends with slave traders. I find it hard to connect with beings that see me as clear profit." She was still looking at the statue while aware of Ferrin's position and attitude.

"I am not the type of slave trader you may have imagined, Miss Devarelle. I know this will be hard for you to believe, but I do my best to better the lives of all humans on Zembeth." She turned her attention to him.

"Oh, really. I find it hard to imagine life without total freedom, as anything other than slavery, plain and simple." She challenged.

"Thousands of years of distrust and social suppression take time to overcome. One elf can hardly be expected to change the minds of the entire population." He offered her a seat by the mantle. "I am hoping to prove to the elfish people that humans are worth, not only saving, but freeing."

"That's quite a big job for anyone, I would imagine. I suppose you do this by cross-breeding and producing better stock." She seated herself in the plush chair. "It sounds more like a bad stag movie than an attempt at the freedom of a people if you ask me." She spoke softly, forgetting the sharpness of elfish ears.

"What is a "stag movie?" asked Rowland.

She stifled a giggle. "Nothing."

"It is clear we have a great deal to learn from each other, young Britteny." Gherkin approached. The red dragon on the mantle writhed down the stones and crawled on to his shoulder, hiding in the mass of white curls.

"Oh! It's alive!" She sprang up to get a better look. The fine reptile like nose poked through the cloud of curls and gave a snort. Britteny reached out her hand slowly, to not startle the creature. Somehow she thought it wise not to frighten a dragon, no matter what its size. She held very still as the brilliant reptile crawled over Gherkin's robes and onto her arm. She squirmed at the feel of the tiny talons; tickle – hurting like a cat's playful swipes.

"Well she seems to adore you as well!" Gherkin was greatly amused. He addressed the animal. "Gilda my dear, meet Britteny." He motioned to the human's face. "Britteny, Gilda."

"Pleasure to meet you, Gilda." She spoke to the creature on her arm. Gilda puffed up her chest and fanned her wings, causing a slight breeze.

"Gawwwakkk!" The dragoness replied. Her bark caused them all to laugh.

"Well off with you lads now, this is my time with the girl, goodness knows I have not much left and I grow older by the moment." He opened the door and tapped his foot.

"Very well father," Ferrin used the familiar term, "I am off to Fairfax to see an old friend." He embraced the older elf. "And to you my dear," He once again extended his hand, "I wish only a fair chance to prove myself. I would like to make up for lost time." He mentioned. She did not understand the lost time part, but found it interesting that he was Gherkin's son.

"Until we meet again, then, happy trails." She grasped his hand and let go, as if it were made of mercury.

"And you, Rowland, I am sure you have much to tell Roderick." Gherkin patted Rowland on the back, and kept talking despite the shocked look he received for his last statement. "Oh bullocks boy, we all know you are going to Ruddy Mudders for a drink and some good gossip. Be off with you, I will send word when we are finished with our visit." He almost shoved the stunned young man out the door. "You tell that scrapper Roderick not to worry about a thing, she is in good hands." And before Rowland could reply, he shut the door.

"Tsk, Tsk…You would think the two of them had nothing better to do." He walked slowly past her toward the next room. "Shall we have some tea then, my beauty? Please bring that little traitor of affections in with you." He waved backwards at Gilda. She barked at his statement. Britt followed him down a few quaint stone steps into the kitchen. Pots and herbs hung from the ceiling rafters. The floor was cobblestone and the thick table was fashioned from some type of ornate wood. He pointed at the fireplace and a flame sparked up under the hanging iron teakettle.

"I don't believe in slaves. Rather do for myself; always have." He sat down. Britt seated herself across the table. Gilda, blending perfectly with the color of her hair, chose to scamper about her head for a time. Every so often the dragon would pop out and lick her nose, causing her to laugh like a little girl.

"I'm glad to hear it. I'm growing tired of the entire thing myself." She offered.

"So shall we cut to the education or do you have more pressing questions?" He asked.

"Oh, well I'm not sure." She stopped playing with Gilda.

"If you want to know, no, you are not in your galaxy, and yes, you are beyond the universal divide." He reached for the teacups.

"How the hell did you know that?" She ignored his offering of cream or sugar.

"You came looking for answers of the stars, did you not? At least that is what Rowland told me. Of course I did not tell him I know where you come from. I gathered you did not tell anyone, or they would have burned you by now." He sipped the warm tea.

"Why would they burn me? Would they think me a witch?" She was thunderstruck and shaking.

"Of course not. They do not fear witches. You met one on the way here that knew who you were as well, did you not?" He raised his brows.

She had to think for a moment. She recalled the insane goblin in town. "Yea, now that you mentioned it I did. How did you know that?" She was totally fascinated by this old elf.

"I am numbering many years dear, there is not much I do not know. Funny thing is, I seem to be the only one, other than your wild goblin friend, that pays any bit of attention." He offered her cream and sugar again, to no avail. "They care little if you are a witch, but…they do care if you are from Earth." He pulled the cup back in anticipation of her reaction. To his surprise she was still. It was clear that he knew more than she had guessed, what was the point in acting surprised? She did, however tear up a bit.

"O.K. Spill it." She demanded.

"Well, where did you think we came from?" He asked.

"You came from EARTH?" She bleated.

"Well, no offense, but I thought you knew more about your own home planet." He huffed and turned sideways to cross his legs, looking away momentarily to allow her to wipe her eyes.

"I know elves were legends from a billion or so years ago, in stories and things, but they were just make believe." She tried to rationalize.

"Well allow me to elaborate. I am a bit over 8,000 years old, so of course I was just a young man then. I was living in Britain near the stone temple at what came to be known as Salisbury." He was deep in thought.

"I know the legend of Camelot and something about Stonehenge!" She burst out. "I don't remember any elves mentioned."

"Of course not. We get no credit until Arthur is betrayed. Morgaine was a fine woman, but only half elf. I felt so sorry for the girl. She tried so hard to save our way of life. You see the world was so brutal back then. We were being slowly shoved into the mist. The Saxons hated and feared us and I do not even want to tell you what those awful Roman Christians did." He shifted, staring at her, he went on: "Merlin told us things would get worse and we believed him. Many of our kind had already fled to Ireland. There we were known as the Sidhe. It was only a matter of time before St. Patrick came along and denied our existence on the emerald isle. So to help us, Merlin opened a porthole to this world so that we may escape, and we did, and took Avalon and the myst with us. Let me tell you now, it was so very hard for my mother. She loved humans and begged our people to keep trying. It was not until the burning times that we gave up all hope. "

"The burning times?" She asked.

"Yes. Again, I am astonished at your lack of information of the history of your own people." He chastised.

"You mean when they burned the witches at Salem?" She felt ignorant and ashamed.

"In a way, but that event was a means to an end. I am talking about the millions of souls lost to the belief in the natural order and magick, which is nothing more than the belief in the spirit of the natural world. Europe was on fire. I was told by those that came later that the humans that still believed in us and held true to the mother goddess were being tortured in ways we could never imagine. I think the last of my kind, the Sidhe, left cursing Ireland to war and violence forever."

"Since then, we have shut the porthole and have lived here. Of course you understand that all that bitterness put a wall between our races that has only grown over time. It was ordered by the high elfish counsel that all humans that had come over with us would be kept under constant observation, in the fear that the same ignorant notions that once nearly destroyed our entire race were brought back to life. Regardless of popular opinion, not all elves are sadistic demons. In the old days we rarely used our powers for pain and domination. At first the humans resisted our rule and decided to start their own colonies. It did not last long. I think it took a whole 100 years before they were warring with one another. Enough was enough and after that they were enslaved. Within that enslavement, germinated the bitter hate that could only come from the betrayal of Earth." He looked at his hands, truly saddened. "I cannot say that there have not been times I did not understand it. We gave them magick beyond their mortal powers. Some of them truly loved us and died for that love. We lived in peace and beauty for so many centuries. I think it was because the elves of old did not understand murder and hate. It was completely foreign to them. I imagine it was also foreign to our human brothers and sisters, and for that they were taken innocent to their deaths, unable to enact such violence, having lived in the light of magick and the balance of nature. Yet the nature of violence is the very nature that supports the nature of peace, one must sustain and balance the other. Life and death proceed and follow a pattern. Growth of any society is measured by its ability to create and encompass, if you will, either one in a balance, or tend to rely on one or the other. I suppose the hope was that violence would only be enacted when it was necessary for survival and peace and reason would prevail. I wake in the night of sweat and horror when I see them still, being taken away in carts by the hundreds. I can still see them reaching to us and screaming for us and we unable to help. You see, my dear Britteny, we were simply rendered extinct and the only way to do that, is to lose belief in us, all of us." He hesitated a moment to let it all sink in. "So now you see where the fairy tales come from, what do you think?"

She was in a spot. "I don't know. I never knew all about that." She admitted. "In truth, I was not on Earth all that long. I was 8 years old when I was taken from Earth to live on Zeneria. My mother always told me stories about elves and magick, but she had to keep them quiet." She reflected.

"Why?" He spoke softly.

"Well, one day I told the priest at her church that I believed in them and he called my mother up. She was really embarrassed and apologized to me and told me I must learn to make believe and not take it serious." She looked at his exquisite slanted eyes and pointed ears.

"Do you believe now?" He smiled.

"Well, I have changed a great deal since then. I've seen things that would make my preacher pass out. Of course I believe. I'm really sad about it too and sorry, if that helps?" She felt her stomach twist.

"Why child? You were not alive then, you had nothing to do with it?" He pacified.

"Yea, I know, but you were not around when I was. You wouldn't want to know what the human race became. If you think the burning times were bad, you should have heard about the world wars." She felt ashamed again, and even against all she had been taught about slavery, understood the dilemma these people faced. No amount of time can heal a wound like that, only trust, and that was hard to come by for humans.

"How is Earth?" He asked.

"You haven't heard?" She dreaded going over this again, but saw no choice in the matter. Previously her speeches had been to science classes and galactic culture historical seminars. They were purely for research sake. Gherkin was a being that remembered stone age England. He had been born on Earth, as she, and he deserved to know the gory end.

"It's gone. The only thing left is a rock of gasses and ice and a mixture of other interesting things. Humans just couldn't get along with each other and I guess they felt the need to end it. Some suicide, huh?"

He reached across the table and placed his cool hand on her arm. She was aware that her body was forcibly deflecting the pain in his eyes. It had to. To see those eyes, the eyes of one born of soil and stone, given the news that the living planet had been murdered, would be to see the end of one's own mind. Gherkin's mind was much older and in immortality held a respectable tolerance for such torture.

"Britteny, it is time for me to tell you why I think you were brought here." He leaned over the table and began as she stared wide-eyed and waiting.

"We have three moons. One of them is new." Gherkin blurted out.

"New?" Britt commented. "That's nearly impossible."

"Nearly?" He asked.

"A moon is a satellite that orbits a planet. Many planets have more than one. Each moon effects and is effected by the gravitational pull of the planet and its inertia." She lifted two fruits from a basket to illustrate. "If a third moon were to have just appeared it would have thrown things way off base. Like a large rock in a fast running stream, it would have knocked the flow of the river off." She did her best to explain astrophysics to a being that had limited resources.

"I knew it!" He slapped the table. "I tried in vain; I beseeched the elfish elders to listen to me. They would hear none of it. They have passed this moon off as a blessing of hope to our people." He leaned closer. "I believe whoever brought you to us knows what is going on and knew you could help in a way no other could." He informed her.

Britt leaned back in her chair and contemplated.

"Does it come in regular cycles?" She asked.

"Yes and no. It has really not been here all that long. The first time we notice it, it looked like this." Gherkin drug a thick book from a shelf behind his chair, excited that someone was finally listening to his theory. He had taken the time to draw a very detailed image of the "new moon" in its first stage.

Britt shifted the book around and studied the pictures. She took some time pondering then asked more questions.

"Have there been any high tides from the ocean or strange weather conditions?"

"No. Everything has been normal." He refilled her tea. "I have attempted to talk to the scholars and they all think I am mad. I am the only being on this rock that believes it is not flat. Can you believe that?" He threw up his hands in disgust.

"I would have to see this moon to be sure. If it is what I think it is, we still have the problem of how to get me home. I can't do a thing from here."

Gherkin smiled a bit. "Perhaps you would fare better if you knew how do to a bit of magick." He offered.

"What?" Britt asked, now thoroughly confused. She had just regained a small glimmer of hope that the moon was indeed some type of space station. From the pictures it seemed that it was being built in phases. Her main concern was the shape. Building stations that looked like moons was the oldest trick in the book and usually used by environmental pirates hell bent on raping primitive planets. She smiled a bit when she recalled sending her gauntlets into orbit. That would have put a kink in their plans.

Now she was being asked if she wanted to learn magick. How it would help her communicate with a space station was still unclear. She was searching for ways to extract information from this old elf, such as, how he knew her. How did he know she was coming? How did he know she was qualified to assist in this type of situation?

"So how do you suppose this is going to help me? If it's so great why haven't you used magick to find out what is going on up there?" She started her questioning from the last point of conversation.

Gherkin gave her a disappointed look. "It is my hope that you are smarter than that last statement. I was so looking forward to being proud of you." He sounded pitiful.

"What do you think we could do, even with magick? Do you think I have even the most remote idea of what that thing is? I may end up causing more harm than good. No one here believes me. Besides, I gather if I teach you some magick then it will level the playing field. It will at least give you the advantage as far as Sholendor is concerned, and help you navigate our planet." he offered and continued. "Magick is not some toy, Britt. I know that most humans believe we elves just go around waving our wands and making things happen, but it does not work that way. You must learn to separate fable from reality if you are to master any of our skills. Magick is like having the ability to generate an incredible amount of energy and have it course through your body to enact your will. That is not as easy as we make it look. It takes a certain mental and physical constitution to do it wisely. As well, our people know that magick is not always the answer. Before you take that step, you must realize what the outcome of your actions will be. There are always ripple effects." She listened to his words intensely. She had not had the opportunity to truly contemplate the ability to shape matter with your mind. Just wrapping herself around the entire concept would be a job, let alone performing it.

"But I am not an elf." She mentioned. His expression made her uneasy.

"Well I suppose if you coupled with an elf that would give us a start." He said it as if he were grasping for things to fill in a space for an answer he was keeping hidden.

"I think I got that one covered." It slipped out.

"You have coupled with a male elf?" He stood up in shock.

"Ya know...some things are better left under the rug. I can't believe I just told you that." She winced.

"You have only been here one day! How did this happen? Who did this happen with…?" Then he froze. "Roderick! Was it Roderick? Please tell me it was not Rowland!" He visibly paled at the notion. "No, I would have seen it in his face the minute he opened the door." He sat down as if relieved.

"Why don't you want your grandson with a human?" She was a tad offended.

"Do not change the subject, you wily woman. Rowland is just not the best of choices. You will understand in time. Besides, I saw it written on the two of you the instant you stepped into the garden. Roderick. I should have guessed. I must be getting old."

"Are you sure you don't know who brought me here?" She glared at him.

"I have some theories, but they are all wild. Even if I did know who, I am at a loss to know how, but as I stated, I can now safely guess to why." He seated himself again. "Are we in that much danger?" He asked.

"That depends. It could just be a science station. I doubt it though. They don't tend to hover or be seen by primitive civilizations. They like to observe from afar, allowing the inhabitants to live naturally. I think this may be some type of environmental pirate. If that's the case, yes you are in big trouble." She settled in to explain further. "You see a planet like this is worth more money than you can imagine. Being primitive as you are, it is a sitting target for someone that has the means to just steal all your natural resources. Planets like this and, more often than not, people like yours will pass it off as an act of some type of god. The pirates come and pretty much strip the planet of everything worth anything and leave you starving. You better hope they don't figure out that elves can do magick, or you will find out in short order what its like to be a slave." She watched his worried look.

"I'm gonna help you if I can. I would never sit back and watch a place like this go down the toilet. Whoever brought me here must know that my people are very opposed to stuff like that. As a matter of fact, we make it our business to preserve planets. We find the long term wealth more satisfying. But I have to tell you, when I find out who yanked me from my flight hangar and just dragged me here, I am not going to be a very pleasant person." She warned.

"I hope you can understand it was out of desperation. I can only guess that whoever it was has some type of knowledge of your world. You must understand he or she probably knew of no other way than to yank you. We do not exactly go flying around the stars as you do. For whatever reasons, though, I can say this, there is more than one reason you are here. This all will be divulged in time. I can promise you, dear, I will do whatever I have within my power to help you get home and make things right." He laughed. "I knew it was scientific. I am not thick like some of these country astrologers. I wish we had more time to talk, there is so much I want to know." He stared off into space before he asked the next question.

"Are you a Christian?" He blurted out.

"Well…I don't know. I guess not. I've only been to church when I was a child, and even then I kept getting asked to shut up and sit down." She snickered.

"How were you educated?" He kept on.

"I was first educated on Earth in elementary school. I was kidnapped at eight years old, like I mentioned, then I was taken to Zeneria. I was schooled there for the rest of my childhood and became a squadron pirate for the Zenerian Empire. On Zeneria we never stop being educated. We can't. In our line of work it takes more than one lifetime to learn everything, so I will be going to school up until I can't think anymore." She expounded.

"You are a pirate? Like those harming our planet at this very moment?" He growled.

"No. Not that kind of pirate. We were just given that name a long time ago. We don't necessarily follow the same laws that the rest of the galaxy does. We do things our own way and we are strong enough to get away with it. We would NEVER rape a planet." Britt assured him.

"How many of you are there?"

"My squadron, or Zenerians as a whole?" Britt tired to clarify the question.

"Your squadron first." He wanted to start small.

"There are ten of us. Myself, Siggurd, Canga, Byron, Billy, Monika, Meadows, Boomer, Loco and Orin."

"Canga?" He asked.

"Yea, she is our physical defense specialist. We all have specific duties within our squadron. Billy is her twin brother. They can do stuff I could never dream of." She opened her eyes and pointed at her pupils. "Their eyes are yellow, like a cat's and they have pupils like Gilda's."

"I should like to meet this woman and her brother, yes I should." He insisted. "Tell me of your other friends." He settled in as though his need for urgency had been sated by his curiosity of space pirates.

"The human ones, or the other ones?" She asked for specification.

"All of them. I am just overflowing with curiosity. Imagine learning of creatures of other worlds. I should think this will make old Berdium quite jealous!" He glowed.

"Well there's Siggurd. He is from Iceland. He is big and blonde and second in command. He's the calm one and very strong. He is kind of the one that keeps his wits about him at all times." She began.

"Who is first in command?" He asked. "You should always start with the leader, it is only polite."

"You 're talking to her, silly. I am Captain Britteny Eden Devarelle. I'm the leader." She smirked and crossed her arms.

"YOU? How impressive my child! I am honored to meet you El' Capitan." He made a silly bow of sorts.

"Oh stop it, you old fool." Gilda was on the table eating nuts and Britt was stroking her slick scales.

"Then the next team is Byron Dawson and Canga. I already told you about Canga, she is of the feline persuasion. She makes a great fighting partner. I think she is my best friend, not only in the group, but in the whole universe. We understand each other quite well. Dawson is her partner. He is an Italian Indian, 100% Earth man. He is the best crook in the three systems and a hell of a chemist to boot. We never thought he would amount to anything but trouble, let alone a prize-wining engineer. He reminds us daily that he had reached his ass saving quota for years to come.

"Next in line would be Boomer and Loco. Boomer is from Ireland. His name is Liam Webb. We call him Boomer because he really likes to blow things up. Needless to say he is our chief explosives technician. He and Dawson designed our ships. Loco's real name is Maria Losensez. Loco means crazy in Spanish. She is from a place once known as Puerto Rico. She is our weapons expert and she takes "no sheet from no body, no time!" She mimicked Loco's thick accent, confusing Gherkin. "Forget it, inside joke." She laughed and went on.

"Then we have the neat little combination of Billy and Monika. Billy is Canga's brother. He's very quiet, very strong, and as fast as they come. He is a man I truly admire."

"Why is this?" Gherkin asked.

"He has a way of making you smile while still being very intimidating. He never has to try and prove he is a man. He is the most well balanced male I have ever known. I go to him for advice often. He is educated in language and politics but his strong suite is planetary geology. He is the one we send to negotiate and test the soil. If his intelligence doesn't work his appearance will. He is quite the picture of raw strength. Monika is a sea creature. She walks on legs, but she was sent to us from the oceans of Zeneria. We all learned quite a few tricks from her."

"What do you mean?" Gherkin was a bit jealous.

"Monika can make sounds that travel through water hundreds of miles. She taught us to make them. Of course not like she can, but the results are sound that can shatter material. It is almost deadly to creatures with heightened hearing. To a creature like an elf I would hate to see the outcome."

"Can I hear?" He asked.

"Gherkin, I have a feeling even at its most subdued it would shatter your eardrums. I don't even know what it would do to Gilda." She kissed the little dragon on the nose.

"Monika is also a language expert, but with her talents, she is able to communicate with a much wider range of beings. Billy is great for telepathy and supernatural things. They can both see in pitch black and Monika can breathe under water. Sometimes Billy thinks he is an immortal and does things that would kill the rest of us just to prove it." She worried.

"You are immortal in a sense now as well." Gherkin added.

"Nah. I'm just a loud-mouthed girl from Ohio." She informed.

"No. You joined life forces with an elf. You will now live as long as he does. That is if I am not so old I do not remember the act of coupling." Gherkin patted her hand.

"I will? He never mentioned that." She tried for a moment to absorb immortality without success, again thinking that the idea of immortality may be very different. Her mind rocked a bit when she remembered the age of the man sitting across from her. To keep sane, she set the thought aside. The deluge of information was slightly beginning to wear on her nerves.

"I doubt the lucky bastard had his wits about him. I look forward to my next meeting with him." Gherkin injected.

"Very funny. Anyway, the last, but not least, pair in my family consists of Orin Wolf and MaryAnn Meadows. They are both from Earth. Mary was from Boston and of course Orin was from the southwest. I don't know what tribe for sure. They are our healers. Orin is well versed in herbal and spiritual healing and has a number of degrees in psychological counseling, not that it's possible to figure a group like us out. Mary is a Medical Doctor. So you see, we all fit together." She smiled quaintly.

"What do you do?" He asked.

"That's just the thing, I don't know. I lead. I guess most people in management don't really know the definition of their jobs. I have adapted to each of their talents and can perform them with some level of proficiency. I can fly a spacecraft like I was born in one. I have had to achieve more education and understanding of ambassadorial duties. Goodness help us if they ever put Loco in charge of planetary treaties. We would all be at war." They both laughed at that statement. She rubbed her forehead. "I have no clue how to contact them. I was hoping that by coming here you could tell me a bit more as to my exact galactic location." Her face was still calm.

"I am amazed at your composure." Gherkin observed. "I know few that would take what you have so gracefully."

"It's not the first time I have had to deal with constant chaos. I know better than to lose it. When I am home, alone in my cottage I will lose it. Now I can't afford that kind of luxury." She relaxed for a moment looking at him with her head down and eyes raised.

"Magick will help you survive here long enough to complete this task and find your way home. I feel it important to teach you this as well. Knowing you are Earth born, it is only right that you know and understand the magick that was born there." He rose and started clearing the table. "Shall we get started?"

"I guess so. It can't hurt." She bit.

"You sound angered." Gherkin observed.

"Ya think?" She snapped. "My people probably think I have been killed. Did the person that zapped me here consider this and leave a little note saying "Hey, took your captain. Have her back after she saves our planet single handedly with no technological assistance. Oh, by the way we're not going to tell her why she is here. We'll leave that to the old guy with the dragon." Yes, I'm worried. I have more to think about then myself." She got up and started walking for the door.

"It would not be wise for you to go into this lesson in the mood you are in." Gherkin warned.

"Do you blame me? The next time you people need your planet saved, all you need to do is ask."

Gherkin grew solemn. "You do not understand magick so I will forgive you this. I will tell you, however, that I know for sure the reason you were chosen. Who ever sacrificed their lives, and believe me getting you here from where you come from would have been a life sacrificing magical feat, could have only found you because you are one of us."

"One of you?" She turned to look at him.

"Tell me then, how many children of Earth are out there in the stars that are descended from the Celtic islands, our last home, with the knowledge of space warfare, are left?" He asked.

She froze in her tracks. "You were wished for, Britt. The one who called you here had a blood link to you and called in desperation, this much I know. You were called by family." He was grave as he passed her and walked for the door. He turned and addressed her once more. "This great feat was done with the will alone. I hope you can understand the desperation and magnitude of this action."

Britt looked at the floor, rubbing her hands together breathing deeply.

"I do not even wish to think of how long he or she had to search to find you. I only know that every living creature on this planet owes them a great debt." He walked to her, putting his hand on her shoulder.

"If you do not wish to do this we will find another way." He offered.

"No. I'll do it." She started walking out the door wondering where her next steps would take her on the wild ride that was her life.

Chapter 10

Initiation

Her skin was beginning to tighten with suspense, naturally foretelling of something on the other side of conceptual reality. She followed Gherkin through the cottage and out the door. Gilda alighted beside her, fanning Britt's cheeks with reptilian wings. They passed through a simple gate and into a lightly furnished enclosed garden. Gherkin looked different now. He had adopted a new aura, one of power and presence. He walked to the center of the yard and turned to face her.

"We will be entering a parallel dimension. You must prepare yourself for this test. No human has ever entered the magick concept of an elf sorcerer. I do not know what reactions will occur."

She walked to him and nodded. He encircled her with his arms and closed his eyes. She did the same, and when she opened them, there was nothing but Gherkin. Her first reaction was defense. To calm herself she turned her full attention to the elf before her, calmed and reassured by his long white hair and wise elderly features. He stared into her eyes for a long moment as if building force then raised his thin arms and extended his fingers.

"All life belongs to the greater divine." As he spoke, colors shifted until she was at home among the stars. Her heart leaped with joy as they floated in the blackness of what she believed to be a fabricated vision. "Universally we are all connected and pull our lives, as well as return to them, to the constant strain of the living presence." Britteny watched as a million sparks of colored light danced around her forming a galactic spiral. "Each life form, no matter what location, is a mixture of all that has come before, all that will be lived, and what they pick up on the other side, just to return again to the circle." He hesitated. "I can hear in your thoughts that you believe this to be some type of illusion?" He interrupted his own lesson.

"Of course. That's fine though. I have some grasp on the powers of the mind. Go on." She looked off to the mesmerizing view of infinity.

"We can not continue until you cease your ignorance." He folded his arms patiently.

"You expect me to believe we are actually floating around in space?"

"Why would you believe any different?" He demanded.

"We would die in space Gherkin. We could not breathe."

"This is a most distressing set back." He shook his head.

Britt was suddenly crushed with the pressure and vacuum of the outer reaches. She clutched her chest and clapped her mouth shut. "How do you know that is not a trick of the mind as well?" He snidely asked her. "We do not live in flesh child. We live in conception. You must understand this to enable your human mind to break free."

She could breathe once more, yet her body felt no effect of the trauma. She looked to him humbled.

"You must learn to not live life but live within life. Rules are merely parameters that we set within our individual matrix to make sense of it all. Your rules differ from mine. For example, you believe that some type of instrument is required to travel through the void of space. Without this tactical assurance you are grounded to whatever solid surface you may inhabit at that moment. I have expanded my parameters. Furthermore, these limitations were never engrained into my psyche as a child. I can travel in space without a ship because I understand that my limitations are within my own understanding. These walls are then easy to break down at will." He held her hand and continued with the lesson.

"All life is made up of five primary elements, earth, air, fire and water." Visions of volcanoes, rushes of cool waves and blasts of air, causing an exhilarating sensation that made Captain Devarelle's hair stand on end, replaced the colored sparks. "The fifth element, of course, is conscious energy or the waking of the conscious, the ability to reason if you will, or you may even choose to call it God." Spinning slowly she was in a womb of sorts.

"So are you telling me there is no God?" She asked.

"I have no idea. I am an infant in the cosmos. But intellectually speaking, from a human viewpoint, as a race you have no concept of what the power of infinity suggests. As a race you must place a simple three-letter label on this inconceivable energy in order to begin understanding. Sad as this is, in an apparent effort to understand, naming something that is inherent in every reality, dimension and fabric known and unknown has also grossly limited your overall understanding of something that is right before you."

She looked down to see a newborn infant in her arms, asleep. Her mouth went dry and she started to shake. She could not overcome the astounding magick and beauty that she had managed not to notice before this very moment.

"So you see creation is a constant form of magick." He stepped back. "As for humans, I will show you three examples of why such magick that we posses has failed with humans, and vise versa." He took the babe. "It is her time to be born. Wish her luck." He kissed the infant and it disappeared. Britt wondered if the babe would remember this moment in future dreams.

Lifting his right hand he produced a flame above a small tree. In his left hand he held a perfect blue bowl of water with a dove above it.

"When our races were created in this whole of infinite possibilities we were each given equal amounts of magick. The elf people held the power of the winds as well as the magick of the water. We were more of the air, with the freedom of flight. We were the color of the new clouds of spring. Our magick was of the mind and logic." All around her flew fairies varied in a spectrum of colors. A large white female floated before her, the perfect pale face ghost like in the black. "You can see our early forms were quite mysterious. This may be why humans thought us celestial and spirit like. I think they called us Angels at one time." The vision was gone, replaced with a dark forest. Britteny could smell the mud and moss; it made her feel alive and primal.

"Humans," Gherkin demanded her attention. "on the other hand, were given the spirits of the earth, and fire." She spun slowly to observe the native people in a cave. They were making a fire and some of them were dancing around it. She watched as they danced faster and faster, the spirit taking them over. Then the scene changed to a pair of lovers, embraced in the throes of passion. She felt her breasts grow warm and her natural sensuality rise. "For thousands of years, this is how we lived, in harmony with the earth and all of life. At times we were each envious of the powers of the other, but soon realized we were a part of each other. Innocence and harmony prevailed."

She was in a village of trees. Far above her head she could see homes built among the strong boughs. She assumed it must be India judging by the darker color of the humans and the foliage in the jungle. "Can we travel through time or is this an illusion?" She chose to ask risking further reprimand.

"Time is an illusion. This is not. Again it is a parameter that your mind clings to. With practice you will learn to be the master of your own universe." He pointed to the tree dwelling people and continued seemingly not offended by her query.

"But there was a flaw." He held up a finger. "The total division was obvious but unlike humans, we were designed to hold the magick. It was natural for us as was survival in the natural world. Humans had to work at it." He gestured to the right. A woman squatted down over a wooden bowl. Her face painted and eyes wild, she mixed the brew and chanted quietly. "These humans were very interested in us and magick. They would spend their lives in pursuit of obtaining both forms of energy. This was no problem to us. We were willing to share and share alike. But alas it appeared to work better in human females than the males." He held his angled chin. "Perhaps the males did not see that their magic was just as strong…or perhaps it was the lack of the ability to give birth." He pondered for a moment. "Whatever the case, it started to cause a rift among the two."

He waved his arms again and called for blackness. "This power is apparent in all humans but remember, your spirit as a baby is innocent. You will live and grow. The choices and circumstances of life affect everyone differently."

He produced a radio, causing Britt to jump in surprise. "I was able to keep in contact with the land of humans up until about 1966. After that, things either got fuzzy, or I just got old." The radio disappeared. "I will now show you examples of what the lack of human balance can do to an individual and why we chose not to merge completely with humans." He stepped away from her leaving her alone on a hill. Above her was a man who had been nailed to a cross. She gasped in horror.

"This is Jesus." She could only hear Gherkin's voice. The scene was so real she could taste the metallic tang of blood mixed with desert sand. This man was the color of aged wood and old earth. His eyes deep pools of ebony, his hair rings of blood soaked coal. When she walked closer he looked down up at her. For some strange reason she felt like weeping. It was as if she were witnessing a precious work of art being destroyed. Her first instinct was to take him down; hunt down the people that had done this to such a man and seek revenge.

"Jesus was a phenomenon among the earth humans." Gherkin began. She faltered at the possibility of witnessing Christ's crucifixion. "His heart was blessed with a magick beyond his own understanding. This was a heart of kindness and beauty. Yet contrary to popular belief, also one of misguided aspirations that would be later disfigured into wild stories and self proclaimed prophecies. I will have you know that I was alive at this time. I was quite young but I remember the lad." The scene changed and she was among the followers of John the Baptist. She was dressed in a toga of sorts and standing on the bank of a river. She could see Jesus standing in the water. It was no wonder people were captured by his dark wondrous character. Their eyes locked for a long moment, leaving her sure he could see her. Just then a woman came to him. She was begging for his help. Britt watched as Jesus put his hands on the woman's face. She had never seen such blind devotion and assurance.

"Jesus did not understand who he was, he only believed that he was gifted and people followed him. In truth, the Jews, the people he proclaimed to be of and hoped to save, never really believed in him as their savior. Yet the people he preached against, the Gentiles, ended up producing a book, largely adopted from the long time beliefs of the Jewish nation, full of tales of demise and blood shed making it their "Bible". I could never quite figure that out? He was an example of what a truly pure soul, in its greatest form can accomplish in a human and yet the tragedy of corruption and the disbelief of true magic was the downfall in the end."

The scene changed again to a Roman court. Gherkin was now next to her. "But alas, there were things a soul like his had no concept of. He had been so convinced in his own imagined reality that he was willing to see the prophecies he had been taught as a child through to the bitter end." She walked up to the seat of the Roman Emperor. She stood next to the large man draped in white. She felt a hand on her shoulder.

"You see Britteny, Jesus may have began to understand the magick he possessed but he let it get out of control. He let it consume him to the point that he truly believed he was the ONLY son of God. Mind you, I feel he, even in his own skewed vision, really believed he was helping humanity."

She started when the Roman yelled and a slave was shoved to his feet and beheaded. "Jesus had tapped into quite a magick and the Roman Emperor wanted to steal that from him. You see, as you already know, anyone can beat a person into devotion. All Jesus had to do was reach out a hand. Hungry and suppressed people were waiting on the brink of losing hope. Jesus gave them hope, even if it was solicited in the end for the personal power of those less worthy. Those people needed a hero and that is exactly what he gave them. You can only imagine what this meant to the one race of people that longed to control the world entire."

"So, your saying he started out with good intent, had an ample supply of magic, and got out of control?" She asked.

"In a manner of speaking, yes. Jesus made many believe he was the son of God and he believed in what he was preaching. He did not understand, if you will excuse the term, the nature of the beast."

"Well, was he?" She asked.

"Was he what?" Gherkin did not follow.

"Was he the Son of God?"

"Well of course he was. But then again, we were all the sons and daughters of the divine. He just had the ability to effectively communicate on both levels. It was kind of like being a favorite among a large family. Regardless, when he died the Jewish people were blamed. As in many instances in human history, he gathered quite a substantial following after his death and his legend grew more astounding. Legends often blossom only when the stuff they are made of is no longer tangible and prone to scrutiny. And the Romans? Well those slick characters went on to embrace the faith of God and his son. I highly doubt the actions that were carried out in the name of Jesus had anything to do with whom the man actually was or what he had hoped to teach. I kept seeing his face depicted as an Arian, like you, and we both know that was not the case. It is noble to follow the cause of such a good man but not to kill in his name. Let this be your first lesson in the evolution of the imagination. We cannot see the spiral of tongues and tales. We can surely experience their effect. And the Bible, well, we shall not elaborate on it." He seemed frustrated.

"Why not?" Britt asked.

"Have you ever actually read the Bible?" Gherkin asked.

"Well, not actually." She had to think about it.

"When all is said and done, I will produce a copy for your educational consumption. I would be very interested to learn what someone such as yourself takes from the pages of such a book."

The scene was again deleted and Britt found herself standing in a humble abode among a crying woman and a little boy. The woman was draped over a dead infant. Britteny could only draw the conclusion that this was her younger son. The boy in the corner was distant and unmoving. He showed no emotion, yet exuded an energy that nearly knocked her sideways. Britt walked over and bent down to look into his eyes. The lad stepped back. His birdlike features gave way to the knowledge that he felt her presence but did not see her. Just then a man came into the room. He spoke in a language that Britt recalled but did not know. He called the boy Adolph, and took his hand to lead him from the room. Another man walked in and Britt noticed the small black yarmulke that noted his Jewish lineage. He was the family doctor.

"Now this child," Gherkin began, "was blessed with much the same gift and even promoted the use of a religious righteousness of sorts but with a different twist or means to an end." They were now walking the streets of Austria sometime in the late 1920s. Young Hitler sat at a café table drawing pictures on small pieces of paper. "Can you believe that anyone who aspired to be an artist could come to such an end?" Gherkin sat next to him and Britt listened. "Adolph had everything Jesus never had, yet lacked many things one would not expect."

"How so?" Britt had already drawn some conclusions but was eager to hear Gherkin's evaluation of the situation.

"Well, from what we know, Jesus had a rather loving family. Adolph, well his family was less than desirable. Both believed themselves to be, how shall I say it.... special. Both were constantly terrified of their individual daemons if you will. Both truly believed they were doing what was right and in many situations used communication, charisma and any means possible to sway others to their way of thinking. I was not on the earth to really get to know Adolph. By the time his generation was produced we were a fable. His mind was as sharp as any wild beast, yet compassion was not in his makeup. He only realized revenge through his own shortcomings. He wished to be as you and I are." Gherkin sighed.

"What do you mean?" She asked.

"White, or of a supposed pure race. I believe they called it Arian. He was not Arian. The fact that he had everyone believing he was is just amazing. Why just look at him. He has none of the predominate features of a true Arian." Gherkin shook his head with disgust. "He also lacked any of the vision to see the fantastic beauty of other races and peoples. Now Jesus, he knew how to truly love people of all walks of life. I have often marveled, and I may say fell smitten, to women of dusky persuasions. However he did have the mind of a mad genius, and the ability to sway a nation of people. Much like Jesus he was able to hone in on the needs of the people. Call it need, call it weakness, in any case it was just the right mixture of desperation and devotion.

But unlike Jesus he used it for all the wrong reasons. Jesus, again, was truly capable of love and I believe, as one who knew him, held an undying love for humanity as no other. Adolph's end came in a bunker, hiding like a coward and full of hate and regret. At least Jesus died with dignity and did not scurry into a hole in the earth. Yet Adolph had a fire Jesus lacked when he was at his peak and unlike Jesus, very few people had the stomach to appose him."

They were standing in mud and gray. Impact perception overloaded to another scene. Before she was aware of where she was, her instinct was tuned to the sadness. She was as an antenna of emotion and energy consuming the power that radiated from the lives around her. A small boy, dark of hair and empty of spirit, stood next to her. He reached to hold her pale hand. His eyes reflected a soul older than the earth herself. He was covered with mud, rainwater and ashes. His background was a painted brick building below biological-stench-belching silos of smoke and ashes. His people were in the clouds, floating over their home country and past his face.

"You feel them. You feel his magick." Gherkin interrupted the trance.

"I've felt this before. I've seen his eyes and know his desolation." She spoke to the unseen elf. "Where are we?" She already knew but somehow needed to confirm it.

"Auschwitz." His voice seemed repelled like oil in water among the death. "My people watched for years in horror, unable to understand the motive and the madness." His voice shook. "The faith of Jesus was no different, just delayed. Millions burned in fires, as well in the name of a religion that preached salvation and a shining new life. I see little difference. Death is death; domination is domination and hate the same in any language."

Britteny walked to the gates and grabbed the barbed wire. "I understand it. It's a beast that grows in you little by little with every victory. You come to think nothing can touch you and you distance yourself from the rest of society." Her hand dripped blood on the cold metal.

"These were not your people. Adolph was not of your blood, yet he believed that somewhere, somehow, he was chosen to enact these crimes. He named himself superior among men and thus alighted a nation." Gherkin said.

"There's no such thing as superior." She yelled to her surprise causing everyone in the court to turn to her. "My people, your people, OUR PEOPLE!"

She started shaking the gate with furious convulsions. "It's all going to be for nothing, you ignorant bastards. None of your great grandchildren are going to survive! NONE OF THEM!" She reached down and picked up a stone, preparing to rocket it towards a guard. She quieted and disappeared into the black. "They will not see it, even now." She dropped the stone and held her hands to her eyes and wept only slightly.

"Yes, and this magick and these actions brand a race for the bad and the good. So you see what human magick can do? Shall I show you the Native American people?" He asked.

"No! I can't bear to see it. I know their story. I can't stand the fact that the people that I share blood with could do such a thing. I feel dirty enough already." She was ashamed.

"These things you must fully realize in order to understand the responsibility of combining the magicks into one person."

Before she could reply they were standing in the deep wood. Her chest still heaved with the pain of suppressing such emotions. For a time Gherkin stood near her. His energy was a bath of comfort and support, quelling the anger that threatened to render her uncontrollable.

"I don't know if I can do this, Gherkin. Why did you choose these things to show me? I haven't set foot on earth for years." She absently held her chest.

"Yet you still weep." He stroked her cheek. "With all our magick there is still the light of instinct that binds you to that planet. You have seen billions of other such situations. I am wise enough to know that I can dote about all I wish but if I am to open you to what you must learn, first I must know where the door is."

He moved to a pair of stumps, seating himself and motioning her to do the same. "This lesson, I am sorry to say is not over. It will become more difficult for you. I do not wish this. I do not wish to weaken you to the point of breaking, but you must understand I have to open that wound. I have to let it bleed and the infection that lurks within your soul spill out before what is to become can become. Do you understand?" He asked.

"Yea. I'm not sure how much worse you can make it than that." She wiped her eyes and regretted her statement.

Britt instantly wailed in pain when entering the next vision. She was seated in the corner of a small attic, painted pink, adorned with fairies and butterflies. A five-year-old child crouched in the opposite corner, sullen and frightened among the princess décor. There came a loud knock from beneath. She scurried down the short ladder to a crawlspace and listened.

"Britt, let me in, it's Aeyden." A gentle voice permeated the paneling. The frail child unlocked the bolt and backed away from the trap door. She started up the ladder to allow her older brother room to climb into her pink prison. She was so pale and thin, more hair than body.

Settling next to her "Winnie the Pooh" lamp, she attempted to feign indifference.

"So when do I get to come down?" She asked the blonde teenager.

"I think it is better that you stay up here tonight, kiddo." He produced a glad bag full of carrots and crackers with a small carton of milk from the pocket of his jacket. "He is passed out in the barn but Mom is still afraid he will get up sometime tonight. She told him you were staying at a friend's house." He set up her little table as if they were in a nice restaurant or a family table full of love and open feelings.

"I don't have any friends." The distant little girl reminded her brother.

"Hey! What am I, chopped liver?" He tried to act overly hurt, teetering to the floor, clutching his chest.

"Stop it you big idiot." She jumped on him and started poking his strong stomach. He acted as though she were killing him. They ended the wrestling match laughing and out of breath. In the corner, a grown galactic captain was barely able to see through the tears. Aeyden pulled the frail table to her lap.

"Here, you little scarecrow. You better eat before you melt away." He joked.

Little Britt picked at a carrot. "Why does he hate me so much, Aeyden?"

Aeyden messed her curls. "Aw booger, he doesn't hate you. He hates himself."

"Huh?" She chewed the carrot, her pink cheeks puffing full as a bunny's.

"I know this is hard for you to understand, scooter, but Dad is really sick. He isn't a real man; he's a bottle and a bunch of regret. Me and Mom love you more than anything."

"Do you think he will ever stop trying to hurt me?" She asked, milk mustached.

"I'll never let him hurt you, sis." Aeyden looked at her filled with love. "Now hush up and get into the sleeping bag, you have school tomorrow." He opened her Cinderella sleeping bag that he had brought home for her the week before. She crawled inside and pulled the pastel nylon up to her chin. Her porcelain face was framed in little girl lace.

"Sing me our lullaby?" She asked.

"Ok, just once though. Then I'm going to go downstairs and you have to bolt the door until morning. I will be knocking really early, so you better get your little butt up." He cradled her head and began to sing a song he had heard on a Billy Joel cassette that he learned just for her. It had become their song. Aeyden loved to sing and wanted to be in a band. His father thought it a girl's profession and so Aeyden only sang to his mother and sister:

"Goodnight my angel, time to close your eyes and save these questions for another day.

I think I know what you've been asking me, I think you know what I've been trying to say.

I promised I would never leave you, and you should always know, wherever you may go, no matter where you are, I never will be far away.

"Goodnight my angel now it's time to sleep and still so many things I want to say.

Remember all the songs you sang for me, when we went sailing on an emerald bay.

And like a boat out on the ocean, I'm rocking you to sleep. The waters dark and deep, inside this ancient heart, you'll always be a part of me.

Goodnight my angel now it's time to dream, and dream how wonderful your life will be.

Someday your child may cry and if you sing this lullaby, then in your heart there will always be a part of me."

The child was asleep and Aeyden kissed her little brow. Britt felt as though she wanted to die. The pain was nearly the most excruciating she had ever experienced. She knew he would sleep in the room that night, watching over her.

"Gherkin, this has to stop, I can't stand it anymore!" She begged sobbing.

"You must see more, I am sorry." He instructed.

She was seated in a P.T.A. chair in a warm tent, striped for the circus. It was the county fair. The grass was trampled by country children and their parents come to see the sideshow. She took a deep breath inhaling the smell of popcorn and sweat. In front of her she saw the aliens. OmJolb looked much younger than she remembered. From her left came a rustling of the tent flaps. Two green eyes peeked through as the child crawled under the canvas to get a free show. Young Britteny walked past Captain Devarelle and said, "Excuse me Ma'am."

Britt moved her legs. She could not resist touching her own hair as she passed by. For some reason this was not a sad memory. She was kidnapped on this day, yes, but she did not regret the abduction. Her life on earth would have been uneventful if not minimal to her life in space. Her education that of earth and thus tainted with the emotions of a solitary planetary civilization. Fortune had smiled on her this day and it came in such a strange form. She knew Aeyden was somewhere in the horse barns talking to Michelle Manning. He was completely in love with the girl and she could see why. He would not notice she was gone for some time and then it would be too late.

Little Britteny walked to the sectioned-off portion of the aromatic canvas where the aliens were displayed. She had always loved Star Trek, Star Wars, Battle of the Planets and any other type of sci-fi input she could get. She cared little if Santa Claus was real. The Easter Bunny was a waste of time. Captain Devarelle giggled and crossed her arms as she watched the scrawny child in Osh Kosh overalls shove her way past hips and beer bellies to see if her dreams were real. It was quaintly nostalgic to see that first meeting from another angle. OmJolb spotted her instantly. She had not noticed him until later. Little Britteny Devarelle pulled out a wax pop bottle from her front pocket, bit off the top, sucking out the juice, chewing on the wax and watching the show before her. She walked from alien to alien, asking pointed questions, drawing amusement from not only the crowd, but also marked interest from the visitors from very far out of town. She approached Dallex, a water dweller from Zeneria, much like Monika.

"Hey mister, can you breathe under water?" She pointed to his gills. This observation commanded the attention of the leader of the expedition. OmJolb bent down to address her.

"Why do you ask this, child?" He asked gently.

"Well look, he has gills and his skin is like rubber. He looks like a dolphin and a fish all in one." She pointed to the almost invisible gill slots under Dallex's jaw. Dallex bent down.

"Would you like to touch my skin, dear?" This child did not poke fun at them or call them freaks. She chose not to hide behind the overexposed housewives searching for their youths.

"Sure, thanks!" She reached a tiny hand up and lovingly stroked Dallex's cheek. Behind her, Captain Devarelle was now standing in the crowd. She was tall enough to see over the heads of many of the townsfolk. She had never considered what she was like as a child. She had all but forgotten touching Dallex that day. OmJolb looked up at her. He knew who Little Britteny was. She had not known it at the time but the Zenerians had been watching her for years and planning this meeting. They avoided abducting children from functional, loving homes. The woman in the crowd was not her mother but the resemblance did not miss his keen eyes. Britt smiled at him in a knowing way. She loved OmJolb so much. When she got back to Zeneria, she was going to hug the old bastard and neglect to tell him why.

"Would you like to see our spaceship?" Dallex whispered into Britt's ear.

"Wow, could I?" She tried to stay quiet, knowing Aeyden would have a fit.

"That day, you left one reality for another. In all this, even with my criticism, I must admit that your ability to comprehend those things that are not of your immediate reality is above average." Gherkin noted.

"I didn't really have much of a choice. My world is all about change." She commented.

"In this first lesson of many, you will be asked then to think upon all that you have seen. I want you to let go of what you know and understand that, to do magick, you have to crack all the concepts you now hold as factual. There is no reality. There is only conceptual reality. You are not separate from the divine power of the universe. You are an intricate working part of that which is the mystery of the all, just as you have thousands of organisms within your own body, working to support the universe that is, too you, simply you.

This lesson has primarily been focused on history and magick as it is and has been reflected through humans. The actual goal of this lesson, though, is to help you understand that if you so wished you could travel through space without a ship as well."

"If you can travel through space, can you take me home?" She asked.

"No. I may be able to take you back to where the earth used to be. Alas, I have no idea where Zeneria is. Now comes the failing of my people. You have studied space. Because you do not posses the powers I have, or so you have come to believe, your people dig in and earn the knowledge they possess. This is a strong magick in itself. What good is floating around if I do not take the time to lean the names of these stars and the lives of these people?" He rose. "One more thing you must see before this first lesson is complete." He saw her wince. "This will not be as emotionally brutal as the others." He promised.

She was standing in a tavern full of fairy creatures. It must be Ruddy Mudders. The place reeked of Zembeth and she knew of no other place that she could see a centaur drinking a beer with a goblin. Osizio burst through the front door, tears running down his face. Tables went flying and the structure rattled from the weight of the ogress that bounded around the bar. Britt imagined that she would have gone right through it if necessary.

The two, hairy, smelly, overweight creatures embraced in the most wonderful hug she had ever seen. Love has no form; it shows no favoritism, not real love. Even in her invisible state, the emotion struck her and warmed her. This was exactly what influenced her to be a leader; this hug was a sample of the reason she kept going though all the days of stress and thankless work. Censci wailed with joy as she placed slimy kisses all over Osizio's face. Britt could feel a strange pang of loneliness in the pit of her stomach.

Next she was seated in the arena at the palace, watching slave Britteny and Rowland, sparring. "I would hate to see her when she is really angry." Gherkin interrupted her dream only to shift scenes again. She was walking with Roderick through the lane before the village of elders. They were licking the flower and laughing.

"Why are you showing me this?" She looked at Gherkin. "I thought you didn't want me hanging out with Roderick anymore?" She insisted.

"I may not, but alas, who am I? I am playing this more for me than for you." Gherkin held out his hands. "But of course you would need to know Roderick to understand."

"By all means, enlighten me." She ignored the scene she was in and challenged the laughing elf for an answer.

"Well, think of the irony! It just slays me! If you were I, you would see things differently." He walked to a picture frozen image of the scene. "Britteny Eden Devarelle, I would like to introduce you to Roderick of Darmuth Anor." He spread out his arms in an over the top display. "Roderick is the most unnoticed natural well of power in Zembeth. Like you, he harbors the power to rule all that surrounds him. As a matter of fact, even though he is a bastard and has, to the knowledge of the court, not a single trace of royal blood in him, I am sure he would be our best King yet. The peasants love him and at a whim and a word he could overthrow the entire social structure of this planet." Gherkin whined comically. "And he chooses not to! HA!" He jumped to the other person.

"And here we have a woman that could wipe out the whole planet with a whim and a word and neither of them has a clue to who the other is. And here they stand like two infants playing with flowers. Ahahah! It is too brilliant!" He slapped his knees. "To make matters more hilarious, I now find out that they have already coupled in a passionate knot of flesh....hoo...hee...and they just met that very day! Imagine! What a scandal! Ah, to be young again!"

"O.K. That's enough. Haha." She walked to him and took his hand. "Very funny. I'm glad to see my sexual urges and lack of knowledge amuse you so much."

"Imagine! I would love to see all their faces if they only knew what you really are! Especially Sholendor! Now that would be truly worth remembering!" He tried to stop laughing. "Oh, I am so sorry, I just could not help myself." He calmed down. He was feeling the bubble weaken with his lack of focus. Britt was looking rather ragged from the emotional roller coaster she had just lived through.

"Yes, back to business." He straightened his frail frame and closed his eyes. They were back in the garden. "I have sent for Rowland, he will be here shortly. I think it is time we allow digestion of all that has come before us." He was alarmed to see Britt sway and set herself on the bench. She was pale and weak.

"My dear! Are you not well?" He was petrified with fear.

"Yea, I'm o.k." She waved him back. "I just have a monster headache and I am so tired all of a sudden. It must have been all that crying. What a rush!" She put her face in her hands and her elbows on her knees. "I feel like I've lived a hundred lifetimes in a matter of minutes without resting."

"Do you have any questions? Is there some way I can help?" He begged.

"No. I don't want to talk anymore, no offense. I just want to sleep for a while." She said. "And I really need to take a pee. Where is your bathroom?" She asked.

"The pot is this way." He took her elbow and helped her to her feet.

"You people really need to get simple plumbing. The whole pot thing is so stinky." She observed.

"We don't stink." He said seriously.

"Suuuure ya don't." She shook her head. "Just get me to the can."

While Gherkin waited for Rowland to return, Britt sat on the pot, head in hands, trying to make her mind stop spinning. In reality, she did not have the urge to urinate. Nearly everyone knows the bathroom is the best place to be alone and collect oneself. She stood bloomers down and skirt up, and turned to vomit in the pot. She pounded her chest as if it would help the heartburn go away. She did not know if she was ill due to something she ate or because of recent experiences. There was no sink or water in the room. "God damn it!" She cursed under her breath. She felt almost crippled. She was sure there was some way to use water if she knew the trick to it. There is nothing more miserable than puke mouth and a wet bottom when you are on a strange planet. She wondered if it was the remaining alcohol in her system, then decided against it. She was sure she had puked it all out in the meadow. "GHERKIN!" She hollered irritably. The elder elf rushed to the door.

"Yes dear? Are you well?" He shouted through the door.

"Where the hell can I get some water around here?" She tried to keep her voice calm. It was not his fault she had not fully adapted to his world. He must have done something. Behind her appeared an overflowing fountain of cool water that drained into a veritable bottomless basin.

"Thanks." She offered over her shoulder and she splashed the water on her face. When she stood she noticed he had added a mirror. What a nice elf. She looked like some maniac witch on a rampage drug overdose. She pulled up her undergarments and wiped her mouth on her skirt. It was going to take a miracle to comb out her hair. She hoped she was dead or asleep during the task. She pressed her hand to her sternum. She still had a slight cramp. She just needed some sleep.

When she walked out, Rowland was waiting for her. She hugged Gherkin and thanked him and then kissed Gilda, hoping only a dragon could appreciate breath like its own and proceeded to walk out the front door. Rowland lagged behind to inquire of her health, only to be told to get her back to her room and let her sleep. He knew better than to argue with such an esteemed member of the elfish elders counsel and his grandfather. He hovered close to the human but did not disturb her. He was deeply concerned now that he was aware of all involved. If Roderick knew she was this ill, he would tear down the palace doors and murder the prince, Osizio in tow to burn down the rest. His visit to Ruddy Mudders had been just as disturbing.

He could have said it was uncomfortable, because at first no one chose to talk about the situation. Roderick was a zombie and Amaranth had left for the day without notice of return. He attempted to talk to Donavan, who seemed to avoid the entire subject for some time before Roderick came to the table. When he did, he inquired about Britteny. Rowland felt the fear grow in his gullet when he realized that he had told the Black Elf of Darmuth Anor that his new friend was a picture of strength and vitality. He glanced at the sullen, weak image of the former mentioned, that barely walked next to him. He devised the safest way into the palace avoiding all attention from anyone remotely elf or noble.

They entered the rear of the kitchens, to the surprise of the staff. Britt could feel a strong set of hands on her hind end. She could barely hear the gravel strong voice of the little woman holding her up.

"Rowland of Sid O'Sala! Whaddya thinkin' yer doin'! The poor beast is near dead! Do ye want us all killed!?" Sara scolded the elf.

"It was not my doing, Sara! I beg you, help me get her to the tower and to bed safely." He put his arm around Britt's back. Her head fell onto his shoulder in a near unconscious state.

"For the love of Ren'Fordel, man, pick her up!" Sara insisted. Rowland bent over and hooked his strong arms under the human. He could feel his heart sinking and somehow knew it was not out of fear of punishment.

"You! Git offa yer lazy arse and fetch me some chamomile!" Sara barked at another slave.

"And you! Cold rags in the room now!" She reached over and hauled a gnome male off of his chair by the shirt. "Mugwort for the lass's bath, back forest garden, and make it quick!" She rolled up her coarse sleeves. "Come on, Rowland, let's get her up to the bath afore she dies." Sara pushed past him and up the slave passage to the tower.

He tried not to watch as Sara stripped off the dress and chemise. She ordered him to pick Britt up again and keep holding her upright while Sara crawled, clothes and all into the steaming tub to clean the naked female.

"What in the name of Giddion's demon did ye do to her? Are ye daft?" She ranted.

"It is as I have told you, she was fine when I left her at Lord Gherkin's home." He pleaded as he cradled Britt's head in his hands. "This is Meriden's new companion slave, Britt." He announced.

Sara stopped scrubbing the bottom of the human's hair. Standing in the water, clothes full of suds she looked up at the elf.

"No! To think I was a gettin' used to ye commin' into the slave kitchens carrying giant mutant human females!" She put her stout hands on her hips. "Who'da thought?"

Rowland scowled. "O.K. Sara, let's just get her cleaned up and in bed before Sholendor or Meriden get here. Where is Meriden?" He inquired.

"Wit her mother. I was lucky enough ta be sent fer early. I ave not told her about this half-assed decision of our Lord Soggy Bottom yet." She hoisted herself out of the bath and walked behind the dressing blind dripping wet. "Dry that up for me lad, will ye?" She asked. Rowland looked at the tiny water puddles on the floor, willing them to evaporate. "Get her out o there and wrap her in the blankets I 'ave laid on the bed. I must a change afore I am ill as well." She reached for the shift that Minakshi was holding out to her while she stared at Rowland as he lifted the soaking human from the warm water. He hesitated for a moment to evaporate the water on her body, rendering her dry before she reached the warm bed, doing his best not to stare. He was male after all. He would surely be considered quite mentally ill for ogling a human, even this human. Somehow, although he admired her naked body, he was surprised to find he felt a bit dirty to his relief. Perhaps her magick only worked when she was conscious. He would not want to be in the same boat Roderick was in now.

"Minakshi." He called, causing the shy girl to jump. "Finish covering her, I must be off." He began.

Sara appeared from behind the blind. "And just where are ye off to so fast?" She barked.

"I am off to Ruddy Mudders. I must inform Roderick of the past events before gossip has her dead and him breaking down the palace doors."

"Creepin' Death! What does he have to do with it?!" She walked to the bed and pulled the mass of hair off to one side, placed a towel on the floor and started feeling the woman's brow and listening to her breathing.

"Let's just say you can expect him here tonight, and it would be better if he did not blame Sholendor for this mess." He was at the door.

Britt moaned and babbled about regeneration engines and strawberry milkshakes.

"Fer shit's sake! It talks?" Sara shouted.

"Yes, you will find she is quite intelligent, and what ever you do, if she wakes up while I am gone, DON'T anger her or make her feel threatened!" Rowland insisted.

"Fer the love of Ren'Fordel, why not?" Sara was beside herself.

"Trust me Sara, it will not be pleasant. Just promise me!" Rowland demanded.

"Sure, sure! What 'ere ye say, red! After all, 'tis just another day in the palace fer old Sara." She slammed down a wash cloth and got to work. "This human has the look of a spell on her. I only hope I can bring her about." She stopped examining and walked to Rowland. "At least tell me what it is I'll be in store fer when it wakes up, and if ye know what Gherkin did to her."

"I think Roderick will be here when she does, unless the palace is full of royals. Besides, she is quite entertaining, and believe it or not, I get the feeling Sholendor will be a bit disappointed as to how she gets on with Meriden." Rowland winked. "I know not what my grandfather did to her. I have a feeling he may have put some type of protection spell on her and the strength of that much magick in her system has made her ill."

Before she could ask her next questions the elf was out the door, only echoes of his light footfalls on the stairs. Sara huffed and turned to look at the flushed human sprawled out on the bed. She was sure the lass had a fever. Absently she reached in her pocket and produced the leather pouch she had found in the woman's bodice. She turned, just in case the human was able to see her, empting the hidden treasure into her strong yellow hand. She dropped the gem as if burned by its' coolness. Had the human stolen such a prize? She hurried to pick the amulet up, quickly putting it back in the pouch. This was an affair she wanted no part of. She walked to the bed and placed the pouch on the stand. She had not shown it to Rowland. She was not sure why. Sara sprung to her tiptoes and placed a hand on the human's forehead. As she did, the wide green eyes opened to stare beyond her.

"Please? Close the door and leave me alone, I am so tired. I just want to hide away." Britt choked.

Sara reached for a cold cloth. "There; there now, lass. No one's a going to hurt ye here." She soothed. It was going to be a very long night.

Chapter 11
The Big Decisions

Sara of Sid O'Sala was a very strong woman. She had been born on the gnome slave farms of Sid O'Sala and was taken to the royal palace as soon as she was weaned. It was noticed by the king that she was a very special soul. He came to this conclusion the day he observed her ordering around a group of ogres in the south gardens. The ogres were listening. He named her personal slave to the expected princess that very moment. Since that day, even as a child, she had shouldered the responsibility of total care for the Princess Meriden of Fairfax. If asked, she would admit, life had been all but boring. She remembered Ren Fordel sitting on the throne waiting for news of the slave revolution. He called her forward, alone.

"Tell me Sara, do you wish to be free? Do you even understand the concept?" Later he would call her to his private chambers and request that she, a simple gnome, care for his only love, his daughter Meriden. He did not have to explain that he was leaving. The queen may have been ignorant to the goings on of the palace, but Sara always knew the current game.

She ran interference as Sholendor plotted time and time again to humiliate the princess. She had even been known to steal the princess to the slave quarters, if only to shield her from her fate.

Now she stood on a human dampened carpet, (Rowland had missed a spot) staring at what she thought just may be the end of them all. It would not be long before Roderick of Darmuth Anor was standing in just this spot. She must make haste and do her best to lower the fever. She was only slightly inept at curing humans. Her life had been spent learning to cure other gnomes and the occasional elf.

She opened the slave door just as Minakshi was laboring up with a bowl of water in her hands and a satchel of mugwort over her shoulder. Minakshi tried to bow to her superior, and in secret, her personal hero, and almost spilled the water.

"Steady there lass, I'm not the bleedin' queen." Sara took the bowl. "Ye know, of course, ye could have waited ta fill this up here." She commented, hoping the child would note the inefficient mistake.

"Yes Sara, I am so ashamed. It shall never happen again." She almost cried.

"Enough 'o that now. I need yer help, not more trouble." She opened the mugwort and began dumping it in the water and rags. "It's good to have, but I'll be needing some white oak bark and cool towels to take down the lass's fever. Best ye go to the slave quarters and get me daughter Hannah and tell her to be off for a fever cure and fast." She instructed Minakshi. "And I suppose ye know Roderick is about to be comin'?" She asked.

"Yes Sara, he visited last eave for most of the dark hours." Minakshi backed towards the door to be off for Hannah. She was jumping inside at the thought of meeting Sara's only child. It was said the girl was unusual among gnomes, as wise as her mother, but almost human-like in beauty.

"Oh did he now?" Sara walked back to the human on the bed getting a closer look at her. Things were getting worse by the minute. "Eye and toe! No matter. Off wit ye to fetch my daughter." With her command Minakshi disappeared down the slave stairs.

Sara lifted the thin blankets off the human's thighs. "Na, canna happened." She dropped the blankets and stepped back rubbing her chin. "Na. Any one 'o those sharp-eared bastards, 'cept Roderick. I just canno' see it." She toyed with the notion of slipping her finger in the female's vagina and smelling it, then decided against it. The girl had been though enough already, no sense making matters worse. Even so, Sara knew she did not really want to know the truth of it.

She was deep in thought when Hannah appeared with an infusion of white oak bark followed by Minakshi toting more towels.

"Hello mother." Came the sweet voice of her beloved child. Hannah was tall and thick for a gnome. Her hair was full and honey colored and her eyes were blue. Her skin only held a hint of yellow, yet her smile could warm the very morning. "I have been told we have a sick human to look after." She confirmed, walking to the bed.

"Hello girl, 'tis been a long time and a torture fer yer old ma." Sara embraced her daughter, her heart overflowing. Hannah had been raised by the elfish elders to work in their community as a general slave, far away from the world of her mother. Her speech was perfect and her education far above that of a simple gnome slave. Sara was more than proud of her only child, but rarely spoke of it, thanking the very Gods that Hannah had been given such a life by Ren'Fordel at Sara's request and not left to be a common slave.

"Yes mother, far too long. We must be to work and visit later if we are to save the giant." Sara beamed at the practicality of her child. "She is no doubt a beauty of a strange breed. The entire city is abuzz with news of her."

"News or no, Roderick will be here soon and I dunna wanna be here to keep him company." Sara began steeping the oak. "Oh shite, I dinna call fer the garlic. Off with ye, Minakshi, fer some dried garlic powder." And so they worked for as long as they were able until the black elf arrived.

Sara stayed with Roderick and Rowland as they tried to determine the cause of the illness. She spoke little to the quiet dark lord and his scarlet friend, instead fussing over the feverish human. Roderick paced about the balcony, asking obscure questions of Rowland. The night wore on and eventually Rowland left, but Roderick stayed. He positioned himself next to the bed and stared out at the deep blue sky. Sara kept watch with him until Hannah insisted that her mother go rest before dawn, knowing all the while that her mother had, just a few short hours ago, expressed her discomfort of the situation. It seemed a night from a dream that was never supposed to happen to Sara as she supported herself on the cool walls. Lives go forth and come round again. Why did it have to be her time? Why did this human pick her life, of all lives, to disrupt?

********* * * * * * * * * *************

Britt stretched like a cat in a sunlit window. Her mind was a bit hazy; still she kept her eyes closed. She could feel a cool breeze blowing like milkweed silk across her naked hip and thigh. She could not recall a time in her life that she had slept so soundly. She was still aware of her situation and, for this reason, allowed her mind some time to absorb this moment of peace and innocence. There were many times that she wished she could stay just so, asleep, alone, while the troubles of the universe flowed by her like a living dream she was not really a part of. The air on Zembeth was superb. She breathed in deeply, filling her body with the refreshing unpolluted oxygen. Slowly she rolled over to face the open window. Pulling the pillow snug under her chin, she dared open her eyes to see a gnome standing on the balcony, smelling the sweet potted flowers. She squinted her eyes and looked though her thick lashes. She had no desire to be bothered at this moment. The gnome turned as if sensing her awakening. She walked to the bed and touched Britt's forehead.

"Oh, I do hope you will be well, dear." She said in a remarkably eloquent vocalization for a gnome. Britt held still. She could feel another presence in the room. Its energy forced its way through her chest into her soul. Roderick stood next to the gnome. Britt was sure to play opossum now. She did not wish to face him again until she felt sure of her emotions.

"It is dawn, Hannah. I must be off." He reached out and touched Britt's curls. "Please take good care of her." He requested.

"I will do the best I can Roderick. I know little about humans. Needless to say, I have never taken care of one like this. I only wish we knew what ailed her." She stepped back. "No need to fret though, Mother will be back soon."

Britt was still tingling from his touch long after he left the room. She remained covert behind her masquerading lashes. A few moments later the slave door opened and she could hear a strong set of footsteps soldier across the room.

"What is she still doing lying down?" Asked the strange voice.

"Mother, she still sleeps." Hannah protested.

"Bull asses! She is wide-awake. Come now, ye wily wench, let's have a look at ye then." Sara slapped Britt's bare bottom.

"Alright! I'm up!" Britt giggled and opened her eyes. She did not know this gnome, but guessed her to be the one and only Sara.

"So yer what all this fuss is about? Humph!" Sara walked up to the side of the bed and felt Britt's forehead. "I just hope ye are as wise as ye are wily fer the sake of us all." She turned to Hannah. "Thank ye for all yer help, child. Ye must be off afore Meriden comes up to have a look. I am thinking ye are goin' to be her new servant afore the day is out. Trust me, ye will need some rest. I can handle this one fine." She hugged the slightly thinner, taller female. "I take it that you know who is gone afoot to the tavern." She speculated.

"Yes mother, he left a short time ago." She was a bit embarrassed for her lack of insight.

"Ah." Sara turned to Britt. "Dinna want to face him this day, did ye, wily?" She chided.

Before Britt could answer, Sara grabbed her hand and pulled her into a sitting position. "Sure we must get ye dressed afore Meriden gets here. 'Tis all she needs to see is those jugs 'o yours swishing about to make her even more sickly."

Britt was not sure how to react. She was certain the gnome could not harm her, and even enjoyed her "matter of fact" personality, but Sara was borderline demeaning. Sara strode off to the wardrobe and began rummaging though. Hannah quickly shot before Britt to assemble a bowl, a cup of weeds and some rags, and then retreat out the slave door. Sara turned back to look at Britt.

"Stand up. I need ta see how tall ye are." Britt stood slowly, still a bit shaky. "Gods! Ye must be half ogre." She produced a simple forest green bodice tunic dress. "Here we are. Simple, but cool." She tossed it to Britt. Captain Devarelle put her hand on her chest. "What's the matter wit ye now?" Sara trod over and looked up at her.

"I have this weird acid reflux problem all of a sudden." Britt admitted.

"Have ye had allot of ale?" Sara asked.

"No, I have barely eaten or drank since I arrived." Britt sat back down, weak with hunger.

"I oughtta blast those idiots!" Sara walked to the silk cord that summoned the servants. "You'da thought they knew better than to starve one of their own." She was disgusted.

"One of their own?" Britt asked.

"Ye are a slave aren't ye?" She asked the obvious.

"I guess that's what they're calling me." Britt said.

"We do what we can fer one another, even those of us that are a bit strange." She winked and started helping with the dress.

"Then you don't hate me?" Britt asked.

"Daffy wench, I donna even know ye. All I know fer sure is that ye are causing a horrible stir. Meriden is beside herself with worry. Roderick is acting like a dolt and Sholendor is more of a slinky creepy bastard…if that be possible."

Minakshi appeared only to be scolded brashly by Sara. She was sent whimpering back to the kitchens to obtain as much food as she could carry. Britt watched Sara with amusement. She was dressed and moving slowly, accommodating strange body aches. Sara noticed her looking around the room, growing increasingly frustrated.

"Would ye be missin' this, lass?" She held up the pouch she had placed on the table.

"Yes! Thank God you found it!" Britt gained muscle control and walked to the gnome to retrieve her gift.

"Tis quite a trinket, I'da think it well to know where ye acquired it." Sara asked cautiously.

"Roderick gave it to me the other night. He got it from a shop in the city." Britt ignored Sara's glare and walked to the bed. She plopped down and dropped the gem in her hand. It was clear that she was not going to be able to fool this gnome as easily as she fooled some of the others. Instead of commenting further, Sara walked to the bed and scaled the mattresses. She gathered Britt's hair and attempted to finish the task of neatness in an unmanageable forest of frizz.

"Well, that's nice." She popped off finally. Britt ignored her and sat still between winces. "The way I figure it, ye must a come from so far off that even Roderick woulda know yer haim."

"Why do you say that?" Britt asked.

"I do know that elf fer the better part 'o his life and I nev'ra known him ta give treasures to humans." She tugged harder. "As well ye donna act like any human I know, much less look like one."

"Why don't you just come out and say what you are thinking, Sara?" Britt barked.

"Really now? Tis that what ye are after, the truth?" Sara jumped off the bed, showing not the slightest sign of hesitation. "It seems ta me that ye mighta bein willing ta give it afore ye expect it." She put the brush down and opened the door to yell for Minakshi. Britt sat stunned.

"All right Sara, ask away." Britt crossed her arms.

"Where are ye from?" Sara challenged.

"Outer space."

"Really now."

"You asked."

"I was hopin fer the truth." Sara huffed.

"Look at me." Britt demanded. "I am from another universe, from a planet called Zeneria. I don't know how I got here, or how to get home. I'm not happy about it either, so work with me here. I just spent the last few hours having my mind melted by an elf. Well actually no one else, except Gherkin knows what I went through or has a clue of where I came from. If anyone else finds out, I'm afraid I'm gonna have to kill a lot of elves."

Britt stalked to look down at Sara. "You and I have been shoved together for the time being. I would rather be friends than enemies. I don't expect you to be my slave and I didn't ask for it." She reached for Sara. "Furthermore, I didn't ask for Sholendor, Meriden, or Roderick. I can't help the way I look and don't intend to become Sholendor's little sex toy if I can avoid it. I have no intention of harming your precious little Meriden, if she doesn't get in my way. I just want to play nice and go home, got it?" Somehow she felt better after getting all the frustration out. She soon realized that she was holding Sara off the ground by her tunic. She felt a bit of pride and admiration when she also realized that the gnome was not intimidated.

"I see. I wonder if ye would mind PUTTING ME DOWN NOW!" She yelled in Britt's face. Britt lowered her to the ground. "That's better, ye brute. So 'tis the long and the short of it, aye." Before she could go on, Minakshi appeared with two other slaves and a trove of food. They arranged it on the tables and bed and left quickly. Sara stood aside as Britt dove into her feast. A few moments into the gluttony, Britt looked up.

"Aren't you hungry?" She asked.

"I am not a companion slave, lass. I am yer slave. 'Tis not right for me to eat such foods. I will wait till yer finished and eat in the servant's quarters later." She folded her arms.

"Oh, bullshit! Here, I insist you have lunch with me." Britt pulled up a chair and pointed to it. Sara grinned and seated herself next to a leg of lamb. The women ate on and talked like sisters. Sara asked a number of pointed questions about Britt's home that the human fired off answers to without hesitation. She knew Sara was testing her. After a time Britt decided to see if she could make the gnome laugh.

"You people don't laugh much do you?" She observed.

"I am a slave. I am ugly. An' now I have a giant pain in the arse to care fer. I have nothing to laugh about." She grinned.

"Ha, Ha...Oh...You're a pistol, Sara. I'm glad I got stuck with you too." Britt said mirthfully. While the two chatted on, Meriden floated up the tower steps with elfish stealth, deciding to eavesdrop as was her nature. She could hear the husky laugh of what must be her new companion slave. The idiot was going on about fat goblins and smelly ogres. Eventually, to her disbelief, she could almost swear she heard the light sound of laughter coming from Sara! She had been briefly told of this human and was not excited. Furthermore, Sholendor's decision to award this slave with a servant of her own was outlandish at best. And of all slaves, HER slave! She had tried to ignore the chatter in the main hall. The talk was of a giant of indescribable beauty. Meriden frowned now as she silently pressed her ear to the door. She knew her protests to her mother and the counsel when she was told Sholendor was her mate were a waste of time. Now she must learn to deal with his treachery. So this was just the start.

"Come on! I'll show you how to knock one down." Britt was teaching Sara how to knock a troll off its feet! Meriden could hear both of their footfalls across the plank floor. Her mouth dropped open in disbelief. What a liar this human must be. No human had the strength to knock a troll to its knees. She could not believe Sara was buying this load of rubbish. Clearly she had lost what was left of her little yellow mind. Next she heard the unfamiliar sound of play. She peeked through the keyhole. Sara was on top of some type of large animal rolling around on the floor like a court jester.

"Wanna see if we can spit on anyone from the top of the tower?" Britt giggled. Meriden watched in horror as the uncommon female jumped up and ran to the balcony.

"I'll give ye a silver piece if ye hit an elf!" Sara shouted with glee and followed.

Meriden stood upright and closed her eyes. This was going to stop this minute! She mumbled a freezing spell to stop the insolent servants in their tracks. As soon as the incantation was over she bobbed down to see the effects. Sara was glued to the floor, a mask of terror on her features as was expected. Britt, on the other hand was jumping forward to reach the wall, oblivious of her companion. Meriden stood up. How could this be? She could hear Sara inside the room now.

"Oh blessed mother! Britteny ye gotta come away from the wall child!" She begged.

Britt turned to see Sara riveted to the floor, waving her arms to keep her balance. "What the hell is wrong with you?" She giggled at first. Realizing that her new friend was in distress, she started toward Sara in concern.

"Shhhh! Someone magickal knows what we are about! T'will be the death of us both!" Sara's voice trembled. "I have nev'ra done something so stupid!"

"Whaddya mean, someone magick?" Before Sara could answer her, she heard the door creaking open. She turned to see a frail ghost of a female elf holding it open.

None of them moved at first. Meriden was distressed. She had worked to build her nerve outside the door but found, when face to face with the newcomer, it had all been in vain. Sara could feel her face going numb with panic. Meriden had never used magick on her that she had been aware of. After what seemed hours, Meriden moved with caution to step into the room. She was concentrating on retaining every amount of courage she had worked so hard to find. She bravely shut the door and paced to the two slaves standing, staring at her in the middle of the room. She was hoping she would actually see the enormous human female move in the same way one watches a horrific accident with morbid curiosity. Her wish came true when Britteny stepped between her and Sara, as if shielding the gnome. Meriden's white brow drew together. How could this be?

"Why do you still animate?" She asked.

"Animate?" Britt retorted.

"Yes! How is it that you can move when I set a still spell upon the both of you?" Her spirit was spiraling to a frantic point in the midst of the unknown. Responding to the situation, she searched her memory for any type of just such a situation. Never had a spell like this failed for her, especially when directed to a simple human. She glared up at the woman, not in anger, but deep thought. Her jewel like ruby eyes scanned over the figure before her. The truth hit her like a cold blade in her chest. She staggered back to grasp for the chair behind her.

"You gestate a magical life!" Meriden blurted out.

"I what? I WHAT?!" Britt bent over to look the rail thin elf in the eyes. "Did you say gestate, like pregnant?"

"Yes! You carry a magical life inside your body! How can this be?" She looked past Britt to Sara. Sara avoided her gaze and looked at the ceiling. "What has happened here?" Meriden demanded.

Britt was lost in thought and overwhelming feeling. Perhaps that is why she had been so ill. She was half sure it could not be true, yet again; it was probable that standard birth control did not work on elf sperm. Part of her was desperate for answers and a way out and part of her was warm and strange. Her daze was shattered by Meriden's screeching voice.

"That is why the spell did not work! You are protected by the life within you!" She raged.

"You might be wrong, Meriden. I am protected against such things. I mean babies, not magick. It would be a very long shot to have gotten knocked up on the first try." She was talking more to herself than to Meriden.

"What do you mean, "first try"? Dragon pups are ingested into the stomach and feed off acid. You just swallow an egg! It is that simple." Meriden explained.

"OH! Well, there you have it. Whew! Yea. A dragon ….A DRAGON?!"

"Yes, you idiot! You carry a dragon pup in your gut! What did you think I was speaking of?"

"Nothing!" Britt was quick to cover up. "I just misunderstood you is all." She tottered back and plopped down on another chair against the wall. Her deception and guilt did not go unnoticed by Sara, who had been forgotten about for the time being. Was she really carrying a dragon pup in her gut? How the hell did she get pregnant with a dragon and what the hell was she going to do with it?

Meriden released Sara from the statue like stance and kept an eye on Britt. "I need to know where you got the egg." She pried.

"I honestly have no clue. I don't even know what a dragon egg looks like. Is this going to kill me?" Britt asked frantically as she placed her hands on her stomach.

"I don't know. I don't think so. All one must do is carry the pup for nearly two moon cycles and then vomit it up. You can vomit?" She had seen humans vomit but they were standard slaves.

"Trust me, I can vomit. I can projectile vomit actually." Britt felt a bit better knowing it would be that simple. The thought of expelling the pup from her body flashed momentarily in her mind, bringing her brief sorrow. She kept thinking of alien births gestated in human bodies. More times than not, they were brutal at best. The majority of these situations resulted in the gruesome death of the human.

"Well, you will just have to cough it up now! A human is simply not permitted to bear such an honor. Start vomiting." Meriden poised herself for the show.

"No! Start vomiting?! I'm not killing it. Get your own dragon." Britt laughed.

"Clearly you fail to understand!" Meriden's voice elevated to a pitch that would cause a dog to howl. Sara had opted to stay neutral and silent.

"A dragon's egg is a gift of great honor and prestige. It is simply not fit for a slave. You have to kill it." Meriden had started to hop with every word in her anger as a spoiled child in a fit of rage. Britt started laughing openly at the site of the petite white elf having a tantrum.

"O.K. Make me." Britt stood and crossed her arms, still giggling under her breath. If what she assumed was true, this pup's magick could protect her from magick. If what she had heard were true, Meriden was probably the most powerful magick worker around. The situation was sounding better and better. This was aside, but not to be measured against, the fact that now she possessed a life within her and it would take a much larger, more experienced individual to sever that bond than Meriden.

"Make you?" Meriden physically backed down, unaware that she had given Britt a physical message that she was trained to note.

"Yea. This dragon is MY baby. Mine. My body. My baby. My dragon. If you want it, you will have to kill me to get it." Britt, grounded with an overwhelming feeling of motherly love starting to grow, knew she meant what she said completely.

Before Meriden could reply, a servant rapped at the door.

"I beg your forgiveness, Your Highness. The carriage awaits to escort you to the games."

"Yes, of course!" Meriden yelled. "We will be down shortly." Meriden dismissed the gnome with a wave of her hand. "As for you both, make ready for the ride through the city. Sara, finish grooming her quickly and bring her about to the carriage. I will meet you both there." Meriden walked stiffly to the door.

"I must be off to thank my groom to be for this generous gift." She turned to them both, her face like marble. This set Sara on edge. She had seen

Meriden frightened, angered, and often melancholy, but never seeping with venom. "I would advise not a word of this reach Sholendor, lest he invents a way to extract this mess from all our hides." She slammed the door behind her.

Chapter 12
To Fit In

Zeneria Prime was a planet of primeval forests, vast oceans and pirates. There were only four truly apparent signs on the surface of advanced civilizations. They were four simple white communications towers that spiraled elegantly from the four corners of the planet. All other complexes had been under the largest of the continental shelves or buried deep beneath the mountains and oceans. Waves crashed against a thick wall of treated glass. Inside the compound, Canga could hear their rhythm. She absently placed her hand on the glass to touch the azure blue. Lower she could bend to see the beauty of the bountiful life on the reef. The room was dark and alone. Behind her, a white suspension tank glowed a cryptic aqua offering no comfort. She longed to be in her beach tree house with Britt, drinking cold ale and telling stories. Later they would strip down and head for the surf to swim with Monika under the stars.

They had all been summoned to a meeting. She had chosen to arrive early. Intrusive emotions had severed her grip on logic. Thought was painful. Communication had become difficult. Each action was wrapped with pain, leaving her vulnerable and insufficient. She had gone underground since the assassination, opting for isolation over confusing comfort. Canga had never been the type to soften under pressure and she almost loathed sympathy. In times of crisis, her gift was solitary confinement. Her embraces intimidated most and worked only to expose an uncomfortable awkwardness within herself. Instead, she hovered close to those she loved, naturally emanating strength and assuredness. Britt was much the same. Each possessed the aura of authority rather than nurturing femininity. One was more likely to receive an embrace from Orin or Monika. Her dark face twitched and flexed with stress. She was a leader of worlds and trained so. Even among her squadron members, the emotions that threatened to evolve into blind rage were not welcome. Losing Britt was real. It brought home the naked truth of incompletion. Heroes may be hard to harm; yet when damaged, deep is the wound.

She backed away from the glass. Dressed in her black fighter uniform, she was almost invisible outside the illumination of the tank. She stepped to the control panels and touched a viewer button. The ceiling of the conference room lit up with the stars that she called home. She wandered past the Andromeda and touched on the Eliptica.

The door slid open behind her admitting Siggurd, Boomer and Monika. Each of them greeted her and took a place at the conference table. It was strange; no one chose to comment on the current events. Canga could only imagine it was pure infuriation that kept them clammed up. She walked to the conference table on the lower level of the spacious room and sat next to Siggurd.

"Dawson, he is out but will be back at any moment." She referred to her squad mate. "Where is my brother?" She asked Monika.

"He is right behind us. He stopped to make a call." She kept staring out into the sea. Canga knew Monika wished nothing more than to plummet into the depths of her natural home and not return for a time. The door slid open once more and Billy walked though followed by Orin, Loco and Dawson.

"I think Meadows is coming. She has been locked in her lab ya know for some time now." Billy informed them.

They all sat at the oval shaped table in front of the glowing tank. Zenerio was no longer capable of surviving outside the weight bearing therapy of water. His liquidating bones could no longer uphold his massive frame.

"It's gonna get ugly." Dawson stated.

"We know." Siggurd was not inclined to discuss the situation until Zenerio was present, feeling it important to organize all the facts.

Zenerio emerged through a tunnel that emptied into the stark tank. He was being wheeled in by his personal servant and was positioned in front of the tank facing the table.

"I am sure you all know why you have been summoned here today. Before we begin any discussion, there is pertinent information that I have asked Meadows to organize and present for this squadron. I feel this information is necessary to a complete investigation and resolution of the current situation".

Meadows entered the room. Placing a folder on the table next to Billy, she lifted the remote for the visual monitor. Fondling the instrument as though it gave her comfort, she began.

"As we are all aware, the political situation that has erupted within the last few days is a direct result of continuing efforts on the part of Jeff Kolbert to obtain jurisdiction and legal rights to designated locations within the rim systems. I know that all of you, as should be, were aware of Britt's involvement with Mr. Kolbert. This, however, as some of you may be aware, was only the beginning or shall I say, top layer to a much larger conspiracy. It has been speculated that Jeff Kolbert was only a smoke screen. Captain Devarelle made a formal statement prior to the attempted assassination. In her report, she provided solid evidence of political maneuvers orchestrated by Prime Minister Szelezenda to incite conflict in the rim systems.

"It is our belief that this is being done to obscure the "special" relationship that the Zenerian Empire now shares with the mid-core and primary core galactic governments. Prime Minister Szelezenda is very well aware of our Emperor's failing health. The elimination of Captain Devarelle is merely the next step in a plan that will set a chain reaction. Our decision to retaliate this tragedy will open or close the doors to an impending multi galactic conflict." She paused to allow for comments and questions.

"So you don't think Jeff was the one who had her snuffed?" Boomer asked.

"I believe Jeff was under the impression he was following orders to eliminate Captain Devarelle. I, however, do not believe that Jeff realized that the person that he attempted to assassinate was indeed his fiancée. Furthermore, I have a hard time believing that Jeff Kolbert would have chosen to risk his entire amassed fortune to dip into the thick of such a, how shall I say it, galactic entanglement." She offered.

"What are you telling us, Meadows?" Monika asked outright, as was her nature.

"The Eliptician government manipulated Jeff into believing he had a chance of continuing his reign of assimilations within our rim systems. Basing information on combined sources from each of you and other field pirates, we now believe that Mr. Kolbert was provided with that fleet that we so conveniently wiped out not long ago. In doing so we have, in their eyes, drawn first blood. Because we operate outside the standard Galactic government, we believe that the Eliptican Government will suspend action in anticipation of our retaliation. At that time, we believe the Eliptica will declare war. Not on Zeneria but against the primary Andromedian formal governments."

"On Andromeda prime." Siggurd echoed.

"Precisely, sir." Meadows concurred.

"That's one hell of a fight they're picking." Boomer said.

"This will not be a war of two Galaxies. The Stinette is partially governed and operated by Eliptica. She will be subdued into service. Andromeda prime will then be forced to make a choice of joining us or negotiating with Eliptica in order to avoid such a conflict."

"This is not good." Billy observed. "Andromeda will insist we operate under galactic regulations. Dis or she may turn us over to Eliptica."

"The question is, can we win a galactic scale confrontation against Eliptica and Stinette?" Zenerio added.

"As I see it, man, we have limited choices." Loco stated. "We got not too many options amigos. If we strike back, our own galaxy hangs our hides out to dry or they insist we give up our sovereignty. If they don't feel like that, we get fed to the wolves. Either way we lose."

Meadows raised the remote and pointed at the screen, commanding a specified view of the systems Thernix. She touched her left weapons gauntlet, producing a thin pointer.

"We have even considered staying neutral. Alas, this will fail as well." She circled the systems in question. "You see there is a little loophole we have neglected to sew up; Thernix." She could almost see their minds working out the details. "Not just the mother planet but the entire solar system. The Thernix system is not under Zenerian contract or protection. Even though we have a very strong influence and presence there, technically they are sitting ducks. This is very well known in all three galaxies. Let's say we choose to stay out of it. Does anyone here think that is going to solve anything?" She asked.

"Of course not." Canga supported her unsaid theory. "Dey want us. We are what is holding dem from all else and until it is we that are gone dey will not be happy. Dey will use the Thernix system to coax us into battle." They all nodded in agreement.

"Even with the support of the merchant's guilds, legally we are not responsible for Thernix. This means that, legally, they belong to the Andromeda." Zenerio offered.

"So we evacuate." Orin said.

"We, as you know Orin, we have already begun evacuations. Yet it will do little good. Possession of that system would put their military forces right at our back door." She pointed again.

"If they take us, they take us. We are not part of Andromeda. It is a very large stepping stone." Said Monika.

"We have been at peace for so long." Orin reminded them. "So many lives are going to be lost if it gets out of hand."

Monika changed the picture on the screen to a full sized picture of Captain Devarelle. "Now for the interesting part." She started. "These galaxies are banking on the fact that Britt is dead. They already know that Zenerio is very ill. The truth is, there is reason to believe Britt survived the assassination attempt." None of her squadron partners appeared surprised. "As you all know, the site was examined in great detail by not only galactic forensic teams but ours as well. All information has been kept top secret at the request of both Zenerio and Prime Minister Trudent. Upon detailed research, it has been confirmed that the hangar in question was completely void of interstellar unidentified remains."

"What the hell is that supposed to mean?" Siggurd barked. "What about human remains? The report I read stated that they had found humanoid remains at the site. It's not like there are millions of us flying around." He stated.

"The information I am about to give you is very sensitive. For some time now it has been documented that our captain is not completely human." Every member of the squadron began talking at once. Meadows set down the remote, signaling to her teammates that she would wait until they subsided to provide more information.

"Yes Siggurd, human remains were located on the site. This is also the information that was given to the press and to Andromeda prime. No one outside this room knows that Britt is not 100% of earth."

"For Christ sake, did she know?" Dawson's voice was dry as a funeral drum.

"She was informed at the age of fifteen. At that time the physicians that were in charge of her health followed standard Zenerian procedures and Britt chose to keep the information completely confidential."

"Well there were at least fifty other interstellar life forms in that hangar. Did we check all of them?" Boomer asked.

"There was no need." Meadows sat down and rubbed her temples. "Not only did Britt decide to keep it confidential, she also refused further testing. As you all know, by Zenerian law everyone, even pirates, have the right to refuse testing of any nature."

"You must have something. Dey took a sample, dey did. Dey found out dat she was different?" Billy pushed. "Why are you making us dig, sister?"

"Because we don't know what she is, Billy. No one does." Zenerio came to Meadow's defense.

"She had a really rough time. From the reports I have been given recently it seems she went through a long period of denial and did her best to fit in." Zenerio informed. A lull fell as each of them felt just a bit sad and ashamed.

"Well now that the cat is out of the bag, there has to be some way to check DNA and samples to find her, right?" Dawson asked.

"Dawson. I don't think you completely comprehended what Zenerio said. We don't know what she is. I have spent the last two days searching every form of life in this galaxy and a few others. Zip. Zero. Nothing. I'm going to have to have a bit more time to do research on what we do have of her to even get close." She stood again and walked to the picture. "I can, however, tell you what we do know. I'm breaching a confidentiality code right now, but I think we all agree the situation is urgent enough to justify my invasion." Pointing to Britt she began.

"What we know so far. We are all going to search. Tissue samples that have been maintained for medical information have revealed that our captain stopped aging around the age of twenty. Her cells possess a regenerative property that allows them to withstand the aging process. When tested they resist, so far, thirty thousand different forms of disease."

"I have seen her sick." Boomer piped in.

"You have seen her hungover. Do any of you ever remember her having a cold? Flu? Any sickness known to be common in humans?" She asked. No answer. "So when testing samples, be aware and test for a high regenerative rate and a killer immune system." She stepped back for a moment and seemed to falter, her exhaustion of three days of stress and research showing. She took a deep breath and soldiered on.

"I have taken the time to go over videos that we use in cadet training." She changed the picture to illustrate. "This video feed was taken three years ago during the evacuation of the X13 fuel facility." She pointed to Devarelle jumping out of her fighter and running towards the engulfing flames. "Any of you remember that?" Meadows asked.

"Yea, sure. What was the big deal? We did a bunch of runs like that." Loco was very eager to understand.

"All of you have taken physics. Figure it out. Here are the equations." She flashed statistics on the screen. "I was watching this feed and it occurred to me that she was in the inferno long before some of you even left your ships." She was interrupted.

"Holy shit." Dawson seemed to pale. "She would have been running at what…around eighty miles an hour to get to the blast zone as fast as she did."

"Correct. If we would have witnessed that speed in an open sprint, Britt may have reached speeds of over eighty miles per hour. Any of you willing to race that?" She shifted to the next screen.

"This was taken a year ago in the Kekta system during the riots." She moved the frames in slow motion. "Watch when she comes into the area of action." She stopped the frame. "There were, as far as we can see, at least three Kektians in pursuit. See here?" She allowed the frames to move in slow motion.

"What the hell is that?" Siggurd asked.

"I think it is some type of force field." Meadows offered. The company watched as Britt moved. Each of the attackers seemed to be propelled or forced backwards. Some appeared to be knocked unconscious.

"So. From what I can hypothesize thus far, Britt seems to have some type of natural ability to project or propel herself." She reversed back and again played it in slow motion. "Notice anything else?"

"Her feet aren't touching the ground." Orin was the first to notice. "She's floating."

As if some type of sedative had been pumped through the air ducts, the 23rd squadron went numb with information overload. Monika leaned against the wall.

"This may be the reason she chose not to elaborate on her findings." Zenerio woke them from the trance.

"What do you mean?" Boomer asked.

"Look at how it is we are acting." Canga whispered. "Dat girl never once asked us for help. She never needed it. But she does always let us shine. I tink she just wanted a family. I tink she should be allowed to have a family dat won't poke at her with sticks and cringe in fear." She closed her eyes to fight back the tears. "How can dis have happened? How could we have done dis?" She was still in control.

"You did nothing, Canga. Britt chose to keep her secret. Perhaps she kept it because being human was the only thing she had left?" Siggurd comforted Canga.

Zenerio moved in the tank. "Now my children, we must take this information and work with it. We know that she did not die in that explosion. I have spoken to Dom at length. The day of the explosion, Celeste learned that he felt Britt. He has assured me that she did not die. He was close enough to that hangar to have use of his gifts. The rest of the universe, however, believes that she died that day. I suggest we keep up the farce that she is gone for reasons I should not have to expound upon. I have decided to allow one of you to search for her out of the systems. We have always worked in pairs, yet if I send two it will start intrigue."

"I will be da one going." Canga stated.

"I was hoping you would volunteer, Canga. It will be easy for us to report that you, of all of us, is stricken with grief and has chosen to stay on Zeneria prime and mourn." Meadows said.

"Siggurd. You are now the leader of the Zenerian Empire. It will be up to you to delegate further undercover research missions. As well, you will be the face of our empire in my absence. It is imperative that we contact every Zenerian outpost with procedures. Remember, no one outside this room is to know what we have discussed here in regards to Britt. Hopefully she will be found quickly." With this he bowed and signaled his servant to wheel him back into the tunnel.

"He has grown so weak. This trauma has left him near incapacitated." Meadows informed them.

Siggurd stood. "Well, the good news is she may very well be alive. The bad news is we have no clue where to begin looking for her."

"Loco and I will start by shaking down some of Jeff's contacts and offices. Maybe she got wind and back tracked." Boomer was aware, as were the rest of the group, that Jeff had left the galaxy shortly after the explosion had occurred. He had been followed. From their reports it was known that he was now cruising at break neck speed toward the divide systems.

"Excellent call. I need to get working on informing the systems. We need to make sure the Thernix systems are totally evacuated before Eliptica finds out we are on to them. Billy, I will need you and Monika to take charge of Thernix prime. We need to scour that crime scene. Bring back every form of tissue you can come up with. Don't leave any stone unturned." He ordered.

"I need to get back to the lab. I should be all right. I am going to download all of your ships with chemical and tissue testing software as well as coded information channels on any new developments I come up with. Check with me when you leave so we can get you all installed." Meadows had been hoping for a few hours of sleep soon. It would have to wait just a bit longer.

"Dawson, you do what you do best. I want every underbellied crook in this galaxy pumped for information." Siggurd had no doubt that Byron would find information no one else could. He had a way of convincing thugs to talk and was not above blackmail.

"Orin. I am afraid it is up to you to go through Britt's personal possessions. Dr. Meadows is going to need all the pure tissue samples and hair samples you can come up with. Go through her files, the works, and see if you can find anything that could lead us to her." His squad members were filing out the door when he touched Canga's arm.

"Anything you need, Canga. Take anything you need. As soon as you find something let us know. If you are in any danger send word. I am not too comfortable sending you out like this." Siggurd held her arm with intended admiration and love.

"I would have it no other way, my brother. It is that I can travel much quicker alone. I will only have to follow my own heart."

Chapter 13

Anger Management

Britt and Sara were placed in the back of the Princess's open carriage. Sholendor had returned from his urgent errand. He had not seen Britt since he had left her in the throne room to run off to Havaland. Meriden noted her fiancé's hungry appraisal of the human but, to her comfort, noticed the human was interested in everything but.

Meriden ascended gracefully into the white carriage to the plush royal blue seat. Britt wriggled against Sara, crammed in the snug compartment at the back of the carriage rumble seat. She had stowed a few pieces of cheese and handed one to the gnome, winking. Sara had warned her on the way down the stairs that they were not permitted to speak unless spoken to. Britt could see the fear wading behind her eyes. The afternoon had clearly reevaluated a facet of the relationship between Sara and Meriden that Sara was horridly uncomfortable with. Britt knew appropriation of such situations and honored the request. This insignificant drama was marked as trivial when compared to all else that had befallen her since her arrival. Life had magically turned on in full force, blasting her in the gob, spiraling out of control. In her ignorance and confusion she admitted impotently that she had done little to stop it.

The carriage lurched forward down the palace lanes. Sholendor had mounted a great black steed and rode ahead of the carriage, as was customary before the marriage. Devilishly Britt's mind replayed imprinted scenes of Roderick in that same lane not but a day or so ago. Time, she could not get time out of her mind. She had been there just short of 3 days. That was, in her interpretation, three days too long. What must be going on in the Zenerian Empire? Would they search for her or had they simply left her for dead? She reached up and touched her chest. Her expression set as she surmised the current events within the Zenerian Empire. Canga was surely experiencing a hell that Britt would have never wished. Realizing this brought about clarity of duty. In the slave's seat crammed next to Sara, her thoughts began sifting through a chain of deductive reasoning in an attempt to foresee the chaos that was surely disrupting the Andromeda.

She had been in her hangar. She had been inebriated, but she remembered approaching Opus and preparing him for liftoff. That was all she remembered. Her hair had been singed and in the light of observation it now occurred to her that her body had been sore when she had come to at the lake. She shifted, uncomforted in the knowledge that her people may very well believe her dead. They would search the site if this were the case. They would only have one option. Britt stiffened. It would be necessary for information as to the origins of her innate DNA to be disclosed for any substantial investigation to bear fruit. Even if they discovered she was not dead, it was going to be a rude awakening for her squad partners to know she was not fully human. The situation just got better and better.

Loud cheers and the smell of primitive culture broke her trance. As was customary, her mind shifted gears. She leaned over and addressed Sara.

"What does it eat?" She asked.

"What are ye talking about?" Sara whispered harshly.

Britt pointed to her chest. "The baby, what will it need to eat when it is born?" She asked again.

Sara clapped her hand over the human's mouth. "Hush up, you daffy bitch! Do ye want Sholendor to hear?" She hissed.

"He can hear me all the way back here?" She squeaked.

Sara nodded her head and frowned.

"Damn!" It seemed she would have to be more sensitive to such abilities. She should have had a better idea after Meriden had "sensed" the life in her. Why was it Sholendor had not when they walked down the front steps? Perhaps it was because Meriden was a female. It was clear she would, in the future, be wary of her assumptions. Then again, she had absolutely no idea of when she had swallowed the egg. Her face lit up when the realization hit. It must have been the fruit she had choked on her first day in the palace. She had eaten little else and had only become ill after that incident. Now she had to wonder as to how a dragon's egg had ended up in her bowl of fruit?

The crowd was held at bay by the palace guards. She was the Corositian Dev Cat in the zoo, on display for all to see. She was taking part in a royal parade around the city only to circle back to the area directly behind the palace. Britt turned her head to see Meriden's tiny white hand waving to the onlookers perched in the apartment balconies of the great wall and lining the streets and shops. When she looked back they had passed a large swinging tavern sign that read Ruddy Mudders. She scanned the crowd and in a short time saw Osizio waving to her with glee. He pointed to his wife next to him. She however did not seem as excited to greet Osizio's rescuer. The female ogre smiled weakly and waved at elbow length. Next to her stood a rather well built human with dark hair and sultry eyes. Britt raised her hand and waved to Osizio and offered her friend a brilliant smile. It caused the human to step back and the ogress's attitude to chill all the more. She expected these creatures to be wary of her, she was different, and this was a natural reaction. A few minutes down the road she heard a loud "Hello Britt!" and to her joy saw Amaranth jumping and waving. Roderick stood in contrast next to his shorter brother. He chose not to wave, as was his subtle nature, yet smiled and nodded his head. She nodded back and produced a smile that came from the very bottom of her emotions all the while aware of the impact he had upon her senses. Donovan could be seen tipping an invisible topper and bowing in her direction. Britt giggled and waved back. When she looked down, Sara sat, arms crossed, shooting daggers at her.

"Are ye havin a grand time, lass?" She huffed.

"Yea, this is kind of cool." She chuckled, stopping short when Sara's glare grew darker. "Oh all right, have it your way." She stopped waving and put her hands on her lap. "Besides, I don't know anyone else." She protested. This declaration ended in a few moments when they had circled around town and were on the way back. They were passing the elfish district for business and commerce. She spotted Ferrin, Rowland, and Gherkin standing together and once again waved her hello. The elder elf hopped up and waved, holding Gilda high allowing her to loft a bit and bark out her enthusiasm. Britt touched her stomach and smiled. Perhaps Gherkin had given her this gift. It calmed her a bit to see Gilda again. It would be very cool to take a dragon like Gilda home, once it got past quarantine that is.

They would be seated on the opposite end of the great area from the prince. Sara whispered to her that it was custom for the couple to be separated thus until they were wed. High in a balcony seat that overlooked the main entrance arena proper, Britt was placed on the right side of the princess and Sara sat behind them in a small wooden seat. Directly in front of them, Britt could see animals being lead out of the bowels of the arena to prepare for the opening of the Beltane games.

"I wonder where my mother is?" Meriden said to herself.

"Maybe she got tied up with business." Britt said.

Meriden shot a look of hatred at the human. "You will never speak to me as an equal if you wish to live." Her voice seethed.

"Yes, Oh Royal Premenstrual One." She mumbled.

They watched the opening ceremonies in silence. Britt enjoyed the rustic music and cultural dancing of the simple folk of the plains. Dwarves provided a statue and performed a droning number that had the sound of mountain halls. Some obscure tribe of Arosa dwellers danced with colorful feathers around the ring. The drums were invigorating. Britt noticed the colossal building was filling up to its full capacity. She had no idea there were this many people living in the city. She considered the fact that a great number of them could have come from other settlements for the occasion. Meriden sat still as stone, save for the occasional wave to the masses. It took some time of pomp and circumstance for the actual games to begin. Servants bowed before Meriden with food and drink, which she waved away. Britt's mouth watered, yet she did not think it wise to reach for food that the princess had been offered.

An announcer rode a fine horse to the middle of the arena to introduce the first combat game. He spun around in a spectacle and bowed to usher in two very large creatures, heavily armed. So it was to be raw carnage. Britt sat back and folded her arms looking bored. In reality she was scanning the crowd to find Roderick. She spotted him just below her to the right, in the front row. The creatures were at it now, bounding around the ring in a fumbling brutality of blood and steel. A fight can be defined. As a jeweler knows a stone of quality to a ditch pebble, so does a honed combatant in such an occurrence. She showed little interest until the larger of the two ogre-like creatures cut the other in half, sending pulsating streams of thick blood spackling the lower rows. The carnage continued as other creatures charged into the arena, making it a blood bath.

"I take it the rules are rather vile? Perhaps nonexistent." She stated.

"What is the point of playing if the outcome is not final?" Meriden snipped.

Captain Devarelle chose to ignore ignorance. She was disturbed by the waste and barbaric thirst for death that was being allowed to masquerade as sport. Before the servants could clear one body, another beast jumped into the ring and gave a savage cry of war. One appeared to be of the same species as Donavan. He bared his fangs and went down on all fours, fur standing on end.

"Ooh. He looks wicked." Britt commented. "So what is the gist of this, if there is one?" She asked.

"It keeps going as each warrior defeats the other, until the Prince announces a Prime Victor of this event." She bit coldly. "Perhaps you would like to do me a favor and participate?" .

"Na, It would be unfair to the rest of the participants." Britt said with total sincerity. "Besides, I don't just kill for the sake of killing. Only the mindless are capable of such a thing." She popped a stolen cookie in her mouth. Meriden stared at her for a moment in self-motivated anticipation. Britt did not notice when she shifted to call one of her servants over.

"Take my companion slave and have her put on the dock. She is of the assumption that she is a great warrior. I wish to allow her the chance to show her ability." Meriden ordered.

"Oh really?" Britt looked at the much smaller woman. She could feel Sara tense behind her.

"Yes really." Meriden hissed.

"Sholendor will have a FIT." Sara tried to warn her.

"I care little for what he thinks. She is my slave and I will do with her what I wish. I dare him to stop me before all of Garath to save a human." She snapped her pale face back to the ring.

Britt stood and turned back to Meriden. "So this is how we're playing it then? No problem there, little miss. I'll be right back and then we'll see who is going to be intimidating who." Britt surprised both Meriden and Sara by going with the arena servants with little more than an evil giggle.

Britt was put into a line of servants behind a small boy. She hoped it would not come to allowing such a small lad out in the ring full of vicious killers. So it went for a time. The wolf creature had done fine, killing two beasts, before he simply got sloppy and had his legs severed. She had been keeping track of him in the midst of flying body parts and pulsating blood geysers.

Britt noticed the small boy was up next.

"Hey, what are they gonna do with that kid?" She asked, sliding to the edge of her seat.

"He is going to fight." The guard said without a second thought.

"You're kidding, right? He can't be older than what, 12?" She blurted out. The terrified human boy grabbed a rattan and started running against the wall, trying to avoid a giant ogre waving a spiked club. The crowd was going wild.

"So, do you think Sholendor will call an end to it soon?" Britt asked.

"Of course not, at least not until the boy is dead. Where is the sport in that?" The guard jested.

"I am going out there to save him." She announced to the guard.

"Go ahead. I could care less. You will be doing me a favor, human." He laughed.

With that, Britt approached the gate. Spinning her body with unspoken grace, she landed catlike in the ring. Meriden moved to the edge of her seat, gripping the stone before her. She glanced to Sholendor. His face was twisted in rage, yet she knew he would never dare stop the games to save a human slave. Not even this one. Nevertheless, she felt frightened and almost called Britt back.

A commotion erupted when Roderick of Darmuth Anor nearly vaulted into the ring. He was halted by Rowland of Sid O'Sala's apparent confidence that the fight was equally matched. Rowland looked at Roderick as he gripped his companion's arm.

"Sit tight, my brother and watch how it's done just remember to pray for mercy for those poor bastards unfortunate enough to be in the ring with her."

Meriden looked back to her new slave walking calmly toward the human child. The boy stood frozen at the sight of the tall woman advancing toward him. An ogre had cemented in his tracks, too stupid to process this much information so quickly. He was amidst the pile of entrails from his last victory. His club was still dripping brains. The arena was shaking with the din of fevered blood lust. Britt gently took the rattan from the boy and escorted him to the nearest door. She tousled his hair before he disappeared, running through the dark arch to safety. When she turned around the ogre was smiling at her, with obvious sexual intent. He grabbed his loincloth and laughed with anticipation, fondling his genitals openly. She smiled back and walked a few paces toward him purposefully dropping the rattan. Her body seemed to shift, the green tunic dress blowing slightly in the wind around her. She placed her legs a bit apart and held her arms relaxed, but ready, her eyes never leaving her prey. She appeared to breathe slowly as if calming herself. Meriden stood up and walked to the wall, Sara next to her. She was aware that every individual hovered on a hair's breath awaiting her signal to end the impending slaughter. She was held fixated and unable to deduce such an action.

The ogre let out a cry of excitement and charged. Dropping his club half way to reaching her, he confidently began pulling down his drawers. She closed her eyes for a moment. Later, Meriden tried to recall what occurred next. Such precision was unexpected and being so had succeeded in evading even elfish logic. Britt stood solid. Grasped in her right hand and held slightly aloft, the ogre's still beating heart bled streams down her elegant arm. The big creature, dazed, had not noticed the gaping hole in his chest. He swayed back only to look down at his blood-cloaked skin. As the dirt crusted color drained he started to teeter forward. Britt simply stepped aside and allowed him to land with a rumble in the sand. She hopped a bit to avoid the pool of blood that was produced from still pumping arteries. The pulsations were powerful enough to nearly lift the mass of him from the arena floor.

Interesting, Britt thought absently. She looked at the heart in her hand and still holding it, half expected Canga to approach and take a bite out of it. Sadly she realized that this was not to be, so she dropped it. She started to wipe her hand on her tunic and grimaced. As common as you will she chose to wipe the thickening fluid on the ogre's britches that were knotted now around his knees.

Now the fun began. The other creatures in the arena had stopped their bashing and took note of the human female. Some of them attempted to fight others off for the chance to kill the now standing prize. The crowd was going wild. As if born to this type of mayhem, Britt sprang to action and ran for the wall, being chased by a large wolf like creature. To the amazement of the onlookers she ran up the side of the wall to kick up a pike off the hooks, spinning midair and forcing the heavier half of her body downwards, implanting the tip of the spear into the wolf's unsuspecting brain. Using the inertia she pulled the body, pike and all with her as her feet hit the ground, sending the body flying into the next assailant. A human male ran up behind her. She never even looked backwards, yet without hesitation leapt into the air and swung her leg like a hammer round to knock the man in the teeth, sending blood splattering over the unlucky attendees in the front row. They only screamed louder as they wiped the blood from their faces.

She was a machine. Even Rowland was shocked. He knew she was skilled, yet she had not shown him this dark side. She had not opened the door to the killer she was clearly trained to be. Her face was purposeful, as if set to a daily task that was programmed into muscle memory. The grace of her movements seemed a ballet as she lopped off limb after limb with precision cruelty. Meriden realized, once the immense shock wore off, that Britt was not killing the victims, or at least not all of them. They were running out of slaves to throw into the ring. Britt stood alone by and by.

"Just like that." Sara whispered next to Meriden. "The wench dropped them all like turds in a tub. In all me years I near 'o imagined such a thing."

"Just like that." Meriden echoed numbly.

In the heat of the battle, Meriden had lost control of her senses and began wailing encouraging shouts to her slave. If Sara's cheers had not surpassed her own volume she may have continued on so. Gathering some composure, she reluctantly slouched back to her seat dragging Sara with her. They were both at the point of hyperventilation.

"I bet ol' soggy bottom had no idea she could do that!" Sara hissed cocking her head sideways and slapping her knee. Meriden contemplated this profound revelation and the world began to brighten.

The last creature entered the ring. He was dark. He had a sword. He walked as if he knew how to use it. Britt wiped blood and sweat from her brow and prepared for real action. The opponent threw her a sword as he walked by. She caught it with ease, trying to make out what race he was. He was scarred all over. Apparently he had been in a number of these matches. His eyes showed the life of a slave born to fight against his will. He enjoyed it. It had kept him alive and made him famous. She could tell by the way the crowd erupted at the site of him that he was the finale. She also noticed both Roderick and Sholendor growing very apprehensive.

"Gogogth! Gogogth"! The crowd chanted his name. He looked at her with a cold stare.

"First I kill you, then I rape you, then I kill the child, then I win." He said loudly.

To his shock, she laughed. "Really now?"

He launched toward her, sword flying above him. As he approached, the human female dropped to the ground in a perfect split and raised her blade up, driving it into his groin to the incredible, audible discomfort of every male in the crowd. Her hands hit the dirt and she sprang up and over herself again, bending and flipping into stance. Without hesitation, she threw a dagger she had lifted from the blood soaked sand, into the air and spin kicked it into his thigh. As he bent to pull the dagger out of his bleeding leg, she approached him, kicking him in the jaw and knocking him out taking a few more seconds to lop off both of his arms ever so efficiently. Her rage was visible.

"Well it doesn't look like you'll be killing innocent creatures anymore, now does it?" He woke to see her standing over him, scrutinizing him like some insignificant insect.

"KILL HIM, KILL HIM, KILL HIM!" Came the insistent demand. She ignored the chant and made her way back to the seat above the entrance doors. Leaping through the air she secured the ledge and landed with barely a bounce. Smiling at Meriden, she bowed and took her seat.

"You have to kill him!" Meriden instructed.

"Nope. I'm afraid that's not an option." Britt informed her frankly.

"You have to! These are the rules! I demand it." She ordered.

"It seems we're having communication problems. I gave you the options." Britt stated firmly.

"You do not presume to give ME options!" Meriden roared.

Britt spoke slowly. "How would you like to get your little white ass dumped in that ring? It can be arranged." With this Meriden hiccupped. She sat down instantly and smiled at the crowd.

"I am merely trying to educate you to the tradition. Only one leaves the ring alive." Her attempt to reason was feeble at best.

"I don't care about your traditions. Besides he'll be punished enough living out the rest of his life like that." She reflected. "Maybe I should've killed him. He may have been happier."

The three women were well into a dispute when a weight crushed the arena. Sholendor was up and alive at the other end of the games.

"THESE GAMES ARE OVER!" He stormed from his plush lounge, knocking over a guard. Meriden instinctively rose like a ghost. She walked without talking towards the exit, surrounded by guards and servants. Sara grabbed Britt's hand and led her to the carriage. Meriden's terror did not go unnoticed.

"What the hell is going on? Why does Meriden look like she's gonna die?" She asked Sara.

"Iffin I guess right, she is in for a good whipping from the prince for allowing ye to fight." Sara reported. "I think she wasa hopin ye would have died."

"What?" Britt ducked and whispered.

"Ima guessin Sholendor figures Meriden knew you could do that and has made a right near arse out of him in front of all the kingdom." She said. "Tis either that or he is hot at her for almost getting his best prize killed. All I am sure of is he is going to throw a king-sized fit whenna we get back."

"I'll tell him I went on my own." Britt insisted.

"You can try, but Sholendor is always a looking for an excuse to thump her around and make her feel like a scullery wench. This is just perfect fer him." Sara looked ahead, dismissing more conversation, pretending she did not see the glower clouding Britt's features.

They were escorted into the palace swiftly and led to the prince's private library. Meriden tried to maintain composure as the guards led Britt and Sara in behind her. Meriden was trembling so badly, she was forced by Sara to sit before she fell, only to rise again and start pacing the floor. The three of them were left alone for a moment but said nothing. Meriden looked at Britt after a time and spoke.

"By all that is magical, where did you come from?" Meriden spun in the circular room of countless volumes. "I have never, ever, in my 200 years, seen the likes of you." She paced back and forth, one hand running through her hair, the other on her hip.

Sara was equally stumped. "Fer once in her life I hafta agree wit the white one. Ye are a devil in a goddess's mask."

Meriden stopped pacing. "This changes things. Everything is happening so fast. I feel faint." She sat down again. Britt stood still and allowed the other females to unwind, knowing full well the impact of the performance she just gave must have had on them.

After a few seconds Meriden looked up from her lap. "You must let me put a spell on you to hide that dragon from his sight." She begged. "If he sees it, we are all doomed. The babe will protect you from all magick yet he can still sense it."

"I'm not afraid of that skinny white bastard." Britt said.

"He is not the only skinny white bastard that you need fear." Meriden's voice lost its usual high pitched squeak. "You can not imagine what the high elfish counsel will do if they find that a human is gestating a dragon, not only to you but Sara and I as well. Sara was with you. She will be killed for sure for this treachery. I knew about it and chose not to tell anyone. We are all in this together now. You must tell NO ONE of the pup." Meriden rose to look up at Britt. "Do you intend to fight the entire elfish race?" She asked.

"No." Britt answered understanding the logic of her statements.

Please let me hide the pup for all our lives." Meriden begged. "That display in the arena will be enough to explain. I implore you."

"Does this mean we're gonna be friends?" Britt allowed a space for silence.

"If it is possible. I make no promises, yet I believe you have a clear head. I know now you are very capable of defending yourself. I can only lay bare my trust."

"That seems fair enough. I couldn't ask for more considering the circumstances. O.K. What should I do?" Britt agreed.

Meriden walked to her and moved her hands over Britt's face. "Say these words to me and mean them. Open is my heart, elf friend. Willing is my mind. Protect me with your magick, strong and kind."

Britt repeated the words and closed her eyes. A foreign sensation washed over her. In the next instant she opened her eyes. "I can hear him coming."

"The dragon babe has heightened your senses. This may be a good thing." She stepped back. "I can only hope trust is among them."

Sholendor burst through the door slamming it behind him. "What in Ren'Fordel do you think you were doing back there?!" His voice pitched unnaturally high for a male. He shoved his way past the mahogany desk. "Do you think you could keep such magick secrets from me, you little witch?!" He boomed.

Meriden cowered. "I had no idea she could perform such magick. I have only just met her this morning!" She insisted.

"Oh really! Do you enjoy making a fool of me?" He started for her. "Do you think it is wise to endanger such a precious gift? Knowing the history of my family, you knew I would do nothing to risk scandal!" He cocked his hand back, balling it into a fist. It flew toward the princess's frail face.

His rage was stopped short a few inches from Meriden's nose. Britt's hand was wrapped around the prince's wrist like a vise grip.

"Hey, now. Hold on there, big guy. I went into that ring willingly." Britt said.

"Unhand me at once! How dare you stop me from disciplining my wife!" He was frantic.

"Last time I checked, the wedding is next week. She's not your wife yet." She twisted his arm till he bent in pain. "Here's a news flash for ya, no one will be slamming anyone around while I'm here. Got it, soggy bottom? You wanna spar, I'll meet you in the ring."

Britt put her face within spitting distance of the prince. "You were the one who let me in here, smartass. Remember? That's what you get for thinking with the wrong head."

Sholendor waved his other arm as if trying to kill a violent insect. He grew more hysterical with every swipe. "You have cast a protection spell on her!" He squawked. "How dare you!"

Meriden leaned down coming equally close to his pink face. "She is my slave. Did you think I would not protect such a precious gift?" She stood back up. "You can let him go now, Britt. I think he understands that there will be no more playing 'punch the princess'." Sholendor shot up. He backed away and bumped into the desk.

"Remember Sholendor, I can choose not to marry you. I can always choose to live alone and carry out my reign as sovereign Queen of the Realm." She gained confidence and walked to him. "You would do well to remember that, Prince Soggy Bottom." She put her hands on her narrow hips and shot her fine little nose into the air in defiance.

He walked for the door. "Yes, Your Majesty." He bit. "I will remember this, for a very long time." He slammed the door.

"I don't like the sound of that." Britt observed.

"I thought he spoke quite clearly." Meriden commented.

"No. I think he's up to something. He gave up way too easily." She walked to the door and put her palm on the cool wood surface. She could somehow sense that he had gone.

"You have turned pink in places." Meriden observed.

Britt looked at her arms. "Yea, I get burned easily. I'm very white. I eventually tan a little, but rarely." She dismissed the trivial conversation. "Listen, what else do we have to get through today?"

"Oh, I canna wait fer this." Sara quipped.

"Hush, Sara!" Meriden poked her servant. "We must attend the royal ball tonight."

"We? Like me and you, we?" Britt squirmed.

"Yes, you and me, we. And you will be expected to be on your best behavior. No doubt the entire elfish community will be terrified of you." She stopped and organized her thoughts, then began to giggle.

"What's so funny?" Britt asked.

"Well, it occurred to me that for the first time as a member of the royal family, tonight I will actually have a small amount of respect." The door opened and a sea of servants swarmed to the princess. "Now off with you both to dress. Sara?" She began.

"I know, try and make her look suitable and be sure she wears black." Sara grabbed Britt's arm playfully.

"No." She turned as the servants were bustling about her like bees. "I want her in our finest black velvet gown. It is the least I can do."

Sara nodded and pulled Britt, still a bit hesitant, out the door.

Chapter 14
Don't Make Me Dance

It was a stroke of good luck that she was pregnant with a dragon at the time. Otherwise, Sara may have broken her spine getting her into the thick velvet corset. As the gnome fussed over her piles of thick hair, interlacing it with gold ribbon, Britt protested and spouted obscenities and gripped the bed frame. "I hate this kind of stuff! OUCH! I'm gonna skin you, you little dominatrix!"

"Fer the love of Ren'Fordel! You'da thought I was that ogre in the ring with ye!" Sara slapped Britt's flying hands from pulling pins as soon as Sara placed them. After what seemed the longest time of true torture in her life, Sara tugged Britt's bodice lace and pulled her by the waist to the long mirror.

"Heh! And they say I'm not a miracle worker!" Sara swatted her backside through the layers of velvet and satin. "Ay, I have forgotten something." Britt kept looking at the strange woman in the mirror. "Here ye big sot, bend down fer an old gnome." Britt bent slowly, constricted by the whale boning. She looked at the almost bald head of her companion, trying to figure out what she was doing now. "Stand up and take a look a' that!"

Britt straightened and gasped. "Sara!" She touched the sapphire amulet Roderick had given her. Sara had attached it to her own necklace with a tiny piece of silver crafted like the other ivy leaves on her necklace. "Where did you get that?"

"You just ferget about that. I hadda kill a few elves but no one's the wiser." She huffed. For a moment they both just stared into the mirror. When Sara spoke she voiced something profound. "I always a thought 'tis a great magick women have. We can change with the flip of a stitch to another creature all together. 'Tis usually not fer the good of men, but who cares?" She walked behind the dressing screen and flopped around, exiting in a simple black dress, made for a being her size. "At least I donna have ta look like a stuffed cock tonight." With that she sat down and patted the chair next to her.

"Here ye are lass, 'tis time fer me to make sure ye do not make an ass o' yerself nor Meriden." Britt sat down slowly, every moment worrying her nipples were going to pop out of the low-cut bodice. "First off, ye are a companion slave and a good one at that. Ye donna have the same rules us simple slaves have. Ye are allowed to dance and talk. No eating though. Ye must stand behind the princess at the meal and when she is done eating, ye follow 'er about the hall. In order fer ye to dance, a suitor must ask permission from Meriden, do ye understand?"

"Sara, this isn't nuclear science, I get it." Britt scoffed.

"What? .... Ferget it. All the same, ye may be asked to perform some things." She added.

"Perform? Like what?" Britt's interest was peaked now.

"I 'av only heard stories. Once ye are both in I musta leave. It is said that humans are, at times, asked to do some near to beastie things." She backed away in anticipation of an eruption.

"We'll just see about that." Britt stood up. "Let's get this silly shit over with before I lose my temper."

"Oh, and Britt." Sara called from behind the voluminous skirts. "He isna gonna be here."

"Who?" Britt asked.

"Ye know flat backed well who I'm a talking about." Sara pushed past and opened the door to start hopping down the stairs. Britt followed grinning. Very little slipped past Sara. With each step she surmised aspect of escape. With every breath a new hope her people searched for her. The palace may not be the prime location for her to achieve her goals. She lifted the black satin and velvet skirts and trudged down the steps behind Sara.

They were to meet Meriden and Sholendor behind a curtain and await announcement. Walking through the kitchens, all the servants stopped to let them pass. Britt noticed many of them were very young. Most of the humans were children. The kitchens were thick with steaming pots and roaring fires. The smell of bread and cooking meats hit her, making her mouth water. Thankfully Sara stopped before a tattered wooden table and placed a bowl on the scarred chopping surface.

"We had better sup now, nar else ta feed on till it ends." Sara climbed onto a stool next to Britteny and started slurping hot cabbage soup. Britt bent down to bite off a chunk of meat while looking around. "I dunna even want ta think of the fear in these buggers now. After that show today I am thinking they all see ye as a spirit or goddess."

"Yea, I was kinda wondering how everyone was going to take that. I wasn't going to sit back and watch that kid get killed." Britt gulped a mouthful of sweet wine.

"Bullocks and brime! Idda nev'ra thought anyone could fight like that! Ta think o' it! Best damn show I'll be seein fer some time. Ye wiped out a whole arena full of big 'uns! A whole fecking arena!" Sara explained loudly, hoping the rest of the kitchen staff were listening to things that were not their business, as usual.

"Yea isn't that funny and you still don't even wince from me." Britt shoved her playfully.

"Killin' me would be a favor. Besides, ye are a kind hearted creature, not a murderer, no matter how well ye can kill." Sara finished her soup and stuffed her bread in her mouth. "Come on then, off with us now ye lanky oaf." She mumbled.

Britt bit off another healthy chunk of bread and swept off her cleavage with a napkin. She rose and followed Sara through the small door, avoiding the stares of all the other servants. At that moment she set a time. Tomorrow night when the palace slept she would steal into the night and search for a way home. She would search the sky until the new moon made another showing, hoping it would send down freighters for materials so she could get a good idea of a location to a land station. She would need time to gather food. She would have little or no idea of the open environment. It occurred to her to swing by Ruddy Mudders and attempt to learn something from Osizio. She decided against that option. He had already become too deeply involved. That would be the first place they would hunt for her. Roderick came to mind as he often did. Her heart jumped, warning her against another interaction with such an influential being. She would be forced to survive on her own wits. It was certainly not the first time.

They kept to the back corridors and low spaces until they reached an antechamber behind the plush blue curtain overlooking the main ballroom. Meriden was waiting for them. She was peering through the curtains with a rather distant look on her pale face. When they approached she turned to look at her companions. Britteny hiccupped sharply.

"WOW! You look great!" She said honestly. Meriden was dressed in a ball gown of liquid silver and white. Along with her perfect white hair and skin, she was the vision of heavenly magick. Her immense ruby colored eyes added a bit of sinister intrigue to the ensemble.

"Thank you Britt, and as usual, you are breathtaking enough to stop the very music." She smiled in spite of herself. The three of them peered together through the long gap, Britt on top, Meriden below her and Sara at the bottom. "I can not believe my eyes." Meriden commented.

"What?" Both Britt and Sara asked simultaneously.

"Roderick is here." Meriden informed them.

Sara sharply elbowed Britt in the thigh. Britt barely noticed. She stayed still, standing over Meriden looking out into the crowd. She could see Roderick standing against the far wall. He was speaking to Gherkin and Ferrin of Sid O'Sala. She felt her dinner sink. Trying to shake off the feeling, she told herself it was a perfect opportunity to question him about the lay of the land, like she should have done the first night they were together, instead of indulging in elfish hospitality.

Sholendor cleared his throat. "Hello ladies."

Britt and Meriden stepped back from the curtain. Meriden bowed. "Blessed is the evening, my lord. I hope it finds you well." Her politeness almost sounded genuine.

"It finds me in deep apology for my earlier ill manner." He reached for Meriden's hand placing a cold kiss at the end of the slender fingers. "I am not yet accustomed to life with a woman, and surely not one of your stature. I must beg your forgiveness." He implored. He noted the glare from Britt.

"Forgiveness is the least I can offer my future husband and king." Meriden offered sweetly.

Britt suppressed the splay of vomit shock. She did not want to believe Meriden was this gullible. The court herald approached and bowed to the royal couple. He then turned and stepped through the curtains.

"OH YAY! OH YAY! Gentle Lords and Ladies! I give you their royal majesties, Sir Sholendor of Garath and his betrothed; High Princess of the realm, Lady Meriden of Fairfax!"

The royal couple entwined arms and stepped into the light, followed by their slave. Britt felt like a prize cow at the county fair. She tried to keep her eyes on a point in the ceiling ahead of her to avoid the stares and comments. It was amazing how such trivial things could be so annoying. She mused that this situation was possibly more trying than disemboweling a Gungulieian Zuzawhats. She started thinking of what she would rather be doing at this moment. Slicing her fingertips open with razor blades then dumping her hands in alcohol seemed a reasonable replacement form of entertainment.

She was accustomed to being different. It was noted that her culture was, however, advanced and accustomed to multiple life forms. She avoided Roderick's gaze altogether. The hall was incredible. She tried instead to focus on the beauty of the vast room.

Above them, small fairies buzzed about suspended frosted lily pads, topped with diamond-like candleholders. Silver streamers hung from each, reflecting the light against one another. The center of the hall was laid out with an enormous banquet table covered in a shining black tablecloth adorned with silver goblets and finely crafted silver diningware. Servants raced around high backed chairs with overflowing platters. The music lifted Britteny's heart. It had been forever since she had been touched by the sound of strings. A deep cello sang a low and sweet melody that made her choke up. She stepped onto the stone floor and was lost in a sea of enchanted beauty. Everywhere she turned she was to be enveloped by the grace of yet another type of elf, each elegant and unobtainable in their unique mysticisms.

Meriden and Sholendor were seated at the head of the table and the feast began. Britt was positioned directly behind Meriden, standing next to another female companion slave half her size. She searched the room trying to get a good look at the other humans. Most of them were barely larger than gnomes. Some ways down the table she noticed Roderick seated next to a blue haired elf female. Without thinking she smiled. He returned her gesture, brilliant and uninhibited. She felt her heart's beat quicken. The female next to him noticed his line of vision and scoffed a bit, playfully tapping his hand. He glanced at her and they spoke for a time. Britt looked away, not wishing to be made a fool of. It was of little matter to her. Soon she would be sweeping through this universe on to her home. Perhaps this was a woman that Roderick was interested in. They made a nice couple. She caught sight of Ferrin of Sid O'Sala and noticed the male human standing behind him. He was tall and pale haired, and staring back at her. He tipped his head hello. Britt looked around to verify that he was indeed tipping to her. She tipped back and frowned, puzzled.

The dinner did not take as long as Britteny had hoped it would. Lucky for the companion slave next to her that had insisted on constantly bumping into her. Actions such as this could end up in the loss of a limb for the shorter of the two. Meriden rose and walked back to Britt.

"My friend, how are you enjoying the party?" She spoke softly.

"Do ya really wanna to know?" She winced.

"Please! You are the most ravishing prize in the pot. You will feel better when the dancing starts."

"Dancing?" Britt asked.

"Yes. There will be dancing throughout the night. Have you never been to a ball?" Meriden asked.

"Well now that you mention it, no." Britt admitted. She leaned closer to Meriden. "Who is that women Roderick is talking to?" She asked.

"That is my cousin De'Loriea of Havaland. They are to be married anon, or so we all hope."

Britt appeared taken aback. She shifted uneasily and looked away from the elf couple. "Funny, in the times I have talked to him he didn't mention a fiancée'." She mumbled.

"Why should he? I am sure he is quite certain everyone that needs to know does. It is our way. We are assigned our mates at birth. It is judged by the high council according to the position of the stars." Meriden turned to nod at approaching elves. "Why is it you ask?"

"Just wondering." Britt acted nonplused.

"It matters not, you will be asked to dance by many of the healthy human males. I think every slave trader here has inquired to your breeding schedule." She looked away to be pulled back.

"Breeding schedule?" Britt barked.

"Do not worry. I have no intention of breeding you. I think I am wise enough to have assessed that will be your choice alone." She patted Britt's hand.

"Well thank God for that!" She laughed.

During the conversation the room had magically changed. The tables had disappeared and the floor was clear for the guests to dance and socialize. Ferrin of Sid O'Sala was walking towards them, followed by his slave.

"Blessed eave to you, my Royal Highness." He bowed to Meriden. "I see you have acquired your new slave and in no short time to show her off at the games today."

"Yes, well that was a bit of a surprise, yet all ended well." Meriden assured. "She has been quite a blessing and a very invaluable gift." She turned to smile up at Britt. "At least I will sleep better knowing she is here to protect me." They all laughed.

"In all seriousness, I have never seen a display of physical agility and strength to match it. All done without the assistance of magick, I assume?" He asked.

"I was as surprised as all other onlookers." Meriden assured him. "I would not have been capable of a spell even if I would have attempted it."

"Why is that?" He asked.

"I, as you, my lord have yet to see a creature move in that manner. I doubt there has ever been one of her equal." She added.

Britt was growing ever so frustrated at being talked about like she was not present, or worse yet, lacking intelligence enough to speak for herself. Tomorrow was not soon enough. Ferrin's slave was making her uncomfortable. His presence was blatant, his hopeful intentions obvious. She looked at the ceiling and all itsglory, to avoid losing her temper.

"Britteny, this is one of my finest companion slaves, Cameron." Ferrin introduced his prize bull.

"It is a pleasure to meet you Cameron." She bit off with great difficulty.

"I look forward to the day we can meet under more serious circumstances." Cameron smiled.

"How so?" She chastised herself for opening the door.

"I am sure our masters will wish to produce a child from our union and good breeding."

As if a voice of fate, a tune unconsciously pulled her furious attention to the orchestra. The hall fell dim and couples wandered to the dance floor and began spinning in a spectrum of color and silk. Such a song she had never imagined.

Cameron had continued talking as if he had expected her to hang on each word. She had become aware of a strong hand on the small of her back, and not knowing why, allowed it to sweep her to the dance floor. After she was finished spinning she held fast to the lime colored eyes that stared into her caged heart.

The music overtook them. Losing the power of speech and the ability to think, tomorrow was forgotten with each step. She met his steps as they spiraled around the patterned stone of the elfish palace. Oblivion may have well had them dancing alone. Neither noticed. He opened his arms to allow her to spin away, just to pull her back in a flourish of velvet. She held nothing back and met his motions as though their bodies had danced in another reality, planned and precise. The mesmerizing song was nearly over when she heard him speak through the din of whispers and silver strings.

"The amulet looks fantastic on you, my beloved." He complimented.

"Thank you. I mean thank you for the gift and the compliment." She was sure she was blushing.

"May I see you again tonight, Britteny?" His voice was exploding with emotion, yet his face was elfishly calm.

"I would enjoy that. Yea, I think I would enjoy that quite a bit." She smiled up at him, almost tipping to kiss his full lips; she stopped herself and remembered where she was. They had stopped moving. A light wind was blowing through from the high windows. The entire court had fallen still. She let go of his shoulder and backed away suddenly terrified of his sway over her. She had invited him to her room against her better judgment.

She blinked in surprise when she heard the word "Tonight" in her mind but did not see his mouth move. He smiled and turned to disappear into the crowd of stunned peers. She felt a hand on her back and turned to see Cameron behind her.

"May I have the next dance lady?" He inquired politely.

"Sure, I guess." Holding out her arms he took her and they began an awkward dance that would become a small part of an awkward evening.

"I have been told you are new to this part of the realm. Is there anything I can teach you?" He asked with voyeuristic intent.

She looked around. "Where is your master, boy? I think he needs to come get you before you get yourself in trouble." She was not joking.

"HA! I love your spirit!" He pulled her closer. "I was told you put on quite a show at the games today. I would have loved to see it. Unfortunately I was in the breeding house earning my keep."

Britt broke the grip with ease. "I suppose you're proud of that."

"I am very proud that I am in such demand, as I am sure you will be soon. I am also proud to be the first to be bred with you. That is, if Ferrin stops acting so strange."

"What is wrong with you people? Is that all you think about? I'm not breeding with anyone! What, does he want to be there to chain me up and watch?"

"No, as a matter of fact he does not want me near you. He has been very insistent that we only become companions, not breeding partners." Cameron tilted his fine head as if showing off his good looks. "Pity really. I was hoping we could get down to business as soon as possible."

Britt let go of him disgusted and started to stomp off. She was stopped short as he gripped her hand to pull her back. When she turned to look at him, for an instant the creeping feeling that this may not be the wisest thing to do, settled in his mind. The thought was overridden by ego.

"I'd let go if I were you." Britt warned.

"No. You see, I have come to think I am the male that will tame you down a bit and teach you a few things about being a good servant." He said it so brashly it made Britt laugh out loud.

Britt's face twisted in a comical grimace. "Boy, you're a real piece of work." She continued laughing out loud. "You sound like some retarded super hero from a cheesy romance novel." She held her hand to her breast and raised one eyebrow. "What ho she wench!" She thrust her other hand forward as if holding an invisible sword. "I shall tame your wild fires of passion until the very fiber of your being explodes with the hot fury of my lusty loins!" She laughed on. Soon she was snorting and her eyes were watered. "Ohhh…Ehhh. Stop, you're killing me!" She walked off, leaving Cameron staring after her.

Meriden was watching from her seat on the throne, never bothering to interrupt. She did notice Ferrin of Sid O'Sala nearly interfere with the dance itself. She watched as Britt attempted to talk to some of the other human slaves. She was met with strange glances and looks of fear. Britt then leaned against the wall, shifting to and fro in boredom. Meriden felt strangely sorry for her new slave. There would be no place she would fit in. The future Queen of Zembeth smiled as her long time slave Sara approached the stranger. She pulled up two stools, offering cheese and ale. Sara was traditionally not permitted to attend such a function. However Meriden felt it important for Britt to keep occupied and out of trouble. Her glance drifted to Roderick of Darmuth Anor, who was talking to the trading merchant lords from the north. No doubt he did more business on a daily basis than her entire royal staff. He was nodding his head and listening to a very insistent dwarf that was offering a fine silver dagger for inspection. She tuned her elf ears to the conversation that was taking place across the hall.

"Here, ye son of a black whore!" The dwarf laughed. "Compare this to any elfish silver, ye cannot find better!" Roderick chuckled and held up the piece, obviously not offended by the earlier title.

"Tis a wonderful display of workmanship, Olrick, indeed. I am sure you will find a strong open trade here in Garath for such treasures."

"From the very looks of it I'm a thinking I'll be needing to get into the slave trading business afore long." His knotted beard swayed in the direction of Meriden's new slave.

"No." Roderick patted the dwarf's stout shoulder. "I think her chances of breeding before anyone dies are very unlikely. Stay with silver, my fine friend." With that Roderick walked off to confer with a group of young elfish warriors engaged in discussion of upcoming initiation rituals.

The night went on with dancing and singing. Silver flutes played as an elfish sonnet was recited of wars and magick. Britt continued to sit with Sara, enjoying the conversation of the quick-witted palace servant. None approached her and most gave her a wide berth. She seemed not to notice. Soon she stood and walked with Sara to the throne.

"Hey Meriden, you look bored. Wanna come talk to us?" She asked. At first Meriden was shocked at her boldness. Sholendor had long before left to fawn about with the ladies and lords of the court, leaving Meriden to her sadness and solitude. "We could go out to the gardens and get a break from all this hullabaloo. Whaddya say?" Britt nudged.

Looking around, it was not surprising to see the women of the court whispering behind closed hands. Britt turned to follow her line of vision. "Will ya look at that?" Britt said.

"Look at what?" Meriden remarked sharply.

"Not a one of them would give you the time of day before. They've all been walking around whispering about you. Right in front of you, as if with those big ears you couldn't hear them. Now that I'm up here actually talking to you they act like this." Britt turned to the princess. After a short deliberation Meriden rose and smoothed her dress.

"You are right, Britteny. A true friend would have spoken to me long ago. Thank you for finally coming to my rescue." They walked down the steps together and headed out to the garden. They sat under the stars amidst silver fountains and diamond pathways. They spoke of ogres, wars, food, men, astrology, geology, government, culture, magick, and even family. Britt found that she was able to acquire just as much information from Meriden in this nice chat, and with much less discomfort, than she would have from Roderick. Meriden seemed alive with stories. Sara had fetched some bread and wine and the three of them sat laughing and talking for what seemed hours. They were oblivious to the many faces peering out the large doors, appalled at the sight of the royal princess conversing with her servants as equals.

"You are not going to stay with me, are you Britt?" Meriden injected, to the surprise of both slaves. Britt shifted in her seat.

"No Meriden, I can't. I will have to find my way home eventually." She saw no reason to avoid the pointed question. Melancholy silence fell for a moment. Meriden placed her cool white hand on the strong hand of her friend.

"I know." She looked at the soft grass. "I was once told by my father that sometimes people come along that are too rare and precious to control or obtain. He would say that lives and souls are not for possession or resale. They are priceless and elusive, and ever shining, like a light in the darkest of nights." She hesitated. "Ironically, in knowing you will leave me soon, I can only wonder what I will do without you."

Britt sat back and huffed. "Whaddya mean?" She touched Meriden's chin and lifted her fine boned face. "From what I have been told of your father, he was a hell of a king. And from what I have seen thus far of you, I am sure you will make him very proud, wherever he is." Britt stood to retire to her chambers. She knew she had a long day ahead of her that would start after the long night was over. "You do what your father would have done, except, stick around and be strong enough to see it through. You never know, I may be back some day. I have to get some sleep. I think I'm coming down with something." She bent down and hugged Meriden. The princess held rigidly still. Britt did not let go until she felt the frail body relax and the slender arms wrap around her neck in return. She turned to Sara who had been watching the entire time.

"Are ye ill again lass?" Sara asked with concern.

"I don't think so. I'm just very worn down. I've had a lot to absorb these last few days. Of course then, there is the fact that I'm now pregnant." She whispered the last fact. "You just keep an eye on her tonight, you ornery old witch." Britt playfully punched Sara's arm, then hugged her as well. She turned and strode to the kitchens and up the stairs, leaving the two Zembethians in the garden.

She paced around the room. Somehow in hopes he could not or would not show up, she watched the door, tapping her fingers against her thigh. Perhaps it was that this would be the last time she would hold him. She should not hold him at all. He was betrothed and this was his world. She had no right to interrupt. She knew very well the strength of social structures and the need to stay neutral. She rubbed her hand hard against her forehead. It was a little late for that. Roderick may be in her quarters at any minute. Even if their coupling meant nothing to him, she could not stop the growing feeling that it meant far too much to her. What was a fling before marriage? She could give him that. Give him that then be gone again, as so many times before.

She paced around the fine carpet. The last time, this would be the last time she would make love to him, talk to him, laugh with him. She had only known him a very short time. It had been difficult to walk away from Meriden and Sara. Strangely, somehow more difficult than it had been to leave many worlds she had become part of. The captain in her rolled the scene in her mind's eye toward the future. If she made it home it seemed prudent to never return. Knowing one's heart was a staple to being a productive leader. She had lost that knowledge in record time. It could be Roderick. It may be the enchanting aura of Zembeth. Addictions were better snuffed early on. If she could be so easily affected then it would be fair to assume her people would undergo the same transition. It would be vital to do what she must to shield both worlds from one another until further observation. If what Gherkin had told her was true, historically she may be obligated to disclose this information. Who was she to close the door to the last vestige of Earth based life? She had been clipped to discover they spoke an old Earth tongue. With Gherkin's information it was clear that they had been doing so thousands of years before even the smallest recollection of Zenerian documentation had been established. Zembeth was so much like Earth, from the smell of campfires to the sounds of the people; it was very much like old or rural Earth and that was all she remembered of it. The nagging question lay within her. Would she make the choice to keep this world a secret to preserve it, or because of her fear of Roderick?

She had nearly fallen dumb while they danced. There had been no argument. He announced he wished to visit her tonight. She accepted without even the slightest protest. She touched the necklace on her chest. Her hand balled into a fist around the sapphire. Perhaps it was best if she left it behind. Split personality captions rummaged through her conscious and subconscious mind. She was aware that her actions were negligible and unprofessional. As she started to emotionally climb the hill of reason, an unknown facet of her personality started to drag her back to ignorant lust.

She felt strong hands on her shoulders and her heart leapt. She turned to look at Roderick once more. She knew she had felt him some time ago, and was not startled beyond the passion that raced through her. As if the entire emotional episode had never taken place, she melted into his arms without a word. He stroked her hair lovingly and for a time they stood so, holding and hoping. When she pulled back, his kisses warmed her neck up to her cheeks, kissing tears and soft eyelids. Before he could ask her, she engulfed his mouth in an urgent kiss, not wanting to speak, just feel. They walked hand in hand to the bed where they sat for a moment before Britt stood to allow Roderick the special privilege of unlacing her bodice.

"Roderick. We both know that there may never be a future beyond these moments for both of us. You have your life and I mine." She sat on his lap naked and kissed his forehead, running her fingers along his sharp pointed ears. "Promise me, no, tell me there is no more to this than a natural urge or a quick fix."

He pulled her hair back and kissed her shoulder. He kept staring at her skin as if finding the words within. "I know not what to say my lady." He pulled her closer. "I have never felt like this for another. In reality, I have never known feeling of pleasure and pain mixed with such fury. I have never ached so. I have never experienced infantlike uncertainty. It is all new." He kissed her. "If I am to live in pain then let it be so, if only for our short time." He lay back and pulled her atop of him. She untied his tunic and kissed his firm chest. Over and over they rolled, in and out of each other's souls.

When Roderick rose to leave she tried not to grab his arm and pull him back. He dressed slowly as if hoping she would. She lay in the linen, filled with his smell and warmth. He turned and spoke softly. "I will leave day after tomorrow. I shall only be gone a short time. I go to find a future for us. I need to know if you will be here when I return and if you will go with me." His voice was shaking.

Britt sat up, pulling the sheets over her breasts. She could feel her gut tighten in anticipation.

"I can't promise that, Roderick. I don't know if it is a good idea for the two of us to be together."

"Why do you say such things, when I know this is not what you feel?" He bent down to his knees before her. "Look at me, Britt! Tell me why!"

"I can't!" She insisted. "I just can't!"

"Do you have another?" He inquired.

"No. There's no other, none like you." She confessed. Her pride would not allow her to tell him she knew of De Loriea. She wanted to see if he would confess on his own. This test she must let him pass or fail.

"Are you ill?" He pressed.

"NO!" She tried to control herself. "Roderick, for crying out loud, are you just crazy or have you not figured out that this is not exactly a match made in heaven? You are an elf, I am a human. HELLO! Where could we ever have a remotely normal life?" She challenged.

"I am going to the Shalnas Forest. I have heard that many beings of refuge live there, hiding from this world, in a place secret and safe."

Britt stood up and walked across the room. "What about Amaranth and Donavan? Don't they count, don't they matter?" She started dressing.

"They will understand. I plan on leaving them word."

"Just like that? A couple hundred years of friendship, blown over one woman?" She tugged her chemise over hear head. "Besides, don't you think we are moving a bit fast? Are you really ready to make this kind of commitment after only knowing me for a few days?

Roderick spoke. "Yes." Britt turned to look at him.

"What?" She asked again.

"Yes. I am." He crossed the room. "I have been limited to few choices in this matter. Apparently unlike you, I have chosen to admit it. I did not choose this. I did not ask you to come into my life and I do not know how to explain the irrational way I am behaving. I do know that I am willing to risk everything to be with you. At this point I only have the choice to either have you with me and risk loosing the life I know now, or losing you and being forever plagued with your memory. I have made my choice."

Britteny was stopped short. "Look Roderick, there are so many things you don't know about me."

"Such as?" He folded his arms, half naked.

"Such as, I can't stay here. I have a home and people, like I told you."

"Well if you wish not to invite me to go with you, please tell me now. I would rather you allow me the dignity than lead me astray."

She blinked. "Well hell, I didn't think you would consider it."

"You never asked." He retorted.

"You would consider leaving with me?"

"What do I have here? I can either roam from town to town for the rest of my very long life, being called a black bastard. Always having responsibility and never having respect. Or I can marry that shrew of an elf bitch that I really despise and spend my days a puppet for an ice queen."

"Well, now that you put it that way. . ." She sat in the stuffed chair. "O.K., well how about this, we wait for a few days until you can arrange things, we head for this forest, and if I find a way home you can come with me, if not we hang out in the forest and take it day by day." She waited for his reply. Her hunger clung to the possibility of having him close despite the obstacles she foresaw.

"That sounds fair enough." He continued dressing. "I will be back tomorrow eave to tell you of the plans. If the situation arises you must not breathe a word of this to Amaranth or Donavan. I wish to tell them goodbye in my own way."

"No problem, I understand." She hugged him. "Just for the record, I think we are both nuts, but hey, who's keeping score?"

He walked to the slave's door and turned to kiss her. "Until tomorrow, my love." And then he was gone. She slapped herself in the head.

"I have got to be OUT of my freaking mind!" Was there some reason she just acted like a total idiot when he was around? It was clear that she must keep her word and if all went as she hoped, she would be leaving in a few days with someone who knew the land. Explaining him to everyone was not going to be easy. He was immortal. He was magical. Space travel had never entered his reality. Winging it. She was just winging it. Meadows would be fit to be tied. She could hear the good doctor.

"We don't wing it. He is not winging it material! Have you lost your mind? He's not a puppy, for god's sake!" She crossed her arms and grimaced. That would, of course, be before she announced her pregnancy.

Chapter 15

Corpse Spelunking

She was a piece of leather, worked into a belt. She could smell herself. She smelled good. From leather she turned to a walking dream and was following an opossum through the woods. He was dressed in a tux and talking about cinnamon and sugar while tapping his cane along. His friend, the well-dressed raccoon, was pushing an old fashioned baby carriage. In it slept a mother of pearl embryo. They walked on through the lush forest until they came upon a cellar door. Britt knew it looked familiar but she could not place it. Walking to the metal handles, she placed her foot on the left door and pulled hard to open the creaking right door. The hinges moaned as flakes of old lumber fell to the moist soil around the sandstone base. She was alone now; her small friends had long since continued their parade. She could feel her bare footstep on the old coarse stone. She waved away dry sand and cobwebs from the ancient passage way.

Before she descended further, she reached up and shoved the other door open, allowing what light she could down the passage into the earth. There was something in this cellar. She could hear it breathing far off at the back of the room. She took a moment to look down at her torso. She was dressed in a light yellow sundress, with small pockets at the hips. She remembered this dress from her childhood. The dress was of her childhood yet set to fit her adult body. She came to stand next to shelves lined with mason jars filled with peaches, tomatoes and other common preserves she once helped her mother with during harvest. Her grandmother's old metal crock-pot was placed on the bottom wooden shelf, along with an array of junk her mother could never seem to toss out. She bent over to pick up a coffee percolator. It was dated 1908. She set it back on the shelf, all the while aware of the person in the dark corner. Somehow she did not wish to speak to it. After all, it was her dream and she did not have to. It grunted.

"Who the hell are you?" The voice belched from the dark.

Her spine straightened and her skin prickled. It was her father, skulking in the dank of the cellar. Did he know who she was now that she was grown? She was thinking of ways to take advantage of the situation when he came into the dim light.

"Oh, so you have decided to come home, you little whore." He grinned, showing his missing front teeth. "And I see you've taken the time to finally grow some." His hand started to reach forward. "Maybe now that you are grown, you'll appreciate your old man."

In that instant she burst into laughter. Perception was a wonderful mystery. With the force of too many years of abuse she shoved him into one of the shelves. She initiated a strange dance around him. "What's wrong, Dan? Cat got your tongue?" She spun about and slapped him hard across the face. "You think that's bad? I can show you everything I have learned while I have been away." Her fists were flying. Dan Devarelle was being bounced around the cellar like a rag doll. Bottles shattered on the grit-covered floor, mixing with Dan's blood.

She was moving in for the final strike when the earth moved beneath her, sending her toppling backwards over a sawhorse. She reached out and braced herself, striking a picture of a Holstein cow hanging on the wall. From the door came a strange wind. It housed a scent that was not completely unfamiliar to her. She had witnessed nuclear fallout. She had smelled charred flesh.

"See what ya have done ya little bitch!" He lunged for her.

Britt jumped out of his way with ease. He was drunk, as usual, and would never be able to catch her. Far back in her memory she could recall tornadoes. Her mother would scuttle her to the shelter numerous times in the spring and early summer with the first signs of any violent storm. Her attention was drawn from the impending disaster when one of the mason jars fell to her feet. She jumped in horror. Small people of all races crammed inside the glass, frantically attempting to break free, had replaced the fruits and vegetables. The cellar had grown unbearably temped. The faces started melting against the glass. Britt leaped toward the jars, only to be stopped by a gust of fire that shoved her to the wall. She pulled her head from the stone and squinted her eyes against the wind. She could see the mushroom cloud beyond the cellar opening. The fallout spread, reaching her. There was no pain. Her hand went to her face and returned with a large portion of her facial epidural mixed with burning strands of hair.

Dream scene change. She was suspended on a cloud, her head cradled by a rainbow. All around her, as if guarding her, she looked up at tall white statues of mythical beauty. She must be dead. She was so tired. She wanted to stay here forever.

"My lady." A voice interrupted. She swatted it away, not wishing to wake.

"My lady Britteny!" The voice came again.

She opened her eyes to squinting width. Sitting bolt upright she grabbed the covers and wiped her hair from her face.

"What in the hell is going on?" She panted. Her chamber had been invaded with what appeared to be a battalion of pale elves dressed in simple silver armor. Each carried a healthy stock of weapons. It took no effort to deduce these males were void of compassion. Each face was morbid and unmoving, each glance was cold and calculating.

"My lady, I must bid you to the main chamber. You are under arrest, by royal decree." The elf soldier chose not to speak to her directly. Instead it was as if he addressed a child or small animal. She got the feeling this task was beneath him on many levels. She wiped her hair back again and tried to think of what she had done. It did no good to jump to conclusions. She had, after all, been arrested for crimes she had forgotten about, did not understand the law of, or had been to drunk to care, in the past. She mumbled as she itemized the evenings' events.

Could they be arresting her for sleeping with Roderick? No. Gut instinct told her it was much worse.

She was preparing to protest. Sara was produced. One of the guards held a dagger to her neck.

"Perhaps this will sway you to behave?" The unknown silver and white ghost hissed. These gentlemen meant business. She could only assume these were the Queen's guards from Fairfax. Sara did not flinch, yet her eyes were pleading.

"All right! Can I get dressed?" She demanded more than asked.

"I would command it, human. We do not wish to be sickened by your animal form." Britt suppressed her "overgrown glowworm from hell" comment and pulled on a pair of snug black breeches, her bra, a pair of knee high boots and a loose fitting white tunic. She was thankful that these elves did not know her for they ignored her like the obtuse animal they believed her to be. She tied her hair back and walked to Sara. Taking the gnome's hand, she started for the door followed by the royal guard.

On the way down the stairs, she tried to hold Sara's hand as firm as she could to reassure the shaking servant that all would be well. They were escorted into the main chamber. It seemed that in a matter of hours, the once beautiful dance hall had been turned into a courtroom. At the head of a large white wood podium, resided a creature of ancient magick. His white hair spilled from under a pointed pale gray cone hat. He regarded all entering with distance and malcontent. It was clear that the two cities hosted somewhat different breeds of elves. The hall was now partially populated by such elves. It seemed the law of Zembeth was comprised solely of celestial ancients. She glanced about searching for the familiar jeweled toned elves of Garath. Few could be found. Those that she did pick out were silent and submissive. Sholendor was seated to the right of the chief wizard. This would explain the ease of the battle seemingly won by Meriden the day before. The two apparent breeds of elves had separated and aligned the walls. As the doors closed, both breeds of elves parted. To the right congregated the ghost elves. To the left of the hall their kin from Garath were seated in silence.

Before them, in a minuscule pile of night clothes, knelt the princess. Britt rushed to her, dragging Sara behind. When she reached Meriden it was apparent that she had been forced from her chambers. Britt picked her up with ease and supported her feather light frame. Her head snapped to the council of elders. She made no attempt to hide her anger.

The cruel guard that had escorted Britteny and Sara spoke. "The princess's servants, my high lord." He bowed and backed to a line directly behind the three women.

"Are these the servants you wish to retain, Lord Sholendor?" The eldest spoke.

"I care not for the gnome. In reality she may have assisted in the deed. However the human is far too valuable to eliminate and was here in my charge at the time of the crime."

The wizard fondled his staff and nodded. "So be it. Take the three of them to the oubliette. On the morrow the human's documents are to be scribed over to the ownership of The High King Sholendor." The guards rounded the women up and herded them towards the dungeon.

Britt found herself carrying the unconscious princess. Her anger was reaching a boiling point. Down and down they went, through a large chasm that appeared to have no bottom, into the prison chambers. They were locked into a small circular room with nothing more than a single candle, a stool, and a badly stained rug covering a filthy floor. As soon as the guards had locked the door, Britt placed Meriden on the floor, lowering her gently.

"Hey kid, wake up." She lovingly coaxed. She turned to Sara. "You wanna tell me what in the Sam hell just happened?"

"Meriden and I are to be hanged on the morrow for the murder of her mother, the Queen Alisi." She bent to assist the princess as well.

"What? How the hell did they come up with that bullshit?" Britt insisted.

"I was there fer the trial. The bastards were afeard to rouse you, thinking of a thumpin' proper. Sholendor and his royal arse kissers told Lord Dolphin of yer show at the games." She wiped Meriden's cold brow. "He says our child here left her ma in the palace of Fairfax, dead, smothered, afore she jumped in her carriage fer Garath. Said she tried to steal the necklace of the Shalnas and when her ma would not give it up she smothered her." Sara pulled Meriden's head into her lap. "So they yanked her skinny lil hide from her bed, after stripping her of her magical powers, and sentenced her."

"They stripped her of all her magickal powers? Why?" Britt knew the answer before she got all the words out. "Never mind, I already know. Is she going to live?"

"I am hopin so. Tis almost all that was in her, her magick." Sara began to weep.

"Aw. . . come on Sara, this is no time for tears. We have to figure a way out of this." Britt stood and paced the circular room. "Killed her mom, huh? Somehow I think this has been planned for quite a while. Besides, you were here with me before Meriden got here. How can they pin this on you?" Meriden moaned and was coming around a bit.

"I feel so ill." Meriden choked.

"Hush now lass, ye need yer rest." Sara looked at Britt. "Ye donna think they care about me, do ye? 'Asides I have not a right to protest. I am a slave." She was holding back tears as best she could. Britt bit her lip and continued looking around the circular cell.

"What is going to happen next?" She asked Sara. Meriden was sitting up against the wall now, mumbling.

"Well, I suppose the bastard will get all the scrolls signed over fer you. It would seem ye have nothing to worry about. 'Tis myself and the elf here that is going to the hangman on the morrow."

"You really think I'm gonna let you two die, don't you?" She shot Sara an evil glare.

"Na, 'twas just testing ye." Sara said as Britt's head snapped erect.

"I hear something." She sniffed. "I smell a bunch of elves coming this way."

"By craky, yer getting rather good being half dragon," Sara whispered, moving closer to Britt. Devarelle hesitated for a moment then hastened to whisper something to her friend. Her instinct had not failed her. She pressed her face to the bars to see a group of white soldiers being led down the spiraling staircase by Sholendor.

"Sara!" She whispered harshly. "When I wipe my brow and tip my head back, cover Meriden's ears and do the best you can for your own."

"What fer you daffy idgit?" She protested.

"Just do it!" Britt demanded and turned just in time to see Sholendor mount the final step to the landing in front of their cell.

He had no fear in opening the door, assuming he could control the human now that Meriden had lost her powers. Sara moved Meriden to the far end of the cell. Britt stood in the middle of the room. Sara watched as Britt's entire disposition changed as if a wind over wheat.

"Have you come for me so soon my lord?" She said sweetly. "I grow tired of this weak company." She was hoping to draw him closer.

Sholendor's eyes squinted to long slits. "Tis a queen among women I see. Least a thief in the night." He approached her and put his hand in her hair. Pulling her head back, he kissed her. "Soon you will be mine, legally and spiritually." He backed away. "Do not think for one moment I am not working with Dolphin to erase that protection spell, my wildcat. He will begin the spell removal after the executions tomorrow." He patted her cheek. "You did not think I would not remove the sharp claws from my fine feline." He chuckled.

"Dolphin, that is quite an interesting name." She remarked innocently. "We have animals where I am from called dolphins." She absently wiped her brow. "Wanna hear what they sound like?" She seemed gleeful.

Sholendor crossed his arms and wondered at this new playful attitude. Perhaps she had been worked into submission by the judgment alone and finally knew her place.

"If it amuses you my pet, I would hear it." He turned to give a snide slide glance to his guards.

Britt tilted her head back and concentrated all her power to reverberate as much energy through her human skull as could be withstood. She opened her vocal cords and shoved sound though them, demanding the waves to run deep, mimicking the distress call of a small whale. Every guard fell to the floor clutching their skulls in agony, Sholendor among them. Meriden and Sara both screamed and held on to their heads for dear life. When Britt stopped for mercy sakes, the entire dungeon echoed screams of pain from creatures of heightened hearing capabilities. Sholendor staggered up in time for Britt to shove him out the door and slam the solid wood and iron in his face.

As he started to protest, Britt raised her finger and opened her mouth, "Opp." He tried to speak. "App." She stopped him. "You best get that spell working, because here's another news flash for you bud, I am either dying with my friends, or getting out of here. However, I am NOT going to be your bitch. Not now, not tomorrow, not ever."

She noticed one of the guards pulling his bow and quiver. "Not so fast, Spock! Pull that arrow and I swear to God I will split your skull!" She took a deep breath.

Sholendor held his hand up towards the guard. They started backing away slowly. "Good boys. Now you run along and get those ropes ready. We'll see you all tomorrow." She poked her head through the bars. "Pleasant dreams!"

Turning back to her companions she jumped back as Sara came off the floor. "Where in the name of sweet Giddion did ye learn to do that, ye beast?" She screamed.

"Just don't you worry about that Sara. We have to find a way out of this place and we have to find it fast." She started looking around the room.

"Well ye genius, ye locked us back in the very room." She noticed.

"Do you really think we would make it out that way even if the door was open? Come on Sara, work with me." She took a moment to notice Meriden was drooling on her gown now. "Man she's in bad shape. We need to get her to some type of elf doctor as soon as possible."

"There is only one I know that can help her now, and I'da be flipped in me grave iffin' I know how that one will work." Sara shifted a bit. "Who is it ya suppose could do such a thing? Who coulda killed that queen?" Sara questioned.

Britteny turned, exasperated. "Sara, please don't make me slap you."

Chapter 16
Shake Down

Boomer had paid a visit to a certain organization he had heard about through certain sources. He had worn his best uniform, slicked back his wild Irish hair, and even shaved. For an instant the receptionist had the nerve to tell him that one Mr. Baxter could not see him, and that he could make an appointment for a later date.

Boomer took the liberty of sitting on her desk. "So, what yer sayin is I'm to be handed me hat. Is that it lass?" His evil smile set her rolling in her chair. She glided away from her terminal. "Ye see that lass over there?" He pointed to Loco, who, unlike himself, was dressed like a Zenerian Pirate. "Heh. . . Well I'll be telling ye something bout that there lass. She is just going to be a terrible mess when I tell her we have to," He held his hands up in comic quote marks, "make another sitting fer this." He rubbed his fine square chin. "Perhaps ye would be willing to discuss the matter with me, dear Maria?"

"Can. . .can I ask whom is inquiring as to this meeting?" The receptionist choked.

"Why sure ye can! Just tell the fine lad 'tis a few pirate friends o his comin to call." He rolled up his sleeve absently exposing a large "Z" emblem tattooed on his forearm complete with a Celtic tri-knot. "Have ye ever heard of Zeneria?" He scooted farther on to her desk. "Jesus, Mary and Joseph! Sure ye have! Here I am a making ye sound like a git!" He bumped her computer off the desk. "Oui! Did I do that?" He pulled out a sizable blade and slammed it point first into the woman's desk. "I'll get that. Would you be willin to hold this for a poor lad?"

As he bent down to pick up the monitor the receptionist yelped. "You are cleared to go in. Please, it's all right, I can get that." She tripped over her files that had fallen.

"There, there now lass, 'tis no reason to get in a fluster." He gently helped her up and damaged her with his deadly smile.

The other visitors had long abandoned the office. Just the sight of Loco had been far more motivation than was needed to spur them to other appointments of a less dangerous nature. The receptionist had a sick feeling that this was going to be her last day on the job. She decided better that, then what the Zenerian would do to her. She would leave, inform security and catch the next shuttle home.

The pair strode into the abandoned office, knowing that the receptionist was running for security. Boomer moved to the desk and turned on Baxter's computer screen.

"Baxter. Baxter. I know that name from somewhere man." Loco started rifling through files and turning over tables. Boomer turned to look out the large picture window.

"Tis sure. I think I have heard of the bloke before. Looks here like he is an aerospace engineer." Boomer pointed to scribbled plans that had been left on the desk. "Ya know, someone that smart isna' going to leave behind any fecking big clues." He noted.

"Well that means we're going to have to do a background check with the system." She started toward the door. Neither one of them were expecting security to show. This was a neutral planet and, as of yet, out of the ranks of galactic conflict. As long as they left the building in one piece they would be clear.

Back at her ship, Loco contacted Meadows. "So we have one lead. Baxter. He is some type of aerospace engineer. Most of Jeff's employees were fired prior to the desertion and assassination. It seems he took a small faction with him and shipped out on a freighter full of equipment. The other reports were right man, he was headed for the divide." She watched as Meadows manipulated her keyboard.

"Baxter. That does sound familiar. Hold on a second." She read with intent. "It says here that he was once on the list for our aerospace program. The man is a freaking genius. He has a family, a wife and a daughter."

"What's he doing working for a gringo like Kolbert?" Loco asked. She noticed Meadows concentrating.

"Yea. I remember him now. I met him once at a science convention. He was a really nice guy. Did the office have any signs of forced vacation?" She asked.

"No. Boomer and I messed it up a bit. Where is his family?" Loco asked.

"I think that will be something I will have to look into." Meadows sucked down a gulp of black coffee.

"Hey chica, you don't look so good." She reached up and tapped on her conversion engines and prepared for take off.

"I haven't been sleeping. I can't." Meadows admitted.

"Ya gotta sleep, doc." Loco had little room to talk. She and Boomer had been knocking heads for too many days to count with little or no sleep.

"I'm obsessed. I really miss her. In a kind of unnatural way." Monika admitted.

"What do ya mean unnatural?" Loco asked.

"Can you remember what she looks like? I mean without looking at a picture?"

"Sure I can doc."

"O.K. Try. Think about it. Tell me what you get." Meadows waited.

"Well. Ya know. She was. . . Well, I know what she looked like." Loco was surprisingly perplexed.

"I know I would know her if I saw her, but somehow I feel like she was a dream or a figment of my imagination. I grew up with the woman. I think I'm going insane."

"No. Now that you mention it doc, if someone asked me I doubt I could actually describe her." Loco called over to Boomer and asked him the same thing. He floundered as well. "Now that is weird."

"Loco. I'm going to let you go. Report back and let me know everything you find. I have to keep in touch with Canga. I'm trying to check in with her at least three times a day to keep her level."

"Keep her level. That kitten is the most level cat I know." Loco tried to sound positive.

"Loco, I asked her the same question. She couldn't answer." Monika frowned.

"Have you asked Zenerio or Siggurd?" Loco asked.

"I can't. I can't do that to them. It almost killed me to do it to Canga. I advised her to keep a picture of Britt up at all times. I would advise the rest of the team to do the same. If you talk to the rest let them know."

"Doc, what's going on?"

"Loco, I wish I knew. I wish I knew".

Chapter 17
Impotent Execution

Roderick was yanked from his bed with a force that sent him tumbling across the wooden floor of his room at Ruddy Mudders. He quickly lunged to his feet and spun about with dagger in hand. His mind cleared in time to hear his brother screaming in panic as he thrashed about to find the older elf's clothing.

"Dearest goddess of the morning star! Where are your boots, man?" He thrust a shirt and breeches into the arms of his baffled brother.

"What in the name of Ren' Fordel are you about Amaranth!" Roderick pinned the boy to the wall.

"Well, if you did not sleep like the dead anon, you would know! There is to be an execution in a few short shades! I was thinking perhaps you would wish to attend." He pushed the clothes at Roderick. "Meriden has been sentenced for the murder of her mother and she, AND her slaves are to be hanged in the public square in short order." Amaranth whisked past Roderick to pull the boots out from under the chest of drawers.

Roderick waved his arm above his head and was dressed by way of magick. "I see you have been practicing. Tis a good thing, we will need all the help we can get." Amaranth bolted out the door, followed closely by Roderick. The two glided down the narrow stairs and were through the dining area before their presence was detected.

"Rowland and Donavan have already left! I sent them ahead while I took the time to rouse you, though it be beyond me why you feel the need to sleep like an infant human."

"Where is Osizio?" Roderick questioned.

"Beriub locked him in the cellar. We thought it safer that way. No need in rescuing an ogre atop this mischief."

Roderick shoved his way through the growing crowds already forming around the platform. Sholendor was atop the wooden death tool addressing the onlookers.

"It saddens even me to think of such a crime. Be it known that our gracious Queen will not die in vain. Be it known that greed and power will not win the day!" He was surrounded by large, black-cloaked executioners mounted on horseback below the encircling platform.

"Roderick!" Rowland shoved past a herd of centaurs. "Thank the goddess you have come! I know not where these accusations arise from, but I have word that the Queen is dead and she was smothered to death."

"And the fools think Meriden did it?" Roderick was still making his way to the platform. Rowland stopped him.

"They have taken away all her magical powers, Roderick. I have been told that very late last night Britteny almost killed the prince in defense of

Meriden. I can only assume this means she is to hang as well, along with Sara." Rowland informed him. "Due to one of the guards informing the high counsel of her actions, it may have been decided that she is too dangerous to be permitted to live." Rowland seemed equally distressed that not only Meriden would hang, but Britt as well.

"When was this decided?" Roderick demanded.

"It was formally decided yesterday morning, not long after you returned to Ruddy Mudders, that Meriden and Sarah would hang for the crime. It was not announced outside the palace. Britt's fate, however, was not decided until very early this morning. I came as soon as I heard the news."

Roderick looked angered and Rowland looked to the sky. It was a well known fact that Roderick was born a weather elf and any severe mood shift would affect the current climate. Storm clouds were gathering. Rowland thought back to the events of the previous day. Roderick had returned to Ruddy Mudders in the very early hours of the morning. He had slept most of the day and the rest was spend in the merchant area purchasing goods that he quickly stowed in his private chambers. The weather had been superb yesterday while the women were on trial, unbeknownst to the common people of Ruddy Mudders and Roderick. In his private room he lay abed with thoughts of escape. He had even announced to his companions that they would need to have a meeting the very next day because he had something very important he needed to tell them.

Rowland took his arm as the wind began picking up.

"Calm yourself friend, lest your emotions for the human become known to all. This is not the way you want Amaranth to find out." The wise young elf told his dark friend.

"What do you mean by this?" Roderick was pulling away from him to head closer to the gallows.

"Do not be a fool, friend. I am not. I have spent time with that human. I know what has transpired between you both. I see it in you and I see it in her, so let us not be vague for the sake of vanity." He released Roderick's arm with a push of disgust.

"So you despise me now, friend?" Roderick stopped short and whispered to Rowland.

"I blame you not for your lust, 'tis what any male being would want. I only question your true motive. I would think you less rash and more able to think of her safety first if it be that you care for her future and her LIFE even in the slightest." With that Rowland turned and was done with the conversation.

Roderick did his best to still his emotions. Things were spiraling out of hand at breakneck speed. It was clear to him that Rowland cared deeply for Britt. Other than him, Rowland was the only one that had spent any time with her. It was sure that Britt's defense of Meriden helped to strengthen this bond, for in the act of putting herself between Sholendor and his prey, Britt had sealed Rowland's love and loyalty surely. He was wise to warn Roderick of the selfish actions that had been dangerously played upon of late. It seemed Rowland of Sid O'Sala was the only being able to withstand the whirlwind that was Britteny. Roderick followed deep in thought.

The citizens of Garath were a pungent bunch. As with many masses, they loved this type of scandal and were flocked like starved jackals around the constructed monument of death. Many of them, in truth, were hungry to see this human that had sparked such commotion among the royal court. This, the very same human that has laid to waste their best game fighters with little or no effort, was to be hanged. Surely entertainment of this quality came round rarely. All in all, it mattered not which city, which people, their talk was rattling the very buildings in hopes of observing the fight of a lifetime. A young halfling hoisted himself up onto his elder brother's shoulders.

"I say she takes the lot of them! I say she spits like a wildcat and tears the hearts out 'o em all!" His brother agreed. They cheered in anticipation of this new celebrity and an assumed live show.

Sholendor stood like an ivory tower and raised his arms.

"Hear me people of Garath! Hear your King!" The mob stilled in the wave of his aura. "I stand before you shamed! I stand before you an elf of trust who has been betrayed by his own intended! For, as of today, I am to the task of once and for all taking control of our once proud realm!" His arms shot out in glory. The crowd boomed. "Soon you will behold this wildcat you speak of! Soon you will know the truth of our shame. You see, the shame lies not in the innocent and ignorant but within our own family." He pointedly addressed the elves gathered not far off. "Many years ago I was put to the test of the life of my own brother! This is a test I wished not to repeat." He bowed his head for effect. "I have always held compassion and mercy as a true show of great magical power. It was for this reason I spared the life of your own Osizio of Garath, in the wake of my brother's bewitchment. Now, I am once again challenged!" He scowled. "I must not sit by and watch the innocent die. I must not allow the power of my bride to grow to a gross use and neglect of her position and power over the common folk. This woman has committed a murder that will never be wiped from the face of the elfish race. She has taken the life of her own mother to advance her ascent to power and evil magic!" He sent a chill wind into the crowd, whipping his hair around his dead face.

"When she came to Garath she had intent to spill the blood of your king. Do not be fooled by her silence. My father once told me that it was silence that does mark a killer. The mozeta are silent. They must be to ambush their prey, as is your princess!" He stepped to the edge of the stage and pointed a finger that swept over their heads. "Now she has created a killer of epic proportions with her magic. Many of you have paid witness to her wrath! You have witnessed the innocent beast mutated by the magic of a sick heart! She has turned a gift of love into an assassin! What power comes from a HUMAN female such as has been displayed at our own games, without the use of deep black magick?" He turned his back and walked to the hanging ropes, his thin fingers sliding over the rough skein, hesitating on the neck hole. He lowered his tone for the masses to barely hear.

"What have we come to? The mutation of an innocent, for the power of the corrupt." He reached into the crowd and pulled a healthy young female woman to the stage with him. The woman fell to her knees as he held her arm, suspending her top so the crowd could see her tearing eyes. "This is a HUMAN woman! She is but an ignorant, innocent beast of burden. When used right, she can be, not only a service, but also a companion. I ask you, does this look like the beast we witnessed at the games!" He bellowed. "If the Lady Meriden can transform a simple human into what we witnessed, what else will she do? I ask you the people of Garath?"

A lobolack howled his anger, creating a catalyst for the rest of the crowd to spiral into frenzy. Sholendor raised his thin arms once again. The woman groveled at his feet. "Her mother trusted her! This murder was simple. Trust makes for interesting bedfellows." He giggled. "And whom do you think she intended her new tool of destruction for? Do you think she dared try my death with trust?" It is I who would have perished. And what is worse is she would have done away with the evidence and the danger once I was disposed of. She would have turned on her most loyal companion and eliminated her as well!" He hollered so loud his face turned ever so slightly blue.

"Today I will once again prove to the people of Zembeth that I am a merciful ruler. Although this very human chose to attack me in ignorant defense of the princess, I choose to spare her life. I choose to take pity on her ignorance in hopes that when the princess is gone, her spell of demonic possession will leave this poor creature to the more suited life of a companion slave, as it should be. I will spare the life of the innocent, and spare my people the evil that would, one day find ruin to us all! I show to my people that we will pity the simple creatures put here to serve us with mercy, and we will not tarnish the pride and majesty that is ELF with a white witch bent on evil!" He threw his arms into the air as if begging for mercy from an unknown source.

An earthquake would have been less obvious. Creatures started shoving and kicking. Whoops and screams bounced off walls. Hot air circulated and stirred the thatched roofs of the simple huts on the square. Sholendor eyed his silent elfish brothers that swayed in the din.

"You!" He boomed. "You my brothers!" The crowd stilled. "I sense the doubt in your minds from here!" He was at the north edge of the stage in a flash. "Do you think it wise to live within our simian circle of creatures as their guides and lawgivers when the whole of our own royal house feels free to murder their own family?" He screamed. "And who do you think she will send it after when I am gone? Do you think she will allow anyone to stand in her way?" He balled his fists. "NO! When I am gone she will have eliminated her last hurdle. Then my brothers," He glared down at Roderick. "Then she will spill the blood of her own cousin." He shot a bony finger at Roderick. "Your future wife, black elf! How will it be then when my Britt tears apart your future wife?"

To the shock of Sholendor, Roderick jumped atop a nearby well. "Fine to me! Fine to us all! For each man and woman in this realm knows well that Princess Meriden is no more capable of murder than my Ma Fafella!" His voice was much deeper than that of the prince, his presence a shock to the system, his superior physical strength, obvious.

Roderick turned in a circle to address his equals of all races. His voice needed no plea for silence. On a well top, dressed as a rover, he needed only open his mouth for command of the throng. The mention of the goblin sorceress was enough to strike respect and fear into each and every being. Roderick spun to face the contrasting elf on the hangman's platform.

"No more shall we play these games that hold back the people of this land! Your greed and passion for this human distorts only your vision!" Roderick drew his sword and held it ready. "Listen, then, all to me! Listen, then, to the son of Zembeth, your brother and equal! I have known the three of these females! I watched Meriden grow into the quiet passive woman she is today. I was there the day the human was sacrificed to your enslavement and went willingly so that one of the common people may be free of a curse brought on by the sick passions of your brother!" He pointed up to Sholendor with the tip of his blade.

Amaranth, Rowland and Donavan did not dare interrupt this blinding rage yet braced for a cyclone. In many ways each of them had seen this moment at one time or another in their dreams and in the prior dealings with the prince. Sholendor looked to his executioners and guards for assistance. To his dread, he found none.

"I have witnessed the gnome Sara stand loyal to the royal family for her life." Roderick's face twisted into a terrible mask of anger. His eyes glowed with green energy that naturally signaled aggression in the elfish race. "Do not tell me of your ideas of lies and poison for you are the king of lies ONLY! You are the prince of deceit!"

Sholendor hovered above the angry mob. A wide circle had been cleared around the well now, causing the onlookers to pack tighter. Many of them chose to hide within shops to avoid Roderick's anger.

"She has stolen the necklace of the Shalnas! She means to use it to gain power supreme over the lives of us all! How can this be moral or just? Tell me this, ruffian? Besides, YOU know NOTHING of this human, you barely spoke to it. How would you have any idea as to its ability or mind?" Sholendor screamed.

Rowland looked up at Roderick in concern that his emotions for Britt would betray him.

"I know all I need know of that human, and she is not the issue, Meriden is. I say better she has this power than it lay in the hands of one not deserving!" Roderick's voice boomed. "She is the daughter of Ren'Fordel! She is the rightful heir to the throne of Zembeth! I say it is her right to wear such power! I say all three are innocent! Meriden has cast no spell on the human! She was born as such! You stand in fear of three of the Goddess herself! You stand impotent and shamed! I will not believe your accusations! I watched Britt defend a human child that day in the arena! I know she protected the princess from you on more than one occasion! And Sara! What should we say of the strength and loyalty of such a gnome?" He shouted into the faces of the common people. "That gnome fair near runs that palace and it is a damn good thing she does!"

At the mention of Sara and her ability, the crowd went absolutely wild. Some in anger, some in support, all lathered to a frenzy, yet none of them had missed the fact that Roderick of Darmuth Anor stood before them committing treason to the crown before the prince and the royal guard, with no show of hesitation or fear. This was the mark of open rebellion. A slight twist of fate moved the raving masses, for as he was shouting out the last of his testament, declarations could be heard from the west side of the droves of civilians hailing riders from the palace. Peeling away like leaves in a harsh wind, the people of Garath parted to allow three lone riders to approach the stage.

Upon dismount, a wiry elf soldier approached Sholendor and begged a private audience. The prince grudgingly accepted and bent to hear the news this distraction brought. His face went ashen. The crowd was caught off guard when Sholendor jumped in a fit of rage.

"This is impossible! Escape from the oubliette is not possible! They must still be in the palace!" He bellowed louder than intended.

Behind him he could hear Roderick's laughter rising above the din of confusion. "Find them at once!" Sholendor bellowed.

"So it seems we all play the fool now, Sholendor. So it seems we have only begun this round of tricks."

Sholendor ignored Roderick. He was far too busy demanding action and instructing his minions to be off. "You!" He pointed at one of the tall executioners. "Back to the palace with the guard to search the dungeons!" His cloak swept over burning torches, unharmed. "You!" He projected. "Out of the city gates and on the road to search the Arosa, make haste!" The mounted, cloaked rider kicked the thickly muscled black steed to charge through the confused residents of Garath and head for the east gate of the city. "You!" He pointed to Roderick, standing among the scattering inhabitants. "You will know now how true banishment feels. I will not let today's words go unheard by the royal counsel of elders!" His hand clenched into a fist then spread out. Osizio appeared in chains on the platform. "I have used restraint until this moment! Find the princess or the ogre and his family perish the most painful death imaginable!"

Roderick prepared to bolt for the stage only to be held back by the strong hand of Donavan.

"Think before you do this, Roderick. He has the backing of the counsel, right or wrong." Donavan advised.

Sholendor was poised in the fading light of the sun to enact the magical power he was afforded as a future member of the royal family. Although it was against their ethics to use this power against a fellow elf, it was public knowledge at this point, reflected in his words, that Roderick of Darmuth Anor was now an enemy of the crown. His assault on the prince would only lead to a decision by the powers that be to end the life Roderick and all that were associated with him. He pulled his arm free of Donavan's grip. Every individual in the crowd stood as still as Osizio, numbed by magick, lying on the stage in chains, each participant fearful they would be next.

"I shall find your princess, and her companions, and we shall see who lives and who dies when the truth is revealed!" He did not wait for a reply. Instead he stormed in the direction of the tavern to ready for the race against the palace guards to uncover the mystery of the missing females.

Sholendor floated to the back of his white steed and reined it to the western gate road. He was suppressing his fear with great difficulty. He could draw no other conclusion for the disappearance of the trio, save that of the possession of the fabled necklace in the grasp of the princess. Magick alone could free anything living from the bowels of the palace of Garath. If this were so, he would need to act in haste to recover the device. Without her natural magick the necklace would, at the very least, afford the princess the ability to remain hidden from his sight. It would allow her the strength to conjure a spell strong enough to override the will of the counsel in time. The moment she was at full strength he would be the first to feel the wrath of her anger.

Nightfall was descending much quicker than usual, or so it seemed. Hunting in the dark was best left to the deadly skill of the orakai and demons. Even in his anger, the voice of dysfunctional wisdom spoke. He could not afford to send elfish fleets out. He could not risk revolt in the city at this time. He would need to rely on Roderick's skill and weakness for the ogre. Demons may be a waste of time if the necklace were in play. He must be shrewd. She would kill Britt to spite him. He continued to be perplexed at how the princess had gained access on the location of the necklace and had the courage to do so with such secrecy. He would have never imagined Meriden, of all elves to be wily enough to remain a step ahead of him. He would not underestimate her again. If she did not possess the fabled necklace his race was won at a cost. It was a simple fact that the women would not survive a day on the open Arosa plain, why waste guards to find dead bodies?

********** * * * * * * * **********

The horse's hooves pounded like spastic hammers on the uneven road leading out the colossal gates of the city's west side. Word had been sent to leave the doors open only to let the palace executioners through, not before would they be closed and barred as usual, locking out the predators of the Arosa plains for the long night. The opening that had been allowed barely fit the girth of the beast and rider. For a moment the giant killer swayed and pulled in his cloak, seeming to shrink or duck down. Past the safety of the city walls the beast kept this pace for some time, in fear of its possessed master. The tree line, at times, ripped at the animal's flanks and yanked at the master's cloak. It was not until the grasses towered overhead and the light of the moon was barely enough to see by, that the rider slowed. The horse's chest was heaving and its body lathered with labor. A sharp tug pulled the unwilling stallion closer to the black forest line that bordered the Deneb Swamp.

As the horse danced with new found energy its rider separated. At first the tall figure appeared to bend over in illness or pain, as if the ride had been too strenuous for him as well. Slowly his long legs shoved his buttocks back and allowed his torso to separate. Britteny slid from the prancing horse's hindquarters and stepped lively to avoid being trampled.

"Come on Sara, lower her down slowly. We gotta calm this horse down before it kills itself." She reached up to embrace Meriden. Meriden reached down and fell into the arms of her slave.

"What shall we do now Britteny?" She asked weakly. "Where shall we go?"

She placed the princess on the cool grass and stopped to listen for a moment to ensure their safety. "I think we are gonna try to find this goblin sorceress." Without realizing it, she had held up a hand and calmed the steed. She helped Sara down. "We have to rest for a moment and I am going to scrape this horse and walk him for a while. The last thing we need to do is kill our transportation." She used the side of her hand to scrape the lather and sweat from the animal. With very slow and gentle movements she placed her hand between his front legs to get an idea of how heated he had become.

"O.K. We walk for a while. When he has had a chance to cool down, we water the horse, let him feed and then we put you two back on him and keep going until we hit the home of Ma Fafella." She announced.

"Are you sure this is a good idea?" Meriden asked.

Sara answered as Britteny continued her care of the priceless animal. "Ma Fafella is the only creature alive what can give ye back some 'o yer juice. That and I doubt that son of a sow Sholendor would dare ta go near the meadow."

"But will she help me, of all creatures?" Meriden sounded doubtful.

"Well, she raised Roderick and Amaranth. I suppose with me and the brute here with ye she might consider it." Sara speculated.

Meriden started shaking violently. For a moment Britteny was sure she was having a seizure. "What in the hell is wrong with her Sara?" She hissed.

"The lass is scared out 'o her pot." Sara held Meriden.

"My mother is dead. How can this be?" She squeaked as she pulled a ridiculous turban from her head fashioned from her own gown.

"Sholendor had his people kill your mother, Meriden." Britt affirmed. "It was either that, or he did it himself." Meriden looked at her blankly. "Now come on, up on your feet. We have to keep moving. We are going to stay close to the tree line. Here." She handed them the cloak. "Cover up and stay as close to me as you can. Sara, you hold the horse, he seems to be calmed down." Sara looked up at the black head. Her head was nowhere near its still flaming nostrils.

"I am hoping there is a surely good reason ye think I can handle this monster." She took the reins timidly.

"He is going to stay on that side of you two. I am going to be as close to anything that jumps out of these trees as I can get." Britt raised her head and sniffed the air.

"Should we not set fire and rest for the night?" Meriden asked hopefully.

"I can tell you have never been outside your tower for too long. NO. No fires. No resting. In a while you can ride the horse. For now, we walk and try to figure out what the hell we're gonna do next." She straightened her tender legs and started herding them all forward.

"I don't get it, why would Sholendor feel it necessary to kill your mother? He was almost king anyway." Britt asked, almost to herself.

"I do not believe Sholendor had anything to do with the murder of my mother." Meriden whispered. Britt stopped walking and sighed.

"O.K. If we are gonna be stuck out here together, how about you try to act like you have some common sense." Britt's frustration and fatigue was starting to seep through.

"Elves are simply not allowed to kill other elves!" Meriden demanded.

"Yea, and they are not allowed to sleep with humans either." Britteny huffed.

"As a matter of fact, they do not." Meriden volleyed. Sara did not like the direction this conversation was taking. She kept walking in hopes her companions would follow.

"Meriden, I've been sleeping with Roderick from pretty near the time I hit the palace." She took Meriden's hand and started pulling her to catch up with Sara and the horse. Meriden planted her feet, stopping Sara, the horse, and pulling Britteny short.

"Then all hope is lost." Her eyes covered in glass like moisture. "Where has my world gone?"

"Stop it! Just stop it! Forget you are an elf. Forget about magick, because you don't have it anymore. You're not in Kansas anymore. You need to deal with the fact that your little idea of how things should go is totally innocent and ignorant." Britt demanded. "Tell me you didn't know that Sholendor was planning to do something evil. Tell me you didn't know why he agreed to keep me and let Osizio live in the city again!" She waited. "Come on, tell me! You can't be that stupid!"

"I am NOT stupid!" Meriden started jumping up and down in anger. "I am not taking orders from you! Who are you? It was not until you came here that all this started!" She continued hopping with her fists clenched. "I DEMAND that we stop right here and right now! We are going to see my cousin De'Loria! I am not going to see a GOBLIN!" She was actually flushing blue in the cheeks.

Sara slapped her own forehead. "Here it comes." She muttered.

Britt started walking back towards Meriden and proceeded to pick the princess up and tuck her tiny white frame under her own arm and carry her like a spoiled child, kicking and screaming all the way.

"PUT ME DOWN RIGHT NOW!" Meriden bellowed. Her small fists flailed causing not even the smallest reaction to her captor. Britt set Meriden down but did not let her go. Instead she wrapped her large human hand around Meriden's stick like neck.

"Listen here Casper, we are NOT going to see that blue haired beast that you call a cousin." Meriden began growing pale as Britt's hand tightened. "Are we clear?" Britt asked. Meriden did not reply. "We are going to see that damned goblin and I am getting off this damn planet and neither Sara nor I am going to hang for your stupidity!" She loosened her grip a bit.

Meriden choked a bit before speaking. "You are not an elf. I do not have to obey you."

Britt started laughing hysterically. "Well, well, it appears you are not as much of a pussy as people think you are." She picked Meriden up again and this time took the makeshift rope that they had fashioned while escaping and began tying Meriden to the horse in a bundle. Sarah had to look away and walk forward to suppress her laughter.

"NO don't bind me! Please, I promise I will calm down! I promise!" Meriden begged.

Britt stopped momentarily. "If I let you go and you start running, I am not coming after you." She stared directly into Meriden's eyes. "I don't give a shit what eats you out here, you are on your own." Britt released Meriden. For the moment they all seemed relatively calm.

"The way I see it, we have no choice but to stick together Meriden. I figure Sholendor wants something. Why else would he kill your mother? What could he want?" She was happy to see that Meriden was actually mulling over the question instead of having another fit.

"The necklace." Her fine features shadowed. "By the love of the mother Goddess, he is searching for the necklace."

"Where is it?" Britt asked.

"My mother did not know. She died for nothing." Meriden reflected.

"Well, who knows where it is?" Britt pushed.

"Only I." This answer surprised Sara.

"And how is it ye know?" Sara asked astonished.

"Before my father left, he came into my room and told me. He knew where it was and he did not want my mother to have it. He told me and then he left forever."

"Why didn't you go get it?" Britt wanted to know.

"I do not know. Perhaps I was frightened of the power it possess." Meriden reflected.

"Well where is it?" Britt whined in frustration.

"In the Shalnas forest." Meriden answered.

"That's the really scary magickal forest? Of course, where else? Where else would it possibly be? Silly me." Britt put her face in her hand in complete frustration.

"Yes. Now you see why I am so distressed."

As soon as Britteny looked up she froze, staring into the sky. She abruptly started running for the nearest tree.

"What are you doing?" Meriden followed yelling. "Do not be afraid, 'tis just our blessed mother, our new moon." Meriden assured her.

Britt kept climbing. She had seen only one other station of this design and it was protected under Belthan law. She searched for branches strong enough to hold her weight. Her heart beat in her mouth as the prospect of going home drew closer with every step. Gherkin had been right. Over the canopy she hissed the need for silence down to the frantic elf female below and squinted to get a better look at what could be her salvation. The satellite had orbited close enough to the planet for her trained eye to access enough visual information to confirm the fabled moon to be a space station.

She landed with a strong thud next to the princess. "I think we may just be saved after all!" She reached up to feel her singed hair giggling with glee.

"Britteny, do not fear our mother, she is a sign of hope of the future." Meriden patted her back.

"That's not a moon, Meriden. That's a space station." Britt paced back towards Sara and the stallion.

"This is gone far enough!" Meriden screamed, shocking Britt and Sara. "For the love of God, I want to go back to the palace." She slid started marching back towards the city.

"What did I just get done choking out of you, you stupid albino?" Britt picked her up, only to be slapped sharply across the face. For a moment Sara feared she would have to get between the two of them. Britt got hold of Meriden's flying arms.

"HEY! There'll be no slapping! Don't make me open a can of whoop ass on you, little miss!" Britt encompassed both of Meriden's flailing hands in one vise like grip.

"Is it that ye were asleep at the games, you daft idiot?" Sara walked over and asked her ward. "This big oaf is gonna wear your guts like a crown iffin ye donna stifle." Sara said slapping Meriden's face. Britt's own face opened up in a comical shocked look as she set Meriden down.

"Awww, you got nailed by the gnome." Britt put her hand over her mouth to stifle even more laughter.

"Sara, you hit me." Meriden could barely get the words out due to her shaking lips.

"Yer damn straight I did, ye bleedin idiot! And Illa do it again iffin ye don't settle down. I shoulda whapped yer ass more often ye spoiled bitch!"

Now Sara was truly angry. Britt backed up in spite of herself. "Now YOU, you big whore!" Sara pointed at Britt. "What the FECK is that if it's not a moon!"

"It's a space station. There are people living on it." Britt crossed her arms. "I know it sounds crazy to you hillbillies, but it's true, and if I am right we are all in big trouble."

Meriden started to say something only to be stifled by Sara's glare. "One more word out of you, whitey, and I swear on my dead mother's grave I will shove those pointed ears up your ass." Sara told Meriden in a very serious tone.

"Have you ever seen lights falling from it toward the horizon?" Britt asked, hoping Meriden would say something, if only to see Sara make good on her promise.

"Sure we do, but the stars shoot ov'r the forest ev'n when she is not about." Sara was willing to assist Britteny in any way she could to get out of this mess.

Britt rubbed her brow hard. "Let me guess, the Shalnas Forest, right?" Both women nodded. "Of course." Britt sighed. "O.K. new plan." Britt clapped. "I wanna go home, right?" She asked. Again the women nodded, more from confusion and helplessness than understanding. "We have to agree here and now to work as a team. I wanna go home. You want that necklace and I bet you just want to be left alone. Right?" They all now stood in a small circle, the horse chewing soft grass behind them. "Either way we go, as I see it, we have common and unseen enemies that would love to see all three of us dead or enslaved." She pointed to the sky.

"That so called moon could very well be a battle station. I highly doubt it is a science lab. If I'm right, that means the beings on it could easily destroy all life on this planet." She reached for a green locust on a blade of grass next to her. "If that is the fact then I need to get hold of my people as soon as possible. When I say all life, I mean ALL life. There will be nothing left but a barren waste land of burning flesh and parched soil." She let the insect jump from her hand. "If it is a science station, well, then all the better. Either way I have to get up there." She looked at Meriden.

"Sholendor is not going to stop until he gets that necklace. When he does, you're as good as dead. No one will oppose him and live, correct?" Meriden nodded, eyes wide. "If that is a battle station, even if I can stop the people on it, you're all still in grave danger." She bent down on one knee. "I promise I won't let that happen, but you both, for the first time in your lives, you must trust a human. We gotta trust each other." Sara reached out and touched Britt's shoulder as Meriden watched.

"I suppose ye have been right this far and I sure as lot do no want me life any worse than it already is." She playfully slapped Britteny's head.

"Meriden?" Britt asked.

The Princess of elves took a deep breath. For a moment she glowed with a light that emanated from somewhere foreign to Britt and Sara. She looked to the moon, reflected in the blood red of her iris. "I see few other options." Folding her arms she huffed. "I can only hope this will not be a completely uncomfortable adventure." Sara stepped in front of Britt before she strangled Meriden.

"Oh. This is gonna be a blast." She took the horse's reins. "Trust me, Meriden, this journey isn't going to be over soon enough." Britt assured her.

"Why are you acting like a troll?" Meriden whined.

"You could freaking say thank you, you selfish little bitch." Britt's face was pink with anger.

"Thank you for what? Dragging me through a pile of corpses?" Meriden seemed oblivious to her ignorance. "I would not be surprised if I do not have some criminal's eyeball stuck in my hair!" Sara knew the princess was arguing for the sake of argument. It was not in her emotional make up to answer to a human.

"Oh hush up, you!" Sara barked at Meriden as she stormed forward not wishing to waste more time.

"Sara! How can you speak so to me?" Britt started walking after Sara looking over her shoulder in surprise at Meriden, who clearly did not remember the "ear up the ass" remark made earlier.

"Ye flappin bag 'o wind! Yer not mad about the corpses! Ye got a bug under yer bonnet because here ye are, wandering though the plains with two slaves what got more sense than all yer sharp-eared traitorous relatives! Donna give me yer load of sheep shit!" Meriden's mouth flapped open and closed. "Ima not goin' to hear another word of it, you spoiled skinny git! Iffin ye wanna go back to Garath then GO. Ima goin' to Ma Fafella's with Britt. I know where my friends live. Do you?"

Sara spat at Meriden's feet and started walking the steed onward ripping the reins from Britt's hand. Britt frowned comically and followed her. Meriden stomped her feet and folded her arms in revolt.

"Fine! I will venture back to the palace! Someone will listen to me!" She neglected to turn around and start back. Her arms fell to her sides. "I mean it Sara! I am really going!" She screeched.

"Well, shut your pie hole and start walking, stupid!" Sara yelled back. "Keep yellin like this and ye'll have a royal escort real soon!" Again she bravely led the horse on. Britt followed choosing wisely to stay neutral. If she were prone to gambling though, her money was on Sara. "Ye'll make a fine snack for some hungry mozeta." Sara added over her shoulder.

So they walked. Eventually they lost sight of Meriden. Britt was amazed that Sara had not opted to turn around. Her will and determination seemed boundless. For a short time she contemplated talking her down and going back. A journey with Meriden was not exactly appealing, yet she felt guilty leaving her standing in the middle of the road.

"Oh stop it!" Sara seemed to read her mind. "That washed out little witch's got no love fer nobody but her own arse. You shouda gagged her when ye had the chance. I am sick 'o fighting with her and playin at these fits. Iffin she's got the nerve to act as though we are the buggered enemies after all the arse savin we have done today then feck her! Let her rot!"

Britt touched her arm, causing Sara to stop and look. Meriden was begrudgingly trotting up from behind.

"I have decided to travel with the likes of you both. I will allow you to assist me." She stated in a matter of fact manner. Now it was Britt's turn to step in the middle of a possible fight.

"Hold on there, Meriden. I don't think we want you anymore." Britt sounded as condescending as she could muster under the comical circumstances.

"Why not?" Meriden squealed.

"Well, for starters you're a huffy little selfish bitch. Second, if we are going to risk our necks for someone it's gonna be for someone that appreciates it and third, you are clearly too stupid or too stubborn because thus far you have been choked, tied and slapped, and you are still stupid."

"I do appreciate it. Really I do." She pleaded.

"You sure as hell don't act like it." Britt informed her.

"Well, I am sorry! I am so sorry! Perhaps I am not accustomed to having my whole world ripped apart!" Meriden cried.

"And yers is the only world that matters, is that it?" Sara asked.

"O.K. I'm getting sick of this drama. Meriden, get over yourself and get a grip. Are you coming or not?" Britt insisted. Meriden started to whine again. "No. I am sick and tired of your bitching. Are you coming or not? If you are, then shut the hell up and act like you give a flying rat's ass about something other than yourself. O.K.?" She gave the impression that this was the last of the argument she would hear.

"I agree." Meriden offered begrudgingly.

"Now say you're sorry to Sara like you mean it." She reached out slightly. "Don't make me choke you again, because nothing would make me more happy right now." She warned.

"I am sorry." Meriden clipped off.

"Did you see the size of that gnome's ears? I know she didn't hear you!" Britt lifted her hand as if to reach for Meriden's neck.

"I AM SORRY! I mean it. I really am. We are all at odds. I am sorry I am fretting, I think under the circumstances I have every right to be upset." She fumed.

"Na Britt, don't kill her." Sara said before Britt could club Meriden in the face. "Trust me, that is as warm as it gets for them." She turned to Meriden. "I can forgive ye always. Iffin ye keep it up though I may not be able to forget." The sturdy woman soldiered on.

Britt scowled at her. "Get used to fear, princess, it is about to become a daily event."

Britt picked up Sara and put her on the horse, then watched as Meriden hopped up. Once the two smaller women were seated, Britt, deciding to ride after all, gracefully mounted the animal with a leap from the ground. They all settled in and Britt took the reins to urge the stallion forward. At first he jumped and pranced, until Meriden touched his withers, calming him only slightly he continued at a brisk walk toward Ma Fafella's swamp.

Left to her own thoughts as they trotted on, it occurred to Britt that it may have been Ma Fafella that transported her to this planet. Perhaps the goblin sow foresaw the destruction the station could ensue and worked a spell pleading for someone of her professional talents. If so, this would still not explain her singed hair. She would have to schedule a private chat with Ma Fafella. She wondered if Gherkin had guessed this as well.

The night was as full of color and life as the very day. Britt noticed that Meriden had settled against her and seemed to be dozing off. Her mind drifted to Roderick. It seemed Meriden had chosen to ignore her statement. Perhaps that was for the best. Britteny knew that, at times, denial was sometimes the only foundation for sanity. If Meriden was so opposed and even able to block such validation of human and elf actually coupling, it was only a sign of what the rest of this civilization felt. A gamble to a gun, Thernix was an astounding distance from this place, even from the perspective of someone like Captain Devarelle. That had to be a hell of a spell she thought, letting her mind wonder, yet keeping her senses tuned to the grass and trees around them.

Britt took a deep breath and winced. They all still smelled like rotting corpses. Perhaps they would need to rinse off in the meadow. It would do no good to show up to a goblin sorceress's home smelling like last year's grave. How lucky it was that neither elf nor ogre had noticed their stench at the lynching. She smiled a bit to think of Roderick's brave confrontation with

Sholendor. A true friend was best judged when they had no idea they were being observed. The display had earned Roderick yet another place in her heart. This one, that of respect and to Britteny, respect was the paramount constitution of any relationship, next to trust.

Their escape had not been rocket science for Britt. It was apparent that they could not simply fight their way through the guards. Even with her voice capabilities, elves were just too good with a bow and quiver to attempt dragging a sick elf and skittish gnome out the front door of the royal palace. Once that plan was trashed, Britt tried to concentrate on how to get out of the room without magick. Meriden had roused a bit and had started mumbling. This made Britt and Sara very nervous. Meriden was drooling on herself and had taken to rocking back and forth. This spurred Britteny to pace faster and eventually catch a whiff of the dungeon below the oubliette. She instantly pulled up the filthy rug to find, against the wall, a sizable air duct. Sara protested at first sight of Britteny pulling off the iron grate and climbing down the passage. She was silenced by the venom in the human's eyes and did her best to keep Meriden quiet.

When Britt returned her face was wrinkled in disgust. She wasted no time gagging Meriden and instructing Sara to rip Meriden's dress into long strips. They would use these to tie to the grate and lower the princess to the sub cell below. Britteny neglected to mention the pile of rotting bodies that had cushioned her fall. Once the three of them were clear of the heap of blood and intestines, Sara was again instructed to keep Meriden calm as Britteny climbed the massive mound once again, slipping from time to time on a detached head or arm. Sara watched in awe as the human leapt nearly half her height to cling to the princess's torn gown and scale arm over arm, back to the oubliette. She was going to pull the rug back over the grate and untie the makeshift rope, then crab walk down the shaft and drop into the flesh heap. It was nearly too dark for Sara to see her come off the pile. When Britt approached, again she insisted that they stay still until she returned. So they waited in the pitch-black chamber full of the rotting bodies consisting of mostly gnomes and humans.

Sara turned to the sound of scraping. She huddled closer to the wall and gripped Meriden's now bruised arms to keep her still. Through the dark Sara could make out a lean figure laboring with some type of burden. Britt hissed to her, letting her know it was safe and proceeded to half carry, half drag the dead body of a court executioner to where the two women were huddled against the wall. She tossed a very large black cloak towards Sara and kept moving towards the pile of bodies. What she did next mortified Sara enough to cover Meriden's eyes. Britt produced a sword of sizeable merit and hacked the body to pieces separating and stashing every limb at various locations in the menagerie of lost lives. In its mouth she shoved the balled up gown-rope they had used to ascend with and shoved the head as far into the pile as her arm and the blade would allow.

She was in no mood for talking and quickly instructed Meriden and Sara to embrace her front and back. She had then produced a cloth rope she must have stolen or made (when Sara had no idea) and proceeded to wrap it around them and bind them together. It took a moment of persuading to get Meriden to do anything after the previous display.

Britt made her point very clear and told Meriden in no short order that she was not dying for Sholendor and if Meriden did not cooperate she would end up in the pile with the executioner. Britt put Meriden in the back and told her to sit high and keep her head up. Unfortunately Meriden has a very small head. Britt took a few moments to contemplate this and a few other important dynamics of her makeshift escape plan. Without asking, she proceeded to finish off what was left of Meriden's skirt, making a turban to enlarge the size of Meriden's child sized cranium to fit in the hood, two slings to fit under each smaller woman's back side to help support them and keep them as close as possible. She even cut a toe stuffer for the oversized boots she must wear to complete the ensemble.

When everyone was tucked in and the robe secure in place, Britt slipped on the stripped man's gloves, slid the sword into the belt and strode off with the best man-like walk she could invent. They were just in time to follow the procession out to the stables, mount and begin the ride towards Garath. This hodgepodge plan worked only for a small number of reasons.

First off, Britt doubted their smell would have given them away. The rest of the henchmen were far from hygienically conscious. Second, riding in such a procession would mean that, perhaps, they would not be required to speak, but listen they could. Of course, having a steed the size of a small transport would only aid their escape. On the ride she learned that the prisoners were to follow due to the extremely sensitive nature of the human. Special slaves were being instructed and given weapons, special slaves, meaning an army of deaf gnomes. They would overwhelm the female and restrain her while the other women were removed to a separate wagon. The gnomes were also instructed to gag the human and leave her bound as such in the cell until further notice. So Sholendor did persuade the council to let her live. It seemed Sholendor was anxious to work the crowd before Meriden arrived and chose to head off early to supervise and prepare for the show.

Britt was so relieved to find that her executioner had been a mounted guard. Why they needed ten men to do the job of one was just another typical display of ancient social dominance and suppression. For a moment she thought she felt Meriden giggle when Sholendor found out they had escaped. In some fashion, Britt now knew that Meriden would choose to suppress much of what was going on around her. If she did not acknowledge it then it did not exist, much like the denial of the murder of her mother. Or perhaps it was in that cold elfish shell somewhere, still present but hidden. Britt was thinking that Meriden reminded her a great deal of a younger Captain Devarelle.

They had ridden a good distance and soon the road ahead started to look very familiar. Britt jumped a bit when Meriden turned and pointed to the moon.

"It has been damaged." She noticed.

Indeed, when Britt turned about to investigate the princess's observation, she too saw the large black area on the otherwise flawless looking sphere. Britt started to laugh.

"What is it you find amusing Britt?" Meriden asked.

"I did that." Britt chuckled. "Boy that must have really pissed them off. I only hope it keeps them occupied for a while." Meriden did not want to ask how. She had experienced quite enough in the past few days. Sara was just plain exhausted.

"O.K." Britt jumped from the horse. "We rest here until full morning. Then I will go to see Ma Fafella and the two of you will wait in the woods for me." She directed.

"Why er we waitin, what's wrong with goin' now?" Sara whined.

"Oh, I see Sara. So you're volunteering to wake a very large and powerful goblin sorceress up in the middle of the night. Is that what you're suggesting?" Britt raised her brows. Sara fell into her hands and was lowered to the ground.

"Well, I'm supposing I should shut my pie trap an' be off to some sleep. Is that what yer sayin?" She winked.

"Yea, I think that's a good idea for all of us." Britt spread the cloak onto the soft grass.

"What if they happen by here and see us?" Meriden asked with more than a little hint of paranoia.

"Trust me, they are all making tracks to the Shalnas Forest to get that necklace first." She positioned herself in the middle of the cloak. "Besides, I doubt they will send any guards after us." Britt informed.

"Why not?" Meriden asked. "I am the princess after all."

"They don't think we will survive long. Why waste time on man power that could be used to get to the Shalnas on three corpses?" Britt walked around looking for a suitable place to bed down.

"Is that not what we should be doing at this moment?" Meriden asked.

"Sure, with a crippled elf, a starving and tired human and a loud mouthed gnome. Yea, we have an icicle's chance in hell of making that trip." Britt waved for the other two to join her in the cloak. Sara climbed in and curled up.

"I will sleep out here if it is all the same with you." Meriden sniffed.

"Suit yourself. If you freeze by dawn I'm not waiting for you to thaw in the morning." Britt yawned.

"I will not freeze, I can . . ." Neither Sara nor Britt remarked when they saw the look on the princess's face. Her mental torment of being without her only self-defense was humbling enough. Meriden walked to the cloak.

"Here, sleep between me and Sara. We should be able to keep you warm." Britt patted the cloak. Once Meriden was in, Britt pulled the other half of the cloak over them completely. The three of them spooned together as Sara tucked the open end of the cloak under her knees. Arms wrapped around each other, the companions dropped into a deep sleep. The ebony war-horse had been relieved of his bridle and was loosely tied to a tree with Meriden's turban. He stayed close and kept guard until the full light of day.

Chapter 18
Ma Knows Best

Britt woke slowly, baked awake by the heat of the day. She was alone in the damp cloak but could sense her companions were not far. She took a moment to hold her sternum. The heartburn was getting worse by the minute. She would make sure to ask the goblin woman if there were something she could take to ease her suffering. As if reading her mind, Sara approached and handed her a fresh red apple.

"Here lass, this will help wit that burning. I should say he is gonna be a rite fine little dragon." She smiled and sat on the cloak to eat with her new sister. From her apron, she dropped a number of roots and berries. "I know it's not much, but I figure 'tis something. After all, we canna have ye starving."

Britt noticed Sara was damp as were her cloths. "I see you have cleaned up."

"As I suggest you do as well. After yer done eating, strip down and jump in. I'll scrub yer garb a bit with some sand." She offered.

"Sara, you don't have to. I can clean my clothes. I appreciate your offer but you won't have the time or the strength to take care of all of us." Britt said gently.

"Oh hogswallow! Iffin it weren't fer ye, I would be dangling from the palace walls as we speak!" She insisted. "Besides, was it not ye who said we must stick together now? I canna do much but I can do me share. If that is making sure ye are both clean and well fed, then that be me lot."

"Fair enough." Britt grinned. She was growing very fond of this woman. There was no fear or shame in Sara. She was very good at what she did and proud to be one that cares for others. Britt had a feeling if she were not born a slave, she would have chosen to either be the mother of a whole litter of little gnomes, or taken up caring for others in a medical capacity. Either way, she was a natural. Britt took one more large bite of the apple and stood to undress. She stripped naked and went to the bushes to relieve herself. When she came out to the open she ran for the lake. She could see Meriden sitting naked on the same boulder she had sat on when she arrived, dipping her tiny toes in the clear water.

"Wahoooooooo!" She yelled as she headed for an embankment. With one incredible leap she aimed for the dark blue water. For sometime she did not resurface. Meriden stopped laughing with amazement and scanned the crystal waves. She had never seen a naked human female, let alone a naked diving, swimming human female. As a matter of fact, she was not sure humans could even swim before today. Finally she saw a massive red cloud approaching the surface right before her feet. Britt surfaced and flipped her hair away from her face. "MY GOD, THAT FEELS GOOD!"

"That was wonderful, Britt!" Meriden clapped. Britt smiled and put her hands together, creating a suction cup and squirted Meriden in the belly. "Eeeekk!!" She squealed.

"Bet ya can't catch me!" Britt challenged as she flipped backwards into the water and accelerated into the lake. Meriden rose to her feet and vaulted off the boulder into the cool water after her friend. They played so for a time, until tired and laughing too hard to breathe and swim at the same time. Sara sat watching in amusement and fed the horse an apple, silently noting that Meriden, her Meriden, was laughing.

"What do ye think we should call him?" She yelled.

Britt and Meriden quit splashing to think on this question. The stallion nudged Sara lovingly.

"Hey, he likes you Sara. You name him!" Britt yelled as she climbed from the lake.

"Well, I know this is gonna sound a wee bit silly, but when I was a lass I fell in love with a dwarf lad." She confessed. Meriden was shocked and stopped mimicking Britteny in the act of shaking like a dog to dry her hair.

"Really! You were in love once!" She was astonished.

"Of course. Where do you think Hannah came from?" Sara huffed.

Meriden blushed hot. "Hannah is half dwarf? Why did you never tell me?"

Sara kept stroking the stallion's soft nose. "I suppose because before ye were my master, now yer my friend." She winked. Britt smiled warmly behind her mass of curls. "I'm thinking I will name him after Hannah's father and call the boy Murdock."

Meriden gasped. "Murdock, the stone carver! The one that worked on the temple in Fairfax?" She asked.

"The same." Sara replied, now deep in thought. Britt was braiding her hair and listening intently.

"Oh Sara, I am so sorry." Meriden looked ashamed and awkward at the same time. Britt looked up.

"Tis not yer fault, yer mother was the one that ordered his death. I put it aside long ago." Sara straightened. "Well enough lollygagging about. We need to get outta here." She started shaking the cloak out.

Britt said nothing and walked to the boulder to put on her still damp cloths. She looked around for a moment.

"What is it Britt?" Meriden asked.

"Well, the last time I was here this place was crawling with little people. Ya know, fairies."

"REALLY!" Meriden switched moods. "I should so love to see one. I have never been close to one. They are a bit shy around elves."

"I thought you were related somehow." Britt guessed.

"Yes we are, but we live in awe of one another I suppose." She squatted and tried to peer through the grass to find a pixie.

"Somehow I don't think they want to come out. If they did, trust me, they would be here by now. I met Ma Fafella in the meadow the day I arrived here." She informed them.

"Ye have already met the goblin witch?" Sara asked.

"Yea. I think it was her. She told me to call her Ma Toad."

"That was her." Meriden remarked. "I have been told she looks like a great giant toad. Does she?"

"Yea. Actually she is sharp. She was the one who suggested I go with Osizio to the city."

Meriden and Sara looked at one another. Britt busied packing and with no further ado, hoisted the women onto Murdock.

Murdock trotted like a foal down the dirt ruts that passed for a road. Britt was amazed he could lift his giant feet that far off the ground. He reminded her of the draft horses the Amish farmers used for fieldwork. After about one hour as the sundial moves, Sara pointed ahead to a barely visible cottage nestled against the black cliff wall.

"That is the place for certain." She informed.

Britteny jumped from the horse. "Well, wish me luck." She kissed Murdock's nose and started walking.

"Britteny." Meriden called.

"Yea."

"Please take care."

Britt waved off her concern with a comical hand gesture. In truth she was rather rattled. She had seen goblins in Garath and they were very nasty characters. She had only spent a short time with this goblin and at the time she did not actually look like a goblin. Britt wondered if Ma Fafella knew her disguise had only partially worked. She had killed a few of them in the arena at the Beltane games. This goblin was female, which made her smarter from the start, and she could work serious magick. This would have to be handled with care. She only hoped Sara and Meriden were smart enough to get out of sight. She remembered Murdock and felt better.

Walking closer to the goblin's lair she was pleasantly surprised. The cottage was small and mound shaped with connecting corridors that attached a number of like mounds to the main cottage. The door was round and solid, boasting iron hinges and stays. The doorframe was adorned with bright green tiles. Every perfect round window was complete with a flower basket of varied shapes and sizes, filled with brilliant blooms. A cobblestone sidewalk, neatly trimmed and cared for, led up to a charming stone fence with a trim iron gate. The road nearly met this gate and turned sharply to the north, heading toward Kloter Mass Arosa. Strange that the road should nearly come to her door and still many rumors were told of how people avoided Ma Fafella. A little chimney sputtered sweet smelling smoke. Britt took a deep breath; it smelled like cedar and cookies. She held for a moment and observed the fantastic gardens that surrounded the extended dwelling. The black walls of the Kloter cliffs brought the wet green of the foliage alive. Sunflowers were already beginning to reach above the gate and, to Britteny's delight, morning glory vines sprawled over the fence and house.

She approached slowly. When she reached the iron gate she hesitated. Perhaps this was a trap of some sort. She looked around. From somewhere behind the main hut she could hear a very deep humming. The tune was pleasant enough, although the voice was almost too deep for such a light ditty. Britt closed her eyes and reached out with her feelings. She could detect nothing but love and warmth from this place. It if were a trap it was a damn good one. She chided herself, and asked what would someone this powerful have to fear? She gently pushed the gate open. Walking to the door, she decided that going around to where the humming was coming from might be a better plan. She boarded the third hut and peeked around to see the green goblin sow bent over in a flower garden pulling weeds.

"Britt dear, hand ol' Fafella those shears on the table like a good lass." Without thinking, Britt walked to the stone table and picked up the iron pruning shears. She handed them to the goblin and waited. Fafella looked up at her with eyes as orange, and almost as large as a pair of pumpkins. "Let's have a look at ye now." Fafella labored to stand. Britt willingly reached out and helped the older woman to her feet. She braced her legs, the goblin had to go nearly four hundred pounds. "Well yer a good girl, and a brave one I would wager. You look well enough. I see the palace was the prudent plan then?"

"Well not exactly. I am here to ask a favor of you." Britt bowed with respect.

"Of course ye are. And yes, I knew you would figure out my little disguise." She winked her lantern like eye. "We are one in the same, you and I. Granted I could not chase a dead cat and catch it, but I could teach you a thing or too about magick." She walked to the portly stone seat that had obviously been built to fit her girth. "And then there is the fact that we both love my son with all we have in us." She slipped in.

Britt sat down opposite her. "Yes, I think that is true Ma Fafella." She admitted.

"So ye know he is my son, then? Well of course he is not my natural son. I found him in Kloter Mass Arosa. He and his brother were left at my doorstep. I fell for the lads from first sight."

"Me too." Ma Fafella seemed to demand unconditional honesty with not so much as a word.

"He is a looker, that Roderick. Always was. 'Course I knew he would require something a bit more than your average run of the mill mattress dragger." Britt laughed out loud.

"There is no asking necessary, my child. The law of magick is easy, we help, and we are helped. We hate and we are hated. It is such in this circle."

She moved her dirty wart covered hand in a circle motion, producing a beautiful blue light ring. "Meriden is always welcome in my home. Her mother would be another matter. I don't allow negative energy past the gate." She insisted.

"I suppose you know her mother is dead?" Britt asked.

"As sure as the frog croaks. Good thing." She offered Britt a cigar. Britt accepted and bit off the end with pleasure. Fafella lit the end with her finger aflame for a moment. Britt leaned over and sucked hard on the tip of the sweet tobacco, drawing the flame inward. "I have already taken the liberty of telling Meriden she is more than welcome here, so the two of them are on their merry way."

"That was nice of you." Britt remarked.

"That Sara has always been one of my favorites. Tough old crow, that one." Her laughter made the table shake. For a moment she looked deep into Britt's eyes. "Yes. You are a rare one. Never thought I would see the day when a child of the stars would be sittin' in my garden."

"Is there anything you don't know?" Britt wondered.

"I know my son loves you. That is all I really need to know about you." She took a big puff of the stogie and blew a smoke ring. "So open up and let's have a look at that baby." She struggled to keep her balance so Britt knelt down before her and opened her mouth wide. "Hmm. Here." She handed Britt a glass of clear liquid. "Apple cider vinegar. I know it tastes like horse piss but ye need to keep swiggin it a couple times a day for the burning."

Britt gulped it down and winced. "Damn, that's nasty!" She coughed.

"So K. Little bugger is growing fast. He should be here soon." Fafella commented.

"Soon? That quick?" Britt was shocked.

"Dragons do what they wish. Some take longer than others. Some come in one day. Depends on the host, actually." Ma Fafella dismissed the conversation and went on to more pressing matters.

"So about that new moon of ours, how bad is it?" She asked Britt.

"How about I tell you, when you tell me who brought me here and how?" Britt looked all the while at the wet black rock wall.

"I do not know who brought you to us child, but I would imagine you came the same way our ancestors came across." Fafella offered.

"What, some kind of dimensional porthole or something like that?"

"I have no knowing of such things, or at least not in those words." Fafella answered.

"O.K. A doorway to another world, how's that." Britt offered.

"Well yes, but it has been so long I have no idea where the doorway is, no one does, that I know of."

"It looks like that moon is my only way back." Britt sighed.

"Is that a bad thing?" Fafell asked.

"Well yea. If that moon is what I think it is, they may not be very willing to help me. For all they know I am an alien native thingy." She flayed her hand through the cigar smoke. "What's worse is what they could be doing to this planet and what they might do if they are caught." Britt said all this with the type of hesitation a parent uses with a child when there is a horrible truth to be told that will likely scar the child for life.

"Give it to me straight." Fafella took a big drag of her stogie.

"Well you remember the stories of Earth right?"

"Most of them, enough to know it was not going in a good direction when our kind left." She informed.

"Well it got really, really bad. The humans grew in their knowledge of the physical world and so did their weapons. They got so good they made weapons that could burn the entire planet, covering it in noxious gasses and literally eliminating all life." Britt turned to access the damage her worlds held to a creature such as this.

"I cannot think of words to describe such a thing." One goblin sized tear streaked down her cheek. "Yet you do not weep?" She asked the human next to her.

"I did my crying a long time ago. With all I have been through sometime, I think I forgot how to cry." Britt fell silent for a moment. Ma Fafella placed her hand on Britt's knee.

"We will do everything in our power to make sure this home does not go up in smoke. Are ye ken?" She asked her human friend.

"Yea, I'm ken." Britt looked up and smiled painfully.

"My magick will not work on such a force. Now do you see why you were called here?" Fafella asked.

"Yea but it still blows. I mean we could have planned it better. Now I have no ship, no armor, no nothing. I got a skinny white elf and a smart ass yellow lady." Britt giggled.

"I think you have been in worse company afore. Just sayin." Fafella laughed back. "For now we gotta get you to that moon. We have much to do. Do you really think you can do this?" Fafella asked.

"I guess we're gonna find out." Britt stood up when she heard the two women come round the corner.

"Well here they are. 'Tis a pleasure to meet you, Your Highness." The goblin bowed her head slightly.

"No Ma Fafella, really, the pleasure is all mine. In fact, it is an honor to be in the company of such an accomplished sorceress." Meriden knelt down to one knee and bowed to Ma Fafella. Britt and Sara looked at each other, thankful of her mood change.

"No need for all that, dear. Up on your feet. You are, after all, going to be the blasted Queen." Fafella howled again, "Let's see if ya bow to me then." She patted Meriden on the arm to show her intention was only that of humor. "Now here is a woman I fear may just be my match." She smiled at Sara.

"Who, me?" Sara pointed to her own chest. "Seems ye have some might strong weeds in yer garden there, lady. Ye may not want to light fire for fear of strange dreams." She offered.

Ma Fafella burst into thunderous laughter. "Well I will be sending all of you to the bathing pool with some very strong soap now. It is a right sad set of affairs when a goblin is ailed by the stench of the likes of you." She huffed. "Now off with the lot of you. When you are done I will be in the main house making something besides berries and roots for lunch. You can come help me." She waved and the three women got up and walked to where her ham fist pointed. In the far corner of the garden was a lovely hot spring, complete with a bathing table and scented soaps. Britt noticed a small brush with a long handle and decided even if it was not a toothbrush, at this point she was using it for that anyway.

When they were done scrubbing each other, they took turns combing out the other's hair. Naked in the garden they set about looking for their clothing. It was nowhere to be found. Meriden panicked for a moment, until she noticed Britt walking towards the cottage as if being a nude human was one of her favorite pasttimes. When she did not return, Sara and Meriden followed, Meriden all the while gripping a pine bow to her midriff.

They arrived at the back door to find Britt dressed in a simple gown of cotton sitting at a rustic wooden table, drinking something warm. The inside of the goblin dwelling was total comfort. The floors were split leveled by a mere two steps. The cooking area was slightly higher than the dining area. Off to the north of the room another level housed a pantry full of sweet-smelling drying herbs.

The floor itself was worn but clean gray cobblestone and the ceiling, white mud and dark hickory beams from which a variety of pots and cookware hung. The table seemed to be the very center of the entire hut and one must walk a few steps down to enter the stone circle of the dining area. Above, a wonderful window of pure clear glass allowed beams of light to illuminate the entire dwelling. If one chose to walk again to the opposite side of the rotunda, one would ascend two steps and be in a walkway connecting the cooking area with the pantry. In another two steps, be on the platform to the front door. To their left, Meriden noticed a closed door that she assumed was the wash closet and to the right and left were two well lit corridors leading to the adjoining huts lined with paintings and wonderfully colored rugs.

"I should say this is the sweetest little place I have been in." Meriden remarked.

"Perhaps you would find it sweeter if you were dressed." Ma Fafella pointed to the left tunnel. "There are clothes waiting for ye. Then come join us for a chat and some lunch."

The rest of the afternoon was spent talking of tales of outer space and wonders beyond Zembeth. It had taken sometime for Meriden to absorb the reality of Britt actually living among the stars. They had not discussed her life other than the brief argument in the palace tower and the moon argument on the road. Now Meriden and Sara found themselves in awe and a bit ashamed.

"You are an Empress?" Meriden whispered from across the table.

"Not yet, I hope. I will take the position upon the death of Zenerio, my adopted master and father." Said Britt.

"How big is your empire?" Asked Sara.

"Oh, I couldn't begin to tell you that Sara. I would have to show you."

"Why is that?" Sara asked.

"Well, in your perception, Garath is a big city. Even larger is the whole of Zembeth. To explain a good portion of the outer rim of a galaxy would be very difficult." She attempted.

"So it is that big?" Meriden guessed.

"Bigger." Britt winked. "But I don't want anyone else but the three of you knowing. I don't think anyone would believe me for one, and two, I don't want to effect this reality in a negative way. We believe that it is not our right to expose life forms to technology until the time they are prepared to understand life on other planets."

"That makes good sense." Said Ma Fafella. "But I am getting the feeling we are a bit relaxed here and there are other issues that we must make haste to incur." She reminded them.

"Yes Ma, it seems we are in a very questionable place without my magick." Meriden pointed out. "Soon we must be off to the Shalnas to look for the necklace and needless to say we face a score of dangers along the way."

"I, fer the life 'o me, cannot believe I am a wanted criminal!" Sara almost sounded proud.

Ma Fafella handed Meriden and Britt a stack of dirty dishes. "Clean first, fret later." She pointed to the ample sink in the cooking area next to the clay oven. Meriden almost protested, but was silenced by a look from Britteny, who hauled her load to the top of the stairs and set them on the stone counter. Meriden watched as Britt left the cottage and returned with a cauldron full of water. She hooked it to the iron brace and shoved it gently over the hot coals. And so the females worked together. Once the dishes were complete, Ma Fafella asked Britt to work in her greenhouse. It seemed there were a few jobs that were a bit too lofty for the old goblin to reach. She did not dare stand on a stool and the amount of magick it would take to lift her would tire her before she was complete.

She put Meriden to work on some sewing she had sitting around and then she and Sara started to prepare dinner. Before Britt walked from the hut she noticed Fafella taking out a whole ham and a number of potatoes. She concluded that goblins were big and thus ate very sizable meals. She had already accessed that Fafella was keeping them busy to tire them out so they may sleep the night through. She had asked where Murdock had run off to. Fafella told her she sent the stallion to the fields to recruit some mares to carry Sara and Meriden on their journey. As well she thought it would be a nice thing to see some fine black colts dancing around next spring. Britt only smiled and pulled on a clean apron and headed to the greenhouse. She had also noticed that Fafella seemed to be very calm with Meriden. She had gone to great lengths to explain some of the simplest things to the elf girl and, at one point, was talking to her about the energy in the stones of her floor.

"The love and laughter alone in these stones can heal many wounds." She explained.

The day was wearing on but Britt did not notice. She was felling better than she had since she had gotten here. She labored tirelessly in the garden beds under the fine glass. The house was moist and warm and smelled like pure heaven. She could not help walking past the large fountain that had been set in the middle of the glass enclosure. Someone had placed benches of iron and white wood all around the crystal structure. Behind these benches a number of small Hallafawn trees had been planted from seed and were now to sapling stage. Their trunks were still pink and soft and their leaves brilliant red and only hinting at the mature gold. She did not bother to return to the hut too soon. She would rather work in this garden than be on kitchen detail. She stopped to stare at the fountain for a few stolen moments before the sun set. The house was alive with color as the light hit the many glass facets. She did not sense the presence behind her until it was nearly next to her.

Roderick touched her shoulder. She could see the two of them reflected in the clear water of the fountain. For a time they did not speak. Inside she wanted to run. Her instinct was that of one on the lamb and therefore in constant flight.

"How did you find us?" She asked.

"I followed my heart." He said honestly. "And my mother gave me a few clues." He admitted.

"That sneaky frog."

"That is my mother you are talking about, wench." He slapped her bottom.

Britt turned to embrace him. At first he was not sure how to react. Thus far the relationship had been hidden sex. This was an open display of emotion and affection. He hesitated for the briefest of moments sure she would not notice his confusion. When she pulled away after a time she looked up at him.

"I suppose you got that trip you were asking about after all. Of course I'm sure it's not the luxury package, but oh well." She started putting away garden tools. As if second nature, he followed her and picked up a wooden spade and placed it in its proper place and began putting clay pots and other tools away as well. They talked on.

"Does she have the necklace?" Roderick asked.

Britt looked from behind a half finished statue of a wood elf. "Roderick." She said flatly.

"What?"

"Would we be here if she had the necklace?" She walked past him and made a silly face.

"Probably not. Why are you here exactly?" It had finally occurred to him that he had no idea what had inspired her to come here of all places and he had not asked how they had escaped. He was not sure he wanted to know the latter.

"Sara seems to think Ma Fafella can get Meriden's magick back for her. She also mentioned that it was probably the safest place in all of Zembeth for the time being. The way I figure it, everyone is heading north looking for us anyway." She started for the door. "Well, we better get in with the rest of them before they come looking for us." She waited.

"Ma Fafella is not capable of giving her back her magick." He stated while walking to meet her.

"Oh boy. She is not gonna be happy to hear that." Britt sighed.

"Aside from this, Sara was correct, this is probably the most secure place in the realm for anyone to visit. Ma can conjure up some very nasty magick when the mood strikes her." He held the door open for Britt. "Funny, I have rarely seen her use her magick even for everyday things." He said as an after thought. She did not step outside.

"Is there something wrong?" He inquired.

"Yea, I was just wondering, when we get in there with everyone, how should I act?" She wanted to give him as many options as possible.

"What do you mean?" He was baffled. She reached over and kissed him passionately. "Oh." Was all he said at first, she waited patiently for a better reply. When none came, she continued out the door towards the main house. He followed quickly.

"Wait a minute!" He insisted, almost grabbing her arm. "What?" He asked.

"You didn't tell them yet did you?" Britt asked.

"No. I have not." He admitted.

"Why?"

Roderick took a moment to consider and found that he had not considered in the least. "I do not know. It is not like I have had time to sit them down or anything."

"O.K., then let's get going. I'm sure dinner is waiting and everyone is wondering where we are." Britt turned again and headed up the path.

"That is it?" He barked.

"Is there more?" Britt asked.

"Well of course there is." He insisted.

"So is it sex or is it a relationship?" She asked.

"It is a relationship." Roderick insisted.

"O.k. So we go in and tell everyone." She tried to start walking again.

"No." He stopped her.

"O.K. Then we just get sex now and then." She looked him in the eye.

"No. It is not that either." He was growing impatient.

"Look Roderick, I'm not in the mood for these stupid games. In case you haven't noticed, we have a lot ahead of us. Either you come clean and we remain friends and that is it, or you tell me if you want me in your life. You can't have it both ways. Besides, what was all that crap back at the palace about finding a place together?" She challenged.

"Why not?" He wondered.

"Why not what?"

"Why can we not have it both ways?" asked Roderick.

"Because the first time I decide to sleep with someone else I don't want to hear so much as a word out of your mouth, understand?" She folded her arms.

"I have never told you that you were not permitted to sleep with whom ever you were mated with, have I?" He argued.

"No, no, no, it isn't like that, slick. I sleep with who I want, elf, dwarf, human, whoever. End of discussion." She trotted off only to add over her shoulder. "You feel free to have your fun as well. I won't let it ruin my opinion of you." She had reached the back door of the main house before he actually grasped what she was getting at. He leaped to catch her and missed her arm only to feel the cool wood of the door against his fingers.

When he entered the dining room everyone was seated at the large, round table, laughing and eating. Britt was up at the kitchen fixing herself a plate so she could eat and join the rest of her new traveling companions in the lively conversation. She bounced down the steps and seated herself next to Amaranth, wiggling her way between Roderick's brother and Rowland. Amaranth giggled and handed her a pint of ale.

"Thanks, little brother." She winked playfully. "So I take it we are all traveling together in the morning?" She asked.

"It would appear that way." Offered Ma Fafella. Roderick got a plate and sat next to Ma Fafella.

For some time they talked of things to come. When Meriden told the boys that she did not have the necklace they all laughed. Apparently Sholendor was convinced that was how she escaped. Roderick made a point of asking how they did indeed escape. Britt did not answer; instead Sara went into a detailed account of the entire escapade. When she was finished everyone at the table erupted into a font of questions. Ma Fafella on the other hand burst out in laughter.

"That is, by far, the most excellent display of wily, sneaky, courage I have yet to hear of!"

Britt added. "I didn't hack the guy to pieces Sara!"

"Oh really? And what would you call it then lass?" She yelled across the table.

"I rearranged his appendages for efficient lack of visibility." She bobbed her head. Everyone at the table roared except Meriden. She had not so much as moved for some time.

They continued talking of their travel plans, Sholendor, and what was in store for them. It was agreed they would head for Sid O'Sala and supply up then, from the slave city, go north to the Shalnas forest. Meriden was distant, even when discussing weeks on the road. She did not even go so far as to ask questions or voice concerns. Britt kept glancing at her. When sleeping arrangements were to be made, Ma Fafella offered Meriden her own sleeping quarters, but she refused and said she would much rather sleep with Britt and Sara. Ma Fafella planned to stay up in the night working a cloaking spell for the entire group of rebels that would keep them from the magical view of Sholendor and his sorcerers. She also took the time to fill a water bottle with vinegar for Britt.

Night was black on Zembeth when the moons were hidden. Britt dropped like a stone into the soft bed. After Roderick's display of insecurity she made it a point to trot by him in her chemise and head for the bedroom where Meriden and Sara slept. He regarded her with dark indecision.

Other than being ill, this was the best sleep she could remember. Once again Sara and Meriden were snuggled up to her. From time to time she had to pull her long red braid out from under Sara, who did not so much as notice. She was the first to rise in the morning, slinking from the room in her cotton shift. She could not help the draw of the dawn and the wild open energy of the pure land. She opened the front door, closing it quietly behind her. The stones on the front walk were cold and wet against her bare feet. The light was pale still, not to be confused with the full warmth of the day, this was heavy morning light, light that reaches deep with promises. At this time it was as if magic were born infant pure. If one stood still enough, one could feel the hum of life vibrate through their body. Britt let it fill her. She did not want to miss one chance of taking in the natural beauty of a planet that had been chosen by a magical race to replace their common home of Earth.

Wind nudged the giant stalks and dipped into the cold beneath, only to race toward her and lift her gown as she sped by. She stilled. A tiny tear formed on her pink cheek as she blinked in the beauty. All was silent, all was right. Perhaps if she stayed just so, everything would go away, everything but this place and this moment. Could it be so? Could one just stand and stop time?

She lifted her head to smell the lilac and honeysuckle. Cold air seduced her body as cold water, and she was now clearly aware that she had changed drastically since arriving on Zembeth. She was aware that she had never truly been aware. Her very sight was beginning to confuse her, for now she could see the finest increments of the construction of life. Colors were almost painful in their richness. She could actually hear the soil shifting around beneath her, full of minute beings ever working out of sight. Coupled with the musk of the moss and foliage, it created a full-blown symphony in her mind. The wind, the rotation of the planet, the beating of her heart, all seemed to go on without her mind. Truth be known, it did a sight better when her mind was absent. She walked deeper into the grass and hugged her chest, caressing each blade as she passed with her elbows and cheeks. Being here was becoming being her. She wiped a tear from her ever sharpening eyes. The individual that brought her to this place knew infinitely more about her than she knew about herself. Even amidst the fear of never finding Zeneria again, her desperation was quelled and dwarfed in comparison to the sudden changes in her physicality. She was not an alien to this planet or these people. They treated her thus, because something in her was part of them. She was familiar to them if only on a subconscious level. The pain behind her eyes, burning down her throat to swell to happy tears marked the fact that they were as well familiar to her. No matter how it happened, it had happened. She had never felt a part of any established species, even when she lived as a child on Earth. She was well aware that she was completely ignorant of the how and why and she didn't care, she only wanted the first feeling of belonging to never evaporate. She would cling to it for as long as she could.

Leaving Zembeth would be one of the hardest things she had ever been obligated to do. It would take more courage than she thought she had. It would leave a hole in her soul she may never be able to close and cover. Such is the spasm of realization and discovery.

She stopped, still as death can be and tilted her head to smell and listen. Someone had left the cottage and was following her. She sniffed the air. It was Sara. She guessed these gifts were part and parcel of mother dragon, yet something told her otherwise. She had some of these gifts all her life but until now chose not to willingly use them or acknowledge them. So regardless of sleeping with Roderick and carrying a dragon pup in her gut, there was another link. She waited patiently for her companion. Soon Sara pushed her way though the grass. She had stopped momentary and grabbed a young shoot to chew on the bittersweet nubile end.

"Tis sure grateful ye get up so early." She kept walking past Britt going deeper into the tall grass.

"Why's that?" Britt followed.

"Ye and I have to have a bit 'o a chat." Sara walked on, allowing the human to shove aside stalks and follow her. Finally she stopped and seemed to reach out her senses to determine if anyone was listening. "Smell any elves?" She asked.

"No."

"All the better." Sara reached to Britt's hand and pulled her down to eye level. "Seems we have a bit 'o a problem. I fer one know you are too blind to see it. Seems lately ye are thinking between yer legs rather than that large tub 'o fat on yer shoulders." Sara hissed.

"What're you talking about?" Britt dropped to her knees and scowled at Sara.

"Ye know full well what it is I am talking of!" Sara said irritated. "I suppose ye think it is just a bit 'o luck that Roderick and his merry men just happened ta show up here? Donna ye think they are taking us right to Sholendor?" Sara accused.

"You're crazy Sara. They would never do that." She started to get up. Sara dropped her fist on Britt's shoulder to keep her on the ground.

"Am I? Let me tell ye something, Britt. I know yer in love with Roderick. I know it as clear as I know the back 'o me hand. I know he canna love ye. I also know Sholendor has ways of makin' all of us fools. I would'na be so sure they are on our side. Bloody hell, Rowland is a bloomin' palace guard no less!" She stared into Britt's eyes, hoping to drive home her point. Britt sat on her bottom and broke the gaze looking at the floor of the plains in thought.

"You really think so?" She had a strong feeling Sara would not be this insistent if she did not at least suspect something fishy. So far she had been the most intelligent and grounded creature Britt had encountered.

"If not, then tell me this child, where is that ogre friend of theirs? Do ye think he woulda let the lads go off like this alone after all they have done fer him?" She touched Britt's shoulder again.

"After all ye have done for him? Even true the lads stay at his inn and woulda gone back there ta get their supplies no doubt. Iffin he dinna come, he woulda sent one 'o his own lads at least. I know he has whelped a few and has more than enough family." Sara continued.

"Ye only just got here, so I understand your thickness, but I'm here to set you straight. Osizio has known those boys their whole lives. After the games, and the accusation and all the trouble we be in, do ye honestly tink he woulda sent Roder out here alone?"

Britt frowned. Perhaps she was a bit fuddled. The thought was just absurd. She tried to separate fact from fiction and emotion from logic. She glanced up at Sara and bit her bottom lip.

"Fer the love of God, if ye think any harder the smoke will give us away!" Sara blurted out. "Tis not that hard to imagine, dear. I know ye have bedded him. So what? Do ye think he cares for ye? I mean really now, you silly nit!" Sara playfully slapped Britt up side the head. "Tell me fond fool, is there a man in this friggin land that would'na want to bed ye?" She crossed her stout arms. "Sure 'tis a rite notch in his pole to best Sholendor at the game, donna ye think? Even if he gets us back to Prince Hell, hella be still wearin the thought of having ye first." Sara sat down next to Britt. "And we both know a man will say ANYTHING to get a bump and a rub. Besides, ye may not know this, but elves have a right powerful persuasion over the lot of us. We canna resist many of their strong wishes."

She was right. Britt felt like kicking herself in the face. "Am I really that stupid?" She voiced.

"Na." Sara pulled another young shoot and started chewing the base. "All the lasses want Roderick. Not sayin that he has them all, mind ye. Matter of fact he is a rite fine fellow iffin ye stand him to his kin. But love? Dedication? Tis yer own fool heart iffin ye believe he would to give up his friends and what fame he has scraped fer for the likes of any human woman. 'Tis the long life that has made them so. Have ye never had a lad lie for a chunk of yer pie?" Sara felt like a criminal breaking the heart of a child.

"The long life?" Britt asked.

"Sure. If I were gonna live fer a great long time now, I'm not sure 'tis a necessarily good thing. Most other creatures arna set up for livin that long. Takes a bit 'o a cold heart and a quiet mind to withstand such time. We all form into our own skin. Elves got the way they are due to all that magick and immortality bustin' through their gulleywhats. The lad canno' help it dear. 'Tis the way his workings work. Ken my meaning?" Her sharp teeth crunched down on a firm blade of grass ripping off a strip to suck on.

Britt flashed the events that had lead up to them arriving at Ma Fafella's. He had stood up for them in the town square and he had offered to run away with her, but that was before Meriden was accused of killing her mother and the whole world had turned upside down. There was also the fact that he had not told his brother or friends yet and did not seem inclined to do so. Even still, she could not afford for all they had in store to go wrong due to a chance and emotion. Sara was right, there was only room in this adventure for the three of them. Stick to the plan at hand. This meant Roderick was a risk. If Sholendor wanted her, let him come catch her, leave Roderick out of it. Sara's uncanny logic of evolution, when all was said and done, was what truly planted the seed of reality in Britt's mind. It made perfect sense when she took the time to digest the obvious. She had never encountered beings that survive and thrive for thousands of years. If she had, she would be willing to accept the hypothesis that such a race could evolve in this manner.

Besides, if he had come for them in Sholendor's place, Britt did not doubt that there was a contingent plan in the works. Perhaps Sholendor had blackmailed Roderick, or perhaps Roderick was doing it to save faith in the eyes of his people. Either way, Britt knew that to turn your back on your people and position was more commonly done for money than love. Money, he could be doing it for money as well. She had not a clue to his financial status. From what she could see, it was not the top of the food chain. If he did, why did he live on the road like a bum? Maybe title, something he had never had, according to him. Either way, Sara had made a point without knowing it. Britt knew full well the power Roderick had over her. People in love rarely listen to the advice of those around them, discrediting the advice to jealousy. She had seen it all too often. She could not afford to let her guard completely down and, although at this point she did not intend to shut Roderick completely out, she would follow Sara's wake up call and keep her wits about her.

"O.K. You're right." She stood and offered Sara her hand. "I'm not saying I think that he does not care for me, but I am saying that either way we cannot risk all that sets in the balance for that chance. First chance we have to get rid of the lot of them, we will. For now we play it safe."

"Now that is my idea of a beast with some grey talking! Glad to see ye back where ye belong." Sara patted her ass and started back to the cottage. After only a few paces she turned back to Britt. "Now remember lass, no telling the princess 'o this plan. Fer sure she donna want to travel alone. I donna care what she says. Now that these bastards are here, she feels akin and safe. I suspect we may just havta gag her again."

"Point taken." Britt agreed.

When they returned to the cottage, Murdock was grazing outside the gate, accompanied by two small mares. Britt patted his withers and kissed his warm nose.

"Hello love, glad to see you back." The brute of a stallion shoved his muzzle into her chest, in pursuit of more stroking. If only we could love each other as our animal friends love us, unconditionally and whole, Britt thought. She was aware of the front door opening and could hear the sound of Roderick approaching her.

“We almost started breakfast without you two wandering women.” He joked.

“Shoulda.” Offered Sara. “We can eat fast as any. Why wait for the likes of two slaves?” She did not wait for a reply and stalked into Fafella’s home.

“What bothers her?” Roderick watched Sara slam the door behind her.

“Nothing. She is just a bit worried about the whole “on the lam” thing.” Britt moved around Murdock to slide her hands over his sleek back, trying hard to ignore Roderick and stifle her heartbeat.

“Oh. Well, all the same, we are about to pack and prepare for the journey. I suggest we travel straight north to Sid O’Sala for supplies. Going through the plains is dangerous, but our fastest route.” He informed her.

“Sounds fine to me.” She started for the cottage. Roderick followed, a bit confused.

“Well then, Sid O’Sala it is.” He entered the front room and shut the door behind him. He was under the impression this was her way of letting him know that she was hurt for not telling his brother and friends that she was more to him than a runaway slave. He would have to take the first opportunity available to try to enlighten her and work this out. He did not know how long he could go without her touch.

They ate breakfast as if it were the last they would have. Britt shoveled at least three of the thick omelets into her stomach and was still gnawing on toast a half hour later. Elves rarely required food but Britt, Donavan, and Sara did. She had gone without food and she was sure Sara had, but somehow she did not like the thought of Donavan hungry. She spoke little to any of them. Meriden was racing around packing and wondering which horse was hers. Britt pointed to the taller of the two mares.

“Take her and give Sara the short one. It only makes sense.”

“Then whom will you ride? I thought Sara and I were sharing one?”

“I’m riding Murdock.” Britt snapped as if Meriden were stupid. They stood just outside the front door, tying up their necessities into saddlebags amidst the entire traveling party.

“Surely Roderick will ride Murdock.” Meriden stated.

“Why Roderick? I stole him, I’m riding him.” She hauled her pack to her back and stomped to the large stallion, ears pricked forward in question. She turned to the rest of her companions. “Unless he wants to fight me for him?” She challenged with a sly smile.

“Meriden,” Roderick addressed the princess, “I have a horse of my own.” He patted her back and shot Britt a concerned look walking to his lean sorrel. “I need not prove myself to our bitter companion whom obviously had a spoiled egg in her omelet.” This caused a bit of laughter from the rest of the party. Britt ignored the lot of them and finished saddling up.

She walked through the busy group heading toward the garden to bid farewell to Ma Fafella. She knew the goblin sow would probably come out front to see them off but she selfishly desired private moments of her own. Roderick watched her round the last hut and changed his range of vision when he noticed Amaranth watching him.

Ma Fafella sat in her homemade chair, smoking a pipe and watching the water drip down the side of the cliff wall. She saw Britt and bit off the end of a cigar for the human then handed it to her as she plopped down.

"Almost ready?" Fafella asked.

"Yep. I suspect we'll be shoving off soon. I wanted to stop and say thank you myself for all your help."

"No need, but I appreciate it all the same." Fafella slapped Britt's thigh. "You take care out there. Lots of wild things can steal your soul." She warned.

"I think there are things everywhere than can steal one's soul if they don't take care." Britt sucked in the sweet smoke. She had dressed in a pair of snug black breeches that Amaranth had left at the cottage, a pair of knee high suede boots and a loose fitting black tunic. Around her hips she had secured a belt, complete with a sword, water pouch and a pouch for general purpose. Fafella noticed her human daughter had also slipped a dagger into her boot.

"Well don't you look like one of the boys?" She chuckled low and wet.

"It's about time. I think if I was forced to wear another one of those dresses I'd have to kill someone."

"How's about I tie that hair back." Fafella offered. She produced a long wide band of leather. After braiding the full length of Britt's hair, Fafella started the top, even around her head, like a sweatband then continued to crisscross the rest of the leather down the braid, to tie it off at the end. Britt sat through the procedure still sucking on the stogie.

"These things are great." She commented holding the cigar aloft and blowing out a smoke ring.

"I am glad you like them. I packed a few for you. Roderick can show you how to harvest the weed and dry it for your own later. Course it only grows in my garden. So that means you'll all have to come back for a visit." Britt raised a brow at her comment. She decided not to remark, knowing the goblin mother was playing with her.

"That would be cool." She allowed.

"Now remember, when you get to Sid O'Sala, try to stay out of sight. Those traders get a look at you and who knows what will happen."

"I think most of them saw me at the palace anyway, but who cares. I'm going to get to that forest, and it doesn't matter who sees me or who doesn't."

"Well that sounds like determination to me."

"Desperation, my good woman, desperation. I want to go home where I know the rules and win the game." Britt flicked her ashes.

"Oh. I have a feeling much will happen from now till then and I think you already know the confusion of where is home and what is foreign to you now."

"Yea." She was doing her best at ignoring the blatant facts the goblin sow baited her with. Nothing she could say would keep Britt on Zembeth. That is not to say she would not come back, but she definitely had to leave.

"Hey, how about Meriden's magick? Any luck with that?" She changed the subject.

"I choose not to bless her with her gifts again."

"You mean you can't, or you won't?" Britt asked.

"A tad and a fetch of both. That wee one is the only hope for these lands as it stands. If I were to grant her powers again, we both know she would learn absolutely nothing. Besides if she earns them herself she will be twice the sorceress and a much better queen."

"Have you told her this?" Britt asked.

"Soon enough, my child, soon enough." She re-lit her pipe. "Let's go to the others, I worked long and hard on this cloaking spell. I will have to have you all together to get it to work." She shoved off.

"Do we all have to be together for it to work?" Britt needed to know. She was not sure she would be safe once the dragon was born and she was concerned for the safety of Sara and Meriden.

"Yes, that dragon will protect you and yes the spell will protect you all, together or apart. Not that Sholendor has a chance in Deneb of catching the lot of you." She offered a green paw to Britt. "Not that it matters, you will all stick together, won't you?" She pried.

"You never know what can happen on the road, Fafella." Britt started toward the back door of the cottage. She slowed to hear Fafella's reply.

"Together, apart, it does not matter. You will all find your way in the end. I fear though, that separation may lead to disaster." She warned.

Britt almost asked her what she meant then decided against it. She had enough on her mind and somehow knew she could not afford more stress. She continued walking to the cottage, slowing a bit to allow Fafella to catch up.

They were gathered near the horses when Fafella chose to take Meriden aside. The girl had been a mess worrying about her request being un-granted. The two were gone for some time. In the cottage Ma Fafella pulled out a chair, motioning for Meriden to be seated.

"Did ye think I forgot about you, dear?" She asked Meriden.

"Of course not, my lady." Meriden lied.

"A bird told me you like to scribble the tales of your days. Is this true?"

"Yes. I keep a journal. It is back at the palace, hidden in a sleeping chamber in the slave quarters."

"Well, that will not do." She produced a smart looking leather bound book and quill. "You must be the keeper of legends."

"Excuse me, Ma Fafella. I fail to see how this will restore my powers. Mind you, I am very appreciative of the gift." She was struggling to stay polite.

"Listen up, my Queen. I am only going to be this bold once. You are a worthless little whelp. You are terrified of your own skin. You have not a chance of surviving that snake of a prince of yours. You are here for a reason. I am sure you know that. I could give you at least a portion of your powers back. Or I could send you off into the Arosa Plains with the lot of them. The mother in me wants to give you those powers back. The goblin in me knows you are incomplete. If you do not get some grit in your soul, all the magick in the world will not save the people of these realms from your whims." She waited a moment for Meriden's reply and watched as the girl's thin blue lips started to tremble. "It's no fun to be at the bottom, is it?" She asked.

"I find it disgusting." Meriden hissed.

"That is precisely why I am NOT giving you back your powers. When the day comes when you think me and all my kind NOT disgusting, I have a feeling you will get your powers back tenfold."

She was about to comment further when they noticed Sara at the door waiting to be invited in.

"Enter, dear. We are finished here." She turned to Meriden. "I can tell you this, child, keeping that journal will be a key to your success. When we think of history and what makes one truly magickal, we must think of wisdom paramount to many other traits you may have been taught." She touched the worn leather. "A truly wise queen knows history when it's being made. Time is an opportunity many overlook. Do you understand?" She asked.

Meriden pondered her words. Her years of schooling had been force-fed. Rarely had her professors insisted she answer a question based on her personal opinion. Remembering her classes she noted that they did not treat the other girls so. It was as though they lacked trust in her ability to deduce planned outcomes or imagine possibilities.

"Yes Ma Fafella. I believe I am beginning to understand." If she were to have been gleeful Fafella would have not believed her. She watched as Meriden rubbed the book and frowned.

"We must learn to speak all languages, magicians all. The mouth is a vile tool used too often. It hinders us from the full scope of the language of the universe. I see in your face sadness. I watch the skin twitch and move to the center. I have the whiff of salt in my nostrils that tells me you are thinking on this. I believe you do understand. Do you see?" Fafella asked once more.

"I see that I would have been a fortunate queen indeed to know you as a child. I am embarrassed at my ignorance of complete magick and I am humble with this new knowledge." She bowed to her superior.

"Now little mother what can I do for you?" She addressed Sara.

"Well. I was thinking. I wonder if t'would be out of my line to ask ye if I might stay behind with ye?" She had made sure she asked in front of Meriden. She had not mentioned it to the gang outside. She was hoping Britt would understand her fear and realize this would be her only chance at freedom. She felt strangely odd allowing this decision to overtake her and compel her to randomly and sporadically make for the goblin sow as if fleeing for her life. Fear seemed to be the catalyst to insanity. Meriden was another nut to crack.

"Sara! What brings this betrayal?" She screeched. "Is it my actions on the road last eve? I told you I was sorry."

Fafella held up a giant green hand. "Lesson number two sister, we must listen before we react. Greed is the killer of innovation and innocence. Are you thinking of yourself or are you thinking of another?" She asked.

"Meriden. I am short. I am fat. I canno' defend myself. I would only be a burden. You got to study these lands. I donna know half of what I should. I canna help wondering if 'tis a good idea fer the likes of me to be trailing along." She explained. "Besides, I would be a great help here to ol' ma. T'would be me dream to live with one such as she."

Meriden rubbed her reddening eyes. Her shoulders shook ever so slightly. "I know my answer should be free of selfishness. I will give that answer though it is not what I wish. Tell me ma, how do we act against what our nature dictates?"

"We learn we have little or no choices in this life. By letting go, child, we begin to get hold of a larger world." She rubbed Meriden's back gently. Sara had never seen Meriden so. If she did not know better, she would have sworn the elf princess was near to tears. She was being selfish, sure, but she was admitting to her downfall and swallowing her pride. She put her hands on her hips and grunted.

"Well that settles it. I canna miss this." Sara announced.

"Sara?" Fafella questioned, confused.

"Ya think something like this happens every day? I donna know what ye did to her but I nev'ra seen her so strong. Ima going on this trek. I dinna spend two hundred years raising that stalk of grass to miss her finally bustin out." She dismissed the other women and strode out the door, her decision made. When she approached her horse Britt regarded her. Sara nodded to her friend.

"We're in it for the long haul. I told ya back on the road I was in it. Ima in it. Ima nev'ra gonna get a chance like this again." She assured as she mounted her horse.

"Well all righty then." Britt giggled.

"All right! Each of you up on your steeds now so I can get this spell underway before yer off into the grass. Sorry Donavan." She patted his fur. Clearly Donavan would not be riding a mount. Once they were all whither to whither, lined as she instructed, Fafella walked from one to the next with a bowl of oil. To each she anointed their forehead and the forelock of their mounts.

"I care little what you have learned in the past." She began as she squatted in front of them rubbing her hands together. "Listen now to the ocean. Can you hear it?" They each replied.

"What about that wind? Hear that as well?" Again they acknowledged her statement. "Mmmm. That sun feels good on my face." She tipped her head skyward. Britt watched and followed suit as each member of the party looked to the sun. "I can feel it warming my blood. I can feel it in my heart. Can you?" Again yes. Fafella spread her body over the grass. "The creatures who carry you, the ground that we ride on, the very trees that bring life, can you feel their vibrations? Do you know their connection?" Britt began to feel as though she would be lifted off Murdock with the power of such thought. Fafella rose and slapped her chest. "Join hands!" She ordered. Meriden took hold of Sara to her right and Britt to her left. Britt reached for Rowland and so on down the line. A charge pulsed through each of them. "Love!" Fafella bellowed. "I care little for what you have learned in the past. Love is the greatest of these forces. You all have it for one another. It may be hidden, but trust me it is there. I give you this to shield all that would harm you. I bid the spirits to cloak and bind, cover and hide till this journey does see its end. So mote it be!" She raised her arms.

"So mote it be." The Zembethian members of the party started repeating. Britt caught on quickly and repeated in kind. They spoke this three times.

"Now get out out 'o my yard, ye band of beautiful misfits!" She laughed and waved. She watched the company for a short time. It never took long for anyone of any size to be lost in the grass of the Arosa.

Chapter 19
The Endless Green

Entering the grasslands of the Arosa Plains is to enter an ever-changing crop circle of mazes. Each horse took single file walking rights behind the other, starting with Roderick. Donavan simply dropped down to all fours and trotted along behind Britt. It was rather disturbing to see that he was nearly as tall as Sara's small horse. Britt was amazed the horses were not terrified of him. Roderick had informed them that they would be taking a path less traveled and using as little magic as needed and only in the case of a dire emergency. He did not wish to spare the chance that there was a royal palace elf within one hundred miles of them that could pick up the smallest of spells. No one disagreed with this and so they rode. The way was at times narrow and then again wide enough to allow them to ride abreast. Britt had taken a moment to slice off a few thick stalks and attempt to make a sunbonnet. She knew she could not stay in this heat for long without burning. She struggled a bit of the way until Amaranth giggled and hid behind her to avoid Roderick's gaze. He fashioned three wide brimmed hats to fit the women. Roderick turned and grimaced with displeasure shaking his head, then smiling.

At first there was not much in the way of talking among them for some time. Britt was in her own world. Roderick was doing his best to avoid Britt. Meriden, terrified and remembering all the ghastly tales she had heard of these plains, could barely breathe. Sara busied herself taking inventory of all the interesting plants she could spy from atop her horse. Amaranth was doing his best not to stare at Britt. Donavan's nose was forever to the ground, always watchful for trouble and a quick meal. Rowland appeared to be the only member of the party that was just riding for the sake of riding. From time to time he could be observed staring at Meriden only to look away as if caught with his hand in the cookie jar.

Britt noticed the moist heat of the area and in some insane fashion deducted that with grass this tall it must take an incredible amount of rain to sustain such a crop. She was about to comment, and even made it halfway through the statement. It rained for days after. Their first night was spent sleeping sitting up with their bottoms in mud. Roderick had provided makeshift lean-tos to help shelter from the downpour. The company ate what supplies they had packed. There could be no hunting or fire making in the black wet of the long night. While watching the giant drops assault the ground, the horses munched happily enjoying the cool bath. Meriden had voiced a concern over meals. Sara educated her in short order.

"Look around ya sis. Have ye ever seen a bigger group of brutes in yer life? I'll be happy if wolfy dosna eat the likes 'o me yellow hide." They all laughed despite the torrents of water soaking their breeches. Britt could not wait to go hunting with Donavan. What a thrill it would be to make chase with a creature like him. She pulled Sara closer to her under the cloak. Meriden was leaning against her other side, making it almost livable under the wet wool. She looked to the next lean-to to see Roderick looking back at her. He was a haunting figure in the dark, eyes glowing, pale strong face, a phantom of handsome retreat. She knew she would love nothing more than to crawl through the mud and huddle up in his arms. He started a quiet conversation to avoid impolitely staring at her. So for a time, Roderick, Donavan, Rowland, Britt, and Amaranth discussed the plains and what would happen when they arrived at Sid O'Sala.

The next morning, the rain seemed to pelt them with more fury. They packed and mounted their dripping steeds. Murdock seemed not to notice his sopping mane and heavy tail. He was as frisky as usual and stepped lively along. New definitions of miserable can be derived on a day as such. Britt was growing very tired of smelling wet dog. Donavan stunk, though she would never tell him that. Despite the smell of wet canine fur, he was enlightening company, always the gentleman. He spoke of music and art and the finer things in life. This was often done amidst grooming and eating small rodents. The situation created a vision that burned into Britt's memory instantly. Some time after the noon meal break, the rain let up ever so slightly, allowing shards of sunlight to slip through the green.

The humidity and soil made it almost impossible to breathe. Pungent earth seemed to invade the lungs, even coating the tongue. The grass had become almost tree ike in thickness. It seemed as if they traveled in the line of some parallel dimension. At times they could only get a glimpse of some creature passing. Britt jumped on a number of occasions to see nothing but the legs of a creature that was large enough to walk with its head well above the grass, as it passed them on its own path. From time to time she would glimpse nothing but a set of strange eyes interrupted by the constant repetitive blades as they passed. At one instance Britt spied the odd green child not far from her between the thick undercover. At first she nearly slid off Murdock to attempt contact. The other party members did not seem to see the insect like creature watching from its grass hovel. Its face had the shape of something like a locust. Its body was formed as that of a human child. She could see the sharp teeth from where she sat and turned to Donavan to ask of its nature. He informed her that there were countless of such creatures in this grassland, just waiting for fresh meat. They were called Shahani. He told her they usually hunted in packs and lived in tribes. In his opinion the only reason they were not dining now was riding in front of them and named Roderick. Like most sub-life-forms on Zembeth, these creatures had a healthy fear of giant elves. In truth they were a type of elf, as Britt was to find out. There were many different breeds of elf and/or fairy creatures. Roderick and his lot being the largest of the family and the creatures she met in the meadow being one of the many ranges of the smallest. The malicious seeming creature grinned at her, setting her skin to tickle with anticipation of battle.

It was on their third day that Britt insisted on taking Sara a little off the path for a chat. Roderick protested hotly. Britt pulled him aside and whispered in his ear, his eyes bulged and he agreed to let them step aside for only a few moments. The rest of the party waited, Meriden a bit upset that they would leave her here with the men. Britt, relieved beyond words that she was not pregnant with Roderick's child as well as a dragon, needed Sara's assistance to teach her what was sufficient to use to absorb blood. Sara pulled up two handfuls of thick moss and wrapped them in a dead blade of grass. She told Britt that this would absorb at least a day's worth of blood but at night they would have to wrap it again and burn it. Leaving the bloody moss behind was sure to attract the wrong kind of attention to the party. Sara commented she would rather prefer the company of the Royal Guard to what would follow the scent of this blood.

So the party traveled on. Occasionally they would come to a village. Rowland, Britt, Sara, and Meriden would be made to wait down the road a bit while Amaranth, Donavan and Roderick went inside the tell tale walls and bartered for food and supplies. Thus far the rain had not relented and so Roderick purchased skillfully crafted rain ponchos for the entire party. This made life in a never ending swamp a bit more accommodating. Meriden was thrilled. Her poor chalk face was dismal and Britt fretted that this trip was going to be the death of her. Despite her discomfort, Meriden had been silent. She only spoke to Sara and Britt in whispers willingly, and she never wandered far from Britt's side. Britt did her best to comfort the tiny woman by telling her tales and making jokes to draw what mirth she could from the princess. She also made it a point to stay physically close to her of her own will as if she sought the company of one that would have seen her hang rather than believe her people were what they were but a week ago. Sara did not let this go unnoticed.

After about two full weeks of riding in the rain, it stopped. Britt was so happy she danced around splashing in puddles. She pulled Roderick in with her and they proceeded to fight in the mud, laughing and tossing slick earth at one another. When the rest of the party just gaped at them, Britt picked up a dripping handful of mud and tossed it right at Amaranth, hitting him in the perfect white hair. Donavan rolled with wolf laughter until Roderick's mud slatted him on the snout. This of course was first blood and all out war. Even Meriden raced around the horses giggling and dodging the bombs.

Sara waved her hands. "Now ye silly bastards, stop this at once!" She was then overtaken with mud pies that nearly knocked her from her horse. Britt raced away from Roderick laughing so uncontrollably it made it difficult to move. He followed her into the grass and overtook her with ease. Tackling her, they rolled over one another wildly. When they stopped Roderick was on top. For a moment they breathed deeply. To break the awkward silence she squealed and slapped at him.

"We should get back." He became uncomfortable. Britt waited for a moment, for what Roderick knew not.

"Yeah, sure. It's dangerous out here. You never know what'll steal your soul." Britt started back. Roderick jogged up to walk beside her.

"Hey, what is your favorite color?" He asked. She stopped confused.

"Black, I think. Black or red, I like them both together mostly." She offered.

"I think mine is black as well. Yet I must admit I like the green of the grass, especially after it rains. When I was a boy I would wake early just to see the color of the trees at dawn, and run outside in the evening to see them again at dusk." And so he continued on, talking to her of his life, his loves and in turn asking her of what it was that made her happy and sad. They found a lake and all cleaned up, still laughing. That night they would have a fire for the first time in too long. Britt was thrilled to find that she would be hunting with Roderick for dinner that night. As she pulled the bow and quiver over her shoulder, Amaranth had to almost yell at Meriden to calm her down. Sara jumped in and assured Meriden that if anyone should be full of fear it should be what ever was out in that grass that can be killed and eaten. Sara also told her that it was expected for a team to hunt at dusk for the party and tomorrow night it would be two others and so on. Britt only hoped she got one chance to run with Donavan. Roderick would, no doubt, prove to test her ability. She was more concerned with the growing tension between them. As she parted the stalks before her, she welcomed any vicious beast that would keep her mind off of him. Meriden was told she had a job to do as well. She and Sara would be responsible for cleaning camp and starting the fire as the men set up the lean-tos. Donavan would prowl the perimeter of the camp, marking it with his scent to ward off a number of foes. In truth, it was spring and he was hoping a female would pick up his musk, so he kept his nose to the wind.

Roderick and Britt trotted through the grass side by side. She held a bow in her right hand and a spear in her left. Roderick slowed at the lake and they made a burrow in some cattails. They rolled around in the mud to hide their scent. Britt giggled and whispered to Roderick that they would have to clean up again. He messed her curls and told her to pay attention. The two laid in wait for some type of beast large enough to feed the entire party. It took all the power in Roderick to not slide over and hold her. She lay next to him, eyes watching the lake, body ready for flight. He could not help but think that he would never find an elf female that would lie in the mud with him and hunt swamp pigs.

When a boar came in sight, Britt barely saw Roderick take off. He was quicker than the very wind and before she could stand he had overtaken the wild pig. She could see that there was an entire herd of them and wasted no time in following one of her own. Once successful, they field dressed their game and started back for the camp. Roderick watched in amazement as his human friend hauled the dead pig up over her strong shoulders as if she did it every day.

"We're eating like kings tonight!" She laughed.

"Hey wait for me!" Pulling his own prey up he started after her. They talked all the way back to camp. They even argued. Britt loved to argue with him because he was so quick that she found it difficult to get the upper hand and this was a welcomed challenge. She loved to get him up in arms and watch his brilliant eyes flare and his wide hands sway with expression. Soon he was on to her game of bait and tackle and would ignore her just to get under her skin. He also figured out that if he held his hand up to her face and denounced her subject, she would be the butt of her own irony and this turnabout caused a few wrestling matches, dead pigs and all.

They argued over matters of state. At one point they set the pigs down just to use more hand gestures. They discussed male and female roles in a relationship. Britt was guilty of sticking her tongue out at him more than once. They debated all the way back to camp and when the pigs were flopped into the chopped clearing near the fire; they continued to banter as if they were alone. As the party cleaned and roasted the meat, Roderick ranted about the theory of democracy and its ability to actually function. Eventually the entire company was volleying comments back and forth across the meat and the fire. Sara proved to be quite the debate queen, sharp tongue and all. Meriden surprised them by joining in and even jumping up and down with frustration. Britt tipped her wooden bowl of broth peering over its edge in amusement. It was not until they started to discuss astronomy that things got really interesting.

Amaranth, for some reason, considered himself an expert on the subject. As he spoke of the cosmic blanket that covered their world to keep it warm, he noticed Britt snickering.

"Well my dear, perhaps you have a better theory?" He handed her the thin twig he had been using to illustrate how the blanket shifted with the winds. She snatched the stick from his grip and squatted by the fire to draw in the dirt.

"See here elf boy, this is the long and the short of it." She drew a circle. "You are here." She wrote the word Zembeth in the middle of the circle. "Zembeth is a. . . well it's a big ball. It spins around like this." She drew arrows to illustrate. Next she drew a sun in an estimated location. "And while it spins, it travels around a sun. When it spins, it makes day and night. When you are facing away from the sun you see the nighttime sky, or outer space. On the other side of Zembeth it is daytime. During the day you are facing that sun and see its light. On the other side of Zembeth it is nighttime." She drew a larger circle that encompassed the sun at the center. "Now Zembeth, while it is spinning, is also traveling around the sun like this." Again she drew arrows. Your year, if it is what I have ascertained, is exactly one revolution around this path, or orbit."

The party gawked at the illustration. Sara rubbed her chin and made a strange noise. Britt stepped back and admired her drawing. She reached for Donavan's mead pouch and gulped down a healthy amount of the festive sweet brew, smiling at the clearly impressed wolf.

Amaranth huffed. "You really believe that? Surely 'tis a woman's opinion. Not to mention that of an uneducated slave." His face wore the regret of his words before they were completely out.

Britt, to the surprise of the entire company just waved him off with a patronizing gesture.

"Ignorance is marked better by denial and inability to explore the theories of all that would dare contemplate the unknown." Her words were lilted as if speaking to the village idiot.

"She sure as true sounds a right bit learned to me." Sara offered.

"I would venture to agree with Sara, slave or no, the fact that she is a woman not EVEN an issue, Britt proposes quite a theory." Meriden went so far as to stand next to Sara, in front of Britt and positioned her face directly in front of Amaranth's shocked mug.

"Well," Roderick clapped his hands. "There you have it." He reached for the mead and gulped down his own measure. Meriden reached for the tankard and followed suit. This became the norm for some time after sunset. Before long, the mead was eliminated. Despite the previous battle of wills, the company kept debating every possible subject they could think of. One by one, the mortal creatures began to nod off.

Britt's head tipped back on her rolled up cloak and Sara slumped beneath her arm. Roderick took the time to cover them and ponder the picture of human and gnome sleeping under the Arosa sky. He did not turn until he heard Donavan bark/cough. He sat back down and stared into the fire. It seemed all the elves fell to the spell of the fire deep in thought. Occasionally each of them glanced over at their two unlikely traveling companions. Meriden had obviously become more accustomed to the company of the men, and she continued to take part in the trance-like vigil. She was seated next to Rowland close enough to touch knees not seeming to notice. She jumped ever so slightly when he spoke.

"It would seem we are all learning a great deal on this, of all adventures." The other elves looked down as though ashamed and contemplating deeper understandings. Donavan just snored.

Chapter 20

Officially Unofficial

Dawn found Britt sprawled on her back and rolled in a cloak. She was not awake though her body twitched her to a wary opossum feigned sleep. At the top of her head she could feel that tingle start, signaling an insect like pair of eyes observing her from the grass not far off. In the hair of a moment she absorbed the raw feeling of hunger and malice the creature exuded. She had always been an excellent hunter. With a dragon pup growing inside her, the instinct germinated to new heights. A brief shadow faded in her subconscious and she knew the Shahani hungered to tear her apart, sucking the blood from her skull. Her muscles tightened ever so slightly, as the foe drew nearer. It was the feeling of being the rabbit in the bush hiding from the fox. Her heart quickened with every savage intention reflected in the scent of sweat and the twinge of desperation. Yet this hunt, to the ignorance of the Shahani, was to be one in favor of the rabbit. She felt its interest shift from her skull to that of an easier quarry. Sara lay only inches away, half out of the cloak and well asleep.

A moment, a second, the time it takes to focus your eye, the Shahani was screaming in pain as Britt clenched and snapped its plated neck. In just that much of a whip she was crouched as if to propel her body into the grass. Her eyes blurring to separate grass from predator she fixed on the largest of the waiting cluster. Her hand dropped to the ground, crushing the dead creature beneath her weight. As if it was a trivial thing she poised for flight. The skin on her back felt alive and she became aware of Donavan easing up beside her. Her nostrils flared as she caught scent of his fur.

Sara was awake but smart enough to remain completely still. Meriden stiffened also finding the wisdom in solidity. One breath, two, three waiting to see if this meal was worth the price, the Shahani positioned for fight or flight every movement a test of courage, every blink a flag to fly. Their eyes could not blink. Instead, inside the chest of every evil bug baby echoed the cold fear that these two beasts actually desired this confrontation.

Donavan shifted slightly and it was on. Britt followed suit surging into the deep grass. Within seconds Donavan had beheaded three of the camouflaged creatures. Their exoskeletons crunched loudly spurting out black blood from between his massive fangs. Britt used body weight to roll over the waiting line before her like a ball of destruction. Her weight alone was not enough to do serious damage although her speed was well in the down time to turn about and sever arms and torsos. A number of the Shahani attempted to leap to her back wielding small knives, only to miss and hit the flat grass with thuds, some impaling themselves in the process. Britt spun about and chopped the leader's legs from his body in a swift motion. Donavan continued to use his jaws like jackhammers giving chase to the rest that were fleeing from the sight of their dismembered leader.

The small tribe rustled like wild wind shivers and shock waves into the array of stalks. Britt jumped as high as any human ever had and let out a stomach-cramping howl as she waved the dead leader above her head like a banner of victory. Donavan followed suit till the two could be heard for miles around. Roderick and Rowland had appeared behind their savage companions, compelling any and all that were left to beat a hasty retreat. Screams as those made it known to all other brave tribes that these were perhaps not the best choice on the Shahani menu.

Little was said at breakfast and even less was eaten. The horses were packed in record time and the party was once again off. It would take some time for the adrenaline to seep and dissipate. Roderick, Amaranth, and Rowland seemed to regard the events as all in a day's work. Meriden and Sara however were a bit shaken at the carnage. They had not gone far when Meriden expressed her dismay. Britt turned around on Murdock and took the time to attempt to explain survival without magic to her.

"Sometimes things are not fair Meriden. Sometimes to survive you have to show your enemy your ability to destroy without remorse. It's sad that those creatures had to die and I doubt for little more than an attempt at a meal, but the world of survival forces us, at times, to be over aggressive to prove our dominance."

"But we could have just let Roderick use magic." She insisted.

"They were not trying to kill Roderick. They were hoping to be off with Sara and gone before Roderick knew which tribe committed the theft." She placed her hands on Murdock's heart shaped rump. "When you're starving Meriden, you'll risk just about anything to feed yourself or your family."

"How do you know they were starving?" Meriden asked.

"For one, I don't think they would have dared it with three elves in the camp if they weren't and for another, I could feel their desperation. They needed that meat. Now I suppose they will have to hunt elsewhere or learn to eat greens."

And so they rode, on and on, in the infinite grass and heat. Hours of horseback riding with little to do was not a productive thing for Britt. After her mind was off the abrupt battle of the morning it started to drift in the exotic heat. She was sure the crack of her backside was sweating and was positive her bum would be permanently shaped like a horseshoe. She had been on Murdock so much she would not be surprised if her cheeks were not imprinted into his back. The day was a constant fight with mosquitoes the size of short- range fighters. Of course only she and Sara suffered this. At one point she yanked a stalk of grass out of the ground, split it off into many small wisps and handed it to Sara. She then did the same and Sara copied her motion of slapping her back and arms lightly as they rode. Body parts were sticking together and horse fur was mixed with leg hair. In the end it was just ten kinds of ugly. This, however, did not stop her from the growing urge to jump off Murdock and yank Roderick off his horse, shove him to the soft grass and rip his clothes off.

Just like all people that have an obsession and sailing down the river of denial, she kept trying to make excuses for her urges. She finally decided it was a phase and deluded herself into thinking she just needed to get it out of her system. Also, like most people that are slightly obsessed, she was not aware that even if she had somehow managed to talk herself down, the urge was something that was driven by a much stronger source. She was fighting a battle honed grinding through millions of years of evolution. She looked ahead and watched him from behind. He was only wearing a vest and his breeches. His thick hair hung down to the middle of his back in a mess of black mixed with beads and bones. His arms bulged and moved as he kept his hands resting on his thighs, rocking gently. It was just evil. She could see the blood veins winding over his large hands. That was evil too. Worse, she could hear his musky deep voice blurring her common sense, as he talked casually to Donavan.

The topper to the hormonal cake was that he was not a bastard. He was a gentleman. He was a man. His presence commanded respect. His actions reeked with compassion and strength. Sex had been the first encounter. If it had been the last this war might not be waging. They had become friends. If asked, she would have to admit that without the physical contact and with the pitfalls of everyday life she would still hold him in high regard and seek out his company. She knew that if she had to be stuck out here in "blood sucking buffet for bugs land", it was worth it to be with him. Her thighs clenched. She was hoping they could get to Sid O'Sala soon so she could find some unsuspecting human boy to molest. She may just have to accost Cameron in desperation. She shuddered at the mere thought. Nope. That was just not an option. She looked up to the sky over the monotony of green. She started thinking of fusion and propulsion. Everything came back to body leverage, broad shoulders and eventually to elf sex. She tried remembering school. No help. She tried thinking of the best sex with other men she had ever had: again a wash.

She came to the conclusion that she was just going to have to seduce and abuse him constantly or go stark raving mad. It did cross her mind that it could be the boredom of being in a big green hell of crack sweat and body odor that was driving her to this. Roderick turned around to address her, parting his nasty lips and saying something unfairly evil, but of course totally proper. She did not hear him. Instead she blurted out that she would like to go hunting with him when they made camp. His eyes bulged a bit and for a moment she could almost see the wheels in his elf brain cranking around. He stuttered clumsily and said "Sure". Rowland rolled his eyes and Donavan just turned his head to snicker.

Amaranth and Meriden were, as usual, out there in La La white elf land, floating around in their own happy little elf world of denial. All be it that in Amaranth's world his brother did not lust after a human and he was just concerned about food. This was a great adventure and it would soon be over. Then they would be heroes. In Meridenville every moment was a terror and a new beginning. She was occupied with reminding herself that she was out on this adventure with her subordinates mixing with the common folk and would also be a hero. She was becoming one with the salt of the earth, a daring wild woman to be feared, even if she jumped every time a large stalk of grass moved the wrong way. Sara was too repulsed to care. She thought of them as animals in heat. Britt was just a big she cat mewling and whining, rubbing her backside on everything. Roderick was some dust field cock puffing his feathers out and crowing like a fool. She was more worried about getting some mud and herbs to make a damn lotion to get rid of these mosquitoes. She almost thought they could kill a few and cook them over the fire for dinner and save a great deal of totally unnecessary breeding time for the two horny idiots. Goodness knows the ruddy things were big enough to feed a small family.

When they finally set camp Britt was fair near giddy. People in love are often under the impression they are fooling all present. They also suffer from the delusion that their comical mishaps are actions that they would perform if sane. Just as a drunk believes dancing is a good idea. These theories and observations were, of course, sans happy La La white elf club members. Roderick was running around setting up cover like a mad man, even tripping over camp gear from time to time. Rowland and Donavan were taking mental notes to use as blackmail later, in case such situation should arise that they would need to remind their fearless leader of just such an indiscretion of biological stupidity was needed.

"Well!" Roderick slapped his sides in mock purposefulness, "I guess we should be off to the job of a main course." He started looking for his bow, which as a point of interest, he had never misplaced in over 150 years.

Donavan could not resist the temptation, "Really Roderick, you don't need to go. After all you did go last time. I would be more than happy to oblige." He waited in twisted glee for Roderick's response. Rowland almost spit up with very badly hidden mirth.

"Do not think of it, old friend. I am more than happy to assist." Roderick insisted, so focused on his need the joke eluded him. He looked asinine, nervously bouncing back and forth as if waiting for permission from his two friends to trot off. As if they believed he was going hunting. Donavan could not help but marvel at a man that went from 200yr old elf to idiot in a matter of days. Before he could speak again, the two of them were off into the grass. Donavan hoped they had enough sense to actually kill something and bring it back for dinner.

Not far from camp, a few trees had managed to take root in the plains. They formed a quiet haven in the midst of constantly waving blades. Britt was barely able to make it to the trunk of a tree before her clothes were off. Talking was pointless. If words needed muttered they came out in moans. Roderick pinned her in unquenched aggression, kissing her to nearly the point of pain. Britt landed with a soft thud and wrapped herself around the naked vision of fabled lore. When he was this close she felt like exploding. The possibility of tenderness would be saved for later days. The absolute devastation of desire was knocking now, demanding an answer. Roderick was sure her roar of pleasure could be heard back at camp. She collapsed at his side, breathing as if she had just finished her display at the games in Garath.

As if regrouping, they lay panting in the moss, blankly watching the stars, their minds erased of valid thought. Roderick rolled over and rested his head on his hand. "Marry me." He stated.

"What?" Britt squeaked.

"You heard me. I want to marry you. As a matter of fact I can not imagine my life without you."

"You're just saying that because I just screwed your brains out." She laughed and rolled to face him, kissing him softly. "Besides, wouldn't you be stoned to death by your peers or something?"

"Probably, but it is not as if they have not tried before. I am serious about this, Britt. I know I have acted like a cad about our relationship but I needed time to think it through. Being out here with you has made it clear. I will never be the same without you. I will never find another woman like you. I could never settle for less now." He tickled her nipple. "Besides you know you have ruined me for all other females, elf or otherwise. How can you not know? How can you not see the effect you have on everyone whose life you touch?"

Britt sat up and tucked her knees to her chest. She seemed puzzled and hurt. "I don't know if this is a good idea, Roderick. I mean we're not even the same species. Where would we live, out on the road?" She looked at the moss. "Besides you don't know everything about me. You've only known me a short time." She chose not to face him.

"Consider this instead? We go hunting, get back to the group, make a formal announcement to the party that we have proclaimed our love for one another and see where it goes from there." He dipped his head to look up at her. "Besides, the only lives I care for are in that camp anyway, save Ma Fafella. I am rather sure she is already abreast of the situation." He snorted.

Britt turned finding the need for courage in the face of something she had never known required it. Love was one of the most painful emotions. Even when it was good it was terrifying. When it is real it is overwhelming. It makes one feel like there is nowhere to go but right where you are and even though you want to run, you would rather die than walk away. She swallowed hard, holding back tears. She had never been allowed or able to afford them. In the past they only proved to uncover weakness.

"I want to give you something." He said in a whisper. She watched as he rummaged through his cloths for a dagger. Once in hand he proceeded to slice his chest. Britt sucked in air hard. "Do not worry, it is an ancient taboo custom. I will be fine." His blood was a metallic shade of violet. He backed into the light of the moon that now hung silver in the sky. Lifting his dagger he yelled first in elf – "Benjoin aft odin! Kelisoa ella shaphana!" He rubbed the blood over his eyes. "Benjoin aft Fraya! Kelisoa ella cercialah labella!" He bent to Britt, lifting her to stand next to him. "Benjoin aft Sheeva! Kelisoa ella Britteny shahean trakka!" He put his hand on Britt's chest. She jumped when he convulsed, his eyes rolled. He seemed to light up, his hair blowing like mad about his face. Britt suppressed the urge to scream or move, keeping faith that Roderick knew what he was doing. He was elf after all. He lowered his hand leaving a deep purple print on her chest. When he spoke to her now his voice was full of determination.

"I have willingly given you half of myself Britteny. I have asked the Gods and Goddesses to witness the giving of my mind, heart, and soul to this woman so that I may live in her and she in I for eternity. I give this to you without asking in return. I give it to you openly and selflessly." He pointed to her right ankle. She looked down to see a magnificent black tattoo encircling her limb. She looked up with tears in her eyes.

"What have you done Roderick?" She backed away from him. "I'll die long before you will. How could you commit this to me? Are you willing to spend the remainder of your life alone?" She asked.

"No Britt, you do not understand. The first time I put my body into yours, you became immortal as I. When we shared our life forces, the magick from my body entwined us. This mark is to tell the world that Roderick of Darmuth Anor has found his true mate." He let his hands fall to his sides as if opening himself to her next onslaught of questions. None came. Silence drifted through the treetops and her face was set. Her eyes frozen regarding him as she stood naked and painted with his blood he waited patiently for a reaction. She backed up away and bowed her head after a five-year minute.

The worst feeling to date is the awkward stagnation of resolve quickly slipping away when someone bares his or her soul to you. In that moment of total vulnerability the recipient has precious few options. They can casually dismiss the mortal selfless expression of adoration, or go along with it, if only for the sake of the smitten. In Britt's case the pickle was sharp dill and she was right in the middle. Before her open and astounding stood the man of her dreams and she had not known she had a standard that would benchmark the final overture. The standard was standing before her. He could have sliced open his chest and handed her his still beating heart and it would have been easier to deal with. To deny Roderick of Darmuth Anor this, a sacrifice she was sure he did not offer lightly, would be to crush him as no savage battle could. Would she return this good faith? In the time it takes to focus one's vision, Britt imagined life without him. The realization that one day she would have to spend it in the cold black of space looking back at this moment held no comfort. She hesitated further, that little angel on her shoulder biting at her ear, kept screaming, "You are going home some day, you selfish bitch! You can't promise him this!" Her life was nothing but saying goodbye. Situations would not afford the emotional ties of a relationship. When she left she would spend her years as the ruler of the Zenerian Empire. What was best for him? She had been experiencing doubt as to her ability to handle the stress of such a position. Could she be there for him? Could she stay here for him?

He was waiting patiently, understanding that she was frightened, but still thinking her to be of this world, and therefore available. She was not sure she could, in good faith, conceal this information from him. If nothing else he would still know how she felt about him.

"Roderick, I keep telling you, there is so much you don't know about me. I mean . . . I really do care for you, I can't tell you how much . . ." He put his hand to her lips.

"I know your life is nothing but chance. I choose to take this one. Our fears of the future can not overshadow what I know to be true within my heart. If the future be my enemy then I say back to it that 'tis rather to choose this future than be standing in my skin in 100 years and still without you.

"It matters not to me where you have traveled or birthed. I care even less for where the future takes you, I am not afraid to stand by you. I ask not for things I cannot have. All I ask on this night is if you feel this way for me, then this will serve my desire, to take you as you are forever more. It matters not where we go from here Britt, I keep telling you so. Love like ours shall not stop if we separate for a time, or eternity." He shook his raven curls. "Britt, do you think I do this all the time?"

"No, of course I don't. But I've gotta say I have had men very confused, and around here all of them seem to be. I'm not saying I'm all that, but I do have this strange way of attracting men. They tend to want commitment right off. None of them have a care for the future, or the past, or anything for that matter, other than making me a possession."

"Is that what you think this is?" He whispered cautiously.

"No." She admitted honestly. "No Roderick. I know that's not what this is. You don't strike me as the type to play games or flit in and out of love every day."

"I have never loved. I am an elf." He grabbed her hands and pulled her to nearly the point of touching noses. "Yet here I stand, like a naked fool in the trees." He kissed her softly. "I am no coward Britteny. I live alone inside my soul. I see this world for what it is, the good and the evil. I will not make this offer again. In the light and customs of my people I should have never made this type of offer, even to another elf. If you would not have come along I still would have not made this offer. This is something elves just do not do. I would not have said this to De'Loria. When I met you I had no idea I would make this offer, even at the point I first saw the beauty that so outshines in the true treasure of your soul. Do you know how I first knew I would make this offer?" He asked.

"No."

"When I was standing in the square at Garath. I was looking up at Sholendor and realized that you had pulled off one of the greatest escapes in the history of our people. You accomplished it without the help of magic. I listened to him. His filthy mouth imploring for your rescuing and it occurred to me, we are the same, you and I. Very few really know us, or want to take the time to get to know us, they do not care. They do not understand that we run every day. Our bodies and faces make us different. They love us, crave us, even to the point of murdering our friends to get next to us." He hesitated a moment. "They fear us and want us, but because we are continually hunted we are, and may always be, truly alone. Even after the games, your show of courage, he had no clue what he was dealing with. He never asked, how deep does she run? I want to know how deep you run. I want a woman that knows how deep I run, and is not afraid to dive in." He stepped back and started putting on his breeches.

She wiped the tear from her eye before he could see, but had the feeling he could smell the salt.

"Roderick." She called. He looked up. Shoving aside issues of race, the future, and universal domicile location, Brit repeated Roderick's declaration of fidelity. Her dark red blood printed on his firm chest, next to the metallic purple of his and again next to the larger male print on hers. Her body tingled with the feeling of all the forces of nature entering her fusing like lightening in her cerebrum then rocketing back to the soil. It spiraled up her back and gripped her chest, causing her mind to flash in and out of consciousness. He reached his hand to her chest and placed it on her red print. He then pulled her hand up to his chest and gently placed it on his purple print.

"I will be yours for eternity my love. No matter the leagues we journey, where time takes us, our two souls will be as one, in love and respect. This type of commitment is taboo for my people. It is believed that due to our long lives emotional attachments are fickle. Yet the ritual exists. I believe it exists for two as we. At one time in our history there must have been a love like this one. This commitment is the most binding magic allows. And this pledge I give to you Britteny."

Britt collapsed against his body pressing their palms between their chests she wrapped her free arm around his back tilting her head to meet his lips. She kissed him for an eternity allowing herself to be lost in the time they had. When they parted she spoke in a soft and sure voice.

"I have a feeling somehow, Roderick, that our souls were already bound. I think I knew it the minute I saw you and I know it now. I'm sorry for doubting it."

He started dressing. "We have nothing for dinner. I am sure we will be in enough trouble as it is, what shall we do?" He asked laughing.

Britt pulled on her breeches. "I think we should just try to snatch something small on the way. It's going to be difficult enough explaining ourselves, we should just get back." She seemed to him a distant mirror now. Although they had joined souls Roderick was sure she would change. Her heart was one to rebel. He was slightly amazed she even considered this type of commitment. He watched as she struggled with her hair, pulling it harshly through her tunic. She was troubled from the day she could walk; he knew this, yet he felt he was the person to unlock this sorrow. How and when it would happen was a mystery. Hopefully it would not take a tragic event to bring forth the softer side of the women he loved.

Chapter 21
Sid O'Sala

None had questioned the companions when they had arrived by the fire with a fine stag for dinner. Meriden was busy grinding herbs with Sara for cooking along with some roots they had dug up in the absence of the two. Donavan hauled the beast from Roderick's shoulders and took the time to nod to his friend. Britt had begged him on the way back to camp, not to speak of this until they had reached Sid O'Sala and had time to announce it properly. It was partially true that she wished it to be a special occasion. The pertinent concern was Sara's reaction. She was not sure Meriden would grasp its meaning. The young princess had changed a great deal without her magic and seemed to care little for politics and etiquette now. She appeared totally preoccupied with learning how to survive here in the wild and forgetting what lie ahead. Britt helped the men skin the buck and quarter the flanks as she pulled on her knee high boots to cover her mark before Sara got a glimpse of it. She had asked Roderick back in the grove to show her the mark on his ankle. It was fascinating. So this is what her soul looked like in writing?

Amaranth chewed a stalk of grass with absence of interest. It was a general genetic rule that elves rarely ate meat. He had tried flesh on a more regular basis than urban dwelling elves. He preferred grass. It may have appeared his interest was pinpointed on the crunching stalk in his mouth procuring a shifty cover for his opinions that threatened to seep from his lips. He was happy having the entire party believe he was hapless and clueless, it helped him in the end to appear childish. In reality it made him sick to his stomach. His hopes of it dying down were growing slim. He would not speak of it. He knew his brother and knew it would only cause Roderick to push further. He longed to tell his brother he was committing suicide. He was clouded by lust for the woman. Bringing her back to the prince would make them heroes . . . Then it occurred to Amaranth that this was just what his brother was doing. He was lulling this obviously dangerous woman into his confidence to make it an easier capture. In the interest of all the facts, this did little to lighten his spirit. He stared into the roaring fire, glancing from time to time over towards the three females working together. Amaranth's heart was torn in two, divided by the whispers in his mind of the cold elf logic that would separate his upbringing from his genetic tendencies and the ancestral understanding of his blood line. Had he not fancied her at one time? If the opportunity would have arisen, would he now stand where his brother laid claim? In truth he was quite fond of her regardless. His thoughts were interrupted by the bustle of camp. His heart, for the moment, remained at unrest, as he knew it would be for an unknown time to come.

They ate dinner and talked. The nights in the sheltered grass, up to this point, had been shared with talk of things outside their dire situations. As Sid O'Sala approached reality was again coming into view on the horizon. They had set aside the status of fugitives if only for a glance of sunlight in the cloud that was tomorrow. It was a stolen moment hidden away from those less adventurous and or unwilling to brave the grasslands off the marked and guarded roads. Britt slept little, tossing on her otherwise comfortable pile of stalks. The stars were haunting her and homesickness weighed her flat, crushing her with the pull of circumstantial gravity. Like Amaranth, she was being plagued by the duality of life. She cocked her head to see Meriden busy scribbling in the journal Ma Fafella had given her under a loosely woven blanket of grass. She had even become adept at writing and riding. Britt was happy to see her occupied. The truth of it was simple; they were all slaves to fate. Perhaps Donavan was the only one free of decision and obligation at the end of this uncertain chain of events. How wonderful it must be to live life in the understanding of a purely natural creature. To be focused and centered on the reality of existence. They appeared void of the psychological trash that seemed to corrupt those that chose to complicate their lives with the unnatural.

And so it was on the road to Sid O'Sala. At dawn the company rose and packed. They noticed the downpour in the dark sky to the north; they ignored it, noting the clouds shifting towards the Shalnas. Meriden did comment that this only proved that Sholendor had the necklace as she squirmed in her saddle. On the day they approached the outstretched crests welcoming them to Sid O'Sala, Britt had seemed to brood deeper, riding close to Sara. Roderick had noticed their distant discussions. He was mature enough not to use his hearing to detect the subject of their private conversation. Britt's expression was troubled as Sara spoke in whispered tones in a preaching manner. He chalked it up to concentration. Sara must be schooling Britt intensely on the workings of this world.

All of the mounds seemed to climb to a small summit then disappear over the long ledge of land into a valley filled of thin forest and farming fields. Britt and Sara stopped momentarily to examine this metropolis that had been named the "Slave City". Although this city possessed walls, like all the other cities in Zembeth, its construction appeared more practical. At every point in the wall, small doors were fitted on the ends of alcoves built off the main wall. Each of these were attached to small fences and further, organized blocks of land. It seemed the residents of Sid O'Sala did not fear life in the Arosa with the same paranoid conviction as inhabitants of other cities. Britt began to ponder the regionally and geographically close, but obvious behavior difference between this city and Garath. After a few pointed questions she hypothesized that Garath was far older than Sid O'Sala, thus built by inhabitants very new to life in that particular location on the planet. Often times, primitive settlers feared far greater what they did not understand and would have naturally built larger walls.

Britt and Sara rode together at the rear of the party, still observing the upcoming situation. Sid O'Sala was constructed of much darker clay than Garath, giving it more of a "medieval" appearance. Although its walls were dwarfed compared to the dizzying heights of Garath, this city boasted a sprawling cut of farm lands and flexibility in the flow from inside the walls to the fields. Even this far out, they were passed by a great number of carts and travelers. Roads veined unnumbered, leaving all directions of the fortress as opposed to Garath's four broad roads. The passages in Sid O'Sala were well wooded and speckled with tall graceful tree lines, giving the city a false tranquil appearance.

Britt shifted atop Murdock. "You know Sara, something has been eating at me for a time."

"And what would that be?" Sara asked, unconsciously reining closer to hear the slightly hushed tones of her companion.

"Don't you think our escape was a bit too easy?" Britt asked.

"Easy? Ye call diving into a mountain 'o dead bodies and running as if the fires of Sholendor's dungeon furnaces were under our very back sides easy?"

Britt bent down. "I know I said I doubted they would follow us because they didn't think we would make it, but still, no one, nothing at all?" She sat back up and looked ahead as if to be sure the others were preoccupied in conversation. "I mean; I was led to believe they have some great army and I know they're skilled hunters. Let's just forget the whole issue of legions of beings that can work magic; that I've seen almost none of? I mean how bad could Sholendor actually want us if we haven't seen one elf or soldier since we left Garath?" Her eyes narrowed. "That is one elf other than our traveling brothers."

Sara shot her a look of surprise. Her husky voice seethed from her sharp teeth. "Why does this sound familiar, you lopsided idget? I believe I told you this back at Ma Fafella's?" She looked forward up the trodden dirt road to spy Roderick and Amaranth talking idly as they rode. Meriden was chatting with Rowland behind them. Donavan had bounded off to the woodlands as a scout/meal ticket. This left Sara and Britt behind to their private conversation. "I was thinking ye and ol' Roder were quite the rutting couple of these days, and now ye are changing yer mind? Are ye telling me now I was right?" She challenged.

Britt shifted on Murdock's bare back absently, stroking his wavy black mane. She had come to love the smell of a horse in the last few weeks. "Yea Sara, we have been close, maybe too close. You don't need to remind me of how foolish I may've been. I guess I am just at odds with the fact that we have seen nothing. I know we have been totally surrounded by freaking grass for what seems like forever, but no goblins, trolls, nothing. You would think there would be a price on our heads. We stole the goddamned princess for crying out loud."

Even with this statement, Sara had her doubts as to Britt's conviction to her own suspicions. Sara found it hard to imagine that Roderick and his company would be in league with Sholendor, but then again, she didn't believe that Roderick would ever bed a human, one never knows, does one? There would have to be some logical explanation for why, although she agreed it was very dodgy, they had yet to be attacked or confronted by Sholendor's troops but she completely understood why all else had let them slip by. She may have mentioned the like to Britt, but during their travels she had become quite fond of all the sharp eared males she had been shoved into adventure with. Perhaps her guard had gone down as well. She had been raised with elves, but never befriended by one. They were quite enchanting when they weren't beating you or killing your spouse.

"I'll tell ye why, no one cares. I bet my yellow bottom we are feckin' heroes to a lot 'o these types in the grass lands. Shit to shingles we are worshipped in Kloter Mass Arosa. Some credit has to be given to three wenches brave enough to hightail it outta the palace. But tis best we donna go spouting our ill omens to Meriden. The lass is taking this all rather in a grain an I donna want to jump her unless we have good cause." Sara advised Britt.

Britt nodded her agreement, feeling a bit guilty at not mentioning to Sara exactly how deep it had become. She glanced down at Sara's yellow head and devised a plan to take Sara with her to Zeneria as soon as the situation arose. Apparently wisdom was best when tinted with a dash of salt and just a hint of yellow. The two rode in relative silence as they crawled ever closer to the slave city. They began to pass vendors with greater frequency along the road, t.heir wares bartered and traded under canvas and colorful tents. For sale one could trip across every manner of jewel, bead, cloth and oil. Lamp merchants hung their masterpieces to collect flashing bolts of the morning sunlight hoping to blind the traveler into a sudden urge to buy an ornate oil lamp. The signs before the tents were written in the same type of scribing:

ᛏᚺᛖ ᛏᚱᚨᚡᛖᛚᛖᚱᛊ ᛏᚱᛟᚡᛖ

ᛒᚢᚱᛞᛟᚲᚲ ᛗᛁᚾᛖ ᛃᛖᚹᛖᛚᛊ

Britt craned her neck to observe this writing. "What is that, Elfish?" She asked.

"Nie, 'tis the common fist used by all others." Sara told her. "Iffin ye wish to learn it I can teach ye. That one ov'r there says "Traveler's Trove" and the oder one says "Burdock Mine Jewels." she reported.

Britt was drawing unwanted attention. There were a number of Elf slave traders that inquired in their native tongue to Roderick. He granted respect and declined their offers as they rode on. They were all sure that each that inquired knew full well who these travelers were. It was apparent that they either had no love for Sholendor, were greedy enough to risk it, or were outright terrified of betraying Roderick. Either way it made Sara's previous words ring true. Meriden expressed her longing to stop and shop. She told Britt that she had rarely been permitted outside the Royal walls, much less allowed to mingle with the common folk amidst their own cities.

Britt asked in a whisper. "Yea, but you're gonna be the Queen. You've never been to these cities?" She was surprised.

"Of course not. Really, how many elves of high office or respectable birth do you see here? It would be absolutely an outrage for someone of my station to simply wander among the peasantry."

She noticed Britt waving her off. "What? You disagree?"

"Forget it. I give up. You and your sick ideas of what it is to rule a people. No wonder you're such a closet freak. "

"And how is that?" Meriden ordered.

Britt pounded her index finger square in the center of Meriden's forehead. "You better get a grip if you think you're going to be any kind of remarkable queen, Casper, and stop talking about everyone else like they are dirt." Meriden started to protest only to be shown the palm of Britt's hand. "This isn't the time or the place to debate politics and I'm totally SICK of your attitude."

She reined Murdock belly to back with Meriden's mare knowing it was only necessary to avoid others hearing what an elf could pick out yards away. "You got pretty brave words for someone that's wanted for the murder of her mother and had to have her ass saved by two slaves. I would shut your yap if I were you." Britt hissed.

"Well, we seem to be in a right foul mood!" Meriden jumped.

"What do you expect? Look around you! I'm riding right into a city full of human slaves. You want me to be chipper about this?" Her voice was rising. Roderick wheeled his mount around and separated the two women.

"Ladies, need I remind you of our situation. I think we can find a better time and place to spit and fight." He ping ponged glances from one woman to the other. "You should know better." He calmly told Britt.

They continued to ride, the women surrounded by the men for protection. Roderick rode to Britt's right with Sara just in front of her Meriden to her left. Next to Meriden rode Rowland. In front of Sara, Donavan kept pace on all fours and Amaranth brought up the rear. Each kept an eye for stray individuals that would have a care to their person. It was their first confrontation in a setting of this population. Entering the city as if they were the norm chipped away at Britt's better judgment. Roderick had insisted that the women be cloaked. Even though the men seemed to wish to protect them, it appeared folly to the Captain that they would just march into a city where information to their location could easily be obtained by any spy with a will to benefit from the wealth of the royal prince.

It was not long before Roderick had secured them one of the small utility dwellings at the south west side of the city. They walked the horses through the crowds of farmers and slaves, dodging chickens and ogre children. Straw blinds or ivy walls hid private, paid for, villa yards, small and filled with aromatic gardens. These compact homes were owned by wealthy slave traders and used as a convenience for trading and traveling. They were scattered amidst the rented villa's that were easily identified by the generic appearance of simple stables for the animals visible from the street in some places. Rather than ivy gardens, these walls were unbleached mud and rough-milled unpainted wooden doors.

Roderick had paid for a rather large compartment with a bathing room for the ladies. It was his hope that a few nights of rest and food would better the moods and mindsets of their female companions. As they unpacked, Rowland brushed down the horses while Sara rummaged through the small kitchenette, organizing and preparing the hearth for a suitable fire. Roderick announced that he and the men of the company would be off into town to purchase supplies for the journey to the Shalnas. Donavan would stay behind and protect the women. Britt ignored his statements, instead choosing to gaze out the front windows that looked into the city behind grass woven curtains. The compartment had a small front porch with a rocking chair. She wished to rock, watching the inhabitants pass by. Roderick warned against it, explaining that Donavan would sit here for a time to allow the women privacy.

Inside the apartment, the hodge-podge family behaved as any normal group of travelers might. They flung packs down and shed footwear, even going so far as to shed clothing. Prior to acquiring and settling into said domicile, it took some bit of masquerading illusions to avoid a potential riot. The women all tossed their cloaks gratefully to the floor, sighing and welcoming the coolness of the mud hut. They had been over one mile from the actual city gates when they began to attracted more attention than desired and had to don the cloaks in the warming spring sun. Britt and Meriden, realizing the error of their ways, had ceased their stress-filled bantering and decided, luckily for the rest of the party, not to pick up where they had left off once they arrived in relative safety.

The steward of temporary housing asked no questions. His was a position of logistics and depended on his ability to "ignore" the obvious. Heuw was a creature of mixed breed and therefore already socially calloused and seasoned. He knew Roderick well and barely glanced from his worn record book. Perhaps such cryptic communication was from fatigue or perhaps out of prior education in the school of hear no, speak no, see no. He bypassed the tenant policy papers and took it upon himself to sign a false name without being instructed to do so.

"Here 'n well me lad. Do us a service n keep yer affairs outta sight, see?" For a split second it appeared as if he wished to see what was under the cloaks. Only a fool would do so. Heuw was no fool. Roderick's eyes narrowed in surprise, landlord man had never spoken to him so. "No disrespect to ye, none atall. The road yer walking now is yer own. Word travels faster than feet. Iffin twere not ye Sir Roderick, me coffers would be filled and the street a bed." He implied.

Roderick nodded and slipped an extra gold coin his way. "Well understood, my good man. I shall not forget your kindness in this matter."

Meriden scatted in and out of each room, amazed at the efficiency of the multi functional dwelling. From the narrow eight-stalled stable a door opened to a small foyer for coats, tack and gear. On the other side of the tack–house another door entered into a small kitchen that also served as a family room. Off to either side were three bedrooms and a bathhouse. The companions were relieved to be off horseback and able to sleep on something elevated off the great mother Zembeth. Sara poked around but seemed strange in her attention now to all the men did and said. Roderick announced they were leaving twice as if upset he was not going to be missed. Britt could hear Meriden in the living quarters.

"I am nearly out of paper already. What shall I do?" She fretted.

"I guess ye will have to buy some." Sara suggested.

"I will never be allowed into the city. Perhaps I will be forced to wait for our arrival in Fairfax. That is so distant. How shall I remember this tale as it is lived?" She fretted needlessly. "Ma Fafella will never help me now." She flopped onto a small pillowed bench.

"I'll not hear a word 'o that. I'll be buggered iffin I am letting this story go untold. I'll be out for some parchment. Twill only take me a moment and Donovan willna mind if a simple gnome runs out. After all, we all look alike." Sara assured her. From the other room they heard Britt's sleepy tones.

"Wake me up for dinner." Was all she offered, not caring about journals or supplies. After the men and Sara left Meriden went to one of the bedchambers to lie down and cool off. So it was for a time that Britt sank into the deep tub, one arm hanging over the side and the other resting under her head. The basin was large enough for her entire length to fit under the water so she did not need to dangle her feet off the end. Outside she could hear and smell the slave city.

At some point she tried to focus her mind on all that had happened. She attempted to think of home and its goings on. The warmth of the water coupled with the cool breeze kissing her cheeks was very lulling. The water had been enchanted and would stay warm indefinably, she had seen to it by dragging Roderick into the room before he left and pointing to the tub. He looked at the empty well and in a moment it was brimming with warm scented water. She shoved the door shut and pinned him to the wall, if only for a moment kissing him deeply. He smiled and pulled her closer.

"You become brave my love. Was it not you that wished this love to be secret, to be kept until further notice?" He chided.

"Yes, but you're so damn sexy I just wanted one taste before you left." She kissed him again, digging her fingers into his winged back muscles. She watched him leave the hut hurting curiously. Worry and love tugged a warring in the better half of her mind. She stripped and slid sleekly along the polished stone basin. She dozed off for nearly an hour before Sara crept into the bathing room. Knowing the prowess of her slave sister, Sara took care waking Britteny.

"Britt!" She whispered harshly standing a good distance from the tub. "Ye must wake child!" She sounded weak. Britt rolled a bit and when her face touched the water she jump-started awake.

"What Sara? What's wrong?" She blinked the sleep from her mind.

Sara approached then and spoke as if addressing one on the other side of the lily.

"I 'ave some sad news for ye, my child." She hesitated. "I took the time to follow our lad Roderick into town. 'E dinna know twas me after him fer I was wearing a slave's cloak. He dips behind some wall and twas there I heard him talking to Ol' Soggy Bottom."

Britt rose as if lifted by an unseen force until she was sitting upright in the tub. "I dinna hear the entire conversation mind ye, but appears we were well en to think there was something in the hen house that shouldna outta be there. Sholendor has them to take us to him in the forest. I heard he has Osizio prisoner in the palace and is a usin' this to keep that black bastard to his word." She braced herself on the tub's edge. "Either way, we are being had anna taken right into a trap. Before ye can ask, yes I am sure of what I heard." She stepped back out of instinct.

Britt knew that Sholendor was not in the city. Roderick had used a message globe to communicate with the prince. As if escaping a crushing blow she descended into the water, her face pale as pearl. Sara feared she would need to call for help to lift her prior to suicidal drowning. Attempting to draw the formidable woman back to reality, Sara kept talking.

"What de ye think we should do now?" Sara was moving about the room, laying out Britt's clothing, talking as quietly as she could, yet trying to permeate the water. Her hands hurried to avoid or deny the status she had brought on. When Britt did not answer, Sara shifted. "Well, we come to it then. I am no gonna stand here and chide ye, lass. I know how ye love him, but I remember telling ye he is an elf and elf 'e will always be. Did I no' tell ye?"

She was still unanswered. Heartbreak can be documented as the chief catalyst to insanity. Many would tell tales of such pain. They would be easily noted as liars. Britt was accustomed to it. She once thought if she kept going after enough crushing pain, she would grow immune. Inch by inch she had felt her jaded shell hardening. Roderick had slipped through the cracks as a virus into the skin. A single refugee tear escaped the war torn battlements of her psyche to curve over her cheek and drop to the dingy water.

"Now lass, I canna see ya sob, t'would be the end o me." Sara shuffled to the edge of the tub and handed Britt a dry cloth. Britt studied the piece of material and giggled insanely. "Imma gonna go talk to Meriden and let ye collect yerself. Iffin ye need me just bellow." She touched Britt's bare shoulder and smiled then left the room.

Britt searched for relief but found none. She turned over the possibility and pros of not having to leave him or explain him on Zeneria. She trudged though the "it figures" stage. It was for the best, after all. Her lip trembled. Her mind cracked and she chastised herself for being weak. He was an addiction; this was withdrawal.

She pulled her knees to her chest and buried her face between them hoping they would hold in the pain and help her center her thoughts on the necessary. She half feared she was giving birth to the dragon pup. Her chest heaved uncontrollably in the confusion of betrayal. The pain racked through her from the inside causing her shoulders to spasm.

It was pain that bleeds one's resolve into putty causing one to draw oxygen in as if sucking down the universe pushing the soul flat and lifeless. Breathe, just breathe, she told herself. Her mind sadistically flashed images of them the first night in the palace. The beauty of his unconscious movements mocking her like a foe in a field of fire, a fire lit after the quarry had been lulled into the pit. She began to sob with her mouth smashed against her drawn knees hoping to muffle the moans. Such a short time, so much pain, was it worth it? She shook her head and wiped her eyes, talking to herself. There is a planet at stake and you are missed at home! What did you expect! You were warned and you still dropped your guard. You deserve this for turning your back as if you never intended to go home?

For a brief moment, her mind attempted to comfort her in the illusion of treason and she wondered if Sara was lying. Her twisted face slowly sunk back to her knees as the realization resurfaced. Sara would never lie to her. She was surer of Sara's loyalty than Roderick's love. This was a sign. She reached for a towel. Every step painful, every breath an effort to fight back the tears, and so she dressed slowly, wishing she would vanish into the water.

Meriden knocked on the door. "Britt, may I come in?"

"Not now, Meriden. Give me a few minutes to get dressed."

"Britt." She almost sounded stern.

"Meriden, I mean it. I need a few minutes to dress." She lied, she was dressed and holding onto the wall with one hand wiping her eyes. The door opened and Meriden stepped in. "I told you to wait outside!" Britt barked.

"I know you did. I chose not to obey. Like you, I now do not follow orders well." She stood her ground. "I am not here to judge you. I am here to hear you and to help you. There are ways we can make you forget your feelings for Roderick and forget the pain."

Britt turned away from the smaller woman. At that moment she could not bear the pain of looking at another elf. Meriden walked slowly around her and unannounced, without pride or fear, reached up and embraced Britteny. It was enough. Britt bawled openly into Meriden's silk white hair. The shorter end of the embrace was faring no better. Meriden gripped her companion firmer at the feeling of such pain and such beauty. Perhaps it was her crippling loss of magick that allowed her to understand the need of her friend. She held firm. Sara stood in the door. Her face was now a strange mask of understanding and revelation at the sight of the two women holding on to each other for strength and comfort. It occurred to her that in her lifetime she had known it possible for elf and human to truly care for one another, and to this slave, that alone made this journey worth while.

"No. I don't think you can Meriden. Not this time." Britt broke the hold and whispered.

"I know natural magicks. Herbs and the like. What I am not skilled at Sara surely has mastered."

"Meriden. There're no herbs for this. There's nothing anyone can do for me now." Britt droned.

"I hardly believe that. You are not affluent in our ways. We can at least try."

"Yea, ha…that 's nice Meriden. Well I have a surprise for you. Wanna see how truly stupid I am?" Britt was yelling in tight tones birthed from the insanity of heartbreak.

"Well do you?" She lifted her pant leg to show Meriden the natural tattoo just as Sara walked around Meriden. The elf gasped and Sara yelped.

"Well! How's that for stupid?" She dropped the cloth and started putting on her stockings. "It seems for some ungodly reason that since I got dropped on this God-damned rock I've totally lost every shred of intelligence, courage, and training I've ever acquired. I've made mistakes that no rookie would have dreamed of. I've broken every code of conduct I've ever memorized. So you tell me Ms. "We Can't Feel Love" what the hell that means!" She pointed to her ankle, face red and eyes swollen.

Meriden frowned. "Oh, Britt. " Sara walked out of the room. Britt followed her.

"We outta get afore they come back, start packing." Sara ordered.

"No, we can't just leave. They'll follow too soon. I have an idea." Britt pulled her hair back, dried her tears and got to work.

When Donavan had returned he simply stayed on the front porch for a catnap. He had faith the women would be asleep within the dwelling and he being near exhaustion himself wished to take full advantage of this precious moment without adventure. He did not waste time with a chair. Instead he flopped down and curling his mass into a fur mountain. He woke with a jump to the energy charged sound of Roderick's voice.

"Donavan! Arise! Where are the women?" Donavan raised his giant head.

"Why my dear boy, they are inside asleep."

"No, my dear canine, they are not!" Roderick took a closer look at Donavan. "I believe you have been lull spelled asleep Donavan." He observed.

Amaranth and Rowland came from the dwelling after checking the stables. "The horses are still here. They could not have gone far. Perhaps they just went out to shop the market." Amaranth said.

Roderick looked into the window and noticed many of their possessions still lying about. "For the sake of the Blessed Mother I hope you are correct my brother. We have no time to waste. Donavan! About to the horse masters to see if any strange travelers purchased mounts as of late! Amaranth, you will make swift to the main gate and warn the guards we have missing slaves. Make sure they understand that discretion is insisted! Rowland, to your father's home and find what news of slave theft and implore his advice and magic. I will be off to the market to search the shops." He did not wait for questions. All four males dispersed post haste for the search for the missing women.

For moments that seemed like years, Britt held her breath in fear the straw next to her nose would cause her to sneeze. She was confident Sara and Meriden would lie still, not wishing to confront Roderick or be packaged off to Sholendor. When she was completely sure all their captors were safe away, she gently slid her fingers though the split in the sheets to pull back the blanket on the lower bunk, thanking the gods that the straw had not been changed in who knows how long. The offal odor could only have assisted them in avoiding Donavan's keen sense of smell. She tapped the top bunk and started picking the straw from her hair and clothes, shoving it back in the mattress. Quietly the women worked in the failing light of dusk. They packed haphazardly; shoving what food they could into sacks left in the kitchen.

Meriden and Sara were in the stable tying one of Britt's shirts to the leg of the smallest of the mounts to throw their scent. Britt stood in the living area looking down at Roderick's pack. Reluctantly she reached for the gem on her necklace. She tugged hard and broke the ring that had attached it. She dropped the brilliant stone atop the worn leather. For a brief moment she let her mind linger on the gift. Life is about choices she thought again, a door is closed. She could not escape the images of never ending doors slamming, people leaving, planets…family. She heard Sara behind her and lifted her hand to stand and once again walk away.

It was decided they would only take two horses. The third mount was scented and sent running north toward the outer most rim of the Shalnas forest. Sara would ride in front of Britt on Murdock and Meriden would have her own mount. It had amazed Meriden and Sara that Britt had the nerve to steal Roderick's bow and his arrows, as well as Amaranth's to give to Meriden. She also took the liberty of swiping a large hunting dagger that belonged to Roderick, sheath and all.

"It is the least he can do for me now." She justified.

"He has probably had that bow for more than 150 years." Meriden said.

"Well now he has part of my soul, so I think we are even." She would speak no more of it.

Britt made sure they were cloaked. Although they were anxious to bolt through the outskirts of town, she insisted they take it at a nice slow walk to avoid unwanted attention. She was internally worried the men would return and make haste to follow. Meriden had suggested the scenting spell on the horse claiming that, with her dragon pup, Britt was quite capable of such a simple incantation. She taught Britt quickly how to put the essence of the three of them into the animal thus throwing not only Donavan but also the super sensitive intuition of all three elves. It took only moments, but Britt hoped it would throw them off for miles. They were all thankful for nightfall even if two of the three were terrified of wondering the Arosa Plains without the men. Britt sat rigid atop the black stallion and stared straight ahead. Once clear of merchant areas she urged Murdock on to a canter and Meriden's steed followed. She was hoping to clear the crest before the moon was directly overhead. At the peak of the crest Meriden pulled alongside her.

"I have a suggestion, albeit a rather risky one." Meriden offered.

"Yes." Britt answered in a dead tone.

"There is a very deep and long gorge that extends this far south from the Shalnas. It is actually part of the haunted forest, if not as thick, but very few travel the road that winds through it. If one takes it as far southwest one can either climb the high road and end up just north of the gates of Kloter Mass Arosa, or one can continue on north and into the depths of the far east end of the Shalnas. It is called Widow's Reach."

"Why would we want to climb to Kloter Mass Arosa?" Britt asked.

"My cousin De' Loriea may possibly be interested in helping us or at the very least restore my abilities. She is powerful enough to do so."

"Are you sure? She didn't seem all that warm and friendly last time I laid eyes on her." Britt stiffened at the name of Roderick's intended.

"No I am not sure, but if we can beseech her to at least afford us an escort of elfish soldiers, we may survive our trip to the Shalnas. I know she could not believe I killed my mother and when we explain everything perhaps she will be willing to plead my case to the counsel of elders.

If worse comes to worse and she decides not to help us, we are only a few short miles south of the location of the necklace. We can simply leave in peace and find our own way." Meriden said, glancing back toward the slave city far behind them.

"It sounds kind of iffy if you ask me. Besides I'm not sure my presence would be a great thing." Britt added.

"Yes, the sight of that mark may just be all that is needed to have us hanged in Kloter Mass Arosa and possibly start a revolution throughout the city."

Britt reined Murdock in. "O.K. So even with all that considered, I take it this gorge is dangerous, so that would be a good idea. After all I doubt the boys would think we would risk it." She concluded.

"Exactly, so off we are and hopefully we will be there by dawn. We can take a nap in the light of day at the mouth of the gorge and start off after a rest. I think we should travel during the day in this deep land. I would guess that day and night look much the same under the thick canopy of trees." Meriden observed.

"Yea and nocturnal predators are much worse on the average." Britt scowled and added, "As if things could get worse." Inside, she mused that being eaten by some wild unimagined beast would be a welcoming feeling next to the pain in her heart. Things had steadily gotten worse and she was sinking deeper into the fabric of the plot and farther away from finding her way off the planet and home to Zeneria.

She kicked Murdock in the direction Meriden led them, thankful for the dark to cover her still stinging tears.

Made in the USA
Lexington, KY
24 January 2012